AT ANY COST

AT ANY COST

Jeffrey Siger

SEVERN
HOUSE

First world edition published in Great Britain and the USA in 2024
by Severn House, an imprint of Canongate Books Ltd,
14 High Street, Edinburgh EH1 1TE.

severnhouse.com

British Library Cataloguing-in-Publication Data
A CIP catalogue record for this title is available from the British Library.

ISBN-13: 978-1-4483-1210-8 (cased)
ISBN-13: 978-1-4483-1211-5 (e-book)

All Severn House titles are printed on acid-free paper.

Typeset by Palimpsest Book Production Ltd.,
Falkirk, Stirlingshire, Scotland.
Printed and bound in Great Britain by
TJ Books, Padstow, Cornwall.

Praise for the Chief Inspector Andreas Kaldis mysteries

"Atmospheric and exciting"
Booklist Starred Review of *One Last Chance*

"Will appeal to fans of Donna Leon and Louise Penny"
Publishers Weekly on *One Last Chance*

"An engrossing procedural. New readers will discover the gorgeous aspects of Greek life"
Library Journal Starred Review of *A Deadly Twist*

"As always, Siger keeps readers turning the pages with ingenious plot twists and delicious description of the Greek isles"
Booklist on *A Deadly Twist*

"Siger seasons Kaldis's investigation with abundant slices of Greek history and island mores . . . Armchair travelers will have fun"
Publishers Weekly on *The Mykonos Mob*

"Fans of Adrian McKinty's Sean Duffy books and other police procedurals . . . will welcome this outstanding crime novel"
Library Journal Starred Review of *An Aegean April*

"Brimming with suspense and a distinct sense of place"
Kirkus Reviews on *An Aegean April*

About the author

Jeffrey Siger is an American living on the Aegean Greek island of Mykonos. A former Wall Street lawyer, he gave up his career as a name partner in his own New York City law firm to write the international best-selling, award recognized Chief Inspector Andreas Kaldis series. *The New York Times* has named him as Greece's thriller novelist of record, and the Greek government selected him as the only American author writing novels that serve as a guide to Greece.

He's also served as Chair of the National Board of Bouchercon, America's largest mystery convention, and as Adjunct Professor of English at Washington & Jefferson College, teaching mystery writing.

jeffreysiger.com

To Linda Marshall, with much love and thanks for all those many years you kept me in line.

ACKNOWLEDGMENTS

Michael Barson; Katharina Bolesch & Alexander Reichardt; Diane DiBiase; Andreas, Alexandra, Mihalis, & Anna Fiorentinos; Lora Kampaxi & Manos Kavallaris; Elpida Kampeli, Fragkiskos Kampelis, & Robert Kampelis; Yanni & Flora Katsaounis; Panos Kelaidis; Alex Khalifa; W. Wilder Knight II; Nikos & Sonia Kotopoulos; Dr Georgios Lianopoulos; Nikoletta & Spyros Lianos, Katerina Marangou; Terrence McLaughlin, Karen Siger-McLaughlin, & Rachel Ida McLaughlin; Kathy & Michael Otinsky; Barbara Peters; Liliane Rigouzzo; Terezdina Rigouzzo; Alan & Patricia Siger; Barbara Zilly Siger; Jonathan, Jennifer, Azriel & Gavriella Siger; Rachel Slatter, Ed Stackler; Birgir Steingrimsson; Sebastian 'Savvas' Varthalitis; and, of course, Aikaterini Lalaouni.

'God, please fill my heart with love, let me become one with my true self, overflowing with profound love.'

– Masahisa G

ONE

He regarded himself as a swashbuckling pirate awash in Mediterranean adventures. Part Errol Flynn, part Johnny Depp, and part good old Jacob Diamantopoulos. Trouble was, Jacob lived in Brooklyn, and the only boat he'd ever been on was the Staten Island Ferry, an experience that still haunted him.

One lunchtime, on a warm and gusty mid-October day, Jacob's mother had showed up at his third-grade classroom to take him for what she promised would be 'an adventure on the high seas.' It was the first anniversary of his father's death from a heart attack, and his mother decided that the two of them should spend the afternoon visiting her sister-in-law on Staten Island. Normally his mother took the bus, but today she decided it would be more fun for eight-year-old Jacob if they went by ferry.

An uneventful fifty-minute subway trip from Brooklyn's Brighton Beach brought them to Manhattan's South Ferry, where they boarded the largest vessel in the fleet for the five-mile journey across a choppy New York Harbor to Staten Island. Jacob had never seen a boat that big up close. It stood longer than a football field and could hold 6,000 passengers, though only a quarter of that many people had joined this crossing.

The journey was as exciting as his mother had promised. He sat staring out a starboard window, mesmerized by the Statue of Liberty while his mother softly stroked his hair. She spoke of how tightly she'd gripped his father's hand at her first glimpse of that symbol of freedom from the plane that brought them to their new lives in America.

As the ferry approached Staten Island's St George terminal, his mother hurried them forward on the main deck to be among the first to disembark. 'We're almost there,' she said, bending down to kiss the top of his head.

He knew nothing about boats, so he didn't bother to ask why the ferry hadn't slowed down.

That unasked question was answered a moment later when the

Andrew J. Barberi slammed into a concrete pier that ripped through the ferry's main deck on the starboard side, trapping hundreds of passengers in piles of broken glass, twisted metal, and splintered wood, while others leaped overboard into the sea.

The impact hurled Jacob away from his mother and buried him under the pile of bodies flung forward behind him. He struggled to breathe, shouting all the while for his mother. All he heard were the screams and moans of the bloodied and dying surrounding him. He never knew how long he lay trapped before rescuers reached him.

Seventy passengers were injured that day.

Ten died.

Including his mother.

Never again had he set foot upon a boat.

Special Crimes Unit Chief Inspector Andreas Kaldis sat behind his desk at Athens Central Police headquarters – better known as GADA – waiting for his sister to call. Her text message had read: WHEN CAN I TALK WITH YOU? IT'S SERIOUS.

He'd texted back: NOW. That was five minutes ago. His mind ran to all sorts of possibilities. Had something happened to their mother, or possibly to one of his sister's three children? The two boys were still in public school in Athens, and Anna had just started university in America.

Andreas stared at the phone as if willing it to ring.

Ring.

He answered immediately. 'Gavi, is Mother OK?'

'Yes, she's fine.' She paused. 'It's Anna.' She paused again. 'She's getting married.'

'What?' blurted Andreas.

She stifled a sob. 'I'll never hear the end of it from her father. I convinced him to allow her to go to America for university. She's not even nineteen and wants to marry a boy she met there.'

'But she's only been in New York a month.'

Her voice rose. 'You don't have to tell me. I know!'

'Who's the boy?'

'I know nothing about him other than his name.'

'Did she say *when* she plans on getting married?'

'No, and I'm guessing the only reason she gave me his name is because it's Greek and she thought that would pacify me.'

Andreas paused. 'Are you saying she didn't *call* you to tell you she was getting married?'

'She told me in a text message. As soon as I received it, I called and texted her on her American mobile. She never answered. I must have tried a dozen times – before and after I texted you.'

Andreas slowly let out a deep breath. 'It sounds as if Anna might be a little high.'

'She doesn't do *drugs*.'

'Then maybe she had a bit too much to drink.'

'She doesn't drink either.'

Andreas knew it was useless to debate that point with his sister. The only criticism of her children she would countenance was her own. 'If she sent you that message stone cold sober—'

'*I know*. It's serious. That's why I called you. Anna listens to you. She always has. A marriage at her age into who knows what sort of family could ruin her life.'

Another debate Andreas knew to avoid was any implication that his sister did not know what was best for her children. 'What do you suggest I tell her?'

'That there's no more important a decision a woman can make in her life than who she marries, which makes it utterly insane to marry someone she hardly knows.'

'Same holds true for a man.'

'That's why you've got to convince her to abandon this madness.'

Andreas rubbed at his forehead. 'I know where you're coming from, but realistically that's not going to happen in a phone call. All I can possibly hope to do is get her to talk about the boy and his family, and maybe tell me why she's in such a hurry to marry. Preaching won't work.'

'You've got to do something. You're her *godfather!*'

'Screaming won't work either.' He looked at his watch. Ten in the morning Athens time meant three in the morning New York time. 'I'll call her as soon as we hang up and leave a message to call me back.'

'Thank you.' His sister's voice cracked as if holding back tears.

'I can't promise anything, Sis, but I'll try. What's her American mobile number?'

She read the number to him.

'And what's the boy's name?'

'Jacob Diamantopoulos.'

*   *   *

Andreas called Anna as soon as he hung up with his sister. As expected, the call went to voicemail and he left an upbeat message asking that she call him when able.

Anna's obvious reluctance to speak with her mother about why she was in such a hurry to marry meant pressuring her to call him back ASAP would be the wrong approach. Patience seemed the better way to go. He did wonder, though, whether he could maintain that same laid-back attitude if *his* daughter sent him that sort of text message. Thankfully, his daughter was still in preschool.

Andreas didn't hear back from Anna until mid-afternoon. He was in the midst of a meeting with his longtime chief detective, Yianni Kouros, and motioned for Yianni to stay put while he took the call.

'Is this my favorite niece?'

'It's your *only* niece.'

Andreas chuckled. 'How many times have we done that opening routine?'

'Every time.'

'At least I'm consistent.'

Anna giggled.

'I understand congratulations are in order,' chirped Andreas.

Anna's tone turned serious. 'My mother spoke to you.'

'Of course she did. I'm her brother.'

'I don't want a lecture, Uncle.'

'From what I understand, no one's had the chance to give you one. Besides, what sort of lecture could I give you while not knowing anything more than you've met someone you plan on marrying?'

'I have, and that's all I have to say on the matter.'

'That's fine with me, Anna, but you have to admit that by refusing to tell your mother anything more than the boy's name, you're giving off big-time defensive vibes over your choice of husband. Most women would be proud to brag about their intended mate for life.'

'My mother won't like him.'

'Why?'

'Because he's much older than I am.'

'How much older?'

She hesitated. 'Nine years.'

'That's not so much older. What does he do for a living?'

'He's a software engineer.'

'Is that like a programmer?'

'No, a software engineer is like the architect on a construction project, and a programmer is like a contractor.'

'Sounds good to me.'

With a bit of excitement in her voice, Anna added, 'He has his own company.'

'That should please your mother.'

'But he's Jewish.'

'Is he willing to convert?'

'No.'

'Will you?'

'No.'

Andreas sighed. 'Frankly, Anna, from what you just told me, unless he has two heads, a bad reputation, or a horrible family, I see no reason to think your mother would seriously object to him. To my way of thinking, her only valid concern might be that by getting married at your age you increase the likelihood of not finishing your university studies.'

'That won't happen. He wants me to finish college.'

'Then I see no reason for you to worry about receiving your mother's blessing.' He paused. 'That is, unless there's some other reason you're in such a hurry to marry.'

'I'm not pregnant,' Anna snapped, 'if that's what you're getting at.'

'Good. Then why can't you and your boyfriend come to Athens? It's only natural that your mother wants to meet your future husband before the wedding.'

'We don't want a big wedding.'

'Who said anything about a big wedding? All I'm asking you to consider is whether you think it fair to deny your family the opportunity of meeting your boyfriend and his family before you get married?'

'He's been an orphan since he was eight. His only relative is the aunt who raised him, and she won't travel outside the United States.'

'Good, that reduces the size of the engagement present your Aunt Lila and I intend on giving you.'

'We don't want presents.'

'Maybe not, but tradition puts certain responsibilities on me as

your godfather, and so I'm taking it upon myself to pay for your
and your boyfriend's roundtrip airfare to Athens. Just let me know
when you can fly over for a few days, and I'll book your tickets.'

'I don't think he'll want to come.'

'If you're going to be his wife, this is as good a time as any to
practice convincing him to do what you want him to do.'

She laughed. 'I think Jack'll like you.'

'Jack?'

'It's short for Jacob.'

'Ah, the same as your mother's nickname is short for Gavriella.'

'I've often wondered how Mother ended up with that name. I
don't know any other Greeks named Gavriella.'

'I'll leave it for your mother to answer that question the
next time you see her. I'm sure you'll find the story quite
interesting.'

'You're trying to entice me back to Greece.'

'Guilty as charged. Just let me know when you and Jack can
make it to Athens. I'm sure that will make life a lot smoother for
everyone, most of all for you.'

'I'll speak to Jack this evening and let you know.'

'Terrific. Please say hello to him for me.' He paused. 'And tell
him one other thing. Welcome to the family.'

Anna paused. 'Thank you, Uncle. Kisses.'

Andreas hung up the phone and looked across the room to
Yianni sitting on the sofa. 'So, how did I sound?'

'Like a brother scared to death that his sister would haunt the
rest of his days were he not able to deliver good news on a head-
strong daughter's marriage plans.'

Andreas smiled. 'Was I that obvious?'

Yianni smiled. 'Only to someone whose own family is steeped
in the tradition of longstanding family vendettas.'

Andreas rolled his eyes. 'Anna is the child of a sheltered
upbringing. She still believes in fairy tales with Prince Charming
coming to her rescue and everyone living happily ever after. She's
not like you Peloponnesian-Mani sons-of-Sparta types who'd
simply shoot her for disobeying her family's wishes and be done
with it.'

Yianni grinned. 'We've given up on the old ways. Today we're
far more enlightened.'

'Considering the current state of our world, I think there's a strong argument to be made that what's considered civilized behavior today is rapidly abandoning enlightenment in favor of embracing your kin's unforgiving *old ways*.'

Yianni shook his head. 'Ah, so that's why you get along so well with your niece.'

'What's that supposed to mean?'

'Despite your rather brutal take on reality, you don't dare challenge your niece's belief in fairy-tale endings complete with Prince Charming.'

Andreas bit at his lip, picked up a pencil, and began tapping the eraser end on his desktop. 'At least not until I somehow get a better fix on her boyfriend.'

Yianni cocked his head. 'I take it by *somehow*, you mean me.'

Andreas smiled. 'Sir Lancelot is unavailable, leaving you as my number one knight in shining armor for rescuing a damsel in potential distress.'

Yianni didn't laugh, but he didn't groan either. 'What makes you think she's in trouble?'

'Nothing. But I don't want to risk the possibility of screwing up my niece's life by my not taking a thorough look into his background. I need you to poke around and give me your best take on Mr Diamantopoulos. I owe it to Anna and her parents to get this right.'

Yianni let his arms drop to his sides. 'Fine, but I thought you wanted to talk to me about opening an investigation into last summer's wildfires.'

'I do.'

Andreas took a deep breath. 'The Minister wants us to track down anyone not yet identified as responsible for causing those fires. And we're to do whatever it takes to get it done before next fire season.'

'But why us? It sounds like something for the Fire Service.'

'The Fire Service solved many, like the dozen started by a fourteen-year-old kid pedaling around central Greece and setting them from his bicycle. But last season's fires were more than five times the yearly average, and despite the Fire Service's efforts, a lot of suspicious ones remain unsolved. Including fires that left three as-yet-unidentified victims dead.'

'Any indication the three were murdered or related?'

'No.'

'Then why pick our unit? It's going to cut in big time on our corruption investigations.'

'I'll pass along to you what I was told when I raised the same point. *Those wildfires brought two dozen countries rushing to our aid. At the very least we owe it to them to show that Greece takes the possibility of arson seriously and will punish those criminally responsible for the fires.*'

'Sounds more to me that we're being set up to take the blame in the media for the next round of fires.'

'That's always a possibility when politicians are involved, but those are the cards we've been dealt.' Andreas leaned back in his chair and smiled. 'How we choose to play them is something else.'

'What's that supposed to mean?'

'I've an idea that might give us an edge on locating who's behind the fires, and if it works, turn the tables on any politics at play to set us up.'

'What do you have in mind?'

'Don't worry about any of that for now. I'll deal with the fires,' Andreas smiled, 'while you check out my niece's new flame.'

Tassos Stamatos loved when bright afternoon sunlight passed into dusk, taking with it the heat, wind, and hordes of Aegean sun worshippers who'd long ago discovered the charms of the once-sleepy Cycladic island fishing village of Kini, which he called home. These days, tourists, locals, and their families spread out along the cove's sandy shoreline, on sun beds and under umbrellas, separated by a row of salt pines from a narrow road lined with tavernas and the occasional hotel or kiosk catering to the many who flocked there during tourist season.

He'd grown up in Kini, four miles due west of Ermoupoli, the capital city of the island of Syros and administrative center of the Cyclades. He still lived in the same house in which he was born, atop a cliff at the westernmost point of the northern side of the cove, far up and away from the frolickers below.

West of his home, across the open Aegean, loomed the island of Gyaros, where he'd once served as a prison guard for Greece's military dictatorship. To the east stood a semi-circular wave of bronzed glacial hills, dotted in green and embracing the landward side of the cove.

Tassos's house differed from the traditional, white sugar-cube

Cycladic construction favored by most islanders. When asked
about his home's unusual appearance, he'd say it was in keeping
with his own make-up: compact, sturdy, and uniquely built to
withstand whatever the elements threw at him. Its pale pistachio
color he attributed to an occasional bout of sea sickness during
particularly stormy times.

He never tired of watching sunsets from his porch. There he'd
ponder over what might have been the thoughts of those who'd
looked out upon this same sea so many centuries before.
Archaeological excavations placed an Early Bronze Age civilization
on Syros (3200–2200 BCE), but according to Homer (8th-century
BCE), Phoenicians (1500–300 BCE) were the first known inhabitants of Syros, naming the island from their words for 'wealth' and
'happy.' Later occupiers (including Ionians, Persians, Macedonians,
Romans, Venetians, Turks, and Russians) and immigrant refugees,
each seeking precisely that same prize, brought the island boom-
and-bust times in the millennia that followed.

There were also pirates back then, roaming the Mediterranean
and instilling terror in all who sailed or stood in their path. They
weren't the romanticized Hollywood versions of the breed, but
callous slaughterers, rapists, and slavers.

Innocents who lived by the sea placed their faith in castle walls
and mountain fortresses for protection against their tormentors. At
times defenses held. At times they did not.

Pirates today were different. Rarely physically violent, they
prowled the world in secrecy and disguise, probing digitally for
hidden treasures weakly defended and easily seized without risk,
then hiding their plunder behind layers of misdirection within
entities far more impenetrable than any fortified wall.

Yet, there remained one trait the new breed shared with their
forebears: they gave not a passing thought to the havoc they
wreaked upon the lives of those caught up in their wake.

Tassos sighed. As the long-time chief homicide investigator for
Greece's Cycladic islands, he'd spent nearly a lifetime in 24/7
hand-to-hand combat with evil's minions, wading through the
detritus of unbridled human passions and cold-blooded malevolence. Yet, despite his many triumphs, little had changed. The
ruthless were still out there, displaying renewed confidence and
vigor as they searched an ever more vulnerable globe for new
victims. Only their names and weapons had changed.

Perhaps the time had come for him to withdraw from the battle and leave this endless war to younger champions of civilized society.

He wondered what his girlfriend, Maggie, would think of that. She loved working as administrative assistant to Tassos's long-time protégé, Andreas Kaldis, but perhaps her unofficial role as mother superior and chief confessor for the administrative staff of GADA had tired her of pushing the same water uphill every day.

Long ago, they'd each earned the right to retire and sit together watching sunsets from the porch, holding hands while reminiscing over past adventures.

Yeah, right.

His mobile phone rang. He recognized the number. 'You just ruined a perfectly good daydream.'

'It's my gift.'

'So, what can I do for you, Chief Inspector, that my lovely Maggie cannot?'

'The Minister just dropped a flaming bag of you-know-what in my lap that he wants extinguished yesterday – by me spitting on it today.'

'Could be worse.'

'I'll pass on asking how,' said Andreas.

'Just let your imagination run wild.'

'I did, and you're what I came up with.'

'I'm touched.' Tassos stretched. 'So, what's up?'

Andreas told him of the Minister's order that an in-depth investigation of last summer's fires was now his unit's number-one priority.

'How can I help you with that?'

Andreas cleared his throat. 'We both know there's a long history of opportunists setting fires in protected forests and then innocently claiming that, with the forests now destroyed, let development begin.'

'Damnable, but it almost always works.'

'All that was supposed to change under a new law exempting protected land destroyed by fire from development.'

'Sure was,' said Tassos.

'Then why are there still so many suspicious fires?'

'How am I supposed to know? I investigate homicides, not fires.'

'Come on, who are you kidding? You know more about our country's dark side than any cop I know.'

'Funny, just before you called, I was thinking somewhat along the same lines, but not in the complimentary terms I assume you intended with that slur on my character.'

'Glad to hear we agree,' laughed Andreas. 'I'm looking for somewhere to start.'

'Come to think of it, didn't Parliament amend that law to allow property destroyed by fire to be used for renewable energy purposes?'

'That might explain a lot. But I need names of big-time players who might be involved in profiting off the fires.'

'Wouldn't the owners be of public record?'

'I'm talking about the money and influencers hiding behind shell companies and nominee owners.'

'Why do you think I'd have access to that sort of information?'

'Like I said,' chuckled Andreas. 'Because you're you.'

'Enough already with the Vaseline.'

'What if I say pretty please?'

Tassos exhaled. 'OK, I'll run some traps and see what turns up.'

'Terrific. As Maggie always says, "You're the best."'

'Yeah, right. Then ask her why she spends her weekdays in Athens working for you, when she could be playing full-time with me on Syros.'

'I don't have to ask her,' chuckled Andreas. 'It's obvious. Your absence makes her heart grow fonder.'

Tassos let out a deep breath, said goodbye, and hung up.

So much for retirement planning.

Anna doubted she'd been born with a burning desire to live in New York City, but for as long as she could remember that was her dream. Posters of long-running Broadway shows, glamorous Manhattan venues and events, magical Central Park, and the classic New York City Subway map dominated Anna's bedroom walls. The first thing she saw every morning when she opened her eyes, and the last thing she saw before falling asleep, hung affixed to the ceiling above her bed: a panoramic 360-degree view of Manhattan taken at dusk from atop the Empire State Building.

Anna dreamed of a life far different from the modest one she led with her family in the working-class northeast Athens neighborhood of Neo Irakleio. She'd grown up during Greece's years of financial crisis and watched her parents struggle to project a confident image of financial security for their children. But she also knew that her Uncle Andreas and Aunt Lila had quietly helped her parents cover the costs of education and after-school activities for Anna and her brothers.

She appreciated her aunt and uncle's generosity and loved them dearly. She also felt bound by their acts of charity to chart a life that would please them. They never told her what that might be, and whenever the subject of a career for Anna came up, they'd simply say, 'Do your best at what you like, and fate will take care of the rest.'

But her mother and father were not so open-minded. They had long made clear what they hoped for their only daughter: a college degree from a Greek university, marriage to a Greek man, a home close to their own, and grandchildren. Anna had no quarrel with her parents' goals for her, but she did not see them as ends in themselves. Her goal was a life free to map its own course, unconstrained by traditions and open to adventure.

All of which she imagined within her grasp once she'd convinced her parents to allow her to attend university in New York City. She left Greece committed to creating a life on her terms, while doing her best to make her family proud of her choices.

Which is when fate had stepped in and introduced her to Jack.

TWO

It was Anna's first weekend in Manhattan, and a girl in her freshman dorm had invited her to join some friends on Saturday night for a party in the East Village.

Although there were other foreign students in her dorm, Anna felt somewhat out of place. Not that anyone treated her badly, or was even less than friendly, but no one else spoke Greek, and she feared her English too weak to carry on an intelligent conversation at the breakneck pace of her American dorm mates. She didn't take that personally, because back home in Athens she and her friends spoke Greek to each other more rapidly than a priest racing through his morning prayers.

Her first instinct was to decline. But she'd come to New York to pursue a dream, and she'd not attain it hiding out in her room.

'Yes, I'd love to go. Thank you.'

'Terrific, we'll leave around ten.' The girl looked around and leaned in toward Anna, as if to whisper a secret. 'Dress foxy, it's a party thrown by some grad students, and we want them to invite us back for their next party.'

Anna's face lit up in a smile. 'No problem. I'll meet you downstairs in the lobby.' She might not speak English as well as the others, but when it came to knowing the ins and outs of wild partying, she could keep up with anyone.

For as long as Anna could remember, she'd spent at least part of her summers on the Greek island of Mykonos – one of the world's top party islands. She knew the ploys used by boys, and how to defend against them. She also knew how to dress to entice while behaving like a lady, not a hooker. Savvy Greek girls who liked bright lights, hot music, and fun times learned early on how to handle the continuing barrage of suitors of all ages looking to bed them. It was that or give in to the seduction and suffer the consequences; or avoid it all by staying home and avoiding the action.

Anna couldn't wait for Saturday night. She'd be back in her element.

*   *   *

Manhattan's East Village always was more a state of mind than a place. It runs south (from 14th Street) to Houston Street (zero street, if you're counting) and west from the East River through a section called Alphabet City (after its street names) to Broadway, where the more genteel village, Greenwich, begins.

For decades the East Village was Madison and Seventh Avenues' hidden Mecca for finding trends in style, dress, and music to capture the imagination of kids wanting to be hip, cool, with it, boss, or whatever. The record industry found gold – and platinum – in its clubs.

What made the East Village unique was the people who lived there. It was a neighborhood they could afford because most everyone else wanted to stay away. In the 1960s and '70s, its proximity to major colleges and cheap rents made it a haven for activists of all stripes – including drug dealers. During those years, 9th Street and First Avenue was Manhattan's bazaar for 'soft' drugs and Second Street and Avenue D was the place serious addicts shopped. Police let it be. 'Better there than anywhere else,' seemed to be the policy. Things changed with the real-estate boom of the early '80s.

Art galleries escaping to the East Village from skyrocketing rents of Soho and Tribeca brought with them a renaissance of sorts. That meant tourists and visitors to the neighborhood – and welcome new funding sources for the habits of its drug addicts. The outcry triggered a highly publicized and relentless police crackdown on open drug dealing and sent development and gentrification off and running. In what seemed a rather perverse nod by authority to the neighborhood's wide-open past – but proved a charmingly attractive touch to its new residents – street hookers of all persuasions continued undisturbed at their old haunts.

By the '90s, gentrification was well underway and couldn't be stopped. Rents went higher than anywhere else in the city for similar apartments. If you were young – or wanted to be – the East Village was the place to live.

Then 9/11 hit.

Union Square, at the East Village's 14th Street border, became the City's unofficial gathering place for those seeking word on missing loved ones. Flyers bearing photographs of the missing filled every available bit of space on plywood sheets erected along the park's walkways, and candlelight vigils carried on around the clock.

It was a place of hope that soon turned to despair as the world realized no one had survived the fallen towers. Innocence was gone for the Generation Xers and Millennials who'd made the East Village their spiritual if not actual home.

Two decades had since passed, and new blood now populated the area, many trying to emulate romanticized notions of what they thought the East Village once was, albeit from a decidedly upgraded and sanitized perspective. Yet, if visitors from another planet ever asked for directions to the one place with everything and everybody that makes New York City what it is, a safe bet would still be to send them to the East Village.

Shortly after 10 pm, Anna and three friends headed east in an Uber across 8th Street toward an address near Alphabet City. Eighth Street turns into St Mark's Place at Third Avenue and continues east to Avenue A, where it ends at Tompkins Square Park. The soul of the East Village once resided on St Mark's Place, and though that's changed, there's still action there, especially at this hour when the neighborhood comes alive.

The car stopped in front of a tiny shop, not more than twelve feet wide. A pastel blue and yellow awning framed the top of a faintly lit, multi-paned display window and a similarly paned door. The window was filled with brightly colored stones, crystals, and other 'balms for the soul.' At least that's what was written on the neatly handwritten sign taped to the inside of one of the panes.

Strollers filled the sidewalks, some pausing to check out a restaurant or bar, others drawn to the many stores lit up for business, but none seemed to take an interest in the shop. Perhaps because it appeared closed.

'Is this the right address?' asked one of the girls.

'There doesn't seem to be anyone here,' said another.

'Or a party,' said Anna, stepping forward to try the front door. It swung open and a gentle chime rang out from a bell attached to the inside of the door. No other sound came from within the shop, and the only light emanated from a half-dozen dimly lit glass vitrines haphazardly set about the shop, each filled with crystals, polished stones, exotic carvings, and small tapestries.

Anna was about to call out to anyone who might be inside when she saw a woman walking toward them through an open doorway at the rear of the shop.

'Hi.' Three-second pause. 'I'm Solona.' Three-second pause. 'Welcome to my shop.'

Anna guessed she was on hash or grass.

'Are you here for the party?'

'Yes,' said one of the girls.

Solona stood still for a moment, nodded, and smiled. 'Fine,. follow me.'

It was easy to be distracted by the rhinestone in the middle of Solona's forehead, three nose rings, elaborate tattoos on both hands, spiked multicolored hair, rings, beads, crystals and host of spiritual accoutrements draped or pierced everywhere about her, and miss that she was a genuinely beautiful woman.

Anna guessed she was likely in her thirties, about five feet four inches tall with a stunningly taut figure. Her skirt – a loosely tied cotton sarong – revealed more and more of her bare thighs with each stride, and she wore no bra under her midriff top.

Anna had dressed a bit more conservatively than that, in a black leather biker jacket, black lace bustier top, black leather skater skirt, and black chunky leather ankle boots. She also wasn't stoned and planned on remaining that way.

They followed Solona out into a garden open to the heavens. The faint glow of a washed-out Manhattan late-summer sky, mixing with dull blushes of light drifting down through far-above curtained tenement windows, faded the surrounding walls of century-old bricks into a blur, while distant sounds of a bustling city blended high above them into a comforting muted background din. Solona's garden seemed a tranquil sanctuary of escape from the chaos of lives being lived outside her tiny shop.

It was the perfect setting for getting high.

And into trouble.

Solona sat on a cushion made from a prayer rug and pointed Anna and her friends to similar cushions next to her and across from a group of four men in their mid- to late-twenties. The men sat sharing a joint. Solona lit her own, took a drag and offered it to Anna.

Anna made as if she took a hit – but didn't – and passed it to her friends.

No one spoke.

This was not the sort of evening Anna had expected, and if it continued along this path, she'd soon be leaving, with or without her friends.

'Welcome, ladies,' said a sandy-haired, blue-eyed guy sitting directly across from Anna. 'Thank you for accepting our party invitation.' He smiled at Anna, and nodded to each of her friends. 'Whenever possible, we make a point of visiting Solona in her magical garden. We first met her when we were undergrads and thought the four of you might enjoy spending some time here while we get to know each other better before heading off to the party.'

So, he's this crew's charmer and disarmer, thought Anna. Every group of guys on the make seems to have at least one smooth talker charged with assuring their prey that getting blitzed or stoned was nothing more than an innocent means for making their time together more enjoyable.

'Would you ladies like some wine?' said a trimly bearded, tawny guy wearing tight jeans and a snug-fitting white tee-shirt intended to show off the results of his many hours in the gym.

Before waiting for an answer, he began filling four glasses in front of him from an open bottle of white wine, while the smiling, freckle-faced redhead guy next to him passed the full glasses on to Anna and her friends.

The men picked up their own glasses as a dark-haired fourth man fixed the sizzling sparkle of his sea-blue eyes on catching Anna's attention and said, 'To new friends, cheers!'

'Cheers,' said the other men, quickly joined in by Anna's friends.

All except Anna took a long sip of wine, but she caught herself lingering long enough over the man's stare to elicit his smile. She twisted on her cushion to avoid his eyes and calm the little butterfly in her belly.

She couldn't believe how naive these girls must be. None of her Athenian friends would dare accept a drink poured from an open bottle offered by strangers. Hadn't they ever heard of date-rape drugs?

'You don't drink?' said Solona.

'I'm on antibiotics.' Anna smiled.

Solona nodded and smiled. 'A good excuse.' She paused for a few seconds. 'How about a smoke?' She reached toward Anna with a joint.

Anna forced another smile but did not answer or accept her offer. Instead, she sat quietly, watching her three friends be drawn into conversation with the men. The charmer tried to flatter and

cajole Anna into participating, but all she did was politely smile
and look away.

Solona leaned in toward Anna. 'I see you're a very cautious
young lady.'

Anna smiled.

'I don't blame you. These boys aren't the kind that would drug
you, but men being men, I agree one can't be too careful among
strangers, especially in a new country.'

'What makes you think I'm not from the US?'

'I'm originally from Ukraine, and your English, though very
good, has a slight accent to it.'

Anna nodded. 'I'm impressed at your ear. Our roots have us
almost as neighbors. I'm Greek.'

'A lovely language.'

'Do you speak Greek?'

'No, but I have friends who do.'

'How long have you lived in the US?'

Solona stared off into the sky. 'My mother brought me to
America when I was a little girl.' She paused to take another hit
on the joint and sighed. 'We lived in West Texas oil country. It
was a difficult life for her, a single attractive woman trying to raise
her daughter among so many predatory men.'

She shut her eyes and seemed to nod off. 'Shortly after turning
fourteen, I had my arms around my boyfriend's waist on a stolen
motorcycle fleeing the police. We crashed, he died, and I fled,
worried I might be blamed for the theft and his death.'

Solona drew in and let out a deep breath, her eyes still
closed. 'I drifted for a couple of years through the southwest
living off waitressing, babysitting jobs, and,' she snickered,
'the kindness of strangers.' She opened her eyes and patted
Anna's hand.

Anna had no idea why the woman had opened up to her, but it
was far more interesting listening to her than the back-and-forth
flirting between the guys and her friends. 'What about your mother?
Weren't you worried about her? She must have wondered what
happened to you?'

Solona nibbled at her lip. 'Of course, I missed her. But my
mother told me to stay away. At first because the police were
looking for me, but later because in our small town, I'd never be
rid of the bad reputation I now had among the locals.'

She slowly shook her head from side to side. 'I promised myself that as soon as I made enough money, I'd move her away from there to a place where we could both live together in peace. That's why I ended up in LA, where I found good work in its upscale dance bars as a stripper.'

She waggled her finger at Anna. 'But I was never a prostitute, no matter how attractively wrapped the proposition. By nineteen, I was one of the most popular dancers in town.'

She stared at her joint, paused, and took another hit.

'But then my mother died. I still don't know how. Just that she had a heart attack. I went back for the funeral, gathered together whatever mementoes I could, and returned to LA to free myself from that past. But I couldn't free myself from frequent, deep depressions.'

She sighed. 'Looking as I do, there were always parties – and booze and drugs. A half-dozen years of that life had me desperate to find another way to live, but I had no idea where to begin.

'One day I was walking by a mystical bookstore on Melrose when in a window I saw a poster of a woman who reminded me of my mother. It was an advertisement for a self-help seminar – something I never knew existed. I decided to go. It didn't help me much but I met an older man there who did. He wasn't trying to seduce me, just being nice.

'We became friends, and he encouraged me to find a different life. I said I had no idea how to go about doing that. He told me that one day I would see the way, and when I did, I must take the risk, because I had the ability to change the course of my life if I truly wanted to.'

Solona's fingers felt for a crystal strung on a cord around her neck.

'On the day he told me he was returning home to India he gave me this crystal. He'd found it many years before in Central Park's Strawberry Fields. He said I should allow it to be my guide. I followed his advice and moved to New York City – changing my name to Solona when I did.'

'Ladies, I hate to interrupt,' said the sandy-haired charmer, 'but I think it's time we move on to the party place.'

'Where's that?' said one of the girls.

'A club a few blocks from here.'

'It's one of the hottest clubs in the neighborhood,' added the trimly bearded guy.

Anna turned to Solona. 'Are you coming?'

She shook her head no. 'I've done more than enough of that to outlast a cat's nine lifetimes.'

Anna blinked. 'You're a fascinating woman. I'd love to hear more about your life.'

'Well, some day when you have the time, just stop by and we'll talk.' She took another sip of wine.

Anna bit at her lip, and her eyes darted from one face to the next. Everyone but Anna seemed high, and none showed any inclination for slowing down. If she went to the club, she had no doubt there'd be more booze and drugs to come, with the evening likely ending in a manner Anna preferred not to confront.

'I've an idea,' smiled Anna. 'What if I stay? That way we can continue our conversation.'

Solona shrugged. 'That's fine with me.'

'You can't do that,' said one of the girls, glaring at Anna. 'We need you to be with us. Otherwise, we're one woman short.'

Anna instinctively jerked up her eyebrows in the Greek woman's gesture for no. 'Don't worry, I'll join you there later.'

'But you don't know where the club is,' said the redhead fellow, 'and it's not the sort of neighborhood you want to be wandering around alone so late at night.'

'Just give me the address and I'm sure I'll be fine,' said Anna, forcing a smile.

'I'm afraid he might be right,' said Solona. 'I wouldn't want to be responsible for something bad happening to you.'

'I can take care of myself,' said Anna, a bit testier than she had intended.

The dark-haired man smiled. 'Spoken like a true Greek woman.'

Anna's eyes widened. 'How did you know I'm Greek?'

He smiled. 'From the way you lifted your eyebrows to say no.'

Solona leaned in toward Anna and whispered. 'Jack's one of my Greek friends.'

'But don't worry,' said Jack, 'I'll hang around here until you're ready to leave, then escort you to the club.'

Anna narrowed her eyes. 'I don't need a protector, Greek or otherwise.'

Jack leaned in toward Anna and caught her eyes with his deep blues. 'We all do, whether we know it or not.' He leaned back.

'I agree,' nodded Solona. 'That's the story of my life.'

'You ought to hear it,' said Jack. He switched to speaking Greek. 'You're right about Solona being a fascinating woman. You should take advantage of this opportunity to hear her story. She doesn't open up about her past to just anyone. You caught her in a mood to talk. Don't worry, I won't interfere. Just think of me as a potted plant sitting quietly in the corner.'

Anna scowled, but as if intended to suppress a laugh.

Jack smiled and gestured with his hand as if locking his mouth closed.

Anna rolled her eyes. Allowing him to stay seemed the least worrisome of a multitude of potentially undesirable endings to her evening. And at least he seemed to share her sense of humor.

'Fine, but don't say a word.'

Jack nodded yes; his lips shut tightly.

In a grin.

Once the others left, Solona excused herself and went inside. Anna didn't move, except to glance every so often at Jack sitting quietly across from her and looking in every direction but at her. She thought to say something but felt that likely was precisely what he hoped for her to do, thereby freeing him from his promise. Instead, she stared off into the sky in a comic battle of wills, waiting for Solona to return.

'Here you are, dear,' said Solona, breezing into the room with a bottle of wine, an empty glass, and a corkscrew. 'A virgin bottle of white wine, for you to open and drink from without fear of what may be in it.'

'That's very kind of you, but I don't think I'll be drinking very much.'

'Drink or smoke as little or as much as you like,' said Solona, handing Anna the bottle and corkscrew, 'as long as it gets your mind off the state of our fucked-up world.' She dropped down on to the pillow next to Anna. 'While I tell you all about mine.'

Jack watched Anna fiddle unsuccessfully with the corkscrew. Saying not a word, he held out his hand. She paused, and without looking at him, handed him the bottle and corkscrew. He popped out the cork like a master sommelier.

He must be a waiter, thought Anna.

She took back the bottle and poured herself a third of a glass.

'To life,' said Solona, lifting her glass.

'To life,' said Anna, clinking glasses with her.

'So, where was I?' asked Solona.

'Something about a crystal inspiring you to move to New York City.'

'Oh, yes, my friend found it on his pilgrimage to John Lennon's memorial in Central Park, across the street from where he was assassinated outside his building.' Solona sighed. 'I had no idea what to do or where to stay. All I knew for certain was that I wasn't going back to my old life.'

She took a sip of wine. 'I remember sitting in the park and asking myself, "How can I use my past to change my future?" That's when it hit me.'

'What hit you?'

'Music. I'd spent years in clubs surrounded by music. I knew how the equipment worked. And I also knew the dark side of the club business. So, I started looking for jobs running sound in clubs where I could keep my clothes on.'

She shut her eyes. 'I was working not far from here, in a karaoke bar on 6th Street and Avenue A, running sound on Saturday nights, when he walked into my life.'

Anna had no idea who she meant but decided just to listen.

'He came in surrounded by an entourage of men and women half his age. They looked like a group of Upper East Siders enjoying a night slumming it in the wilds of the East Village. It didn't matter to me. The more people in the place, the more likely I was to keep my job and make some tips.'

Anna took a sip of wine.

'About ten minutes into the set, I felt his eyes on me. A lot of women came there dressed to attract attention, but I wasn't one of them. His stare made me more uncomfortable than when I was pole dancing naked in front of horny roustabouts in West Texas bars.

'He didn't take his eyes off me. At a break one of his companions came over and invited me to join them for a drink. I, of course, said yes. It's how you get tips, and if he wanted anything more than music or conversation from me, he'd be sorely disappointed.

'He was three times my age but behaved like a perfect gentleman. He apologized for staring at me but said he couldn't help himself.' Solona took a sip of wine and smiled. 'He said I reminded him of his first serious adult love.'

Anna giggled. 'Even *I've* heard better variations on that pick-up line.'

Solona laughed. 'Who of us girls hasn't? And I told him so.'

'I take it that didn't discourage him,' said Anna, taking another sip of wine.

'He said he was happy to hear that he could still be considered young enough to be hustling a young woman as lovely as I.'

Anna laughed.

'I laughed too, and we talked through the entire break.' She smiled to herself. 'He stayed to talk with me through the rest of my breaks, even after his companions had left. When the bar closed, we went to an all-night diner on Second Avenue and talked straight through to sunrise.'

'Wow. What happened next?'

'Nothing. He walked me home to my apartment, asked if he could see me again, and said goodnight.'

'That was it?'

'Nope. Later that day he called to invite me to attend a dinner party he was having for friends at his apartment. He said he'd arrange for a car to pick me up. My first reaction was panic. I thought I'm not the sort of girl to fit in with his crowd.'

Solona felt for her crystal. 'But then I remembered what my friend who gave me the crystal had said. It was time to take a risk. Besides, I'd already told him everything there was to know about me, so if this was just his elaborate way of trying to get laid, big deal. He wouldn't be the first or last to con me into bed. On the other hand, if he was as sincere and kind as he seemed, why blow the chance of making such a friend?'

Anna nodded. 'A wise decision.'

'Perhaps the wisest decision I ever made.' She paused, closed her eyes, and leaned back. 'And saddest.'

Anna said nothing.

'He not only was rich – a lot of people have money – but extraordinarily influential. He counted sheiks, princes, kings, US politicians – even presidents – among his friends. Out of nowhere I suddenly was living a fairy-tale life.

'He found me a better apartment closer to his own and paid all my bills. Not as his mistress or even lover, but for companionship. His wife had died a few years before, and he'd been besieged by fortune hunters. I became his first line of defense. With me on his arm, dressed however I wished, I discouraged all but the most determined hustlers. And those I handled in a direct, West Texas way.' She smiled. 'Those were great years. Then one day, out of nowhere, he died.'

'How awful.'

'He was wonderful and kind, with a mind dedicated to discovering what really mattered in life. He was fed up with the all-so-many in the world looking to acquire *things* just to make themselves feel important.'

Both took another sip of wine. 'He told me it had taken him much of his life to realize the simple truth that it's not how much you acquire in life that matters, but how you use it. He said he saw in me someone who'd come to that conclusion early in life, and in living my life the way I did, I bettered the lives of all who knew me.'

'That's great praise,' said Anna, reaching out to pat Solona's hand. 'What did you do after he died?'

'Cried a lot and wondered what I'd do next to survive. So many ups and downs take a terrible toll on one's spirit.'

'How did you end up here?' Anna waved her hands at the garden and in at the store.

'He had four children, all older than I, all of whom he loved dearly, and all of whom would inherit on his death. I assumed he'd leave something for me, at least enough to get started on a new life.' Solona snorted. 'Was I ever wrong.'

'What do you mean?'

'His will provided for me, but not as I'd expected.'

She patted Anna's hand. 'He treated me in his will as if I were another of his children. I received one-fifth of his entire estate.'

She took another slug of wine and shook her head. 'Now I'm the one resisting fortune hunters.'

Anna's eyes darted toward Jack.

'No,' smiled Solona, 'not Jack. I've known him since his university days, when he was just a few years older than you are now. He's a good soul, but like many, is caught up in reconciling his understandable desire to make money with the risk of that becoming the be-all and end-all of his life.'

'And on that bit of amateur psychoanalysis of yours truly,' said Jack, 'I think it's time for me to renounce my vow of silence and suggest that we rejoin the others at the next planned stop on our evening's agenda.'

'As I said before,' said Solona, 'count me out.'

Anna nodded. 'Me too. I'm sorry to have messed up your evening, Jack, but I don't feel like going to a club.'

He shrugged. 'No problem. I'm flexible. Let's compromise and get something to eat.'

'No thanks, I'm not hungry.'

'Come on, you made me promise not to say a word while you and Solona chatted, and I kept my end of the bargain. Don't you think it only fair that you owe me at least a few words over a cup of coffee?'

'That's a pretty good routine you've got working there,' smiled Anna.

'That's kind of you to say, but it's obviously not working unless you say – or nod – yes.'

Solona loudly cleared her throat. 'Now that the two of you have reached the let's-get-to-know-each-other stage, I'm beginning to feel like an eavesdropper. Why don't you two just take off and find a better place to carry on your conversation?'

'Any suggestions?' asked Jack.

'As a matter of fact, yes.' Solona smiled at Anna. 'I'm particularly fond of an all-night diner over on Second Avenue.'

When they left Solona's shop, Jack led Anna east, toward Avenue A and Tomkins Square Park, away from Second Avenue. He was taller than she thought, with an athletic frame she associated with swimmers.

'Why are we going this way?' asked Anna. 'I thought we were going to Solona's favorite diner.'

Jack sighed. 'I truly love Solona dearly as a friend, but on occasion the many drugs in her past take a toll on her memory. The diner she speaks of went out of business a few years back. I'm taking us to a twenty-four-hour diner on East Houston Street, if that's OK with you.'

'As long as you know the way.'

'I do. I've spent a lot of time around here, both in university and since.'

'Why?'

They maneuvered their way through a raucous crowd huddled on the sidewalk outside a brick-faced bar close by Tompkins Square Park.

'I like the energy, especially how it attracts a lot of like-minded types who share my professional interests.'

Anna looked back at the crowd. The scene resembled a movie set hosting an *en-masse* cast call for a dystopian science-fiction-romance extravaganza. 'Just what would those shared interests be?'

'I'm into working on the fringe of the metaverse.' Jack paused to smile. 'Going where no man has gone before.'

Anna nodded back toward the crowd. 'I'd say you've found your element. What are you, a Trekkie?'

'Star Trek was the idealized science fiction passion of my youth. What I do today is create new reality by building virtual worlds that ever more closely simulate our natural life.'

'You're beginning to sound as if you and Solona share a similar psychedelic history.'

Jack chuckled. 'I don't do drugs. Never have. The most I do is alcohol and once in a while a joint. My mind means too much to me to risk it on any of that shit. Excuse me, *stuff.*'

'Yeah, watch how you talk to me, *malaka.*'

He smiled at her use of the most popular Greek curse word. 'Duly noted. So, what are you interested in doing with your life, Anna?'

She felt an unexpected rush when he called her by name. 'Not sure yet. It's my first year in university. All I know is that for as long as I can remember I wanted to come to New York, and not just come here, but make it *big* here.'

'Doing what?'

She shrugged. 'That's the tough part. I don't know yet.'

Jack nodded. 'I get the picture.' He waited until he caught Anna's eye. 'I know the perfect remedy for your dilemma.'

'What do you mean by *remedy*?'

Jack pointed up at a bright yellow and red neon-style sign flickering out REMEDY from its perch above a largely glass-enclosed first story of an otherwise green, brick-faced five-story tenement. 'It's the name of the diner.'

Anna stared up at the sign and spoke through a deadpan stare. 'Let me guess, when you're not reordering the universe, or offering counseling services to those you perceive to be impressionable female undergrads in need of rescue, you're practicing your stand-up comic routine.'

Jack spread his arms wide and smiled. 'Am I that obvious?' He pointed toward the door to the diner and took her hand in his. 'Shall we?'

Anna rolled her eyes and shook her head but didn't let go of his hand as they walked toward the door. 'So, what's your name?'

'My parents named me Jacob, but I prefer Jack.'

'I meant your last name.'

'Diamantopoulos, though Diamond is easier for most people to remember.'

'I prefer the original version.'

'Me too.'

Inside, they found a table by a window looking out on Norfolk Street and sat across from each other talking in English and Greek about their pasts, presents, and hopes for the future.

They didn't leave until dawn.

THREE

After his telephone conversation with Andreas, Tassos spent the better part of the rest of his day ruminating over how to get Andreas the names of big-time players who might have not only profited from the torching of the nation's forests, but were also complicit in their arson. Profiting did not mean the profiteer had anything to do with lighting the match. Some viewed crises as money-making opportunities. Acting on such opportunities did not make them responsible for the tragedy, no matter how morally questionable their perspective on such tragedies might be.

But Tassos had another concern. He couldn't simply reach out in a scattershot overture to the dark side for the names of potential bad guys without risking his own name getting out there as their hunter. He'd have to pick his sources carefully or risk becoming the target of powerful players anxious to keep their arson profiteering a deeply buried secret.

His first instinct was to reach out to Maggie, but Andreas must have thought of that already. Her back-channel network of government clerks, secretaries, and administrative staff offered the potential means for cutting through elaborate property ownership smokescreens far faster than contested court efforts ever could.

Also, making Maggie his point person risked shifting the target from his back to hers. There had to be a better way. The very least he could do was try to narrow down the number of haystacks before involving Maggie.

'Federico?'

'Yes, who's calling?'

'It's Tassos.'

Pause. 'Tassos?'

'Yep, the one and only,' he chirped.

'Oh,' laughed Federico. '*That* Tassos. Sorry I didn't recognize your voice, but it's been years since I heard from you, and mobile reception isn't the best out here in the middle of God's country.'

'Where are you?'

'Some place I want to keep secret.'

'From me?'

'From everyone, but most importantly from developers.'

'I see you're still at war with the capitalist class?'

'What can I say? Like father like son.'

'A good man, your father. I didn't agree with many of his beliefs, but he always spoke the truth as he saw it, and respected the same quality in others, regardless of their political differences.'

'You two had a mutual admiration relationship. He often spoke about how you protected him from the more brutal of your fellow prison guards when the Junta jailed him over his politics.'

'It was the right thing to do.' Tassos swallowed. 'I miss your dad. I think the last time I saw you was at his funeral.'

'I miss him too.' Federico paused for an instant and exhaled. 'So, how can I help you? I assume that's why you called me.'

'Frankly, I think we can help each other.'

'All the better.'

'Your father always spoke proudly of your dedication to saving the environment.'

Federico chuckled. 'He used to say the capitalists hated environmentalists more than they did communists.'

'Why's that?'

'Because we knew how to get the media to paint them as the bad guys.'

Tassos laughed. 'Terrific, because what I'm calling about plays to that strength.'

'What do you have in mind?'

'It's about the wildfires of last summer.'

'Puh, puh, puh. Horrible situation, much of which could have been avoided if only those in charge of preparing for the inevitable summer fires had followed the science.'

'I understand your point, but what I'm interested in at the moment are not the negligent, but those who profited off the fires through arson.'

'Arson? I haven't kept up with the statistics, but as I recall from the last time I looked, over ninety per cent of Greece's forest fires are attributable to three causes: Unknown, Recklessness, and Arson. People have come to accept forest fires as inevitable, and unless someone dies, I doubt anyone cares about their causes. And even

deaths no longer seem to matter, not unless someone's left alive
to identify the victims.'

'I hear you,' said Tassos. 'Three died in the last fires, but the
authorities have yet to identify even one of them.'

'Is that because the government wants them to remain nameless,
or because it hopes Greeks will forget that fires set by the capitalist
class for profit can kill?'

Tassos responded sternly. 'Well, that's changing, and it's why
I'm calling you.'

He paused, waiting for Federico to speak, but he didn't. 'With
your widespread influence and respect among environmentalists,
I couldn't think of anyone in a better position than you to help us
go after those burning down our forests for profit.'

Federico sighed. 'I'm sure there are a lot of farmers and developers who'd make that list.'

'No one's too small – or too big-time – to be on the list, but
we're not looking for uninformed guesses or vindictive-payback
leads. In order to send a truly meaningful message to would-be
arsonists, we need the names of anyone your colleagues genuinely
believe might be behind the fires. And by *behind* I don't just mean
those who actually set the fires or the property owners benefitting
from them.'

'In other words, you'd like me to name the powers hiding behind
the curtain?'

'Yes.'

'How serious about this are you?'

'Very. The directive comes from the highest level of
government.'

'That seems hard to believe considering the government's past
record on the subject.'

'That's why I've come to you. I trust you not only to get me
the names, but to help shepherd this through the press in a positive
way for all concerned, should it come to that.'

Federico chortled. 'I think you're trying to sell me on this.'

'Absolutely. But all I'm asking you to do is share with me what
you and your friends have undoubtedly been speculating upon
among yourselves for years. This is the chance for those who've
seen so much of what they've struggled to preserve go up in flames,
to bring the targets of their suspicions to justice. What's wrong
with selling you on that?'

Federico paused. 'I see why my father liked you so much. You have a knack for turning the most complicated and potentially risky situations into a simple matter of doing one's duty.'

'So, what do you say?'

Pause. 'Give me a couple days to see what I can come up with.'

'Thanks. Your father would be proud.'

Yianni stuck his head into Andreas's office. 'Do you have a minute, Chief?'

Andreas waved him in from behind his desk. 'What's up?'

'I have preliminary information on your niece's fiancé.'

'How preliminary?'

'Let's just say it's close to all we're likely to learn about him through official channels.'

'I wonder if Tassos has connections in America who might be able to help us out on that?'

'Has he had any luck yet coming up with a lead on the wild-fires?' said Yianni, dropping into a chair across from Andreas.

'He's in touch with an environmentalist associate with close ties to activists who keep track of suspicious forest fires and those who might be to blame for them.'

Sounds promising.'

'Fingers crossed.' Andreas leaned back in his chair. 'So, what have you learned about my niece's boyfriend?'

'No criminal record, at least not under the name Jacob or Jack Diamantopoulos, but I found a Jacob Diamantopoulos, age twenty-seven, a naturalized US citizen, born in Athens, now resident in New York City's Manhattan. He has bachelor and master degrees with highest honors in computer science from New York University, and currently operates as an independent computer consultant to a variety of businesses.'

'Any family?'

'Parents both deceased. His only known relative is an aunt who raised him and lives on Staten Island.'

'What happened to his parents?'

'His mother was killed in a ferry accident when he was eight. His father passed away of a heart attack exactly one year before.'

'Both on the same *day*?' Andreas shook his head.

'I know, but he seems to have turned out all right. At least from what I've been able to find out so far.'

'Any idea on how, when, or where my niece met him?'

Yianni gestured no. 'Not a clue.'

'Well, at least there's some good news to pass on to my sister. No criminal record and obviously smart.'

'Oh, one more thing.' Yianni pulled a photograph out of his jacket pocket. 'I found this online. It was taken a few years back at his university graduation.'

Andreas reached for the photo of a dark-haired, tanned, smiling young man, and held it in one hand, purposely shaking the photo as he studied it. 'There's something about him that looks familiar, but I can't put my finger on it.'

Yianni broke into a big grin.

'What's so funny, detective?'

'Maggie told me you'd say that.'

'Does she know him?'

'Nope, but she knows who he looks like.'

'Enough with the games, Yianni. Just tell me who.'

The smile faded from Yianni's face. 'A somewhat smaller, younger, and blue-eyed version of . . .' The grin broke out again. '*You.*'

Andreas blinked and stared at the photo. 'A damn handsome fellow he must be.'

'Ha!' Yianni's smile widened. 'Maggie said you'd say that too.'

Tassos enjoyed his morning routine on Syros. Just past dawn, he'd drive into the port town of Ermoupoli to join old friends for morning coffee and gossip in the same waterfront cafe where they'd met for decades. There he'd learn from fishermen, boat captains, and shopkeepers the sorts of things that never made the newspapers, but often led to arrests for past crimes and prevention of new ones.

Tassos liked to park by Ermoupoli's town hall, by far the island's most dominant building, a striking football field-size neoclassical beauty built between 1876 and 1898 facing upon an even larger town square. Four blocks east of the town square sat Ermoupoli's semi-circular harbor. At the harbor's northern border, a long concrete dock ran in front of the stately customs house and port authority headquarters. To the south loomed the shipyards that once were the busiest in Greece.

Though central police headquarters had long ago moved to a

bluff overlooking the sea, Tassos liked to park by the town hall. It was his way of reminding himself of his island's grand and sophisticated history, while getting in a bit of exercise walking to his office.

Unlike its island, the capital city of Ermoupoli stood barely two centuries old, founded essentially by refugees flocking to Syros to escape Asia Minor, the Ottoman devastation of Chios in 1822, and its victimization of other eastern Aegean islands.

Those refugees included merchants, bankers, shipowners, and industrialists, who, within a decade, helped turn Ermoupoli into Greece's largest urban center of its time, and the birthplace of Greece's first industrial efforts, including iron works, textiles, flour mills, and tanneries.

The great wealth and civic dedication of many of Syros's new citizenry brought unparalleled infrastructure and cultural development, including water supply and drainage systems, a street plan, a pier, shipbuilding facilities, harborside warehouses, a quarantine station, a theater house modeled on Milan's La Scala, Greece's first high school, and an exquisite collection of marble-adorned neoclassical buildings ranging from the simple to palatial.

It came as no surprise that in choosing a name for their new town, the inhabitants chose to name it after Hermes, the god of commerce.

But Syros's great aristocratic run as Greece's nineteenth-century shipbuilding and repair center ended at the close of that century with the proliferation of railroads, the opening of the Corinth Canal, and the harbor and shipyards at Athens' port city of Piraeus – driven by the determination and wealth of other capitalists possessing different visions of the future.

World War II ushered in a brutal Italian occupation of the island, bringing famine and poverty, sharp discord between Catholic and Orthodox islanders, and death to 8,000 of its people. But perhaps the single most significant factor in bringing Syros to its knees was a *Titanic*-like tragedy during Easter week in 1945 that wiped out virtually all the island's leadership class.

On May 2, 1945, a one-time Norwegian whaler turned minesweeper, given to the Greek navy in 1943 for continued service as a minesweeper, sailed out of Piraeus for Syros, Chios, and Samos. By May 1945, the *Sperchios* operated more as a civilian cargo and ferry boat than military vessel, given the toll the Greek ferry fleet had suffered during the ongoing war. The badly over-loaded *Sperchios* sailed that evening with goods destined for its ports of call and passengers anxious to return home from business dealings in Athens. Most were headed to Syros.

Though enemy warships no longer presented the concern they once did, there still were minefields to contend with, and as the *Sperchios* worked its way back and forth through those fields, its captain made a sudden turn, capsizing the ship, and sending most on board to their death.

Among the dead were many from Syros's most influential, successful families, including its most powerful clan, the Ladopoulos family, which had led the island's finance, business, industry, shipping, politics, charity, and social life.

The sinking of the *Sperchios* brought great mourning to many on Syros and soured the future for all. Without leadership, businesses began to fail, bankruptcies followed, banks foreclosed, buildings emptied and fell to ruin. Some said the island still hadn't recovered and point to grand commercial and residential structures once owned by those fabled families that have been allowed to crumble.

Others said things began to turn around for Syros in the early 1980s with the revival of Ermoupoli's shipyards, and that a recent change in ownership of the shipyards promised even more jobs for the island's 22,000 residents, supplementing those existing in agriculture and in support of the island's role as the administrative center of the Cyclades.

The massive tourism influx that fired the development of many of the Cyclades, such as Mykonos and Santorini, still had not yet materialized for Syros – a blessing some said – though visitors looking for a more culture-oriented, family-friendly Cycladic experience flocked there to enjoy the town's Venice-like vibe – sans canals and plus steps – and laid-back holiday atmosphere.

More importantly, an energized new generation seemed to have taken root, intent on gaining more respect for Syros's history as part of an effort to restore its structures and protect the island and its residents from the consequences of indiscriminate development plaguing so many of their island neighbors.

Tassos paused at the harbor, thinking of his conversation the night before with Federico and the never-ending clash between capitalists and their opponents. The arguments on each side always boiled down to the same ones, only the names of their respective proponents changed.

He wondered when Syros's next chapter would be written, and by whom.

Having completed his moment of contemplation, Tassos turned and walked north along a two-lane harbor-front road toward a small square. At the square he crossed the road and walked alongside a line of cafe umbrellas, chairs, and tables perched upon a narrow concrete apron between the sea and the road. Directly across the road were the tavernas, bars, and cafes serving those who chose to sit next to the sea rather than indoors.

It was too early for tourists and most locals to descend on the harbor, but once they did, waiters would dart back and forth among the two-way traffic carrying trays filled with food, drink, and the remains of both. For now, though, all was calm. Or at least appeared to be.

Tassos stopped across from a nondescript *kafenio*. Inside, seven old men sat drinking coffee at three well-worn wooden tables pulled together next to a street-facing window. Two younger men sat playing backgammon at a nearby table, while two others looked on. Back by the kitchen, two men stood talking. One looked to be a cook, the other a waiter.

Everyone glanced toward the doorway and nodded to Tassos as he entered. He returned the nods and patted one of the backgammon players on the shoulder as he made his way to the seven men.

'Good morning, gentlemen,' said Tassos, dropping on to a tattered wicker taverna chair facing the sea. 'Any new aches or ailments to report on?'

'Xenophon's bunions are killing him, Giorgos has a touch of gout in his big toe, and I'm switching to a new blood pressure medication.'

Tassos nodded. 'Thank you, Spiros, for your thoroughness. Any other earth-shattering news I've missed?'

The waiter set down a coffee and plate of biscuits in front of Tassos.

'We held off on the juicy gossip until you got here,' said Spiros. 'We knew you'd make us repeat it, so why bother starting?'

'Why indeed,' smiled Tassos, taking a sip of coffee.

'Did you hear about Lazaretta?' asked Xenophon.

'What's there to hear? The place is in ruins.'

South of the shipyards, along the southern border of the harbor, sat the shell of a stone building known as the Lazaretta. Built in the 1840s to quarantine anyone arriving by sea who might be carrying plague, it later served as a place for refugees, a prison – first for criminals, then for political prisoners – and a madhouse, but Lazaretta had not been in service since 1961 and, as with other once proud structures, had fallen victim to pillage and ruin.

'Someone plans on restoring it.'

Tassos laughed. 'As what? A getaway from the next pandemic?'

'It's not funny,' said Giorgos. 'It represents an important slice of our history.'

'Some slice,' said Tassos. 'It's served as a warehouse for quarantining the potentially diseased, imprisoning the insane, detaining prisoners, isolating dissidents, and executing a few particularly troublesome sorts along the way.'

'Let's not forget it also served as a convenient dumping ground for the drug addicted, homeless, uncared-for old, and any others that the police were prepared to swear posed a danger to society,' said Xenophon. 'It's a place of great sorrow.'

'It's still part of our island's history,' barked Giorgos. 'The structures are a magnificent architectural example of the cultural influences that helped shape our island.'

'I get that, my friend. That's why I'm happy the Municipal Port Fund finally got together with some of our dedicated citizens to finance and arrange to light it up at night.' Tassos took a bite of a biscuit.

'It's our Parthenon,' added Xenophon, 'symbolizing the best and worst of our past.'

'I wouldn't go that far,' said Tassos. 'Besides, if someone is seriously offering to restore it, call me a cynic, but I doubt the motive is solely for historic preservation purposes.'

'I don't agree,' said Xenophon. 'Our national government is behind an international project employing Lazaretta as a symbol for rallying artists around the world affected by pandemic times. Its purpose is to convince them to utilize expanding technologies for creating a new platform of digital culture for the future of our world – one inspired by the historical significance of Lazaretta and the impact of modern pandemics.'

Tassos stared at him. 'With all due respect, dear university professor friend, I have no idea what the hell you're talking about.' He swallowed. 'It just strikes me, as a woefully underpaid public servant, that no one is going to put in the amount of money it will take to restore that place to twentieth-century standards, let alone twenty-first, without a way of recouping its investment. And forget about the government. Encouraging others to do good deeds, yes, but putting in a single euro of taxpayer money into such a project when so much of the country is still reeling?' Tassos shook his head. 'Not a chance.'

Spiros spoke up. 'I agree with Xenophon that something is in the works with Lazaretta. A mutual friend of ours who works with me in city hall said that there's been a lot of interest expressed by anonymous "international investors" over any local regulations and protections that might apply to Lazaretta and its surrounding properties.'

'Interesting.' Tassos paused and took another bite of a biscuit. 'I suspect you used finger quotes around "international investors" because *your friend* suspects there's something suspicious about the prospective investors.'

'Probably money launderers,' interjected Giorgos. 'Who else has that sort of money to throw away on crazy real-estate projects?'

'A lot of people,' said Xenophon. 'We just don't travel in those circles.'

Tassos smiled to himself. *But I know someone who does.*

FOUR

Andreas sat alone on the sofa in his favorite room. He'd made it home just in time to catch the penthouse view across the National Garden of a gold-and-rose-laden sunset slowly enveloping the Acropolis.

From behind him he heard, 'Is this a private moment, or may the mother of your children intrude?'

'Are they awake?'

'All I can swear to is they were in bed when I left them. Would you like them to join us?'

'Yes . . . and no.'

'Aren't you the pensive one this evening,' said Lila, dropping down next to her husband on the sofa. 'What's on your mind?'

'How soon they'll be out in the world, living their own lives.'

'Let me take a wild guess. You were speaking with your sister about Anna.'

Andreas gestured no. 'But her situation has me thinking about how quickly our own kids will go from running around playgrounds to living amid a world of eight billion people, many of whom are nuts or worse. How do we possibly prepare them for what's out there?'

'Are you talking as a cop or a parent?'

'Does it matter? We can't escape reality by ignoring it.'

'If you're right, I see two alternatives. Either we instill in them the best values and good sense that we can while they're with us, or lock them up in their rooms until they're thirty-five.'

Andreas patted Lila's knee. 'I'm for option two.'

'I figured as much.' She kissed him on the cheek. 'Any word from Anna?'

'Not yet, but I'm still hoping she'll agree to come to Greece before she gets married. From what Yianni's been able to find out about the boy, there are no red warning flags – not even yellow ones – about him, but unless my sister meets him before the wedding, she'll plague every marital bump in Anna's life with "If I'd only met him before you got married" lectures.'

'Is that why you insisted on asking my father for my hand in marriage?'

Andreas grinned. 'And such a lovely hand it is.'

Lila cocked her heard. 'Do I detect this conversation now headed in a different direction?'

Ring, ring.

'Hold that thought.' Andreas reached for his mobile. 'It's Tassos. This might take a while.'

Lila stood. 'Send him my love. I'm going back to check on the kids. Our little chat has me concerned they might have packed up and moved out while we were fretting over their futures.'

'Are you about to surprise me with news on who profited off last summer's fires?'

'I'm still waiting to hear back from my source. I'm calling for your help on running down a bit of gossip that, if true, might be the tip of a very rotten iceberg.'

'Never heard that metaphor before.'

'But you get my drift.'

Andreas smiled. 'Yes. So, what's the icy gossip?'

Tassos repeated what he'd heard that morning of potentially serious interest by persons unknown in developing Syros's Lazaretta and its surrounding area.

'I'm surprised you waited all day to call me on this.'

'I was hoping I might get lucky and have some news for you on the fires. Besides, despite my iceberg analogy, I'm only looking to add to the gossip. I doubt there's anything sinister to it, even if my gossip network buddies have it right.'

'I've no problem helping you out, but what makes you think I'd know anything about any of that?'

'I never thought you would, but we both know someone who might. Or at least someone who is more capable than either of us at finding answers.'

Andreas paused. 'Maggie?'

'Come on, Mister Detective. Why would I feel compelled to go through you to speak with my girlfriend?'

This time Andreas hesitated only slightly before exclaiming, 'Lila?'

'Well done.'

'How would she know anything about what anonymous investors are doing on Syros?'

'Because Lila's the wife of a very important man, and the daughter of one of Greece's most prominent families. Similarly situated spouses and offspring tend to hang out together and share gossip. Sometimes sharing information they shouldn't.'

'Lila is not like that.'

'I know, but not everyone is as discreet as your wife.'

A voice heading toward where Andreas sat barked, '*Lila is not like what?*'

'We've been made. I'm putting you on speakerphone so you can get me out of this jam.'

'Hi, Lila. It's Tassos. We were only complimenting you.'

Lila sat next to her husband and smiled. 'In other words, you want something from me.'

'I've often wondered who the better detective in your family was,' said Tassos.

'Enough already; what can I do for you?'

Tassos explained what he was hoping to learn through Lila's contacts.

'I can't say I've heard anything about any of that, but I'll see what I can find out.'

'Thanks, that's all I can hope for. Sorry to bother you.'

'It's no bother. Besides, it gives me the opportunity to chat with old friends. Time just seems to fly by these days.'

'I know what you mean. I wonder what it would be like to remain young forever. Or at least until it's our time to pass on.'

'That's an interesting thought,' said Andreas. 'Imagine what it would be like if we and our children could all remain the same age.'

'Starting, no doubt, with a battle over what that age should be,' added Lila.

'I'd have only one requirement on that score.'

'What's that?' asked Tassos.

'That it be post-puberty.'

Lila groaned. 'Figures.'

'I think it's time for me to say goodbye,' chuckled Tassos.

Andreas draped his arm around his wife's shoulders.

'Sure seems like it,' said Lila.

'Bye.'

Anna woke well before dawn, patting the space beside her as she rolled over.

Jack was gone.

Perhaps he was in the bathroom. She sat up and listened, but heard nothing.

She reached for a lamp on the bedside table.

'Please. No lights.'

The voice startled her. 'I thought you'd left. I was worried something might be wrong.'

'Everything is perfect. I'm just sitting here in the moonlight, watching you sleep and thinking how lucky I am to have you in my life.'

'That sounds like there's something serious on your mind.'

He smiled. 'Am I that obvious?'

'Uh-huh. So what's bothering you?'

'I'm not bothered. I'm thinking about our wedding.'

Anna's voice cracked. 'Are you having second thoughts?'

'Absolutely not. I couldn't be happier at the thought of you as my wife.'

'Then what is it?'

He swallowed. 'I think we should follow your uncle's advice and visit with your family in Greece before we marry.'

'But I've told you, my mother will spend the entire time trying to convince me not to marry you.'

Jack shrugged. 'Frankly, if that's all it takes to convince you not to marry me, don't you think it better for both of us to learn that *before* we marry?'

Anna drew in and let out a deep breath. 'You don't know my mother.'

'That's precisely the point. I don't know her and she doesn't know me. And if we get married without even attempting to get to know one another, I don't think she'll ever forgive me.'

'Why you? I'm the one who doesn't want to confront her.'

'Because you're her daughter and always will be. She might blame you to your face just to piss you off, but in her heart and soul I'll be the one she never forgives. That's a burden I don't want to bring into our marriage.'

Anna smiled. 'You're far too rational for my family.' She waved for him to come back to bed.

The message emblazoned in all-caps across Andreas's mobile read simply: SHE'S COMING! It arrived a little after midnight, but Andreas didn't see it until dawn. He was amazed that his sister had restrained herself from waking him up to share what he took to be obvious good news about Anna.

He waited until reaching his office to call her back. 'Sounds like you're getting your wish, Gavi. The groom will meet the family before the wedding?'

'Yes. Thanks to you. Now we have to find a way to convince Anna that this marriage is wrong for her.'

'Whoa, Sis. That's not what I signed on for.'

'But you know it's wrong. He's too old for her and not Orthodox.'

'I have no intention of prejudging him or participating in efforts to discredit him in Anna's eyes. And if you're thinking clearly, you'll realize that's the wrong approach to take. You'll have far more influence over her if you're not judgmental.'

'I'm *not* judgmental.'

'Yeah, right. Then let's just say it would be better for all concerned if you restrained yourself from offering Anna unsolicited advice on her prospective husband within the first five minutes of meeting him.'

'She's my only *daughter*.'

'That's precisely my point. She knows what to expect from you, which means if you're hoping to have any chance at changing her mind, you better show her you're being fair to him.'

'Hm. I'd say you're the judgmental one.'

Andreas smiled. 'It comes with the job.' Andreas stretched out his arms and yawned. 'So, when are they coming to Athens?'

'Anna has her fall school break coming up at the end of next week. They're aiming for then.'

'Wonderful.'

'I'm so nervous.'

'Now you're sounding like a typical parent. It's natural to be nervous on first meeting your child's betrothed.'

'We work so hard to protect them, and then one day they just up and fly away. It seems so wrong.'

'This topic of conversation seems quite popular these days. Let's just say there's no lifetime cocoon available for protecting our babies. At some point we must let them go – subject, of course, to occasional well-intended moments of parental guidance.'

Andreas heard a brief snicker.

'So, you *do* share my belief in staying involved in our children's lives.'

'Of course I do. It's just a matter of degree – and how you choose to deliver whatever message you have in mind.'

'I take that to mean I'll find a more sympathetic ear in discussing this with the mother of your children.'

'Quite possibly.'

'Goodbye.'

Andreas stared at the silent phone. *So much for offering brotherly advice to a wound-up mama bear on how best to protect her cubs.*

Tassos was heading out to a lunch meeting when his mobile rang. He didn't recognize the number. 'Who's calling?'

'The man you've been waiting to hear from who doesn't want there to be a record of him calling you from his phone.'

'That sounds ominous.'

'Decide for yourself on that point after you hear what I have to say.'

'I'm all ears.'

'You were right about there being behind-the-scenes players profiting off the fires. Some were looking to turn forests into farmland, others to clear land for development. The same old bullshit selfish efforts wrapped in politically correct jargon. Most of them won't get away with what they have in mind. The conservationists are on to them, and willing to call them out publicly.'

'Then what's got you worried?'

'The new players.'

'What new players?'

'If you're looking for names, I don't have them, but they're big-time and heavily capitalized. They're proposing to turn tens of thousands of hectares of scorched earth into wind farms, by taking advantage of a loophole added to the law that prevented development of burnt land.'

'Ten thousand hectares is almost twenty-five thousand acres.'

'And that's just for starters,' said Federico.

'Sounds like big energy has discovered Greece's sunshine and wind as an alternative to gas and oil.'

'But big energy's not behind this.'

'Would you please deliver the punchline already? Who is behind it?'

'You're going to think I'm nuts.'

'Frankly, I'm waiting for you to prove to me that you're not.'

Federico laughed. 'Many of my conservationist friends are computer whizzes who know their way around the internet as well as you know your way around Ermoupoli. They're deeply hooked into the digital world and try to outdo one another over who's more up-to-date on the latest game, fad, news source, and money-making scheme.'

'And your point is?'

'They all agree on one thing. Whoever's behind this wind farms proposal is interested in something far afield from simply harvesting energy as a substitute for oil and gas. Chatrooms have long been abuzz over efforts by unnamed non-EU governments to establish a surreptitious mega-internet presence in an EU country. It's a very hush-hush project that requires huge energy resources in order to operate on the scale they have in mind.'

'In mind for accomplishing what?'

'That's the sixty-four-billion-euro question. But the stakes are great enough that anyone who dares stand in their way is rumored as expendable, which is what has me so concerned about being discovered talking to you.'

'OK, assuming these computer-whiz friends of yours aren't crazy, who else knows about this?'

'Other than my friends and whoever participates in those chat-rooms, I've no idea. The bigger question is who will believe it. Or better yet, who will *want* to believe it in light of the huge amount of capital and jobs the project will bring to Greece.'

Tassos shook his head and sighed. 'Thank you for ruining my lunch.'

'By the way, I'm no longer interested in serving as your shep-herd to handle the media angle on whatever's going on. Too many bad-tempered wolves willing to do whatever it takes to control that flock.'

'I get the analogy.'

'Good. Stay safe.'

'You too.'

Tassos hung up and stared off toward the sea. Staying safe had just taken on a whole new and urgent meaning.

Tassos immediately telephoned Andreas. Maggie told him Andreas had been summoned to a meeting at the Ministry, but she'd have him return Tassos's call the moment he was free.

Tassos decided to pass on lunch and wait in his office for Andreas's call. It wasn't the sort of conversation he'd dare risk someone overhearing in a public place, no matter how careful and circumspect he might be. After all, eavesdropping was a Greek national pastime.

Ring.

Tassos answered on the first ring. 'Andreas, are you in a place where you won't be overheard?'

'That's quite a hello. Maggie said it was urgent but never mentioned top-secret.'

'Cut the funny stuff, this is serious.'

Andreas's tone sharpened. 'Understood. You can talk freely.'

Tassos laid out his conversation with Federico as literally as he could recall.

'*Panayia*, Tassos. Is your friend reliable?'

'Before him, I knew his father, and they've always been straight shooters with me. As for his internet friends who passed along the information he shared with me, he claims to have faith in them.'

Andreas paused.

'You still there?'

'Yes, I'm just trying to decide where to go from here.'

'We have to tell the Minister.'

'What good is that going to do? If we think it's true, we have to take it straight to the *Prime* Minister.'

'But the Minister is our boss.'

'Let's be real. If there's as much at stake for these unidentified foreign powers as your friends say, we need to assume they've allocated unlimited funds toward the success of their project. And we both know how susceptible some of our public-service colleagues are to providing off-the-record assistance for the right price.'

'Yeah, but our Minister? Our Prime Minister?'

'I'm not saying they are, but are you willing to risk that they might be?'

Tassos grunted.

'But even if no one is corrupt, there's another consideration to keep in mind. This project will do a lot for the Greek economy, and there are those in government who think that's all that matters, regardless of the impact it may have on the rest of the EU, if not the world.'

Tassos added. 'And they believe they're right in their thinking.

Many still fault the EU for letting Greece suffer through the financial crisis to protect the economies of the northern European members.'

'Whatever the rationale, be it corruption or revenge, we have to be careful how and to whom we present what you've been told. I just spent an hour at the Ministry getting lectured by a deputy minister on how I'd better move more rapidly to arrest those responsible for last summer's forest fires. There's nothing more I'd like to do than drop this bomb in his arrogant lap.' Andreas shook his head. 'But we can't risk doing that. At least not yet.'

'Then what do you suggest?'

'Determine the properties involved, gather all the information we can on chain of ownership, and get someone in here who understands all this deep internet stuff and can give us a better understanding of what the hell's going on and who's behind it.'

'That's going to require a lot of manpower.'

Andreas chuckled. 'Frankly, I was thinking more along the line of woman power. With her back-channel network of friends in other ministries, Maggie's the perfect person to run with this.'

'At least with the info-gathering part,' said Tassos.

'Let's hope so. At this point there are just too many loose ends and unanswered questions for us to take what we have to a higher level. At best, we'll be told to come up with more concrete, reliable info. At worst, our investigation gets killed before we even get started.'

Tassos cleared his throat. 'Correction. The worst-case scenario is *we* get killed.'

Yianni and Maggie sat on the sofa in Andreas's office while he brought them up to speed on all that Tassos had shared with him, and what Andreas saw as the next step.

'I know it runs counter to official department protocol to keep this from our Minister, but since I once served in that position, I think it's safe to say that if this blows up in our faces, I, not you two, will take the blame. There are no guarantees, but as your superior and a former Minister, I should have known better than to cause my underlings to violate department protocols.' He cleared his throat. 'Now that you understand the magnitude of what's at stake – and the potential risk to your careers – are you both with me on this?'

'As one of your loyal underlings,' said Maggie, 'allow me to say there's no need for you to feel that someday you might have to cover my butt from political fallout. I know a lot of things many higher-ups in government never want to see the light of day. They wouldn't dare allow their compatriots to come after me.'

Andreas smiled. 'You and Tassos are a match made in heaven.'

Yianni shrugged. 'Count me in, too. After all, it's only my pension and entire future I'll be putting at risk.'

Maggie poked him in the arm. 'Don't worry, I'll include your name on my list of who among us will get to keep our pensions come Armageddon.'

'Thank you, ma'am.'

Maggie poked him again.

'How long until you and your shadow army of government agency workers can locate the properties involved, and the identities of their owners?' said Andreas.

'If we get the name of the lawyer or lawyers involved, it will simplify things a lot. Lawyers' names generally appear in the transactional documents recorded in official government filings, regardless of the purchasers' names. Without the names of the lawyers, it's generally tougher to isolate the transactions, because anyone trying to conceal a massive acquisition of properties would acquire each parcel under a different entity's name. But I'm guessing whoever's putting this all together will *not* use different lawyers for each acquisition.'

'So you're saying, "Follow the lawyers."'

Maggie smiled. 'Precisely.'

'OK, I'll pass that on to Lila. Hopefully that will help her get us a lead soon. Assuming she does, how long after that will it take to identify the properties and their true purchasers?'

'As I said, getting a purchaser's recorded name won't be a problem, but determining who's actually behind the acquisition is another story. I'll get my friends organized to move ahead as soon as we have a lead, but don't expect immediate answers.'

Andreas looked at Yianni. 'Since you're the youngest among us, I expect you to be the best choice for finding us a digital guru who might be able to help us figure out what's going on.'

'I don't want to disappoint you, Chief, but I have difficulty putting up a post on Instagram.'

Andreas frowned. 'That's not the answer I was hoping for.'

'I know,' smiled Yianni. 'That's why I have a different one for you.'

'Huh?'

'I have your guru.'

'What? How? Who?'

'Your niece's fiancé.'

'*Jack?*'

'In looking into his background, I found nothing criminally suspicious, but I did come across a lot of professional writings by him on subjects I had not a clue about. He's deep into the digital world and has been since he was a kid. He's also on track to earn a doctorate in that world. Let's just say if he's not your expert, he's certainly in a position to know someone who is.'

Andreas shook his head. 'Amazing how the gods play with us mortals. Who would have thought that convincing my niece to bring her fiancé home to Greece to meet the family would introduce me to a digital expert who just might be able to help those of us still living in the physical world.'

'A bit dramatic, wouldn't you say, Chief?' piped in Maggie.

'Yeah, but you've got to admit it's a pretty dramatic development.'

'When's he going to be here?' asked Yianni.

'She told my sister they plan on arriving the end of next week. Perhaps I can convince them to come sooner.'

'Can we wait that long?' asked Yianni. 'Maybe he can help us remotely?'

'Maybe, but I'm not prepared at this point to risk entrusting potentially explosive information to someone my niece has known for little more than a month, without at least meeting him face to face.'

'Frankly,' said Maggie, 'with all the preliminary work we have left to do in order to have any hope of getting a proper fix on this situation, you'll be better off convincing him to stay longer. Much longer.'

Andreas shook his head. 'In order for that to happen, it will require my sister to be nice to him.'

'Good luck.'

FIVE

'Lila?'

'Yes.'

'It's Georgiana. Sorry for not calling you back sooner, but your message came in this morning while I was getting the kids ready for school, and . . . well, you know what that's like.'

'Even with a nanny, I have my hands full corralling a preschooler and kindergartener. I don't know how you do it with three teenagers.'

'And all girls.'

Lila laughed.

'I wish I could laugh about it. My husband is going mad over the way they want to dress. The oldest sets the trend for the other two and believe me when I say modesty is not in fashion.'

'I'm happy Sofia is only three.'

'Three? Well then, my eldest's skirts and tops should just about fit her, though they may be a bit tight.'

Lila laughed. 'I'm sorry, I just couldn't help myself. I know it's a serious concern, but I'm happy to see you haven't lost your sense of humor.'

'I don't know how else to live with life. In a year, my oldest will be off to college. Lord only knows what will happen when she leaves the nest.'

Lila decided not to mention Anna's engagement to a fellow she met the first month of her first semester in college. 'What is she looking to study?'

'I'm happy to say she wants to be a lawyer like her father.'

'Well, that's a good example to be setting for her sisters.'

'Yes, but she wants to be the sort of environmental lawyer who tries to shut down Stavros's clients.'

'You're going to make me laugh again.'

'Even I laugh at that.'

'Well, while you're laughing, I have a question for you that's likely more in keeping with your daughter's interests than your husband's.'

'What is it?'

'A friend of mine who lives on Syros heard a rumor that a major project is in the planning stages involving the Lazaretta area that could have a major impact on the island. He wants to know if there's any truth to it.'

'What's the rumor?'

'That foreign interests are looking to acquire vast property holdings around the old harbor and convert them for purposes unknown.'

Georgiana paused. 'You know I can't talk about my husband's clients and business affairs.'

'Of course not, and I'd never presume to think that you would. I just thought that based upon your family's deep roots in Syros, you might have heard the same rumor, or know someone who does and would be willing to talk about it. Frankly, my friend is concerned that uninformed locals are getting riled up and he's hoping they don't go after the project based on gossip and cause unnecessary, avoidable grief to both sides.'

'I understand your friend's concern. I've not heard anything about that from anyone on Syros, but I know a woman in Athens who might know something.'

Lila's pulse raced. 'Do I know her?'

'I don't think so. She's the wife of one of my husband's lawyer colleagues. An American trying to establish herself in Athens society who incessantly brags about her husband and his latest *conquests.*'

'Conquests?'

'She means clients but calls them conquests.'

'What's her name?'

'Jill McLaughlin. She kept her last husband's surname. Her current husband is Panos Cirillo.'

'I don't know her.'

'I'm not surprised, but for certain she would love to know you – the famous, universally well-liked, and internationally connected socialite Lila Vardi.'

'You do know how hurtful I find the term "socialite."'

'Accept it, my dear, especially if you want Jill to open up to you.'

'What makes you think she knows anything about what might be happening on Syros?'

'Last week we were at a dinner party together, and she went on endlessly about how her husband had a huge international client actively acquiring properties all across Greece.'

'That's it?'

'I reacted sort of the same way, which seemed to disappoint her, so she added, "Aren't you from Syros? They're *particularly* interested in acquiring prime property in and around its capital."'

Lila swallowed. 'I'd like to meet Jill for lunch. How do you suggest I arrange it?'

'Easy. I'll call her, say how much I enjoyed our chat last week, and ask whether she'd like to join my childhood friend Lila Vardi and me for lunch. I'm sure she'll jump at the opportunity. Then I'll call her on the day of the lunch to say I can't make it but you would still like to meet her.'

Clever. 'That works for me.'

'By the way, when *can* you and I have lunch together?'

'Any time your schedule permits.'

'I'll call you next week, once I know the girls' schedules.'

'Cop out,' Lila joked.

'No. FMS.'

'FMS?'

Georgiana chuckled. 'Frazzled Mommy Syndrome.'

Georgiana had told Jill to pick the restaurant, and to no one's surprise she chose one of Athens' most fashionable places to be seen. Its signature marble, light woods, and stark white decor now occupied the lower floors of its own boutique hotel across from the National Historical Museum.

When Lila arrived for lunch, a tall, trim woman in her thirties sat alone at a table set for two. She wore a fuchsia Chanel suit, with a matching Hermès Kelly bag conspicuously occupying a corner of the table. Her blonde hair and make-up looked freshly done, and the moment she saw Lila she jumped up and waved, causing her strings of Van Cleef & Arpels Alhambra diamond and gold necklaces to sparkle wildly.

Lila hurried toward her with her hand extended. 'Mrs McLaughlin, I apologize if I'm late.' She spoke in English.

'Please, call me Jill, and no, you're right on time. I had another appointment in the area that ended earlier than expected, and only arrived a few minutes ahead of you.'

'We Greeks have what I call an unfounded reputation for never being on time, and I certainly didn't want to play into that caricature on our first meeting. Georgiana would never forgive me. And do please call me Lila.'

'I'm so sorry Georgiana had to cancel, but I take it as a sign we were predestined to meet one on one.'

Lila politely laughed. 'We could say that.'

'From all the good things I've heard about you, Lila, I just knew we'd hit it off once we had the chance to meet.'

Lila smiled as she and Jill sat down across from each other. 'I've heard very nice things about you too, Jill. Where in America are you from?'

'Texas. Dallas.'

'Ah yes, the home of cattle and oil wells.'

Jill laughed. 'And a few other things. But oil wells and cattle were my prior husband's businesses.'

'You were married before?'

Jill's expression tightened as she answered in a clipped tone. 'Yes, is there anything wrong with that?'

'I'm sorry, I meant no offense, I was about to say I'd been married before too.'

'I didn't know that.'

'I was widowed,' said Lila.

'I wasn't as lucky, though I'm not complaining. My marriage ended in a profitable divorce. And I got to keep my rich and famous husband's last name.'

Lila wasn't sure what to say in response and settled on, 'Shall we order? They have wonderful salads and fish here.'

'I know. I've eaten here many times before.'

Lila nodded. This conversation was quickly turning into a major test of her polite small-talk skills. 'How did you meet your husband?'

'You mean Panos?'

'Yes.'

'A dear friend who lives in Greece heard about my divorce and invited me to visit with her in Athens to escape the publicity of it all.'

Again, Lila successfully resisted a nigh overwhelming curiosity to ask for more details about this woman's marriages and divorces. 'Then you didn't meet him in a professional capacity.'

Again, Jill responded sharply. 'What do you mean by that?'

Lila forced a smile. 'I thought you might have met him in his capacity as a lawyer. Georgiana told me he is a very gifted and respected attorney.'

'And rich. His clients idolize him.'

'You must be very proud.'

'Absolutely. Especially for how well he listens to my advice on how to handle his foreign energy clients.' She waved for a waiter.

'Sorry, Jill, but you've lost me on that.'

Jill held up her hand to indicate they shouldn't speak until after they'd ordered. Once they had, she leaned in toward Lila and said, 'He's excellent at his legal work, but a bit weak at developing business. I coached him on how to develop new clients.'

'I meant the bit about the foreigners.'

'Oh, my last husband dealt with all the big international energy players. He knew first-hand that they didn't play by the rules, but he also knew how to turn that trait to his advantage by convincing them he was the perfect fit for their style of doing business.'

'How did he do that?'

Jill smiled more broadly. 'By doing whatever had to be done to get them what they wanted. And they paid him handsomely for his dedication.'

'That's quite a talent.'

'And I've taught those same skills to Panos. Now he's the top lawyer in Greece for virtually every environmentally challenged big-energy player in the Middle East, China, and Russia.'

Lila hoped her heart-racing excitement didn't show. 'He must make a fortune from that sort of clientele.'

Jill smiled as she reached to jiggle the strands of gold and diamonds draped around her neck. 'As do I.'

Lila cleared her throat. 'He sounds like a very busy, globe-trotting man.'

'He used to travel a lot more outside of Greece to the home countries of those he was trying to land as clients. These days it's more about travel within Greece to acquire the local assets his clients need to implement their plans.'

'That all sounds very mysterious and exciting.'

'That's a pretty good description of how my husband describes his clients' projects to me.'

'What do you mean?'

Jill shrugged. 'I've no idea whatsoever what his clients' projects are, other than that China, Russia, and one of those Middle East countries have formed a consortium for a project in Greece.' She broke a breadstick. 'Frankly, whatever their ultimate plans may be is of no concern to me as long as they continue to pay the big bucks.' She popped half of the breadstick into her mouth with a crunch.

Lila forced a smile, along with a look of admiration. 'I'd be so curious were my husband involved in anything that mysterious. I don't know how you can resist asking for at least a clue to what he's working on.'

'Oh, I did, but when he started talking about artificial intelligence I gave him such a blank stare that he told me just to think of it as a project intended to develop a videogame.'

'That's it?'

'I said it sounded like a Nintendo, PlayStation, or Xbox One wannabe.'

'What did he say to that?'

'He just patted my hand and said, "Wait and see." I assumed he felt I didn't comprehend the magnitude of their new gizmo.'

'Do you?'

'Not at all, but it's going to make us very rich. And that's all *I* care about.'

Lila kept forcing her smile of admiration. 'When is all this supposed to happen?'

'It's already underway. Or rather the development people have been working on it for a long time. From what I've overheard, it sounds that now they're into acquiring and building what they need to make it all operational.'

'Sounds like a great opportunity. Is there a way to invest?'

'No. It's all foreign-government financing. That keeps everything secure and away from prying eyes. There's no one to answer to in Greece.'

'It sounds like a life-changing opportunity. My congratulations to you and your husband.'

Jill beamed. 'Yes, I agree. See, I knew we'd hit it off.'

'That we did.'

'I can't wait to tell my husband.'

Lila sat back and smiled contentedly. 'Me too.'

*   *   *

Jill stood at the entrance to the restaurant, engrossed in bidding a fawning farewell to Lila, while Jill's driver, in coat and tie, stood at attention holding open the rear door of a double-parked, brightly polished black Mercedes S560 sedan. As soon as Jill had settled into the back seat, the driver closed the door, and Lila reached for her phone, waving goodbye to her departing lunch companion as she did.

Andreas had been waiting for her call eagerly, though he hated when Lila got involved in his cases. If cops were interested in something, bad guys likely were too, and that meant potential danger, no matter how innocent and risk-free Lila's role seemed to be.

Excited to share all that she'd heard from Jill, Lila rushed into a staccato presentation of her thoughts, prompting Andreas to suggest she take a deep breath, slow down, and start at the beginning.

Lila bristled. 'Are you going to tell me to *calm down*, too?'

Andreas cleared his throat. 'Ms Vardi, just the facts, please. You can beat up on your husband at home later.'

'*Malaka.*'

'Great. Now you sound more cop-like. So, let's start again.'

Lila drew in and let out a long breath before carefully recalling every word, look, and intonation Jill had offered her at lunch.

Once she'd finished, Andreas sat quietly for a moment. 'What's your take on all of that?'

'Isn't it obvious?'

'You were there, so I'd like to hear your impressions first.'

'I don't think she has any idea how much our conversation compromised her husband's confidences and, depending on what she meant by "doing whatever had to be done to get his clients what they wanted," it could cost him his law license, if not his freedom.'

From the other end of the line, Lila heard her husband's pencil tapping his desktop as he thought.

'Any ideas on what the wife actually knows about the mysterious project? Hard to imagine it's all about developing a better video game.'

'I think all she's interested in is whether whatever it is makes her and her husband a lot of money. And there's certainly a lot of money to be made in the digital world.'

'Agreed, but to have a consortium of governments backing a single project screams out that there's a hell of a lot more to this than building a better Minecraft or Fortnite.'

'Since when do you know so much about online games?'

'Since I spent my afternoon online trying to learn what I could while my dedicated wife was engaged in heavy-duty, face-to-face sleuthing.'

Lila cleared her throat. 'Chief Inspector, you sound as if you're trying to get my husband back into my good graces.'

'I can't speak for him, but on behalf of GADA's Special Crimes Unit, thank you for identifying the attorney involved, as that undoubtedly will assist us in narrowing down our search for any relevant property transactions, and thank you, too, for pointing us in the general direction of the potential nature of what's driving all this activity.'

'You're beginning to sound flatteringly in cahoots with my husband.'

'I hear he's a great guy who loves you madly.'

'And apparently knows how to grovel.'

'When necessary.'

'Maggie, did you check to see when Tassos is available for a conference call?'

Without moving her head, she answered through the open door separating her desk from Andreas's office. 'He'll call back as soon as he's in his office, which should be any minute now. And before you ask, Yianni's joining us in your office the moment Tassos calls.'

'What would I do without you?'

'Probably starve to death in the wilderness.'

Ring.

'That's my guy,' said Maggie. 'I'll put him through.'

Andreas hit the speaker button on his desk phone. 'Hi, my friend. I hope I didn't mess up your plans for the afternoon.'

'No, I was just about to finish lunch when Maggie called. It spared me the temptation of ordering dessert.'

'Just think of me as always there to help keep you on your diet, my love,' Maggie called out as she entered Andreas's office ahead of Yianni.

'Hi, Tassos.'

'Afternoon, Yianni.'

Andreas motioned for Yianni to shut the door as Maggie headed for the sofa facing Andreas's desk. 'I've news from Lila that could impact our investigation into the wildfires and potential related activity on Syros. A friend of Lila's introduced her to the wife of a lawyer who liked to brag about her husband having huge international clients particularly interested in acquiring prime property on Syros. Lila had lunch with her today, and just shared their conversation with me.'

'Shouldn't Lila be in on our call?' said Maggie, adjusting her position on the sofa so that Yianni could sit next to her.

'I don't think that's necessary,' said Andreas, shaking his head. 'And frankly, I don't want to encourage her taking any more risks than she already has.'

'What sort of risks?' said Maggie.

Tassos spoke up. 'The kind we have no idea are out there until someone steps on a landmine.'

'My thoughts exactly,' said Andreas. 'I think she's taken enough of a risk in getting the wife of prominent lawyer Panos Cirillo to tell her as much as she did.'

Maggie raised a hand. 'I've seen that name before in records relating to some of the wildfire properties.'

'That's good news. I was hoping there'd be a connection. How many properties?'

'I'll have to go back and check, plus there are still a lot more wildfire properties to research.'

'Now, all we have to do is determine what the link is, who's involved, and why.'

'Did I hear you say, *all we have to do*?' quipped Yianni.

Andreas waved him off. 'Just hear me out on the details of Lila's conversation with the lawyer's wife and speak up if something pops into your head.'

Five minutes into Andreas's presentation, Tassos shouted, 'Stop, I need a break. This woman's a nightmare.'

'Why's that?' snapped Maggie.

'Just listen to what she's been saying. It's all about money, nothing else matters, including the damage she's likely doing to her husband's career trying to impress someone at lunch.'

Maggie replied in a deliberate, determined tone, 'Were she not a she, but a he, you'd be describing him as a driven man motivated to better the life of his family.'

'As a matter of fact, my love, you'd be wrong. I'd be describing him as a ruthless asshole who deserves what's coming to him. I just decided to tone down my language for the benefit of Yianni's delicate sensibilities.'

'Whoa, don't get me involved in your squabbles. I've got enough trouble communicating with my own girlfriend.'

'Uh, excuse me, folks,' said Andreas. 'Can we get back to reviewing the facts?'

'Yeah, why not. I've vented enough,' mumbled Tassos.

'We'll take up this conversation later,' said Maggie, an edge still in her voice.

Andreas resumed Lila's description of her lunch conversation and finished without further interruption. 'Why's everyone been so quiet?'

'I was concentrating on trying to get a handle around all this technical stuff,' said Tassos. 'But what struck me was how neatly the mystery project his wife talked about falls in line with what my friend told me is happening on Syros.'

Maggie nodded. 'I also was hoping to grasp what that project might be about, but I've not a clue. What confuses me is if her husband is involved as the lawyer for whatever's happening on Syros, why does his name appear on transactions tied into wildfire properties that have nothing to do with Syros?'

'Where are the properties?' said Yianni.

'So far, they're all in northern Evia, roughly one hundred and sixty kilometers north-west of Syros.'

'That's a big island.'

'Second biggest in Greece.'

Andreas looked at Yianni. 'What do you think?'

Yianni shrugged. 'The same as I did before. We need a digital expert. We're trying to piece together a puzzle without the faintest idea of what it's supposed to look like when put together. All we have is a non-expert's vague comparisons to a videogame as the ultimate goal.'

Andreas nodded. 'I agree.'

'Where do we find that sort of help?' said Tassos. 'We can't just blindly seek out experts in Athens. If it's as big a project as it sounds, anyone involved in the digital field might be somehow tied into the project.'

'And even innocently so,' said Andreas. 'But I agree with you, we can't afford to take that risk. The last thing we need is word getting back to whoever's calling the shots that we're on to them.'

'Especially since we're actually staggering around in the dark with no idea where we are,' added Maggie.

'So,' said Yianni, smacking his thighs with his hands. 'Where do we go from here, Chief?'

Andreas slapped his desktop. 'The time has come to follow your suggestion.'

'My suggestion?'

'That I seek help from my niece's fiancé. We can't afford to wait until he's in Athens at the end of next week. I'm calling him this evening.'

'Do you think it's wise for us to bring him into the tent with us before we know more about him?' said Tassos.

'I've checked him out,' said Yianni, 'and so far, found nothing of concern. He's been living in the US since he was orphaned there as a child, raised by his aunt, has no criminal record, and no known contacts or dealings with Greece. He's a better gamble than anyone we might reach out to here.'

'Unless someone has an objection, tonight I'll be introducing myself to Jack Diamantopoulos as his future bride's favorite uncle.'

'Correction, you mean her only uncle,' smiled Maggie.

'Thank you for reminding me how often you listen in on my phone calls.'

'I don't have to. You speak loud enough on your end of every conversation for me to hear you clearly through the doorway.'

Andreas stared at her. 'Do I really speak that loudly?'

'Yes, but I only listen when it's interesting.'

Andreas rolled his eyes. 'Armed with that knowledge, let's get back to seeing what more we can turn up linking the mysterious Syros project, this past summer's wildfires, and . . .' He looked to Maggie. 'That lawyer Cirillo.'

Yianni and Maggie stood, exchanged goodbyes with Tassos, and headed for the door.

'Oh, Maggie, one more thing.'

'What's that, Chief?'

'Please shut the door. Tightly.'

Panos Cirillo grew up in the northern Athens suburb of Neo Psychiko, a respectable middle-class neighborhood of well-maintained two-story apartments, small single-family homes, and businesses catering to local needs. Panos and his parents lived above a small fruit and vegetable store owned and operated by his father one block from Kifisias Avenue, a broad and busy avenue separating Neo Psychiko from its strictly residential neighbor to the north-west, Paleo Psychiko.

Athens' best private schools stood in Paleo Psychiko, and many of Greece's most prominent, old-money families called it home. His father took great pride in his reputation among its prestigious residents for the quality of the produce he sold, and he worked hard to instill in his only child a similar pride in the business he saw as his son's future.

But, as the public-school-attending son of a fruit peddler, Panos saw his east-of-Kifissia-Avenue life as demeaning. Feelings of inferiority spawned resentment and festered over the years into a view of life in which all he expected to receive from those who considered themselves his betters was courteous dismissal. It drove him to prove that he was better than they thought, and he threw himself into his studies, gaining entrance to Athens' most respected law school.

The anger came later, when despite his notable academic accomplishments, he could not find a position among Athens' prestigious law firms, many of which included members of families long serviced by his father.

As Panos saw it, none of them wanted to give the fruit peddler's kid a seat at their rarified table.

That's when he vowed to create his own table – a massive, gilded one to dwarf and outshine all others.

Panos opened an office in a neighborhood near to where he'd been raised, catering to the families of clerks, cops, mechanics, shopkeepers, and civil servants of the sort he'd grown up with. People who'd trust a fruit peddler's kid off streets much the same as their own to understand their problems and take care of their needs far better than some fancy lawyer raised in privilege.

He took on matters others deemed too petty or unwinnable and found ways to gain results that pleased his clients and spread the word of his skills. The cases grew, along with his reputation, and he soon found that his mere threat to file a case or challenge a transaction brought settlement offers that pleased both his clients and his adversaries.

In the process, he amassed a coterie of sources and allies – helpful hospital personnel, court officers, notaries, and civil servants – who helped make his practice flow smoothly and quickly through the courts and government agencies. He knew how to keep them feeling happy, appreciated, and loyal. The money he made came not from headline-grabbing victories or mega deals, but through deliberate, orderly efforts at amassing and rapidly moving his inventory of matters to resolution.

He'd found his way to a lucrative, satisfying life, consumed as it was by relentless dedication to his work.

Then he met Jill McLaughlin.

She wowed him. Literally bowled him over. Convinced him to change his style of dress and manner of living to better reflect the financial success he'd achieved. She steered him to the chicest restaurants, introduced him to her like-minded driven friends, and ultimately led him to marry her – without a premarital agreement.

She possessed an uncanny grasp of her husband's deeply held resentment of the long-time rich and powerful, a feeling he came to realize she shared, and she masterfully played upon their mutual desire for suitable revenge to prod him into developing a clientele as powerful as any in Athens. One that would generate untold influence and riches for them both.

She introduced him to the Chinese and their Consortium colleagues through a contact she'd made on the bedsheets of an Athens hotel room. It was the price to be paid for an introduction that proved well worth the cost.

Panos impressed these future clients with his low-key manner, familiarity with the vagaries of property acquisitions across Greece, commitment to secrecy, and willingness to do whatever it took to succeed.

It was only later, when the negotiations for land purchases were underway, that Panos hit upon the idea of using his name as the designated agent for each otherwise anonymous separate purchaser. Otherwise, once the overall project was completed, no one would know the role he'd played in this monumental assemblage. He'd only be a legend in Greece if the world knew. But there was no way for that to be . . . unless Panos innocently did what virtually every lawyer did when acting for an undisclosed client and use his own name as the registered agent.

His wife thought the idea ingenious. She couldn't wait to show him off in all his brilliance to her new friends, and decided the best time to do so would be at the housewarming party for their glorious new home.

In Paleo Psychiko.

SIX

'Hello?'

'Hi, Anna, it's Uncle Andreas.'

Anna's voice dropped. 'Is everyone OK?'

'Everyone's fine. We're all looking forward to meeting Jack and seeing you next week.'

'If everything's OK, why are you calling me?'

Andreas chuckled. 'I'm supposed to be the suspicious one.'

'You're a cop, my grandfather was a cop, and my mother is into everybody's business. I come by my suspicious nature honestly.'

Andreas chuckled again.

'So, why *are* you calling me?'

'Actually, I'm not calling for you. I'm calling for Jack.'

'Jack?' Her tone turned defensive. 'Why do you want to speak with him?'

'It has nothing to do with either of you. I'm calling for his professional help on a police matter where we're in urgent need of expert advice on a specific digital matter.'

'There must be digital experts in Athens who can help you.'

'I'm sure there are, and that's where we may end up after I talk with Jack, but at this point we're looking for preliminary guidance, and don't want to set off rumors in the Greek digital community that my Special Crimes Unit is investigating what could be an innocent matter.'

'You make it sound exciting.'

'That's me, Mr Excitement.'

'How does Aunt Lila put up with you?'

'A question I've often asked myself. But one I'm sure you'll soon be able to answer for yourself, Mrs Soon-to-Be Diamantopoulos.'

'No need for more smooth talk. I'll ask Jack to call you. He had an early meeting. Hopefully, he'll be able to call you before it's too late in Athens.'

'Oh, don't worry about that. He can call me any time that's convenient for him.'

'Even in the middle of your night?'

'If that's the only time he can talk with me, it works for me, and Lila is used to me receiving middle-of-the-night calls.'

'I repeat what I said before.'

'Huh?'

'How does she put up with you?'

'Love you.'

'You too. Bye.'

Andreas's conversation with his niece ended on the same sort of light-hearted note as had most of their bantering chats through her teenage years. It was difficult for him to think of her as about to marry. Perhaps his sister was right. Maybe Anna was too young to set such a course on her own.

A lot would depend upon her choice of captain.

Andreas paused, then laughed at his thought.

Had he said that aloud to Anna, she'd have snapped his head off for such sexist thinking. After all, who's to say Anna wouldn't be the captain of their course? Or at least co-captain? He thought of his own marriage and the path it had followed, more often than not charted by Lila.

Perhaps he'd have a better fix on what Anna might face in marriage once he'd spoken to Jack. *No.* That wasn't the purpose of his call, and he shouldn't look for an answer to that question while seeking Jack's assistance. An individual's professional behavior often bears little resemblance to their home life.

He'd not yet heard from Jack when he left GADA for home. Nor had he heard from him when he helped Lila put Tassaki and Sofia to bed.

Andreas and Lila were watching a movie in bed when his mobile rang. Lila grabbed the remote and muted the sound as Andreas reached for his phone. He held it so that Lila could listen in on the conversation.

'Hello, Kaldis here.'

'Hi, this is Jack Diamantopoulos. I understand from your niece Anna that you want to speak with me.'

'It's a pleasure to meet you, Jack, even if only over WhatsApp audio.'

'A pleasure to meet you too, sir. I'm looking forward to meeting all of Anna's family in person.'

'Next week will be fun, I promise. And, please, do call me Andreas.'

'Anna has talked about you, her Aunt Lila, and her cousins Tassaki and Sofia so often that I feel as if I already know you.'

Lila flashed a thumbs-up.

'I hope that's a good thing,' quipped Andreas.

'Absolutely. I know it's late in Greece, and I apologize for not getting back to you earlier, but I'd agreed with my alma mater to deliver lectures today to three different class levels on three different subjects during three different hours, so this was the first chance I had to focus on anything other than that.'

'No problem, I'm just happy you called. But to be honest, what's on my mind won't give you much of a reprieve from teaching. As Anna may have told you, I'm in dire need of expert guidance on the digital world.'

'She did, and said it sounded as if there might be some dark mystery lurking about in your situation of interest.'

'More likely just an ignorant uncle wandering in the dark.'

Jack laughed. 'So, what's the situation?'

'In a nutshell, we're attempting to determine the motive behind apparent surreptitious interest in acquiring substantial property on a prominent Cycladic island for use in connection with what's been loosely described as the development of some sort of digital product or system, perhaps even a game. The project is thought to be backed by a consortium of foreign governments willing to commit unlimited capital to the project.'

'Can you tell me a bit more about the foreign governments?'

'There's not much to say because we don't know for certain who they are. But a guess would be China, Russia, and an unnamed Middle Eastern state.'

'I have only one more question.'

'Shoot.'

'Is there a massive source of electric power available on that island?'

'What do you mean by massive?'

'Multiple times more than what's needed to meet the island's peak needs.'

'Not that I know of.'

'It could be gas, oil, coal, nuclear, hydro, solar, or wind-generated.'

'Again, not that I know of.'

'Do you know if there are any plans to develop that sort of generating capacity on the island, or to import power from elsewhere?'

'On Syros? Not to my knowledge. May I ask you why that's relevant?'

'The key element behind turning the theoretical I have in mind into operational applications is electrical power. At the risk of getting you thinking your niece is about to marry a crazy person, concepts that even the most far-out science-fiction fans once thought unachievable technology are today viewed as the inevitable direction of our digital age. The burning question these days is, who will first convert the theoretical into operational technology on a grand scale?'

'Um, I think I need a bit more detail.'

'I can't say the technology I have in mind is at the root of your mystery, but there's always that possibility if the nations you mentioned are involved.'

'What sort of technology are you talking about?'

'Technology intended to prey on populations conditioned by years of masked pandemic terror, mandatory lockdowns, voluntary self-quarantines, social isolation, and world economic chaos that had sent their societies into survival-mode hibernation and, at times, violence and even war. On no one did that societal transition have greater impact than on the young denied the opportunity of experiencing the full range of person-to-person real-life interactions so necessary for human development.

'An entire generation had been conditioned to accept a new digital template for living. An unreal one, where no one cared how much they earned or what form of government they lived under, as long as they could find happiness somewhere in their personal dream world, ignorant of real-life wars being fought to control their digital existence.'

'You make it sound as if someone's creating a new world order.'

'Based upon what you've told me, that's a bit further than I'm willing to go, but as a basic proposition, isn't that always the case? After all, individual billionaires from around the world have been trying for years to bring what they conceive as the next generation of the internet into existence. Now they have AI, the metaverse, and a spectrum of rapidly evolving technologies to make the scary into the plausible. It's illogical to think governments wouldn't join forces to achieve ends they haven't been able to achieve on their own.'

'What sort of ends are you talking about?'

'I'd prefer not to speculate until I've got more facts.'

'Evil ends?'

'As I said, I'd prefer not to speculate.'

'But why would they pick Greece for such a project?'

'My best guess is because Greece is a member of the EU, and setting up an EU-based operation gives them credibility in the West.'

'That point I get,' said Andreas. 'Because considering Greece's history of dealings with Russia, China, and the Middle East, those countries can expect a far more accommodating reception in Greece than elsewhere in the EU. Russia is its number-one trading partner, China its number three.'

'You'd know that better than I, sir.'

'Please, call me Andreas, because from the way this conversation is going, I'm the one who should be calling you "sir."'

Jack laughed. 'That's very kind of you to say. But just to be clear, there remains a critical component missing from what you've told me, which, if present, would turn my academic musings into serious concern.'

'What's that?'

'Power.'

'How much power?'

'I can't say off the top of my head, but to give you an idea, the world's largest digital cryptocurrency operation requires power on the order of what is needed to power the US city of Houston, Texas.'

Andreas exhaled. 'If Syros is where they plan on setting up their operation, where do you think the needed power will come from?'

'I've no idea.'

'Any other thoughts you'd like to share?'

Jack paused. 'Not yet, but when I'm in Athens, if you could arrange for me to visit that island, perhaps I'll be better able to answer your questions.'

Andreas drew in and let out a deep breath. 'I wish you could come to Athens sooner.'

'Not sure how that would play with Anna.'

'Just ask her.'

'Is that wise?'

Andreas chuckled. 'I see she's training you well.'

Lila poked a finger in Andreas's side as Jack laughed.

'Funny you should say that. She once told me she learned how to train a husband from the best possible teacher.'

'Her mother?'

'No, Aunt Lila.'

Lila thrust her fist in the air and whispered to Andreas, 'I love this kid.'

Andreas feigned a grimace. 'I get your point. Let's speak again tomorrow. OK?'

'Sure. After I've had the chance to speak with Anna.'

Andreas looked at Lila, resignation written across his face. 'But of course.'

Before they hung up, Jack gave Andreas his mobile number and told him not to hesitate to call at any time for whatever help he might need.

Andreas put his phone on the nightstand and looked at Lila. 'What do you think?'

'I like him.'

Andreas nodded. 'I do too. He's impressive. No doubt about that. I guess my sister can relax.'

'What do you think will impress her the most about him?'

'His respect for his elders?'

'Nope.'

'Then what?'

'His command of Greek. You do realize that the two of you conducted your entire conversation in Greek?'

Andreas smacked his forehead with his fingertips. 'You're right. It was so natural I didn't even notice.'

'Where do you think he learned to speak like that?'

'I guess from the aunt who raised him. But you can ask him when you meet him.'

She picked up the remote and turned off the TV. 'So much for watching the rest of this movie that I've been dying to see.'

'Yep.' Andreas stretched out his arms and yawned. 'Although he didn't say it directly, I took what he said to mean that we've got a real-life blockbuster of a science-fiction thriller to contend with ASAP.'

'What do you mean?'

'I sensed he didn't want to alarm me with what he thought

might be the most chilling scenario. It's an academic thing not to guess but wait for the facts. That's why he wants to see Syros.'

'When do you think he'll come to Athens?'

Andreas shrugged. 'The tickets are on us as an engagement present, but Anna has school obligations, and Jack has a business to run. They might not be able to change their plans. Besides, Jack's given me enough leads to likely keep us busy until he gets here as planned.'

'Get some sleep.'

Andreas leaned over and turned off the lamp on his nightstand. 'Good suggestion, because it looks as if my real-time life, starting first thing tomorrow morning, will be all about figuring out how to kick some big-time international digital butt back to the Stone Age.'

New York City's East Village has hidden treasures that more likely than not survived gentrification efforts by two simple means. One, they delivered desired and appreciated services, and two, there's no landlord to boot them out in favor of higher-paying tenants, or to sell out to a developer. A prime example was the oldest continuously operating Italian restaurant in Manhattan.

The massive mound of white candle wax at the back of the restaurant's rear dining room, close by a pair of ever-swinging kitchen doors, has been growing (and getting shaved back to manageable proportions) since 1908. Its tin ceilings, tiled floors, and walls adorned in frescoes of rustic Italian scenes frame a white-linen-tablecloth candlelit intimacy that's launched many a memorable evening, and continues to draw crowds of loyal clientele packing its simple bar while patiently waiting for a table.

That early twentieth-century, Roaring Twenties ambience has made this East 12th Street restaurant a popular setting for memorably dramatic scenes in some of America's best-known gangster films and TV series. But its celebrity was not why Jack had picked it for dinner with Anna. He found its southern Italian cooking and reasonable prices hard to beat elsewhere in the city.

They sat at a corner table by the kitchen, facing toward the front room. A waiter swiftly brought menus and what remained of the half carafe of red wine they'd ordered at the bar.

Jack ordered the restaurant's famed garlic bread and house salad to share.

Once the waiter left, he said, 'I had a wonderful talk with your uncle this afternoon.'

'Were you able to help him?'

'I don't know. I didn't want to unduly concern him with all the potential scenarios running through my mind after hearing what he had to say. I thought if I did, he might think me mad and blackball me from the family.' Jack smiled. 'He still might think I'm crazy, but he did say some nice things to me. Even asked if we would come to Greece sooner.'

'Can you?'

'That really depends upon you. I don't want to leave without you.'

'But I can't leave before Thursday afternoon. My interview for an internship at the Greek Consulate is scheduled for Thursday morning.'

'Can't you move it up to earlier in the week?'

'The Ambassador is flying in from Washington on Thursday morning to personally conduct the interviews. I might not get the internship, but if I don't show up on Thursday, I'll be eliminated from consideration.'

Jack's chin dropped to his chest. 'I'll just tell your uncle I can't get there before you do.'

Anna reached out and patted Jack's hand. 'If it's important that you go, I completely understand. Knowing my uncle, it sounds as if there's a big mystery on his mind. Is it a secret?'

Jack paused. 'He didn't say it was secret, or anything like that, so I guess I can tell you.'

She tilted her head in toward Jack. 'You better believe you'll tell me. I'm the one who got you this gig.'

Jack laughed.

'What's so funny?'

Jack shook his head. 'Nothing. I just had this thought of your Aunt Lila asking your uncle the same thing.'

Anna gestured no. 'That would never happen.'

'Why not?'

'Because if he spoke to you from home, he likely let her listen in on the conversation. That way he spares himself the third-degree she'd put him through to repeat everything you said in your conversation.'

Jack raised his eyebrows. 'What kind of family am I getting myself into?'

Anna kissed him on the cheek as the waiter arrived with the

garlic bread and salad and asked if they were ready to order their main courses.

Anna looked at Jack. 'Just order the shrimp and calamari pasta in red sauce that you've been dying for, I'll order the eggplant parmigiana, and then tell me everything. *Including* whatever scenarios you left out when you talked to my uncle.'

Jack did as she'd asked, and by the time he'd finished reciting the details of his conversation with Andreas, including omissions, their main courses had arrived, and Anna had gone from smiling to the verge of tears.

'What's wrong?' Jack asked,

'Our world is utterly mad and becoming ruthlessly more so every day. We've got power-hungry technology giants engaged in cut-throat competition to aid and abet the planet's most merciless in taking us in directions only God should control.'

'See, at times a fan of ancient philosophy and a software guy can view the world the same way.'

'It's not funny,' she snapped.

'It wasn't meant to be, but now you see why I didn't speculate with your uncle.'

Anna gripped the table. 'You're talking about universal brain-washing for political purposes!'

Jack leaned in and lowered his voice. 'Potentially, yes, but propaganda's been around since one human first tried to influence another. Until I know more facts, I'm not about to say something that could alarm a chief inspector of the Greek police.'

Anna clasped her hands and rested her elbows on the white tablecloth. 'This is frightening.'

Jack reached across the table to take one of her hands. 'One thing's for sure: the world as we know it isn't going to end before we get to Greece. And in that same spirit, I suggest we finish dinner – including tartufo for dessert – and not delve into this any more now.'

She pulled her hand away. 'I think you should call my uncle tomorrow and tell him everything you just told me. And you should leave for Greece as soon as he needs you there.'

SEVEN

Andreas left for his office far earlier than usual. Despite promising himself that he'd get a good night's sleep, thoughts spawned by his conversation with Jack kept him awake and tumbling for much of the night. The last thing he wanted for his commute that morning was the stress of battling Athens' notorious rush-hour traffic into the heart of the city. So, he was up and on the road by dawn.

Though Andreas's plan worked to the extent of overcoming the stress of morning traffic, his mind filled the void with thoughts raised by last night's phone call. Could forces truly be at work seeking to replace our real-world order with a made-up digital one? As crazy as that sounded, and as much as Jack avoided opining on the possibility, the media's relentless focus on artificial intelligence made it seem as if the stars were aligned to make the threat inevitable.

Inevitable, Andreas's subconscious repeated.

He thought of his children. 'That *can't* be true!' he yelled at his subconscious. 'It's all utterly insane.'

But very real.

'Well, aren't you the early bird this morning,' chirped Maggie, poking her head into Andreas's office.

Andreas grunted a quick, 'Morning.'

Maggie paused at the door. 'Are you OK?'

Andreas gestured no.

Maggie stepped inside the office. 'Are the kids OK? Lila?'

'Yes, and yes,' said Andreas, crossing himself three times. 'It's that digital twist to our wildfire investigation. The more I learn about it, the bigger a nightmare it becomes.'

'I take that to mean you spoke with Jack Diamantopoulos?'

Andreas leaned back and rolled his head from side to side. 'What he told me isn't what got me into this mood. It's what he *didn't* tell me. I sensed he was playing down some of the more consequential possibilities, hoping not to alarm his fiancée's uncle any more than he already had.'

He exhaled deeply. 'Please set up a conference call with Tassos as soon as Yianni gets in. I'll go over my conversation with Jack then. In the meantime, please do your best at running down the specific properties linked to that lawyer Cirillo.'

'I'm already on it. So far his name's popped up tied to properties on Syros near Ermoupoli, the southernmost part of the mainland at Lavrio, and parts of Evia ravaged by the wildfires.'

'Is there a pattern or reason for his interest in those properties?'

'Not that I can see.'

Andreas shook his head. 'Jack told me the key to everything is power. As in energy, not political juice.'

'Why's that?'

'It's a long story. I'll get into it once we're all together.'

'You certainly know how to keep up the suspense.'

'Trust me, it's not by plan, but out of ignorance.'

Maggie turned to go to her desk as Yianni walked past the open office door. 'Yianni, the Chief wants us in his office now.'

Yianni did a crisp military turn, marched straight into Andreas's office, and dropped on to the sofa, while Maggie walked over to Andreas's desk and called Tassos from the desk phone.

Two minutes later, Andreas launched into a description of his phone call with Jack. No one spoke a word until he'd finished. Even then, Andreas was the first to speak.

'Any comments?'

'If there is a new world order coming, heaven help us,' said Maggie, crossing herself.

'I don't believe it,' said Yianni, shaking his head.

'I don't think I've ever said this before,' muttered Tassos, 'but if he's holding back on what he truly believes is afoot, I think this is the first time I can recall being happy to be as old as I am.'

'What's that supposed to mean?' barked Maggie.

'Just what it sounded like. I'm not cut out for this brave new world.'

'Philosophy is down the hall by the coffee machine,' said Andreas. 'This office is all about hard-hitting investigations into matters of national concern, and if Jack's even partially right in his conjectures, this matter jumps straight to the top of that pile.'

'OK, so where do we go from here?' asked Yianni.

'Maggie's already linked the lawyer Cirillo to property

acquisitions around Ermoupoli, Lavrio, and Evia. What we now need to do is determine how those properties potentially tie in to what Jack told me.'

'If I understood everything correctly,' said Tassos, speaking slowly, 'software developers are likely already hard at work somewhere on the planet creating whatever programs and inexpensive user-friendly artificial intelligence equipment are needed to take over the world – be it the unreal or real one – and the planned targets are likely the citizens of EU member countries. Considering how rapidly artificial intelligence programs are said to be developing human-like skills, I'd say the battle's well under way. What's missing – if Jack is correct – is electrical power sufficient to drive a master operations center from somewhere within Greece.'

'Sounds right to me,' said Yianni.

'Fine,' said Maggie. 'Then could someone please give me a logical answer for why the need for power ties into the lawyer's interest in Syros, mainland Lavrio, and Evia?'

Silence.

'That's reassuring,' said Andreas, patting his desktop. 'I have a new project for us. We'll each spend our morning doing whatever we must to come up with potential answers to Maggie's question and re-convene after lunch. I'd like to have the benefit of your thoughts before I speak to Jack this afternoon, if for no other reason than to prove to him that his future bride's uncle isn't as ignorant as I'm sure I seemed in our first conversation.'

Tassos spoke up. 'If that's your goal, I suggest you confine your conversation to inviting him to get his butt over to Athens ASAP.'

Tassos loved wandering about Ermoupoli. Especially the classic old-time market area running up from the harbor along Chiou Street, full of vendors offering the finest local foodstuffs. Such bustle he'd never seen before the day his mother first brought him to Ermoupoli, and he'd carried that image with him ever since. Island city life had captured his imagination, but his roots – and home – remained firmly planted amid the tranquil Kini Bay sunsets of his rural childhood, due west of the capital.

One street south of Chiou Street, and one street west of the harbor, Tassos stood in front of his favorite pastry shop, staring soulfully through the window at the day's delectable offerings. A childhood friend stood behind her cash register waving for him to come in, but he waggled his finger no.

She laughed.

That had been their routine ever since Tassos promised Maggie that he'd stick to a rigorous diet. Each time he passed by the shop he'd longingly admire the window's temptations, summon up sensory memories of their aromas and tastes, shut his eyes for a moment, then walk away, waving goodbye to his chuckling friend.

Another day, another inviting seduction resisted.

He'd usually go on to meet his friends for coffee, but this morning he'd made an early lunch appointment and decided to skip coffee and go elsewhere. He made his way down to the harbor, turned right heading south, and walked toward the Onex Neorion shipyards, a symbol of Ermoupoli's modern efforts at rekindling its industrial past.

The shipyards commanded the harbor through both their physical presence and contribution to the island's economy. He wondered how this real-world operation would stack up against a deep-pocketed digital challenger intent on setting up shop on the island.

At the shipyards he borrowed a friend's motorbike and headed toward the Iroon Square rotary, where roads spun off toward the airport, the southern villages, the general hospital, Ano Syros, and the western villages, including his home village of Kini.

He followed the road running closest to the sea, passing by the ruins of nineteenth-century buildings, though not the ones he was interested in. When the road split, he stayed left, following the shoreline to a small marina, where he continued left down on to a narrow paved road and up through a small cluster of modest whitewashed homes to the top of a rise.

Off to the left, a neatly maintained ochre stucco church, bearing a single white cross atop a blood-red roof soffit, nestled snugly up against the badly deteriorated ruins of a mid-nineteenth-century building. The church's two dark front doors each bore two large white crosses, and off to the right a plaque described the church as consecrated in honor of Saint Haralambos, a martyr who guarded his people much as a shepherd would his flock. It was built in 1945, the same year as the *Sperchios* tragically sank, claiming many Syros lives and much of the island's future.

Thirty meters past the church, the road effectively dead-ended at a sign marked ENTRANCE IS NOT ALLOWED. Simple goat fencing

separated the road from a stone doorway opening into the main
ruins. A well-worn path, running from the fence through the
doorway and beyond, evidenced that few visitors abided by that
warning intended to protect what remained of this one-time
architectural gem.

Today, the Municipal Port Fund of Syros – charged with main-
taining and improving existing port infrastructure and building
new where necessary – regarded Lazaretta as part of the area's
cultural heritage, a treasure to be protected, preserved, and high-
lighted as a symbol of both the long-ago prominence and the dark
side of this one-time commercial hub of the Aegean. From what
Tassos could tell, little if any of that was happening.

Of the thousands of times he'd gazed upon or driven by these
largely stone and brick-and-mortar ruins, he'd never seriously
looked at them, let alone thought to explore them. Lazaretta's
dramatic northern side, filled with enchanting rows of marble-
framed archways commanding a view of the sea, was the image
seen from the harbor and the view most photographed by tourists.
Rarely did visitors glimpse the structure's less recognizable
southern side, with its large rectangular courtyard and main
entrance to the historic facility.

He thought to take a closer look but decided against creeping
in among the rubble and prickly undergrowth without having any
idea what he might or should be looking for. He turned to face
south and scanned the rolling hills, open fields, scattered buildings,
gas storage tanks, grazing sheep, and airport.

Why would they want to build a state-of-the-art facility here?
he wondered. *Especially if they're trying to keep their project
secret.* He shook his head. *And how do they expect to get the
approvals they need, including from the Municipal Port Fund?*

Tassos sighed, turned, and headed back to town. He had too
many questions seeking answers he likely wouldn't comprehend
even if he got them. As far as he was concerned, Anna's digital
whiz fiancé couldn't get to Syros fast enough.

Tassos went to lunch at his favorite place. A cozy little taverna
just off the port, set away from a relatively quiet, marble-paved
side street by a line of oleander and tamarind. He walked straight
toward a table occupied by a bear of a man with piercing blue
eyes and a Santa Claus beard.

'Hi, Mario,' said Tassos, dropping into the chair across from him. 'Thanks for agreeing to meet me for lunch.'

'Since you offered to pay, I figured it must be important.'

'Am I that obvious?' smiled Tassos.

Mario grinned. 'No, stingy.'

'*Malaka.*'

'So, what's on your mind?'

'Let's order first.' Tassos waved to a waiter leaning against a counter at the rear of the taverna. 'Giorgo, send out the best of what's on the menu for today.'

The waiter answered back, 'You always say that.'

'Then why do you always wait for me to ask?'

'Because I live to be surprised.'

Tassos turned back to Mario. 'I know what Giorgo means. In fact, that's sort of why I need your help.'

'I assume you don't mean with the menu.'

The waiter set down a basket filled with bread, two knives, two forks, and napkins, a large bottle of flat water, olive oil in a bowl, and a small plate of cheese and olives.

'I'm hoping that your years working for Syros Power give you insight into a situation that has me terribly confused.'

Mario nodded as he tore off a chunk of bread.

'I'm trying to understand why someone in need of a huge source of electric power would be interested in properties on Evia, Lavrio, and Syros.'

'Sounds like you're talking about the Cyclades Interconnection Project.'

'What's that?'

'Its full name is the *Interconnection of Cyclades Islands with the National Mainland Interconnected Transmission System.* It comes out of a 2005 study looking to connect the Cycladic islands to each other and to the mainland system via marine cable connections.'

'How's that done?'

'By placing substations close to the coast.'

'But what does any of that have to do with Syros, Lavrio, and Evia?'

Mario snickered. 'Everything. A marine cable running between Lavrio on the mainland and Syros was the most vulnerable link in the system, should high load conditions occur on Syros. To assure that power coming from Lavrio to Syros remained sufficient to meet the power demands of Syros and the other connected islands, advanced phases of the project called for buttressing the power supply. That added electricity would come from power generated in Evia and delivered to Syros via Lavrio.'

Tassos shook his hand at his friend. 'Mario, make it simple for me. I'm a dumb cop.'

'Power generated by wind farms on Evia is to be transmitted to Lavrio on the mainland, and from there delivered by undersea cable to Syros in quantities far greater than Syros needs.'

Tassos watched in silence as Mario tore off another chunk of bread, dipped it in the olive oil, and devoured it in one bite.

'Mario, would you be offended if I gave you a great big kiss?'

Mario shrugged. 'At our age, who would care?'

The meeting resumed in the early afternoon, after lunch and an unexpected call from a deputy in Andreas's Minister's office pressing him for an update on the state of the wildfires investigation.

'Progress is going better than expected,' didn't satisfy the deputy who demanded concrete details.

Andreas picked up a five-page document from his desk and slowly read every page to the deputy as if speaking from memory. That seemed to satisfy the deputy, who asked that Andreas 'immediately' transcribe and transmit that report to his office.

Andreas agreed to do so at once. What Andreas did not tell him was that he'd delivered that same report to that same deputy's office two days before.

Aside from delaying the start of his meeting with Yianni, Maggie, and Tassos, his conversation with the deputy served as further confirmation of why he considered any achievement by any ministry packed with cover-your-butt bureaucrats as nothing short of miraculous.

'Sorry for the delay, Tassos. We're all here now and ready to go,' said Andreas into his speakerphone. 'Who wants to go first?'

Maggie looked at Yianni, and both looked at the speakerphone.

'Let's not fall all over one another in a rush to speak up,' said Andreas.

Yianni raised his hand. 'From friends in the construction

business, I learned that wind power contractors are descending on Evia forest areas hit by the fires. Both Greek and international companies. The government has declared its intention to turn Evia into a wind power hub, and there's sort of a gold-rush mentality taking hold among contractors based on rumors that property owners will pay top money to those who can get facilities up and running quickly.'

'Any names on the property owners?'

'No, but a power cooperative has been formed by the owners to handle all contracting arrangements once they get the go-ahead.'

'What's holding it up?'

'They say they're waiting for the government's OK, because the current law allowing forest land destroyed by fire to be used for renewable energy projects is being attacked by environmentalists in lawsuits challenging the legitimacy of the law and raising accusations of wrongdoers benefiting from their role in causing the fires.'

'Sounds like my friend's buddies have been busy,' said Tassos.

'Yeah, but my friends say the lawsuits are going nowhere, and rumor has them on the verge of being dismissed. Something about Greece needing the investment capital and jobs. Also, since it's intended to battle carbon emissions, the environmentalists are far from unified in their opposition.'

'Anything to add?' said Andreas.

'That's it for now, Chief.'

Andreas looked at Maggie. 'Any more to add to what you said this morning?'

'The lawyer's name keeps turning up in real-estate transactions in all three places, but in every case it's for a different buyer. And the buyer is always a foreign entity with no obligation to disclose its principals, provided it names a properly empowered representative in Greece.'

'Let me guess,' said Yianni.

'Yep, in every instance Cirillo is the designated representative.'

'That puts him dead center in the middle of a bullseye,' said Yianni.

'Convenient, isn't it, should the day ever come that those behind whatever's going on decide to eliminate the one person who can link them all together?' said Andreas.

'The linkage has already occurred,' said Maggie. 'By naming himself as their representative, he's effectively done that. Had he not, we'd likely never know.'

Tassos cleared his throat.

'You've been rather quiet, my friend. What surprises do I sense you have in store for us?' asked Andreas.

'I think I have the answer to what links Syros, Lavrio, and Evia together in whatever might be the consortium's plans.' Tassos described his conversation with Mario. 'I didn't press him any further, because he's a well-known gossip around the port, and I saw no need to get that engine fired up and running.'

He paused.

'Are you waiting for applause or is this just for dramatic effect?' quipped Maggie.

'Do you remember back in the days when the power grid in the Cyclades depended upon outdated, poorly maintained fossil fuel plants that constantly failed?' asked Tassos.

'Many a romantic night started out as a blackout,' Yianni recalled with a smile.

'Well, back in 2006, China and Greece signed a strategic partnership agreement initially intended to cover technology and communications, but ultimately led to the privatization of the port of Piraeus to a Chinese entity, and China State Grid, the world's largest utility, purchasing a sizable minority interest in Greece's national power grid operator, ADMIE.'

'Where did you learn that?' said Yianni.

'I do know how to use Google, folks. It's part of China's openly declared global infrastructure strategy. They call it the Belt and Road Initiative and it's meant to give China a greater leadership role in world affairs though investments in foreign countries. As part of that strategy, it plans on benefiting from renewable energy by creating an intercontinental electricity grid, and Greece has turned to China to connect its far-flung islands to that electric grid. In other words, Greece is used to doing energy business with China.'

'But why all the secrecy with this project?' said Yianni. 'With all that power and money, why not just openly acquire the property and build whatever's necessary to generate all the energy it needs?'

'My guess is China's afraid of the real world's reaction to the truth,' said Andreas. 'Greeks are deeply suspicious of the Chinese despite their vast economic dealings with China. Openly revealing China's acquisition of those sites would trigger an onslaught of media coverage and send packs of investigative journalists running in search of a story. Not to mention computer geeks across the internet going nuts with speculation over what they see in China's actions. And let's not forget our vocal Greek nationalists, who'd undoubtedly accuse China of plundering Greece of its heritage and natural beauty.'

'Agreed,' said Tassos. 'Plus, can you imagine what would happen if word got out that Russia and a Middle Eastern country are also in on China's plans?

'China, Russia, and their oil-rich Middle Eastern colleague have a history of banding together to bring grief and pain to the West in pursuit of their global ambitions.'

Andreas nodded toward Tassos's voice. 'From what's being done to keep this project cloaked in secrecy, I'm betting the last thing the Chinese or its consortium partners want is someone poking around looking for their real intentions.'

'You mean pokers like us,' said Maggie.

Andreas nodded.

'How do you plan on stopping this juggernaut?' asked Tassos.

Andreas patted his desktop twice. 'Cautiously, my friend. Very cautiously.'

EIGHT

'Hi, Jack, it's your soon-to-be Uncle Andreas. I hope I'm not calling too early.'

'Hi. No, I've been up for hours. Coffee is my refuge.'

'Mine too.'

'I was about to call you. Anna agrees I should come over to Greece earlier than we'd planned if you think that might be helpful to you. But she won't be able to get there until Friday. She has an important job interview on Thursday morning that she can't miss.'

'Sorry to hear that, and please wish her good luck on the interview. The reason I'm calling is recent developments have me thinking it's important for you to come over as soon as possible.'

'What sort of developments?'

'Well, to begin with, we think we've found a huge source of power being assembled for transmission to Syros.' Andreas told him what they knew about the Syros-Lavrio-Evia connection. 'What do you think?'

Jack did not respond.

'I assume you're formulating your thoughts into an answer,' said Andreas.

In a firm voice, Jack said, 'Another reason Anna wanted me to call you was to share some speculative thoughts I had when we last spoke. I'd held back because I didn't want to alarm you without any sound foundation for my thinking.' Jack cleared his throat. 'You've just given me the foundation I need.'

'Why do I sense that's not good news?'

'Are you familiar with virtual- or augmented-reality games?'

'I've heard of them, and don't want my children involved with them, but I wouldn't say I am familiar with them.'

'The promise of the technology involved allows you to wear a device that theoretically enables you to experience whatever sort of imaginary life you want to live at any particular moment, and interact with images that appear, react, and communicate in real time as if they're human. Whether that will be for good or for bad is another story. The disabled, the homebound, the poor can play any sport, visit any place, live anywhere they desire. It also allows anyone the opportunity of having sex with everyone they desire, without fear of disease or pregnancy, simply by hooking available accessory packages to appropriate body parts.'

'How could that be?'

'It's already happening. Millions have created parallel lives amid digital applications, employing avatars of themselves living a virtual-reality life of their choosing. Some pay huge sums to have a unique avatar created for them, and many pay to outfit their avatars in posh brands at prices rivaling real-life fashion wear. Then there are the crazy real-world real-estate prices many are willing to pay to set their digital life in the home and neighborhood of their dreams.'

'But why would anyone pay so much for make-believe things to live in a fake world?'

'Whether it's fake to them is a whole different conversation. Let's just say that if you're unhappy with where you live, your job, your looks, your family, your friends, your athletic skills, your relationship, whatever in your life you wish you could change, virtual reality offers you escape. At least one futurologist, Ian Pearson, sees us one day connecting our brains to servers so that we can inhabit humanoid androids in different countries, effectively transcending the limits of our puny human bodies.'

'That's quite an intoxicating proposition.'

'Precisely, and with it comes terrifying possibilities. Approximately five billion people use the internet. Imagine how simple it would be to control the minds of hundreds of millions or more if you could offer them just temporary escape from whatever troubles or disappoints them, all the while indoctrinating them with the propaganda of your choice.'

Jack's voice tightened. 'It creates an addiction as strong as any drug, and the opportunity for its creator to influence – if not control – as much of the world population as it can reach with its manufactured version of reality.'

'And I thought *The Matrix* was far-fetched,' said Andreas in a serious tone.

'Think of it this way. First we had radio, then television, and now the internet, all appropriated in some manner by nations seeking to spread their own message. Today China and Russia already control the thinking of much of their populations through propaganda aimed at obliterating what their leaders consider undesirable reality. And the Middle Eastern state is well on its way to legitimatizing its ventures and values in the eyes of the world's masses though aggressive efforts at establishing itself as a dominating force in the world of professional sports and using its highly paid, wildly popular talent as messianic spokespersons for burnishing its image.'

'I get your point. They want to weaponize the digital world.'

'Worse, legitimate technology companies become complicit by battling each other for mastery of what they call 'the metaverse' and offering up their own promised-land solution for what ails humanity.'

'I've always looked upon metaverse talk as just another hype to sell more things. But you make it sound a lot more . . . real.'

'Much of the metaverse talk *is* just hype intended to sell more things. There's not even an agreed-upon explanation for what metaverse means. Personally, I agree with those who say it's a term describing how we interact with technology in a universal and immersive virtual world – not a specific form of technology. Still, there are loads of technology businesses out there portraying themselves as portals to this mystical place.'

'So, where's this all headed?' asked Andreas.

'No one really knows, and with so many rivals out there seeking dominance in the market, the metaverse has a considerable number of hurdles to overcome. For example, metaverse technology companies have no incentive – profit or otherwise – for cooperating with their competitors, and without cooperation, one company's metaverse can't interact with another's.'

'You're reminding me of that biblical story about the Tower of Babel, where God saw the people of the world speaking in a single simple language as a bad thing, and scrambled the one into many in order to prevent humanity from being of one language and one mind.'

'That might be just the sort of intervention the metaverse will require one day, because if powerful nations like China and Russia commit to establishing one *super* metaverse . . .' Jack let the thought drift unfinished.

'What do you think are the chances of that happening?'

'China is one of the few entities who could successfully cajole the major technology giants into opening their virtual worlds to the China/Russia model.'

Andreas exhaled deeply. 'This truly *is* an existential threat to democracy. How bizarrely ironic – or is it planned malevolence – that a consortium of ruthless autocrats plans on hijacking democracy by striking at it from its birthplace.' He rubbed his forehead. 'May history damn us all if we allow that to happen.'

'So now you get why I hesitated to speculate during our last conversation.'

'Yes, and I appreciate that. But now that we're in battle mode, we could use you over here on the front lines.'

'Understood. Let me rearrange some obligations and get back to you on when I'll arrive.'

'Thanks, Jack. Oh, and one more thing.'

'What's that?'

'Your homeland thanks you.'

Andreas made it home in time for the kids' bath time. The ensuing spontaneous water battle resulted in two thoroughly soaked adult family members, two stark-naked, squealing water splashers, and one mostly dry nanny strategically stationed at the bathroom door under orders to keep the junior combatants from fleeing to another room.

Once the water party had ended, and all were back in dry clothes, Lila and Andreas tucked the children into bed and read to them until they fell asleep, then crept away, headed for the kitchen.

'That was fun,' said Andreas.

'That's only because you won't be the one who has to deal with a four- and six-year-old who from now on will think that's how bath nights should be.'

'Well, shouldn't they?' He gave her an impish smile as he opened the refrigerator.

Lila pushed around him and reached for a half-full bottle of white wine on one of the shelves. 'Since you opened the door, you're responsible for dinner. I'll take care of the beverage.'

She turned and headed for the cabinet containing wine glasses.

'I'm terrific when it comes to whipping up a left-over cold chicken and roasted lemon potatoes feast.'

'As I said, you're in charge.'

'Wow, there's even fava in here.'

'See you on the sofa, my chef.'

Five minutes later Andreas appeared bearing a tray filled with neatly plated cold chicken, potatoes, yellow split pea fava puree, and a freshly made Greek salad. 'I thought I'd surprise you with the salad.'

Lila smiled. 'My hero.'

He put the tray on the coffee table in front of the sofa. 'I'll be right back with the silverware and napkins.' Thirty seconds later he appeared with what he'd promised, plus a basket of toasted pita bread and olive oil.

'I thought you might like pita and olive oil with your fava.' He set everything down in place and dropped on to the sofa next to his wife.

She handed him a glass of wine and neither said a word. They sat holding hands staring out at their view of the Acropolis at sunset.

'I never get tired of this,' said Andreas.

'Holding hands?'

'That too.'

Lila lightly dug her nails into his hand. 'How did your day go?'

Andreas took a swig of wine. 'It's better now.'

'Meaning something is bothering you.'

'The upside is that Anna's Jack is arriving in Athens earlier than originally planned.'

'When's that?'

'He'll let me know.'

'What about Anna?'

'She has an interview on Thursday and can't get here before Friday.'

'Too bad.'

'But we need Jack here ASAP.'

'I take that to mean the downside is things aren't going well on that videogame case.'

'If he's right, it's a videogame unlike any other. One that will change the world as we know it, by, to paraphrase Jack, "satisfying everyone's cares, concerns, needs, and desires with but the pull of a joystick. And all we must give up in return is our free will in the real world."'

'That's insane. Tell me more.'

Andreas laid out Jack's concerns.

'And that lawyer husband of Jill McLaughlin is involved in this craziness?'

'If it succeeds, it's not craziness. But yes, he looks to be a pivotal player in Greece for the Consortium.'

'Well, I guess that's one invitation we can pass on.'

'What invitation?'

'In today's mail we received an engraved invitation to join him and his wife for cocktails and a buffet dinner next Thursday at nine in celebration of the purchase of their new home in Paleo Psychiko.' She reached for her glass.

Andreas nodded. 'How nice of them to think of us.' He took a sip of wine. 'I think it would be downright rude of us to turn down such a gracious invitation.'

Lila almost choked on her wine. 'How can you even think that, knowing what you do about him?'

'That's just the point. I don't know enough, and this could be the perfect opportunity to learn more.'

Lila shrugged. 'OK, if you say so.'

'One more point. Do you think you could wangle an invitation for Jack?'

'Will Anna be here by then?'

'According to her, no. But I need Jack's face-to-face take on the husband, because if I can get him talking and it turns technical, he might as well be speaking to me in Chinese.'

Lila rolled her eyes.

'That wasn't meant to be a joke,' said Andreas.

'Good, because it wasn't funny.'

'What about the invitation?'

'There shouldn't be a problem in expanding the invitation, and if there is, Jack can go in my place.'

'Uh-uh. Nice try. But you're going. You're who put us on to Jill and her husband. We need the continuity.'

Lila sighed. 'Fine. Now what?'

Andreas pointed to her plate. 'Dinner is served.'

'Darling, would you answer the door please? I have the maid working on rearranging my closet. We really should have the carpenter build a room just for my shoes. Oh, and for my bags.'

Panos Cirillo turned away from the TV news show he'd been watching to look at his wife stretched out on a sofa and thumbing through a fashion magazine. 'You're closer to the front door than I am.'

'Just answer the fucking door. Ladies don't open front doors when the man of the house is at home.'

He shut his eyes, let out a deep breath, and headed for the front door.

'Thank you, darling,' Jill said, picking up the remote and turning to an English-language channel.

A minute later he was back in the room. 'Hey, what happened to my news show?'

'It was boring. And I couldn't follow the Greek.'

'It's the number-one news show in Athens. It's important that I keep up with what's on the minds of Greece's mainstream media.'

'And it's important I'm not bored.'

Panos walked over to the sofa and held out his hand for the remote. 'I need to keep on top of what's happening in the news that might affect the interests of my clients who pay me what keeps you in shoes, bags, and whatever.'

Jill glared but handed him the remote.

'Thank you.'

'Who was at the door?'

'A courier with this for you.' He handed her a large manila envelope.

'Oh, great, it's the sample menu and place cards for our dinner party on Thursday.'

'Is all that formality necessary?'

'Yes, dear, it is. The danger in entertaining society is not in overdoing it, but in not doing it correctly. Especially if any of your Far Eastern clients accept our invitation.'

'I wouldn't bet on any of them coming.'

'But if they do, don't you want them to see that your wife knows how to entertain properly? And let's not forget we'll be entertaining some of the leading members of Athens society.'

'You mean the lucky winners of the birthright lottery, possessed of big-time inherited names and money, who never had to work at a serious job or make a living that earned them an honest callus?'

Jill shot up from the sofa and waved a finger at her husband. 'That bullshit working-class drivel is no longer part of our vocabulary. You wanted to run with the big dogs and now you are. So, unless you want to go back to chasing after deadbeat clients and standing in line waiting for a table at a souvlaki place instead of living the life you've always dreamed of, keep those suicidal ramblings buried deeper than you do your dear clients' secrets.'

Panos waved his hands in the air. 'Fine, fine, fine.' He drew in and let out a deep breath, before dropping back into his chair. 'So, who are these high-society types you're so anxious to impress? And what makes you think they'll come?'

'I've invited many, but the trick to landing them is to make them feel that even more important people than they will be there.'

'How do you plan on doing that, other than flat-out lying?'

'I've thought of doing that, too.' She smiled, sidling toward her husband. 'But I hit on a better way.'

'Which is?'

'I've let word creep out that a favored member of Athens society who rarely attends such functions will be joining us.'

'Has your lure agreed to come?'

'Not yet, but she will.'

'How can you be so sure?'

'Because I charmed the pants off of her the other day at lunch.' She stopped in front of Panos's chair, blocking his view of the screen. 'Not the same way as I did with you, my darling.' She dropped down to her knees and gently began stroking his crotch. 'But just as effectively.'

Anna sat on the edge of the double bed. 'Have you decided when you're leaving for Athens?'

'The earliest I can leave is Tuesday afternoon,' said Jack, standing in the doorway to the bathroom with a toothbrush in his hand.

'But that only gets you into Athens on Wednesday, two days before I'll be there,' said Anna, a tinge of disappointment in her voice.

'I said sort of the same thing to your uncle when I told him I couldn't leave before Tuesday, but he said it's very important I'm there by Wednesday. Something important is happening on Thursday that he needs me to attend with him.'

'What sort of thing?'

'I don't know. All he said was he might need me to translate technospeak.'

'But where will you stay?'

'He said with him and your aunt until you get there. Then I guess we'll stay with your mother.'

'No doubt about that. She'd never let us stay anywhere else.'

Jack put down the toothbrush, dropped on to the mattress next to Anna, and grinned. 'So, let's make the best of the time we have left alone.'

Panos enjoyed driving long distances, provided he could cover them in his beloved Porsche 911 Turbo, and the trip didn't include long patches of impenetrable traffic. He'd been obsessed with that car since, as a boy, he saw his first 911 pull up in front of his father's store, and a long-legged blonde stepped out. Now he had both the Porsche in metallic silver and the long-legged blonde in gold.

He preferred to drive alone. It freed him to think without distractions – other than those posed by notoriously macho Greek drivers who saw the Porsche emblem as a challenge to their manhood.

It also freed him from his wife's incessant efforts at steering him into doing what she considered best for advancing their joint financial and social interests. He had no quarrel with how much she'd changed his life for the better, but her merciless prodding he could do without.

From the moment they met she'd picked up on his long-held insecurities among those he imagined as seeing themselves his social betters, and how quickly he'd react to a perceived slight with anger or insults – even though the occasion would have been better served by blithely ignoring the comment or offering a bit of humor.

Privately she'd hectored him into seeing himself as far more capable than he imagined, taught him how to turn conflict to his advantage by knowing who to ignore, who to worship, who to cajole, who to embrace, and – above all – who to destroy.

She taught him how to embellish and market the skills he'd developed at catering to the needs and wants of his working-class clients, repackaging him in the process with an upscale appeal to the bigger payers and international movers and shakers.

He came to appreciate that clients are clients, and just because some like to talk in terms of bigger numbers, or think themselves smarter because they're richer, they all want the same thing from their lawyer. To win at any cost.

And that was the magic he offered them.

She also taught him to be ruthless and merciless when it came to achieving his clients' goals. Nothing was beyond the pale. He appreciated that. But he also realized she lived by the same rules. He had to keep her on his team. In part that's why he married her. That and the long legs.

Today, he was driving from Athens to the North Euboean Gulf village of Limni in northern Evia, Greece's largest island after Crete and one of Greece's windiest places. He'd take the new bridge at Halkida and, depending on traffic, would cover the 150 kilometers to Limni in under two hours.

Limni's lushly forested hillsides and deep blue waters once drew tourists to its picture-postcard setting. But no longer. In but a matter of days, the forests, and economies, of a broad swath of northern Evia, including Limni, were ravaged by the island's worst wildfires in recorded history. Trees, livelihoods, and hopes vanished in the flames.

But none of that lingered in Panos's mind.

He had three appointments scheduled for today, starting with holdout members of a group of landowners who'd lost close to a hundred thousand acres to wildfires but, unlike the other members of their group, had refused to sell their properties to Panos's clients.

His second meeting involved local authorities charged with granting property use permissions, and his final get-together was cocktails with the senior officers of the largest bank in the region.

He'd met with all of them many times before. Today it was time to seal the deal. The once-reluctant property sellers were now pleased with the terms of their long-term leases with Panos's clients, leases converting their idle properties into predictable, guaranteed incomes while preserving ownership in their families; the authorities were satisfied that the properties met all requirements for alternative energy development, or would soon receive the necessary waivers and assurances for such use; and the bank was anxious to capitalize on the anticipated infusion of new opportunities into the fallow sectors of their portfolio.

The only aspect of the project he'd not personally addressed was the media. Lawyers were not the best media spokespersons. Especially if they happen to be big-city lawyers driving Porsches. The Porsche worked well on those looking to profit financially from a transaction, because it subtly established bona fides. But to crusaders in opposition, it became a symbol for galvanizing support. He knew better than to poke his nose into areas beyond his expertise. That's why he left the public relations aspects of his clients' project to their grandmasters of propaganda.

That decision had served him well, for when rumors began to circulate that forests in Evia were purposely burned to allow for the installation of wind turbines, Greece's World Wildlife Fund promptly dismissed such speculation as baseless conspiracy theories. He had no idea how that came to pass but was greatly relieved that it had.

Panos's thoughts wandered back to his first meeting with his soon-to-be Consortium clients. He'd listened attentively and without interruption as they explained to him in excruciating detail how critical the Evia properties were to the power generation needs of their project, one that would propel Greece to an international leadership role in the coming metaverse. The Consortium's efforts until then had failed, largely because of the properties' protected status under Greek law.

Once they'd finished, and asked Panos for his opinion, he nodded respectfully to each representative and then calmly said, 'I can make it happen for you.'

When they asked how he could be so confident after so many other lawyers had failed, he smiled. 'Because I possess a burning desire the others do not.'

Now, less than two years later, everything was humming along as smoothly as his Porsche.

The bell on the door to Solona's store jingled lightly when the door opened, but Solona sat immersed in a book, and did not look up from behind the counter.

'Hi, Solona.'

She raised her head and smiled. 'Anna, what a pleasant surprise. Where's Jack?'

'He's working this weekend, so I thought I'd stop by and say hello.'

'That's wonderful news, though I'm not sure I like hearing that your fiancé has already fallen into the New York City trap of working 24/7 and neglecting his soulmate.'

'Oh, it's nothing like that. We're heading off to Athens this week to meet my family, and he's trying to finish up what he won't be able to work on once we leave.'

Solona smiled. 'That's good. So, what's new in your lives, other than wedding plans?'

'We haven't set a date, but when we do, we'd like you to be our maid of honor. After all, we owe it all to you.'

Solona smiled. 'I thank you for the credit, and pray the day never comes that I get the blame.'

Anna laughed. 'That's about the weirdest but sweetest blessing I've ever heard.'

Solona put her book down on the counter.

'What are you reading?'

'*God and Man* by Masahisa Goi. It's one of my favorite tracts. I read it whenever I need to recharge my spiritual batteries.'

'What's draining them?'

'Nothing unique to me, just the world in general. To borrow from the wit of Dorothy Parker, what "fresh hell" awaits us next?'

Anna nodded. 'I know what you mean. Dealing with a "fresh hell" is why Jack leaves for Athens before I do.'

'Would you like some wine? I'd offer you grass, but I know you don't smoke.'

'It's a bit early in the day for me.'

'Why? What else do you have to do?'

Anna smiled. 'You're right. Jack won't be home until late, and I'm all caught up on my classwork.'

'Come, let's sit in the garden.' Solona stood up and tapped the cover of the book. 'Though I sincerely try to live by Masahisa's simple mantra, "*God, please fill my heart with love, let me become one with my true self, overflowing with profound love,*" I know that many in this neighborhood do not share that attitude.'

She gestured toward the front door. 'So, please lock the door and flip the sign in the window from OPEN to MEDITATING while I get the wine and glasses.'

Anna did as Solona asked and met her outside.

They talked of their respective lives and Solona spoke of her hopes for Anna.

'But what of your hopes for yourself?' asked Anna.

'I've achieved mine, and now I'm enjoying the fruits of my successful wishes, prayers, and good fortune.'

'That's a great attitude.'

'Attitude is much of the battle toward success.'

'Jack sort of feels the same way.'

'Too bad he can't join us.'

'I know, but I understand why. My uncle needs his help and asked him to come over as soon as he can get there.'

'Is your uncle OK?'

'Yes. It's not a personal problem. He needs his help on an investigation. My uncle's a chief inspector for the Greece police.'

'Sounds mysterious.'

'It is. And frightening too.'

'Frightening?'

'Yes, it could change our world for the worse. Much worse.'

'I don't think I want to know any more about it, except that I hope your uncle succeeds.' She waggled her glass in Anna's direction. 'That is, assuming he's on the right side of saving the world.'

Anna smiled and clinked her glass against Solona's. 'He is. He's all about keeping the world real.' She took a slug of wine.

'Who isn't?'

She leaned in toward Solona. 'Metaverse people. They want to control us all.' She took another swig. 'And they're on the verge of succeeding.'

'I'm sure your uncle and Jack will prevail.'

'But how can we be sure?'

'Nothing is certain.' Solona stood up. 'Excuse me, I'll be right back.'

Solona went inside the shop.

Anna held up her glass to take another sip of wine but paused. *I'm saying too much. I'm sure Jack and Uncle Andreas wouldn't mind me telling Solona, but I don't think I should say any more.* She put down her wine glass.

Solona came back holding another bottle of wine and the book she'd been reading at the counter. She dropped down on the pillow next to Anna and held out the book.

'If you read this, you'll find answers to all your questions.' She took a sip of wine. 'Although it remains up to you to match them up correctly.'

Anna smiled as she took the book and nodded a thank you.

Solona picked up her glass and raised it, gesturing for Anna to pick up hers. 'To each of us achieving what is best for our world.' She clinked on Anna's glass and took a sip.

Anna did too.

NINE

'Hi, Chief, sorry to bother you over the weekend,' said Yianni, 'but I just got a call from one of my buddies who told me about that alternative-energy construction activity on Evia. He said he had more news for me.'

'Are you in Athens or spending the weekend with Toni on Mykonos?'

'With Toni, but she's still sleeping. She had an all-night gig playing piano at a private villa's mega-party.'

'I thought she worked in that piano bar Lila likes so much.'

'A lot of people liked it. But the place closed. The landlord wanted way too much rent.'

'Too bad.'

'Yeah. It's now just a storeroom. The island's not the same. But speaking of landlords, that's why my buddy called me.'

'I'm all ears.'

'Word is that Evia property owners whose forests were turned to charcoal by the wildfires but refused offers to buy their land are now entering into long-term land leases.'

'Meaning there won't be a record of a new owner because there's not been a sale of the property.'

'Correct,' said Yianni. 'So, there's no way of telling how much land that lawyer's clients actually control as lessee-tenants.'

'Not unless his name is on the lease, but since the money's not being paid up front, it's hard to imagine any landlord's lawyer agreeing to such a deal without ironclad security tied to a deep-pocketed guarantor of the lessees' obligations. And I can't imagine Panos Cirillo qualifies.'

'No, but banks would qualify, and I can't imagine a bank serving as a guarantor without a heck of a lot of information on its client . . . including the name of its lawyer.'

'Good thinking. Perhaps one of Maggie's contacts can get that information for us by going at it that way. I'll give her a call. By the way, how did your buddy find out about this?'

'A cousin of his owns property destroyed in the fires and was bragging about how, once his lease deal goes through, he'll be driving a Porsche like the bright and shiny one driven by the lawyer for his soon-to-be tenant.'

'Did your friend happen to have a name for the lawyer? Or a plate number on the Porsche?'

'He had no reason to ask, so prodding his cousin to get more info could have alerted the lawyer we're on to him.'

'Good point.'

'But when I ran a check on vehicles registered to Panos Cirillo, guess what turned up?'

'A shiny Porsche.'

'Silver metallic to be exact.'

Andreas shook his head and smiled. 'Bless the ostentatious.'

'Toni's waking up. I've got to make the coffee. Bye.'

'Bye.'

Andreas put his mobile down on the black granite kitchen island top and looked across at Lila sipping her coffee. 'Did you know Toni no longer worked at that piano bar?'

Lila nodded. 'She hasn't for years.'

'Nobody told me.'

'No reason to. Everything's fine. She earns more money during the season playing at parties for the rich and wannabe famous.' Lila took another sip of coffee. 'Is Anna's fiancé still coming on Wednesday?'

'As far as I know, yes. Around ten in the morning on the direct flight from JFK.'

'Is your sister OK with him staying with us?'

Andreas looked puzzled. 'Why would she not be?'

Lila rolled her eyes. 'For a chief inspector you awe me at times with your lack of even a basic understanding of women. Imagine how you would feel if, instead of Anna's fiancé, it were Sofia's and we'd never met him before. How would you feel if he stayed at your sister's instead of with us?'

'How many guesses do I get?'

'I'm serious. And regardless of how hurt you might be as the father, multiply it by a factor of ten for the mother.'

Andreas shook his head. 'That's not a problem in this situation.'

'Why not?'

'Because she doesn't know.'

Lila's jaw dropped. 'You haven't told her?'

'I saw no reason to. Jack's here on police business and I don't want him distracted by having to make nice to my sister and the inquisition she'll subject him to from the moment they first meet. I need his full concentration on the investigation, at least until Anna arrives.'

'When will that be?'

'Friday morning. Same flight.'

Lila fluttered her lips. 'It's your family. Good luck in handling the explosion once she finds out the truth.'

'How is she going to find out?'

Lila stared at him. 'You've got to be kidding.'

'Why?'

'Even if Anna doesn't tell her directly, sooner or later something will be said in front of Gavi that will set off her mother's ESP and the truth will come out.'

'If so, I'll deal with it then.'

'What about me? What's my excuse going to be for not alerting her as one mother to another?'

'Just say you thought I'd told her.'

'*Oh what a tangled web we weave . . . when first we practice to deceive.*'

'We're not deceiving. We're practicing mercy.'

'On whom?'

'On Jack, by shielding him from Gavi until Anna's here to run interference for him. On Anna, by not worrying her to death over what her mother might be saying to him during the forty-eight straight hours he'll be in Athens without her. And most of all, on us by sparing us incessant conversations with Gavi over every criticism she'll be looking to level at Jack from the moment they meet.'

Lila put down her coffee cup and threw up her hands. 'OK, she's your sister. Play it as you see fit. Just don't involve me. My story's going to be the one you suggested. *I thought my husband told you.*'

'Good, and in keeping with your fondness for quotations of Sir Walter Scott, just follow this one: "*For success, attitude is equally as important as ability.*"'

'That's nice, but once your sister learns the truth – and she will – I'm betting "*Revenge is a feast for the gods*" will be her motivating quote.'

* * *

Fall afternoons were among Maggie's favorite times of the year, especially when Tassos and she would find their way above Ermoupoli to the medieval upper village of Ano Syros, called Apano Chora by some and simply Chora by the locals. It was the island's first settlement, erected in Byzantine times to help protect its inhabitants from pirates plaguing the Aegean.

They loved to wander among its largely marble and stone narrow streets, maze of alleyways, and covered spaces, passing by old stone houses built so that their walls linked to one another in a barrier against pirates and conquerors storming up the town's steps intent on doing the villagers harm.

Largely because of their inhabitants' respective origins, medieval Ano Syros and nineteenth-century Ermoupoli differed in architecture, religion, culture, and general way of life.

Ano Syros's mostly Catholic roots and centuries-old ways and trades stood in stark contrast to what the flood of new Orthodox refugees brought to the island. Anxious to establish the cosmopolitan, cultured, and sophisticated lifestyles they'd been forced to leave behind, in a matter of decades they'd turned Ermoupoli from a comparatively unpopulated seaside into Greece's leading mercantile capital.

But by far the most visibly evident difference between the two adjoining locales lay in their respective architectures.

Ano Syros was laid out upon a hillside in amphitheater fashion, made up of largely one- and two-story whitewashed traditional Cycladic-style stone structures fitted with utilitarian, form-follows-function modifications, such as half-doors – split horizontally and vertically – allowing fresh air and easy communication with neighbors, second-floor balcony doors built without a balcony for much the same purpose, unfenced courtyards open to the lanes, and other practical alterations, such as slicing away corners to allow laden donkeys and carts to pass by unobstructed.

Down by the harbor lay Ermoupoli's very different world of wide streets, majestic neoclassical public buildings, commercial structures, private residences, churches, marble statues, and elaborate mansions of those who'd brought prosperity to the island.

Ano Syros and Ermoupoli truly were a tale of two cities.

Tassos claimed there were at least a thousand steps from Ermoupoli to the top of Ano Syros, and with severely limited access for vehicles to enter upon its narrow medieval streets, their wanderings these days began with finding a parking place offering the shortest hike to their destination.

Maggie saw none of that as an inconvenience, but rather as a welcome opportunity for a bit of exercise for Tassos.

Today they were off to the Markos Vamvakaris rebetiko Museum, named after Ano Syros's native son and legendary rebetiko musician known to rebetiko fans simply as Marco.

This tiny, striated ochre stucco museum was hosting one of Greece's finest bouzouki players in its beguiling garden, framed by deep purple bougainvillea and a bird's-eye view of Ermoupoli. Tassos didn't want to miss the opportunity of hearing the live performance in that enchanted space. Rebetiko was Greece's equivalent of America's blues music, hatched in prisons, hashish dens, and ouzo parlors. Tassos had had an affinity for the music since he was a kid.

They drove up the mountain from the port along broad Ethnikis Antistaseos Street, and turned left by a parking area at the beginning of narrower Marcos Vamvakari Street. That street took them up to Kamara, the lower entrance to Ano Syros, before winding its way on to the town's upper entrance. They found parking by Kamara, and made their way toward its tunnel-like entrance notorious for forcing six-footers to crouch a bit, something neither Tassos or Maggie ever worried about.

After a few dozen marble and stone steps, twists, and turns, the narrow stone and marble paved lanes opened on to the town's somewhat broader central street, known as Piatsa. Two meters wide, at most, Piatsa had changed a lot in the past five years.

Artists had moved in and added a different vibe to the street, as had the new and updated bars and tavernas. Along this stretch of Ano Syros you'd find most of the town's shops and eateries, along with Ano Syros's city hall, cultural archives, and radio station.

'Are you excited?' Maggie asked.

'I feel like a kid on his way to a Rolling Stones concert.'

'Great, but for the record I think these days the Stones are more likely to attract kids' grandparents than the kids themselves.'

'You're too cruel to this old man,' said Tassos, feigning pain.

'Oh, no, I didn't mean it that way,' said Maggie, patting Tassos's arm. 'Besides, rebetiko is different. It appeals to the mood of today's youth.'

'Meaning?'

She shrugged. 'Kids these days seem so lost, and rebetiko's themes fit right into reinforcing that mindset.'

'Considering the hot topic of conversation in your Chief's office these days, I'd appreciate us avoiding any talk about how to control another's mind.'

Maggie took a few steps in silence. 'So, what would you like to talk about?'

'The usual fall-back topic of conversation for islanders is how drastically tourism is changing their island for the worse, even when they're greatly responsible for making it so.'

'A common complaint among islanders everywhere.'

Tassos nodded. 'They like the idea of raking in the cash they see flooding into places like Mykonos and Santorini but hate the thought of what comes with it. Money, yes. Dramatic lifestyle changes, no.'

'I can't blame them,' said Maggie, sighing. 'Drugs, prostitution, robberies, fights, price gouging, and jam-packed roads and beaches don't make it on to my quality-of-life top-ten list either.'

'Not to mention what it's doing to infrastructure built to accommodate thousands of locals, now bursting under unrelenting pressure from hundreds of thousands of visitors.'

'Not to return to our forbidden topic, my love, but doesn't that sort of explain the lure of the Consortium's project? If our government authorities negotiate the deal properly—'

'That's one hell of an assumption,' interrupted Tassos.

Maggie ignored him. 'Syros stands to gain significant revenue and jobs, plus infrastructure development projects that should benefit locals and tourists alike.'

She stopped and waved her arms about her. 'Imagine what will happen to all these businesses and homes if tourism is allowed to run unchecked here the same as it has been elsewhere in the islands. Especially if nothing is done to improve municipal services.'

'I don't have to imagine. I've seen – and smelled – the results on other islands.'

'So, what do you think we should do?'

'Say nothing more about any of this until the concert is over.'

'Why? Are you worried someone might overhear us?'

'That's always, of course, a reason not to talk about confidential things in public, but no, that's not my concern.'

'Then what is?' Maggie asked as they stopped in front of the museum.

'Because, from this moment through however long this concert runs, I want to concentrate on only one thing.'

'Which is?'

Tassos leaned in and kissed Maggie on the cheek. 'Being a kid again, holding hands with my best girl.'

Maggie smiled and took his hand. 'Deal.'

Monday mornings were far from Panos's favorite, especially when it involved cutting short a long weekend of sailing and partying with some of his well-heeled new neighbors and his wife insisting on staying behind to party on alone.

'It would be rude for me not to stay,' she announced in her most condescending tone. 'How do you expect my many efforts to have us included in Athens' most elite social events to pay dividends, when you walk out early on our hosts simply because you see fit to jump at a client's snap of its fingers. The very least I can do is remain behind and try to make amends.'

It was useless trying to explain to Jill how important this Monday would be in achieving her goals. If he could assemble the remaining real-estate plots necessary for launching the Consortium's project, their net worth would leap mega-levels beyond any of those society types she worked so hard at impressing. As she so often preached, *money changes things*, and if he pulled this off, it would change *everything*.

So, Sunday night he jumped ship on Mykonos, caught the last ferry to Syros, and spent the night in a harbor-front hotel close to his early-morning meeting at the headquarters of the Municipal Port Fund of Syros.

The Consortium had made clear to him its needs, and thus far Panos had delivered on his promises. He'd acquired the Evia properties and the government consents and commitments required in order to erect the Consortium's wind farms upon them, created the master contract setting forth the terms, conditions, and pricing every contractor participating in the wind-turbine phase of the project had to sign, and obtained the government's commitment to allow power from Evia wind farms to supply the Consortium's needs on Syros via the Lavrio cable and any additional or auxiliary cables underwritten by the Consortium.

All that remained for the project to proceed were two real-estate transactions on Syros. One in Ermoupoli and the other in Ano Syros. Panos found it hard to imagine how the island could refuse what he was prepared to offer. Then again, this was Greece and reason often gave way to emotions understood best – if not solely – by their possessor.

It was a five-minute walk from the hotel to his meeting in the commanding two-story Customs House that shared the tip of the peninsula marking the northern border of the harbor with the island's memorial to the Unknown Sailor. It was the first nineteenth-century building constructed in Ermoupoli, and with its imposing marble and red-roofed composition of arched windows and entry-ways, remains to this day one of the first buildings to be seen on entering the harbor.

Up close it offered a different impression, one of badly peeling paint and graffiti.

He entered through the easternmost archway into a busy office space marked by computer screens and shelves filled with file folders. Once inside, Panos was led into a room and told to please wait. He was the first to arrive for the meeting but hadn't expected otherwise. In Greece, many took punctuality as a sign of weakness or insecurity. To his Consortium clients it was a sign of respect and confidence. When acting on their behalf he followed their rules.

Though the light beige room had a small conference table, it appeared to serve primarily as a storage facility for cartons of additional files, and the chairs around the table did not match. Ten minutes later, the Port Fund's representatives arrived en masse, fresh from an obvious chat among themselves. Again, nothing unexpected.

Panos immediately stood and moved aside to allow them to find what Panos took to be their assigned places at the table. Panos remained standing as the Fund's president introduced herself and five other members of the Fund's Board – its vice president, the Port Master of Syros, and three representatives of the Municipality of Syros and Ermoupoli. She also introduced the heads of the Fund's department of administrative and financial services, and its department of technical services. Because of a lack of room at the table, the last two sat on chairs behind the president.

'I'm honored you're taking the time to meet with me. Thank

you.' Panos made his way around the room, shaking everyone's hand.

'I assume the remaining seat at the table is mine,' said Panos, making his way to a chair facing a window looking due south across the harbor.

'Yes,' nodded the president. 'I apologize for the cramped quarters, but our own office's conference room was unavailable today, so we kindly imposed upon our Tech Services to allow us to use their space for our meeting. Besides, they're who we look to for professional guidance on what you have in mind for Lazaretta.'

'This is perfectly fine.' Panos cleared his throat. 'I assume by now each of you has had the opportunity to review our proposal to preserve and invigorate the Lazaretta in a manner that will greatly benefit your island.'

No one demurred. 'Wonderful. So, rather than repeating what you already know – which I am prepared to do, of course – perhaps our time together can be better spent with me addressing any questions you might have.'

One of the Municipal representatives jumped at the opportunity. 'Why should we agree to allow a group of foreigners to desecrate one of our island's most cherished architectural treasures?'

'A very understandable question,' said Panos. 'Let me see if I can answer it to your satisfaction.'

'I doubt that,' smirked the representative.

Panos instinctively knew how to bring this one around to backing the project, but the question gave Panos an opening to explore whether others shared the representative's views.

'I'm certain I don't have to go into Lazaretta's history with any of you, but I'd appreciate it if you'd allow me to offer a slight bit of historical perspective to frame how our proposal not only offers great benefits to all of Syros, but is in keeping with a long-standing tradition of adapting Lazaretta's use to whatever best serves the evolving needs of the island.'

The president nodded. 'Please, proceed.'

'For Syrianos, Lazaretta serves as a proud reminder of their island's rich cultural, sociological, and architectural heritage. Built after our 1821 War of Independence, it has been used for many, many different purposes for more than two hundred years, always depending on the community's needs. Today, this landmark structure stands on the verge of literal collapse, with little hope of saving it unless immediate efforts are undertaken.'

Panos stared directly at the head of technical services. 'I'm not offering that as my opinion, for I am not an expert on such matters, but I am offering it as the conclusion of every bona fide study in recent memory into what must be done to resurrect, if not preserve, this symbol of Syros.'

The tech services head nodded.

'Is that all you have to say?' barked the representative.

'I'm more than willing to offer more information on its state of disrepair if you'd like me to, sir, but I thought you'd be more interested in addressing the financial terms and benefits of our offer.'

'I don't care about any of that.'

'Well, I do,' said the president.

'Me too,' said several others.

'But before you get into any of that,' said the Port Master, 'would you please give us a better understanding of just what you're thinking of doing with the building?'

'Certainly. The property is approximately two-thirds the size of a soccer field, and our intention is to fully restore the exterior to its original glory, while upgrading the interior to twenty-first-century, state-of-the-art computer facilities in a manner that in no way compromises the exterior.'

'What precisely do you plan to do with the interior?'

'We're committed to creating a community performance and exhibition space, but our primary business purpose is to establish a server array powered by transformers housed within the facility.'

'What is the purpose of the servers?' asked the vice president.

'To create a metaverse hub in the heart of the Greek islands.'

'For Greece?'

'No, sir. For all the EU.'

The Board members looked at one another in surprise.

'Are you serious?' said the president.

'Absolutely. We see Greece as offering the perfect environment in every way.'

'But how can Syros possibly supply all the power that sort of operation requires?' asked the tech head.

'Syros won't have to,' said Panos. 'We've taken care of that by arranging to generate our own power on Evia and deliver it directly to Lazaretta by undersea cable.'

'And what if we don't want your servers here?' said the representative.

Panos shrugged. 'We'll build our facility on another island, or a more receptive community on the mainland that sees the benefits of becoming the new tech center for Europe.'

'What sort of benefits?' asked the financial services head.

'To begin with, the many construction jobs it will create. Then there are the technical support, administrative, transportation, maintenance, and let-your-imaginations-run-wild jobs to follow. It goes without saying that every job supports a family and brings new money rushing into the Syros economy.'

Red-faced, the representative nearly shouted. 'I don't like it. It's going to drive up housing costs by attracting newcomers to the island with money to pay more than Syrianos for housing.'

'We've addressed that concern. First of all, we're hoping it will be Syrianos who decide to work for us, but, for those who come from elsewhere, we'll build housing and offer it in line with then-current price levels so that there will not be a spike in housing costs to local residents.'

'Where will you be building that housing?' pressed the representative.

'It's a bit premature to announce that publicly, but I'll be meeting later today with representatives of one potential community.'

'I want to know, and I want to know now!' shouted the representative.

One of the other representatives spoke up. 'Cool it, Florio, this isn't about you angling inside information for your real-estate business.'

'I resent that.'

'Then shut up and let the man speak before I say more.'

The representative mumbled to himself but did not respond.

That bit of a temper tantrum confirmed Panos's take on how to turn the representative into an enthusiastic advocate for the proposal.

'Who is going to pay for all of this?' asked the financial services head.

'We are,' said Panos flatly.

'Everything?'

'Yes, everything.'

'But why?' asked the vice president.

Panos smiled. 'This is not a charitable donation. The world's largest technology companies not only see the metaverse as the future, they're investing in it heavily. The parties I represent – all of whom are disclosed in our proposal – see Greece as the metaverse bridge between East and West. Potential upside profits are both astronomical and uncertain, but what is certain is that there's but one choice to make: Either jump in with both feet, or stand far enough back on the sidelines so that your toes don't get trampled by the hordes rushing by you.'

The president raised her hand. 'I apologize for cutting our meeting short, but we have another starting in a few minutes. I do want to thank you, though, for making things clearer for us. I'm sure we will have more questions for you, but there is one bottom-line question on all of our minds.'

She paused to catch Panos's eye, then, with a no-nonsense stare and tone of voice to match, asked, 'How much are you prepared to invest in this project?'

'A fair question,' said Panos, returning her stare. 'The answer is unlimited funds.'

'*Unlimited?*'

'Guaranteed.'

He waited for the concept to settle in. No one spoke.

Panos pointed toward the window. 'As I sit here looking south across the harbor to the far side, it's hard not to be moved by Lazaretta's commanding presence. Your Fund has made it beautiful at night by bringing long-awaited light to that long dark building. Now you have the chance to do far more – you can literally bring it *back to life.*'

He paused. 'And in so doing uplift the island's economy in unimagined ways, all without sacrificing your island's values or traditions, something you've undoubtedly witnessed other islands suffer in chasing fickle tourism cash.'

The head of financial services sighed. 'By when do you need a decision?'

'Quickly.'

'Why?' asked the president, appearing somewhat less confident than before.

'We face ruthless competition from heavily capitalized

international players intent on attaining dominance in the metaverse. Although I truly respect your traditional approval processes, I would hope you understand that we cannot afford to have our plans put on hold by governments that insist on following those time-consuming routines while our competitors rush ahead unheeded by the same constraints.'

'By when do you need an answer?' the president repeated.

'I was hoping to hear today.'

'*Today?*' shouted the representative.

'The timetable is not set by me, but what I can say from what I do know is that the train to the future is about to leave the station in search of a new place to call home.'

The financial services head passed a note to the president.

She read it and looked at Panos. 'Would you mind waiting outside for a few minutes?'

Stone-faced but smiling broadly on the inside, Panos rose from his chair. 'Not at all.'

Panos sat patiently outside the conference room listening to bouts of wild shouting separated by moments of relative calm. The shouting at first lasted longer than the quiet, but as the promised few minutes wore into fifteen, the shouting began to subside, and by thirty it had vanished. Panos couldn't make out what was being said, but that didn't matter. He could guess.

He'd heard representative Florio's voice kick off the shouting, no doubt in an effort to spike the deal so that he could later approach Panos for a payoff in return for his support. There always seemed to be at least one of those sorts hanging around government contract negotiations looking for an angle on how to personally profit off their government service.

And the world brands my clients' *forms of government as corrupt.*

To Panos, the silence behind the door meant Florio had been beaten down by his colleagues. Perhaps some even threatened to expose his past corrupt acts, likely triggering recriminations by him directed at others in the room. The corrupt are rarely unknown to their colleagues. They know who's modestly corrupt and who's corrupt to the point of irresistible obsession.

Panos guessed Florio fell into the latter category, and if so, his character traits could prove to be of great benefit to the Consortium.

Panos now saw the Lazaretta project as a done deal, leaving only the housing component to address. Though he doubted all the members had read the Consortium's proposal, the only thing that likely mattered to them was the money it would bring to their island via a project filled with twenty-first-century high-tech sex appeal.

No one possessing even a modicum of political sense would dare risk being labeled for life as one who denied Syros the opportunity of becoming a mega-player in the metaverse.

He smiled at his unintended word play just as the door to the conference room swung open, and the president stuck her head out.

'Mr Cirillo, would you please re-join us?'

Panos stood up, smiled courteously, walked briskly into the room and sat down in his seat at the conference table.

He fixed his eyes on the president.

'We are very impressed by your presentation and frank state-ment of your reasons for needing a prompt response,' she said. 'However, I'm afraid we can't give you an answer today.'

Panos felt the color drain from his face as he struggled to maintain his practiced poker face. He fought off an instinctive desire to ask for an explanation. Instead, he waited for the president to say more.

'We can, though, tell you that we are of one mind on one thing. We want to accept your most generous offer but cannot act without the approval of our entire Board, and the earliest we can hold such a meeting is this Wednesday.'

The blood was back in Panos's face.

'I appreciate your candor, President. Though we're disappointed that a decision did not come today, I'm certain your promise of a decision by Wednesday will be acceptable. Thank you.'

Panos walked around the table shaking everyone's hand and thanking each personally. After the others had left, he spoke with the president for a few minutes on details surrounding the preparation and execution of the formal documents.

As he walked out of the Customs House, he heard, 'Mr Cirillo, may we have a word?'

It was representative Florio.

'Certainly.'

'I just wanted to say that I'm sorry we started out on the wrong foot back there.' He gestured with his head toward the Customs House. 'But I hope you realize my first and foremost concern as a representative of my fellow Syrianos is that my actions on the Board unquestionably better the lives of the people of my island. That sometimes gets me carried away with my rhetoric.'

He's desperate to work his way back on to the money train.

'I both understand and appreciate your dedication to Syros, and never thought otherwise for a moment. I didn't mind the give and take.' Panos smiled. 'Even enjoyed it. I like your style.'

'You did? I-I mean, I'm happy you did.'

'By the way, did I understand you're in the real-estate business?'

'Yes,' Florio nodded proudly. 'For over twenty years. If you know someone who wants something done in the real-estate world on Syros, tell them to call me, and I'll make it happen.'

'You sound like a good man to know.'

Florio's chest seemed to puff out at the praise. 'Damn straight.'

'That's terrific to know. In fact . . .' Panos patted him on the shoulder. 'I might be able to use your help with a project unrelated to the Board's upcoming decision.'

'What is it?'

'As I mentioned at the meeting, it's a bit premature to discuss that matter, but if things progress, we'll be in touch.'

'Just let me know what I can do to help out.'

Panos nodded. 'By the way, do you handle rentals?'

'Commercial or residential?'

'Residential.'

The representative nodded.

'Assuming we go forward with the Lazaretta project, there will be lag time between getting the project up and running and construction of new housing for our employees. That means we'll need to find places for them to live temporarily.'

Florio's eyes glistened. 'Don't worry. I can find you all the leases you need, no problem. But you might want to buy up existing properties as they come on the market and use them for your people rather than building from scratch. I know a lot of potential sellers.'

This is the same guy who an hour ago was lecturing me on how worried he was about our pricing his people out of the housing market.

'That's great,' said Panos. 'As I said before, I like your style. Perhaps I could convince you to act as the Consortium's housing consultant . . . for a reasonable per-transaction fee, of course.'

A broad smile burst across Florio's face. 'Of course.'

An even broader, though hidden, smile passed through Panos's thoughts, for he knew Syros was now a done deal.

TEN

Monday mornings to Andreas meant a meeting of GADA unit heads at the Ministry of Citizen Protection. He had no doubt wildfires would top the agenda. As Andreas saw it, the deputy minister running the meeting was obsessed with making a name for himself and had settled upon the fires as his path to glory.

During Andreas's time with the Hellenic Police, the Ministry had gone through four name changes: Ministry of Public Order, Ministry of Citizen Protection, Ministry of Public Order and Citizen Protection, and back to Ministry of Citizen Protection.

Today, the Ministry of Citizen Protection remained responsible for Greece's national police, fire service, agrarian police, and prison system.

The Ministry's various names hadn't changed Andreas's work much. What had a more direct effect on operations was the choice of minister. More than a dozen ministers had served during his years on the force, including his own brief stint in that position. He'd never wanted a political post but was convinced to take it on when the minister under whom he'd served the longest fell terminally ill and begged Andreas to succeed him to save the credibility of their Ministry from the intentions of others seeking his position.

Andreas pulled into the Ministry's parking area off Kanellopoulou Street and turned off the engine. He remembered how much he disliked being Minister and couldn't wait to get back to his old job as Chief Inspector of Special Crimes. Yet when he did, he found his tenure as Minister had made his old job unexpectedly more difficult to perform.

Subsequent bosses felt threatened by him, even though he'd made clear to all that he had zero interest in serving again as Minister, and all he wanted was for them to stay out of his way so that he could do his job. Fearing that Andreas might one day want their job, some tried to undercut his reputation, while others worked at setting him up to fail, but even those who took him at his word were somewhat uncomfortable in having a former peer willingly serve beneath them.

The current Minister took a unique approach to Andreas. He'd served under Andreas as an assistant during his time as Minister and regarded him more as an equal than a subordinate, a situation potentially undermining the Ministry's chain of command management style it openly practiced in group encounters . . . such as Monday-morning unit head meetings.

The solution the Minister came up with was to pass responsibility for conducting Monday-morning meetings to Deputy Minister Dittos, who relished the role.

Andreas stared at the Ministry building. Dittos was a pain in the ass, but budding politicos on the make are often like that, especially when presented with the opportunity of eliminating or mortally wounding those they perceive as potential threats to their own ambitions. Andreas hated the political world. Butt-kissers circling you, each hoping for a lethal shot at your unguarded throat when you least expect it.

Time to go upstairs and join the party.

From the way Andreas's fellow department heads abruptly cut off their inside politics gossip when Dittos walked into the room, Andreas assumed they shared his view of Dittos as someone to be wary of.

'Gentlemen, give me some good news,' said Dittos, bursting into the room, aiming for the head of the table.

'Arrests are up, crime is down,' said the Head of Tourist Police.

Dittos waved him off. 'I don't care about any of that. High tourist season is over.' He looked straight at Andreas. 'I want to know what's being done to put an end to the tragic free reign arsonists have had to destroy our precious forests.'

'I can't speak to what sort of preventative measures or infrastructure improvements may be underway, because as you know that falls to other departments and ministries, but . . .'

'I don't want any *buts*, Kaldis, I want action and I want it *now*.' He pounded the table.

Andreas sat looking at his nails as if waiting for a commercial to end.

'Kaldis, *did you hear me?*'

Andreas kept looking at his nails.

'Do you have *any* idea who you're ignoring?'

Andreas looked up. 'Yep. One very rude son-of-a-bitch.'

Two of the three others at the table struggled to suppress a laugh. The third lost it completely.

'I'll have your—'

Andreas put up his hand. 'Do you really want to go down that road? If so, strap on your helmet. Not so that you'll survive, but to make it easier for your nearest and dearest to identify your remains.'

Dittos clenched his jaw tightly enough to look on the verge of spitting out teeth.

Andreas dropped his elbows on to the tabletop, cupped his hands beneath his chin, and stared straight at Dittos. 'So, do you want to start this meeting over fresh or not?'

No one moved.

Dittos drew breaths at a hyperventilation rate.

Still, no one spoke.

He caught his breath, shut his eyes, and sat quietly for a few seconds. 'So, where were we?'

'You don't want to go back there.' Andreas sat up and removed his elbows from the table. 'I was about to tell you we've made great progress toward identifying those linked to a substantial number of the fires.'

'What sort of progress?' asked Dittos, still struggling to retain control.

'Earth-shattering, but it's not yet ready for prime time.'

'What is that supposed to mean?'

'In this case, it means the potential targets possess substantial power, influence, and wealth, so until we corroborate suspicions with hard evidence, we can't risk naming names.'

Dittos shut his eyes, paused, opened them, and calmly said, 'Chief Inspector, do I correctly understand you to be saying you will *not* share the names of potential targets with your superiors in your Ministry?'

'If a superior can show a valid reason beyond curiosity for needing such details at this critical phase of our investigation, I most certainly will cooperate. But until that time, I prefer keeping the names known only to those conducting the investigation. The targets have no idea we're on to them, and I want to keep it that way.'

Dittos glared at Andreas. 'We'll see about that.' He pushed himself up from the table and stormed out of the room.

'Now what?' said Andreas, looking around the table.

'I'd say you just lit up the room with a Molotov cocktail,' chuckled one.

'He acted like one of those guys who loses a bar fight and storms out making all sorts of wild threats,' said another.

'Yeah,' said the third, 'and five minutes later shows up with an AK-47 to wipe out everyone in the bar who witnessed his humiliation.'

'In that case,' said Andreas, standing up, 'I vote we declare this meeting over and get the hell out of here before the shooting starts.'

'You've got my vote.'

'Mine too.'

'Ditto.'

Andreas slammed his hand on the table. 'Meeting adjourned.'

'Back so soon, Chief? Your Monday-morning meeting usually runs a lot longer.'

He stopped beside Maggie's desk. 'My next one may be even shorter. Like none.'

'Oh, is this another one of those, "Pack up my desk, Maggie, I'm out of here" moments?'

'Could be, but this time it won't be my call. I pushed back a bit hard on that self-important prick of a deputy minister. He's likely right now crying to papa about what that big bully Andreas said to him in front of the other kids.'

Maggie rolled her eyes. 'I'm happy to see you've worked the anger out of your system sufficiently so that when you get the call from the Minister's office asking for your side of the story, you won't allow your temper to prove Dittos's point.'

Andreas stared at Maggie. 'Is it that obvious?'

'Uh-huh. I suggest you think about puppies and kittens until you're back to your simple, understanding, compassionate self.'

'Sorry, but I'm still seeing only cuddly Rottweilers and Bengal tigers.' He headed into his office. 'Tell Yianni I need to see him the moment he gets back.'

'He already is. He caught an early boat from Mykonos to Piraeus and came straight from the port to the office.'

'Fine, send him in.'

'*Yianni, the Chief's in and wants to see you, stat,*' she shouted down the hallway in the direction of Yianni's office.

'And may I have a coffee please?'

'*Please?* Now that's what I call a big step toward being back on the road to the land of puppies and kitties.'

'Growl.'

'Morning, Chief,' said Yianni, double-timing it into the office.

'How was Mykonos?'

'Not nearly as crazy as it was in the summer.'

'I assume that's good news.'

'Not for Toni. At least not income-wise. Her big piano gigs are coming to an end until next tourist season, and the robberies and break-ins that fuel her finder-of-stolen-goods business are winding down too.'

'So why doesn't she move in with you in Athens until springtime and live off the fat of a police detective's elaborate salary and benefits.'

'Lord knows I've tried to convince her but she loves the solitude of the island in winter.'

'Perhaps I'll soon have the same opportunity.'

'What's that mean?'

Andreas told him about his confrontation with Dittos.

'I admire the way you handled the situation with tact and diplomacy.' Yianni nodded toward Andreas's desk chair. 'May I have it when you're gone? For sentimental reasons, of course.'

Andreas feigned a smile. 'So where are we on connecting the fires to properties linked to lawyer Cirillo?'

Yianni dropped on to the sofa. 'So far every property purchased, or as far as we can tell leased, through him on Evia was affected by the fires.'

'Did they burn before or after he acquired or leased them?'

'The great majority, burned after.'

'And the others?'

'You're going to love this. Virtually all properties acquired after they'd burned sat adjacent to land he already controlled, and burned when fire spread from his properties to theirs.'

'How convenient.'

'Yeah, but we still need evidence linking him to arson.'

Andreas shook his head. 'There's way too much coincidence

at play here to be anything other than arson. But I can't believe he'd personally risk lighting even a single match.'

'I know. I've asked the Fire Service to get me a list of all known arsonists and fire freaks with even the slimmest likelihood of being involved in any of the fires. As soon as I get those names, we'll shake their trees big time for any link to the lawyer.' Yianni paused. 'No pun intended.'

Andreas deadpanned, 'Just let me know if you need me to light a fire under anyone to get you those names.'

Ring.

Maggie answered the phone and within seconds yelled through the open doorway. 'It's think-kittens-and-puppies time.'

'Kittens and puppies?' said Yianni.

'The Minister's calling. Just listen.'

Andreas hit the speakerphone button. 'Good morning, Minister.'

'Morning, Chief.' He paused. 'I'm sure I don't have to tell you why I'm calling.'

'Correct.'

'So, what happened this morning that has my deputy on the verge of resigning?'

'Over what? My tone of voice, my telling him not to be obnoxiously rude, or my refusing to reveal names to him associated with what appears to be the most consequential investigation ever undertaken by this office?' Andreas swallowed. 'Regarding the latter, there is no way I'll be revealing the particulars of our investigation, other than on a strictly need-to-know basis. And certainly not to someone whose agenda is at best curiosity and at worst obtaining information for use in furthering his personal best interests, not those of his country, or in this case, the world's.'

'I can see why Dittos is upset.'

'I wasn't trying to offend him, only tell him the truth in terms he could understand. As I told him, if there is a superior with a true need to know whom I believe will safeguard the information, I will fully cooperate. That said, I'd caution my superiors that simply by knowing what we know now opens them to temptations and risks unlike any they'd ever imagined. And even if they refused, I've no doubt the parties involved wouldn't hesitate to terminate anyone they saw as a threat to their plans.'

'Even the Prime Minister?'

'Yes.'

'If I didn't know you better, Andreas, I'd say you've lost your mind.'

'I've thought the same thing about myself. However, the signs are very real, even though we can't yet prove what's underway. But if word gets out prematurely, we never will. We can't risk it. Far too many lives are at stake.'

'I'm not going to ask you to tell me any more about this, except for an answer to one question. Is this something I should tell the Prime Minister?'

'I've thought about that too, and my conclusion is not yet.'

'Then when?'

'We have an expert arriving from the US on Wednesday who we believe can provide the technical assistance we need to confirm what we think is afoot.'

'What sort of expert?'

Andreas hesitated. 'It's one of those things I can't say.'

'Really?'

'I'm afraid so.'

'Kaldis, you're making this very tough for me.'

'I know, but trust me, I don't mean to.'

'And when should I expect to be in a position to brief the PM on this?'

Andreas looked at Yianni and mouthed, 'One week?'

Yianni nodded.

'One week should do it.'

'Next Monday? That's a long time away.'

'Not nearly as long as Armageddon will be if word of what we expect is happening should get back to the bad guys before we're ready to move on them.'

'You're leaving me with little choice.'

'Sorry about that, Minister, but those are the facts.'

A distinct sigh came back over the phone. 'I wish they weren't.'

Andreas bit at his lip. 'So do I.'

'Then Monday it is.'

It was Andreas's turn to sigh. 'Thanks, Minister.'

'But not a day longer. And if you can't deliver, I'll expect your resignation. It's the only way I can see to keep peace in the Ministry.'

'Understood.' Andreas paused. 'Again, thank you.'

'You're welcome.'

They exchanged goodbyes.

'Whew,' said Yianni. 'I really thought for a moment I'd be getting your desk chair.'

'Don't give up yet. We've only a week to unravel a rat's nest of property transactions across much of Greece's second-largest island and tie the strands back to arson committed in pursuit of the Consortium's plans for world domination.'

'Sounds like a bad opening line to a sci-fi horror film.'

'Starring all sorts of nefarious characters,' hollered Maggie from her desk.

'Where do we go from here?' asked Yianni.

'I've an idea percolating, but I'm open to suggestions.'

Maggie came to the doorway. 'From the way you spelled out the risks to those of us in the know, let's just pray word doesn't get out before our ducks are all in a row.'

'What, no more kittens and puppies?' said Yianni.

Maggie gestured no. 'From what I've just heard, forget all about those cuties. I'm getting myself that Bengal tiger to protect me at home.'

'And a Rottweiler for the office?' asked Andreas.

'No need,' she smiled, and nodded toward Yianni. 'We've got him.'

'Good point,' said Andreas, leaning across his desk. 'Mr Rottweiler, I think it's time to turn up the heat.'

'On whom?'

'Everyone.' Andreas began tapping the eraser end of a pencil on his desktop. 'First thing tomorrow morning, I want you to pay an unannounced visit on our friends at Fire Service headquarters and ask to see whatever information they have on those three unidentified fatalities from the fires.'

'What about that list of potential fire-starters I requested?'

Andreas nodded. 'We definitely want those names but I sense it's likely akin to our "round up the usual suspects" list.'

Yianni grinned.

'Something's been nagging at me about those three unidentified bodies. We're talking about horrific deaths in rural areas where just about everyone knows everybody else. And if they were visitors, someone back home must have reported them missing.' Andreas shook his head. 'One unidentified body, maybe. Two possibly, but three . . . I don't see it.'

'Maybe they're all from one family? And there's no one left alive to miss them,' said Yianni.

'Or possibly they were refugees hiding in the forest who couldn't escape the fires?' added Maggie.

Andreas kept tapping away with his pencil. 'Yianni, I want you to get every scrap of information the Fire Service has on those unidentified bodies, starting with when they were found, where they were found, and by whom they were found. And if you sense any resistance from them, let me know immediately.'

'Why wouldn't the Fire Service cooperate?' asked Maggie.

'Because I'm convinced a certain deputy minister who oversees the Fire Service is capable of doing virtually anything to prevent us from meeting our Monday deadline.'

'Between your morning at the Ministry, this Fire Service thing, and Jack coming on Wednesday, it's shaping up to be a very interesting week,' said Yianni, rising from the sofa.

'But Wednesday is two days away,' said Andreas, 'and we can't rely upon Jack for evidence linking the Consortium to the fires. All we can hope for is his opinion on whether Syros is about to become an international hub for the metaverse, or the next-generation propaganda center for the East in its relentless battle for the hearts and minds of the West.'

'A bit flowery,' said Maggie.

'Beats funereal,' said Yianni, heading for the door.

'Let's hope so,' said Andreas.

After his call with Andreas, the Minister sat quietly at his desk for a few moments before asking his secretary to have Dittos join him in his office. Seconds later the door to his office swung open, Dittos marched in, and dropped into one of two leather chairs directly across from the Minister.

'Well?' said Dittos.

The Minister leaned back into his chair. 'I know that you and Kaldis have decidedly different management styles, but you both are very important to me. I'd like to think there is some way for the two of you to navigate through this current crisis together without sinking the ship in the process.'

'What ship and what process? Kaldis is an intolerably arrogant man who has no appreciation of his true status in this Ministry.

He works for me. And if you won't back me up on that, I'll have no choice but to resign, effective immediately.'

'That's not the answer I was hoping for.'

'Well, it's the only one I can give in response to his gross insubordination.'

The Minister nodded. 'Let's play out this scenario in accordance with your resigning. I'm sure you'd agree that the media will have a field day with this, and you no doubt will understandably do your level best to cast yourself in the best light possible.'

'This is not about me, it's about respect for the office.'

'Yes, I understand all that, but please let me finish.'

Dittos crossed his legs and folded his hands across his lap.

'Good, thank you. Now, let's assume you convince the press that Kaldis was all the things you say about him, and the media goes after him in a feeding frenzy. From experience I think I can accurately predict his reaction.'

'I don't care what he says or does.'

The Minister put a finger to his lips. 'He will say absolutely nothing. Instead, he'll let the media punch itself out silly on whatever juicy things you have to say about him.'

Dittos looked puzzled. 'So why is that bad for me?'

'Because,' said the Minister, 'should what Kaldis claims prove correct, and he either brings down this claimed international threat, or fails to do so because the bad guys are warned off by media coverage your resignation triggered, you'll be skewered long and mercilessly by your once-adoring press.'

'I doubt that.'

'That's your right, of course, but trust me on this. I've seen it happen many times before to those who've underestimated his resilience . . . and connections.'

'I have connections too.'

'I know, I hired you, remember? Believe me when I say that I have your best interests at heart. Please don't risk destroying your brilliant budding career by taking on Kaldis simply because you can't wait a week.'

'Wait a week? What are you talking about?'

'Kaldis has an expert flying in from America whom he promised me should be able to confirm his suspicions by next Monday.'

'Did he tell you what those suspicions are?'

'No, and frankly I didn't want to know.'

'Why not? You're the Minister.'

'Because he didn't think it wise. I trust Kaldis to do what he promises, even if I don't always agree with his style. But that's neither here nor there. The question is, are you prepared to bet your career over a one-week delay in satisfying your curiosity at what lies behind the curtain?'

'What curtain?'

The Minister blinked. 'Forget it. The point is, Kaldis has agreed to resign if he can't deliver by next Monday.'

'And if he doesn't resign, are you prepared to fire him?'

'That seems fair.'

'Yes or no?'

The Minister sat up straight in his chair. 'If that's not a good enough answer for you, perhaps I should allow you to learn first-hand the wisdom behind an adage passed along to me when I was about your age by a former Minister who sat behind this very desk.'

'Which was?'

'"He who lives by the press, shall die by the press."'

Dittos chewed at his lip. 'Kaldis said he needed a week?'

'Yes.'

'OK. One week.'

The Minister stood up and extended his hand across the desk. 'Thank you, you won't regret it.'

'I'm certain of that too,' said Dittos, shaking the Minister's hand.

High above the harbor, in Ermoupoli's Tris Hierarches neighborhood close by its border with Ano Syros, sat a large swath of long-neglected fields surrounding the ruins of a storied hundred-year-old orphanage.

In 1922, following the burning of Smyrna in Turkey and ongoing atrocities against Greek, Armenian, and Assyrian victims of the Ottoman Empire, an American humanitarian relief organization established in 1915 confronted the monumental task of moving more than 20,000 orphans out of Turkey. The Greek government agreed to accept 16,000 of the children, but it lacked sufficient facilities to house that number of refugee children.

Based upon the organization's commitment to build a suitable orphanage, the government granted it the use of a large parcel of land on Syros. Through the construction efforts of adult refugees hired by the organization, and massive labor contributions by its future residents, the orphanage was completed in 1923. It could house between 2,200 and 3,000 orphans at a time, with the boys spending half of each day working the fertile land surrounding the facility. Hard work by the residents, and the organization's contribution of equipment and supplies, soon had the orphanage operating on a self-sustaining basis.

The orphanage's primary focus, though, was on education. The second half of each boy's day covered training in popular trades that would allow them to support themselves later in life, while homemaking, nursing, and teaching skills were offered to the girls. By the end of 1924, a hospital and nursing program were up and running, and the American School, as it came to be known, developed a first-rate reputation for education; so much so that by the end of the 1920s, local farmers wanted their sons to study at the school.

In 1929 everything changed.

The organization's focus soon switched from humanitarian relief to development work, and in 1930 it closed its orphanages. But by then the organization had saved the lives of over 130,000 orphans, including 7,000 who lived and studied at the Syros orphanage.

Subsequent years of neglect, war, and pillage turned it into little more than an unofficial playground for neighborhood children, but even those days had passed it by, for now its land was home to pit vipers, scorpions, and centipedes, and its tunnels and wells a repository for construction garbage dumped by contractors building homes snug up against its property line.

There had been talk of the organization – now a foundation – acquiring the property and creating a museum honoring its good works on Syros and elsewhere. There were also efforts by real-estate types seeking to interest investors in building a hotel or similar venture on the property, but a reported requirement restricting any new project to the original building outline made that proposition a hard sell for most potential investors.

But not for Panos's Consortium.

If he could make the deal and obtain the necessary permits for what he privately considered to be but the first phase in development of the orphanage property, once the related Lazaretta project was up and running, the Consortium would be pumping such wealth into the island's economy that no one would dare stand in the way of the Consortium expanding its housing element beyond the current boundaries and restrictions. Especially when expansion would be the sole means of keeping housing costs down for Syrianos in the emerging, metaverse-driven economy.

Panos's late-afternoon meeting with the property's neighbors at a grade school on Sokratous Street, a block away from the ruins, included representatives of activist groups adamantly opposed to altering the position of even a single stone on the property. The meeting went much as Panos anticipated.

He tried to speak, but the activists shouted him down. He tried again, and they shouted louder.

He was pleased the meeting went as it did, because the more subdued types in attendance never had the chance to ask potentially troublesome questions. Many later told him they were embarrassed at the rough treatment his courteous and respectful efforts had received. Some apologized. A few even wished him luck with the project, hoping it would remove a major eyesore and druggie hangout from their neighborhood.

In his most courteous and respectful manner, Panos promised them he would move heaven and earth to do just that.

A lot of earth.

ELEVEN

'Hi Lila, it's Gavi.'

'Hi. Great timing, you caught me just as I'd walked out my front door to meet a friend for brunch.'

'Do you have time to talk with me? It's important.'

'Sure, just give me a moment to go back inside.'

Lila knew what was coming. She'd been expecting Gavi's call from the moment Andreas told her his sister didn't know Jack would be staying with them.

'OK, I can talk now.'

In a slow and deliberate tone, Gavi said, 'Did you know?'

'Did I know what?'

'You know what.'

'Gavi, if I knew I wouldn't be asking you.'

'About Anna's . . .' she stumbled for a word. 'Friend.'

'Know what about him?'

Gavi's voice rose. 'That he's coming to Athens on Wednesday and staying with you!'

'Yes, of course I know that.'

She practically screeched, 'Well, then why didn't *I*?'

Lila calmly answered, 'I think that's a question better asked of your brother or daughter.'

'You're a mother – you know you should have told me.'

'Gavi, if you think I should have, I apologize. But the truth is, telling you would not have changed a thing. Andreas needs Jack's help on a very serious police matter, and with Anna arriving on Friday, that leaves them less than forty-eight hours to work together before family obligations will take him away.'

'He should be staying at *my* home.'

'As I said, take that up with your brother. But it won't do you any good. It will only make Andreas angry and Jack very uncomfortable. Why create that sort of a situation when your daughter is bringing the man she's about to marry home to meet the family?'

Gavi practically shouted, 'He's not married to her yet.'

'Another conversation that I will not be drawn into.'

'He's wrong for her!'

'Gavi, I like you and love you, but you're wasting your time trying to draw me into this.'

'Well, if I can't talk to you, who can I talk to?'

'How about your daughter?'

'She won't listen. She's who told me that her friend is staying with you and Andreas until Friday.'

'Dare I ask what you said in reply?'

'Just what I told you. He belongs in our home.'

Lila knew she'd said a lot more than that. 'And what happened next?'

'She told me that if I insist on making a scene with Jack over this, they won't stay with us at all.'

'And what did you say in return?'

'I told her the truth.'

'At what point did she hang up on you?'

'How did you know she hung up on me?'

Sounding a bit exasperated, Lila said, 'It wasn't hard to guess. You're not very good at hiding how much you resent her fiancé before even meeting him.'

'Please don't call him Anna's fiancé.'

Lila stared at the phone. 'Gavi, you are off the rails on the subject of Jack and Anna. I truly hope you gather yourself together before they come to stay with you, otherwise you'll not only drive Anna closer to him, but farther away from you just as she's striking out on the next phase of her life. Neither of you want that, so don't make it happen.'

'You don't understand me.'

'Wrong, you don't understand your daughter. Be understanding and listen to her. You'll learn a lot more that way than by being judgmental.'

'You're a mother. I don't understand how you can think that way.'

Lila looked toward her daughter's bedroom. 'Because I remember what it was like being a daughter with parents who loved me and always wanted what they thought best for me.'

Pause.

'But you still married my brother.'

Lila hesitated, then laughed. 'Happy to see your sense of humor is back.'

'It's been hiding away amid my anxieties over this marriage.'

'That, I fully understand. But believe me, the boy and Anna are just as anxious if not more so. Approach it with an open mind and go with your honest instincts. That's your best shot at making this all work well for everyone.'

Lila heard a sniffle on the other end of the line. 'Thanks, Lila. I'm happy you married my brother.'

'I am too.' *Though not necessarily at this moment.*

'I love you.'

'You too, Gavi.'

'Bye.'

Lila closed the call, drew in a deep breath, shut her eyes, and exhaled. As she started for the door she murmured, 'Thank you, dear husband, for another exciting day in family-relations paradise.'

With Anna attending class most of Monday, Jack spent the early part of his last full day in New York buying what he thought he might need for the trip, plus little gifts for Anna's family. By late morning he'd caught a bus to Staten Island for a brief goodbye visit with his aunt.

She'd met Anna and adored her, but now cautioned him not to expect as warm a welcome from her family.

'There was a reason your parents left Greece when they did, and some in Anna's family might carry the same sort of attitudes as made it intolerable for your parents to stay. I'm only telling you this so that you're not surprised.'

'Is it because we're Jewish?'

'It is because we're different, and those feelings are not confined to Greece. It's something to be aware of whenever you travel to a foreign place.'

Jack smiled. 'So, you're saying I shouldn't wear a yarmulke?'

His aunt smiled back. 'Since you don't wear a skull cap here, I wouldn't recommend changing your ways for this trip.'

'Understood.'

On the bus back to Manhattan, Jack wondered what Anna's family was really like. Antisemitism wasn't new to him. He'd experienced it growing up in New York City, of all places, but hoped that wouldn't prove to be the case with her family. He had enough anxieties over this trip without contending with the silent all-knowing looks and glances among bigots trying to act as if they aren't.

As the bus started across the two-and-a-half-mile-long Verrazzano-Narrows Bridge spanning the bays of New York Harbor between Staten Island and Brooklyn, Jack's deepest anxiety took hold and his pulse began to race. He refused to look down at the sea, but still knew it was there, and silently repeated the five words he always said to himself when passing over water.

'I'm not on a boat, I'm not on a boat, I'm not on a boat.'

Once the bus reached Brooklyn, Jack's pulse returned to normal, and his thoughts went back to his trip, and worries over meeting Anna's family. *What if they don't like me?* preoccupied his thoughts.

Then a new thought crossed his mind. *What if I don't like* them?

Piled on top of that anxiety was the project he'd been drafted to work on for her uncle. He couldn't imagine how anyone with standing in the world of metaverse experts would ever consider him qualified to pronounce that our world order is about to change by reason of what some cabal of autocrats is planning to set up on a Greek island.

Jack knew he was good at deciphering chatroom talk, but opining on seminal international policy questions was clearly beyond his pay grade. He feared he'd fall flat on his face and forever be regarded by Anna's uncle as a lightweight.

He needed to talk to someone, someone who could help him put his feelings into proper perspective. He wanted to talk with Anna, but with so many concerns tied to her family, the risks of triggering a massive defensive reaction were more than he could bear to face.

That's when Jack decided to pay a visit to Solona.

Yianni stormed past Maggie into Andreas's office. 'Chief, I've got serious news!'

'I was wondering when I'd hear from you.'

'Me too,' said Maggie, stepping into the office and shutting the door behind her.

'The Fire Service was one-hundred-percent cooperative.'

'Great to hear. Their Chief's a good man.'

'He thinks the same of you. I had a slight problem at the start from a clerk who said I needed permission to see what I'd requested.'

'Why didn't you call me?'

'I didn't need to. I told him to call his Chief and tell him I was there at your request. He called and put me on speaker with his Chief. I explained who I was and what I wanted. That's when he told his guy – and I quote – "give him whatever Kaldis wants. After this morning we're all going down in flames anyway."'

Andreas laughed. 'A sense of humor is what keeps us sane.'

'Some of us,' said Maggie.

'So, what's the news?'

'They copied everything I asked for on to this.' Yianni pulled a thumb drive out of his pocket and handed it to Andreas. 'The first three files contain all that they have on the three unidentified fatalities. You'll find it interesting reading.'

'Just give me the punchline.'

Yianni sat on one of the chairs in front of Andreas's desk. Maggie sat on the other. 'All three were burned beyond recognition, with not a remnant of identification on any of them. Not a bit of paper from an ID, residue from a credit card, medallion around the neck, piece of jewelry.'

'It must have been one hell of a hot fire,' said Maggie.

'I thought the same thing, but the clerk told me it's as if the three were stark naked before the flames hit them.'

'That's crazy. I can't imagine three naked men running around the countryside starting fires.'

'Nor does the Fire Service, even though some arsonists get off sexually on the fires they set.'

'So, what's their explanation?'

'At each scene they found scraps of the sort of highly flammable cotton and light synthetic fabric used in clothing made in China that many countries have long barred from sale.'

'That's a telling coincidence,' said Maggie.

'Were they found together?'

'Good question. Nope. Each was found in a different part of Evia, all on properties owned by different entities, and before you ask, none was tied in any way to Cirillo or his clients.'

Andreas sighed.

'Cheer up,' said Maggie. 'Yianni called me from the Fire Service with the locations of the deceased, and I checked for any subsequent changes in ownership of the properties.'

Yianni smiled. 'It's a big yes to all three.'

'With Cirillo linked to every transaction.'

Andreas thrust his fist in the air. 'I knew that bastard had to be connected to those deaths. I'd bet my pension the three set fires for Cirillo.'

'And were eliminated in a way intended to sever any ties to Cirillo or his clients,' added Yianni.

'But the bad guys got greedy and couldn't resist gaining control of the properties the three had died on,' said Maggie.

'All that might be true,' said Yianni. 'Also, everyone on the Fire Service's arson list is alive and accounted for. So it wasn't them.'

Andreas bit at his lip. 'If I were the cautious, lawyerly sort, like Cirillo, I wouldn't want to involve locals in my illicit plans. Certainly not if I intended to get rid of them once they'd done their jobs. That would leave mourning friends and families clamoring for an investigation. But if it's outsiders who disappear, who would even know?'

'Or care,' said Maggie.

Andreas reached for a pencil. 'I wonder if there's any way to determine where the three came from?'

'Why?' said Maggie.

'I might be able to answer your question once I know the answer to mine.'

'Chief, plug the thumb drive into your computer. There might be a way.'

Yianni stood up and leaned in across Andreas's desk to see the computer screen. 'The Fire Service drew DNA samples from each victim and submitted them to our official Greek and EU databases, hoping for a match. When that yielded nothing, they submitted the samples to one of those commercial sites popular with people looking to trace their ancestry. Some of those sites permit us to access their data in situations like this, where authorities are trying to identify victims of a tragedy.'

'So, what are we looking for in here?' said Andreas, pointing to the files on his screen.

'Those ancestry searches did not turn up a match to a name, but . . .' Yianni reached for the mouse and moved it over a file. He clicked on it and up popped three additional files, labeled Victim One, Victim Two, and Victim Three. He clicked on the first file, and it opened to a report from a popular genealogy search company.

'It reads "no match,"' said Andreas.

'I know, but something else in there might be of help.' Yianni clicked again on the file, and it opened to a page captioned *Ethnicity*.

'What's this?'

'A map showing the victim's likely roots in our world based upon the victim's DNA compared to that of millions of others.'

Andreas studied the map. 'Show me the maps for the other victims.'

Yianni opened the other two files.

'I can't make out what you're looking at from here,' said Maggie, 'but I highly doubt any of this is admissible in court.'

'We're not in court,' said Andreas, swinging his screen around so that Maggie could see the three results side by side.

She leaned in. 'Wow. All are from east Asia.'

'The Consortium provided the arsonists, and then conveniently eliminated them in separate fires.'

'Ruthless,' said Maggie.

'But what evidentiary use can we make of this?' said Yianni, sitting back down in a chair.

'Do you have the list of fire-starters?'

'Yes, everyone that's known to the Fire Service.'

'Good, twenty-four-seven from here on out, I want everyone in our unit chasing down every name on that list. Tell them we're not looking at them as targets . . . unless we sense they're not cooperating. Then put the hell-hath-no-fury squeeze on them for names and descriptions of everyone they saw at any of those fire scenes, especially any new or suspicious faces. See, arsonists tend to set fires in areas they're familiar with, and most firebugs can't stay away from a local fire, even if they didn't start it. Maybe we'll get lucky and a fire-starter noticed a suspicious stranger in their midst. Get whatever they can remember. But don't suggest an ethnicity unless you get a bite. We don't want them making up descriptions just to please us.'

'I feel we've hooked on to something,' said Yianni.

'Me too. Now let's land it.'

Jack found Solona sitting behind her cash register, reading a dog-eared copy of *The Prophet*.

'Hi. Sorry to drop in on you unannounced. I hope I'm not disturbing you.'

'Come on. You're never disturbing.' She put her book down on the counter. 'Let's go sit in the garden.'

'What about your customers?'

'If any need me, they will find me.'

Solona came out from behind the counter, hooked her arm in his, and led him toward the rear of the shop. 'Feel free to tell me as little or as much as you wish about why you've come to see me.'

'It shows?'

Solona patted his arm and kept walking.

'I'm heading off to Athens tomorrow to meet Anna's family, and I'm afraid it's going to be a disaster. I'm certain her mother is hoping to find a way to break us up.'

Solona sat in her customary place on the cushions and motioned for Jack to sit next to her. 'I think you should take that as a sign of a mother's love for her daughter, not a dislike of you.'

'Maybe, but it ends up in the same place. I risk losing my soulmate through no fault of my own.'

'It's not as if she's met you or has any legitimate basis for disliking you. She's just speculating over what you might be like and anticipating the worst. That's better than her expecting the best and finding you don't measure up.'

Jack shrugged. 'That's an interesting perspective, but I think in this case it's more of the mother thinking, "I want my only daughter to marry the man of *my* dreams."'

'Why do you think that?'

'Because the father doesn't seem to play much of a role in the family dynamic. Everything hinges on what the mother has in mind and what must be done to get the father to go along with her thinking.'

Solona nodded. 'I understand your concern, but to be honest, I think that's the way it is with most Greek marriages, if not marriage in general.'

'I have no personal experience in that regard, what with my parents both dying when I was very young.'

'Nor do I, and certainly not with Greek marriages, though I did see *My Big Fat Greek Wedding*. Three times.'

Jack laughed hard at that. 'You're right.' And laughed some more.

'Just be your charming self with the mother and I'm certain you'll wear her down into seeing you're perfect for her daughter.'

'From your lips to her mother's ears.'

'Glad to have helped out.'

'Now, if only you could somehow get me out of the predicament I'm in with her uncle.'

Solona said nothing.

'He's a police chief in Athens and I've agreed to give him advice in connection with a highly technical, delicate situation with potentially dangerous consequences.' Jack looked down at his hands, and shook his head. 'I don't feel I'm up to the task.' He looked Solona in the eye. 'Her uncle's going to think I'm a fake, and with his influence over Anna, he'll destroy me in her eyes.'

Solona sighed. 'You have an intense case of meet-the-family jitters. Just accept it as that and move on.'

'I'm not making myself clear. I'm being asked to serve as an expert over matters I don't feel qualified to opine.'

'Now you're sounding like an honest expert who's willing to acknowledge his limitations.'

'What's that have to do with anything? I can't do what I'm being asked to do.'

'OK, let's approach this differently. What *are* you being asked to do?'

Jack hesitated. 'Let's just say it has to do with whether a project underway on a Greek island involving powerful international players has the potential to change our world as we know it.'

Solona blinked. 'I can see why you're concerned. But let's take this one step at a time. First, is the technical subject matter something you're familiar with?'

'Yes?'

'Would you say you're expert in it?'

Jack hummed to himself, thinking. 'Some would say so.'

'Are you familiar with the players involved in the project?'

'Not specifically, but I'm familiar with their . . . magnitude.'

'Are they capable of achieving their purpose?'

'With the right technology and power support, yes.'

'Do they have that?'

'That's what I'm being asked to give my opinion upon.'

'So, what's your problem? You're qualified to give it.'

'I'm afraid I'll be wrong.'

'Are you prepared to guess?'

'That would be wrong. No.'

'Good. Then just share your concerns with her uncle. Tell him that not only might there be better opinions out there, but yours could be flat-out wrong. If he still wants your opinion, give it to him.'

'But the consequences are not academic. My opinion may well lead to the project's demise and international blowback of unimaginable proportions.'

'And your failure to give the requested opinion will result in . . .'

'Her uncle thinking I'm a wimp.'

'Bravo. I suggest you choose between mastering your anxieties by accepting that you're sufficiently expert to give the requested opinion and suffering the consequences of leaving Anna's uncle in the lurch.'

Jack was back to biting his lip. 'That's some guidance.'

'It's what I've got. If you think any of my assumptions are inaccurate, tell me. Beyond that, there's nothing more I can say to help you make this decision. It is your life to lead as you choose. No one can – or rather should – decide it for you. But reach out if you need to talk more. I agree that the two of you are soulmates, and you met here in this garden. So, I'll do whatever I can to help you steer through these trials successfully, and with love.'

Jack leaned in and kissed Solona on her forehead. 'Thank you.'

'No need to thank me.'

Jack smiled as he rose up from the cushions. 'But I do.'

As Yianni saw it, seeking out arsonists for help was akin to asking the same of serial killers. Both were likely psychopaths with neither possessing a scintilla of redeeming societal conscience. Still, his job required a bit of play-acting at times, and this was one of them. So, late Tuesday, he was off to Korydallos Maximum Security Prison in the suburbs of Piraeus to make nice with three recently incarcerated arsonists.

The first two fit the classic arsonist profile of young, Caucasian male with limited education, low economic status, a drug history, and the inability to properly vent their feelings when angry, disappointed, or hurt – all the while claiming to be shy and socially withdrawn. As for motive, that generally fell into three major categories: those seeking to profit off fires by reason of insurance or otherwise; those driven by revenge, excitement, sexual satisfaction, or thoughts of emerging as a hero; and those seeking to stake out political, social, or terrorist positions.

Whatever drove the first two inmates to set their fires, and whether they were psychopaths or not, from his separate interviews with them, it was clear neither was anywhere near the fires that claimed the three men's lives.

The interviews took place in one of the prison's virtually color-less interrogation rooms, with the inmate sitting shackled to a well-worn square metal table anchored to the floor. One could not be too careful with psychos. As much as Yianni prided himself on his ability to defend himself, getting hit by a madman swinging a chair was an experience best avoided whenever possible.

The first two inmates were awaiting trial on cases where surveil-lance cameras caught them in the act of starting their fires. Those two would have done or said anything in exchange for a better plea deal, but they'd had nothing relevant to offer.

The third inmate never sought a plea deal, but instead proudly and loudly pled guilty to setting fire to a bank in central Athens as revenge upon the capitalist class for exploiting workers. Inmate Three did not strike Yianni as a likely candidate for cooperating with the police.

The door to the interrogation room opened and a slim, long-haired, scruffy-bearded man in his early twenties shuffled into the room, escorted by two beefy correction officers. They carefully anchored his shackles to the table leg farthest from Yianni.

'Be careful of this one,' said the older officer. 'He may not look like much, but he's developed a reputation as a troublemaker who never shies from a fight.'

'*Pig!*' shouted the inmate.

'Like I said, be careful. He's into martial arts. A real Bruce Lee fan we have here.'

'Thank you,' said Yianni.

'Shall we stay with you?' asked the other officer.

'That won't be necessary,' said Yianni. He smiled at the inmate. 'I'm a big fan of Bruce Lee myself.'

The inmate glared at Yianni. 'What do you want with me?'

'It actually has nothing to do with you.'

'Yeah, sure.'

'Wait a minute,' said Yianni, raising his hand in the air. 'It just hit me. It has everything to do with you.'

The inmate cocked his head. 'What are you talking about? I've already pled guilty. There's nothing more you capitalist lackeys can do to me.'

'You're right about that, but what I'm here for has nothing to do with your legal situation, and everything to do with helping you get that revenge on the capitalist class you crave.'

'Sounds like entrapment.'

Yianni touched his hand over his heart. 'I swear to you as a joint fan of the same great legend of a fighter, that all I'm about to tell you is true.'

Inmate Three stared at Yianni. 'What was his best film?'

Without hesitation, Yianni answered, '*Enter the Dragon.*'

Inmate Three held his stare. 'How can I get revenge while locked up inside this hellhole?'

'That's the beauty of it. I'll do it all for you.'

Inmate Three's eyes narrowed. 'Let me guess. All I need do is give you the names of my people. Not a chance.'

'I'd never ask you to do that, for I know you never would. But this has nothing to do with you or your friends. Hear me out before deciding if what I propose will give you what you want.'

Inmate Three leaned back in his chair. Yianni took that as a sign for him to continue.

'This past summer, much of Greece's open space was set ablaze by persons intent on exploiting that land for their own selfish purposes.'

'The masses be damned,' said a nodding Inmate Three.

Yianni nodded back. 'And in those fires, three men died. Perhaps you heard about them?'

Inmate Three did not respond.

'What we're trying to determine is the identities of the three, and whether anyone has any idea of why, with whom, and where they were when they died.'

'To destroy the people's land so that the rich get richer.'

Yianni nodded again. 'Now that you realize what's at work here, I hope you'll agree that, by helping us identify the dead men and those who exploited them as workers, you will get your revenge as well as justice for the dead.'

'I don't see how I'm in a position to help you find what you're looking for.'

'Perhaps someone you know, either in here or on the outside, knows something about them. After all, three people dying in three separate parts of Evia, all at or about the same time and in the same manner, would get tongues wagging. Certainly among those in the business of setting fires.'

'Are you suggesting the deaths were related?'

Yianni paused. 'Yes.'

'But they were found in three different parts of Evia. What makes you think they're related?'

Yianni thought of Andreas's admonition not to mention their common ethnicity.

'All three were Asian.'

'From where?'

'East Asia is all we know at the moment.'

'Like Bruce Lee.'

'Hong Kong could surely use him now,' said Yianni, detecting a slight smile. 'So, will you help me?'

'Let me put it this way. There are some who are not arsonists and do not start fires but view a burning forest as a raw canvas being embellished upon by nature through the shapes and colors of fire. To them wildfires are not destruction, but rather nature's effort to create environmental art in the spirit of installation artists such as Christo and Jeanne-Claude. For them it is an artistic happening that requires vigilance on their part to capture.'

Yianni had no idea what he was talking about.

'If, by chance, any of those artistic folk were observing an area targeted by whoever set your fires, they might have something for you.'

'What sort of thing?'

He smiled. 'Trade secret.'

'Come on, don't put me on.'

'Drones. They regularly fly drones over vast areas of forest on the lookout for fires.'

Yianni's pulse was racing. He hoped it didn't show. 'Would they take video of the areas?'

'For sure. After all, video is the only record they have of nature's creation.'

Yianni held his breath. 'What are the chances of my getting a copy of drone footage shot in the areas where the bodies were found?' He paused. 'And of any Asian males or suspicious strangers in any footage from any fire area.'

'Your chances are nil.'

Yianni's face dropped.

'But mine are pretty good. Just give me the coordinates of the areas you're interested in, and where you can be reached twenty-four-seven, and I'll take care of the rest.'

Yianni didn't dare ask how an inmate in Greece's most secure prison planned on getting such information smuggled out to his revolutionary friends. Instead, he asked, 'How long do you think it will be before I hear back?'

'Hard to say. In here I measure time in years. Out there, who knows?'

'Understood, but sooner would be appreciated, as the bad guys behind the fires and deaths are on the verge of winning, unless we can stop them, like, the day before yesterday.'

Inmate Three snickered. 'I know that feeling. I have it every day.'

Yianni smiled. 'But it's all new to me.'

'Welcome to the battle. But be patient, for it's endless.'

And filled with surprises.

Yianni didn't shake hands with Inmate Three when the two correction officers unshackled him from the table to lead him back to his cell, but he did make a point of patting him on the shoulder and saying 'thank you' in front of the officers. It wouldn't hurt the inmate's standing among the prison administration for word to spread that Inmate Three had friends in Special Crimes. And if he delivered on what he suggested might be out there, he'd have very good friends in Special Crimes.

Yianni sat alone in the interrogation room, taking time to carefully read through the prison's official background report on Inmate Three, something he'd not had time to do before their interview. This inmate definitely did not fit the mold of a traditional fire-setter. He came from a prominent Athenian family, graduated top of his class from one of its finest private high schools, and studied at a celebrated Athens university until dropping out to pursue his newfound revolutionary interests.

To Yianni, Inmate Three represented another example of a different sort of sorry tradition – one that had some of Greece's best and brightest young radicalized in their university years by recruiters well trained in drafting youthful minds into their cause.

Yianni jerked his eyes up from the report. *That's precisely what the Consortium plans on doing to entire populations, 24/7, from cradle to grave.*

Wouldn't it be a righteous twist of fate if those revolutionaries whose budding, civilized lives were destroyed by well-rehearsed brainwashing techniques proved to be the undoing of the Consortium's efforts at accomplishing the same in its metaverse?

Yes, that would be very nice indeed.

TWELVE

D ittos had convinced himself that his meetings with the Minister and Kaldis had provided a golden opportunity to destroy them both, and he'd spent much of his time consumed by concocting how best to achieve that goal.

But every plan required him to find a sponsor capable of bending the Prime Minister's ear to his way of thinking. That would not be easy, for not only must his sponsor be a person of influence, but one who shared his passion to rid the government of the pair.

It was not the sort of palace intrigue one could casually raise in an internet chatroom and then ask whether there were any takers. He needed to find the right environment to subtly test the waters for possible takers.

He sat in his office asking himself over and over: *Where can I find such a place . . . and quickly?*

He was about to leave for the day when he saw a message from his secretary asking whether he planned on attending an event described in an invitation attached to the message.

A eureka smile formed on his face, and he quickly scribbled across the message:

A DEFINITE YES!

Lila could sense that her husband didn't want to talk about his rough week at the office. Instead, as they got ready for bed, she raised what she thought a neutral subject.

'Are you excited about meeting Anna's fiancé tomorrow?'

'I don't want to talk about it.'

So much for that ploy.

'Then what are you excited about?'

'Nothing.'

'Thank you for the compliment.'

'I didn't mean you.'

'Then prove it. Tell me what plans you've made to show Jack around Athens.'

'There won't be any time for that. We've got to head straight off to Syros.'

'What do you mean there won't be any time? He's a native-born Greek who's not been back since he was a child.'

'Don't worry, we'll see that he's not arrested for failing to serve in the army.'

'I'm not kidding. How can you not at least show him the Acropolis, the new Acropolis Museum, the Archaeological Museum, the view from the top of Lycabettus Hill, the . . .'

'Stop right there. I think you're missing the motivation behind my decision not to show him those sites the first day he's in Athens.'

'This should be a good bedtime fairy tale,' said Lila, plopping down on the bed.

Andreas sat next to her, taking her hand in his. 'You're right, this is the first time he's been back in Greece since he was a child. He's about to experience emotions he could not possibly have anticipated, and . . .'

'And you're denying him that opportunity.' She crossed her arms. 'For selfish police business reasons.'

'You're really worked up over this.'

'Of course I am. Jack deserves the opportunity to explore his heritage. These are moments he'll remember for the rest of his life.' She freed one arm and poked him in the chest with a finger. 'And you're denying him those memories.'

'That's precisely why I'm *not* taking him on a tour.'

Lila blinked twice. 'I don't understand.'

'As you said, these are birthright moments he'll remember for the rest of his life. They are not ones to share with his soon-to-be wife's uncle, but moments to share with Anna.'

Lila's nostrils flared. 'Do you think I don't realize you just came up with that fancy romantic excuse to placate me?'

Andreas looked shocked. 'After all our years together, how could you possibly think such a dastardly subterfuge of me?' He smiled. 'Besides, Jack is staying with us. He can see the Acropolis from our front windows and Lycabettus from the rear.'

Lila picked a pillow and lightly smacked him with it. 'Don't be so smug. I have an alternative plan. One that you won't find so easy to smooth-talk your way around.'

'Pray tell, what is it?'

'You'll find out soon enough.' Lila crawled under the covers and flipped off the lights, leaving Andreas totally in the dark. 'Night, night.'

On Wednesday morning Andreas was waiting outside customs at Athens's Venizelos International Airport for Jack's 10 a.m. arrival from New York's JFK. They shook hands, hugged hellos in Greek, and exchanged so-happy-to-meet-yous as Andreas shepherded him to where a van waited to pick them up.

'Just leave all your baggage in the van. The driver will drop it off at my home.'

'Where are we going?'

'We're flying to Syros. It'll take about a half-hour, but it's a beautiful trip out over the Aegean Sea.'

Jack's color noticeably changed.

'Are you OK?' asked Andreas.

'Yes, I'm just tired from the flight. I didn't sleep much. Some kid cried the whole way.'

Andreas nodded. 'I know the feeling. Both as a passenger and a parent.'

'What sort of plane are we taking?'

Andreas smiled. 'Through the kindness of the Greek Coast Guard we'll be in an S-70B Aegean Black Hawk, on loan to us for this occasion and piloted by one of our own.'

'A helicopter?'

'Yes.' Andreas noticed Jack bite at his lip. 'It has two engines and is the safest in the fleet.'

Jack stopped biting. 'Is it that obvious?'

'What has you nervous?'

'It's not a fear of flying.'

Andreas nodded. 'Is it tied to what happened to your mother?'

'You know about the accident?'

Andreas shrugged. 'What can I say, I'm a cop. I can't help but learn such things.'

'When I can't see the water because I'm in a plane with the shades down, or in a vehicle crossing a bridge where I can concentrate on the road ahead of me, I'm fine. But put me on a boat . . . I just can't take it.' Jack swallowed. 'I've never been in a helicopter over water, so I've no idea how I'll react.'

'You have the broad-shouldered build of a competitive swimmer. I never would have suspected your aversion to the water.'

'Swimming pools I'm fine with. And yes, I swam in high school and college. In part to overcome my dread of open water. I never did, but my college coach said that anxiety is likely what inspired me to get out of the pool faster than virtually everyone I competed against.'

Andreas laughed. 'I didn't know of your fear. If I had, I'd have arranged for a fixed-wing plane. There are very few scheduled flights in and out of Syros.'

'No need to worry. But thank you. I'm sure I'll be fine. I'm just exhausted. And I know my fear is irrational.' Jack paused, then smiled. 'Besides, I'm about to marry a Greek girl who loves the island life. I'll just have to work harder at getting over my past.'

Andreas shook his head in disagreement. 'You'll never get over how your mother passed away, Jack. All you can hope to do is what she'd want you to do. By that I mean put aside your fear that the same destiny awaits you and live your life unafraid of whatever actually is in store.'

Jack stared at Andreas. 'You sound as if you're speaking from personal experience.'

Andreas drew in and let out a deep breath, then pointed out the van window. 'There's the chopper.'

Jack looked to be waiting for more from Andreas, but he said nothing.

They exited the van and started for the helicopter when Andreas raised his hand in a signal to stop.

'What's wrong?' asked Jack.

'You deserve an answer.' Andreas exhaled. 'My father died by suicide when I was eight. A very different situation from your father's heart attack. And, unlike your mother's tragic passing, my story has no boat to blame. But I know all too well the consequences of a parent dying in a horrendous, highly publicized way. Memories leap out at you in the most unexpected and inopportune moments. And they always will. I've just learned to accept them as subconscious tributes to my father's memory, and nothing more. You can do the same once you're willing to accept that there's no rule requiring you to be sad or blame yourself when your thoughts drift to loved ones who've passed on.'

Jack touched Andreas's arm. 'I appreciate that.'

'One more thing. On this flight, don't worry about the helicopter.

I've got your back.' Andreas stared into Jack's eyes. 'Which means, if we go down, you won't have to swim like hell for shore alone.'

Jack laughed. 'Thanks, Uncle.'

Andreas smiled. 'I like the sound of that.'

'Me too.'

The helicopter and passengers made it to Syros National Airport without incident. Sound maintenance and experienced piloting no doubt accounted for the copter, but it took a bit of creative distraction to assure the same for Jack. As soon as Jack and Andreas strapped themselves into their seats, Andreas launched into a rapid-fire status report covering every known aspect of the Consortium's project and its players. Jack never had a second to focus on anything other than Andreas's words – though, just before landing, Andreas did have the pilot circle and hover over Lazaretta.

They landed on an asphalt tarmac by a small white-to-cream building with a terracotta roof and a sign reading AIRPORT SYROS. No other aircraft were anywhere to be seen.

'This isn't a very busy airport,' said Andreas.

'I can see that,' said Jack.

'It's thirty-some years old with runways way too short for large commercial jets. It covers a hilltop overlooking the sea, south-east of the harbor, not far from Lazaretta.' Andreas pointed toward the terminal building. 'The man walking toward us can give you more info about Syros. He's a native Syrianos and longtime Chief Homicide Investigator for the Cycladic Islands.'

'A lovely day for a flight, gentlemen,' said Tassos, extending his hand to Andreas.

'Jack, this is Chief Tassos Stamatos.'

'Pleased to meet you, sir.'

'It's my pleasure to have you here,' said Tassos, shaking Jack's hand. 'You're an answer to this digital illiterate's fervent prayers.'

Jack smiled. 'That's very kind of you to say, but from what I've seen so far, I'm not sure you're going to like what I have to say.'

Tassos frowned, looked at Andreas, and back at Jack. 'How can you say that? You haven't been on the ground for three minutes.'

Jack shrugged. 'Assuming you love your island as it is, I can say with near certainty that everything about it will change if this project goes forward. And by everything, I mean more than just its physical appearance.'

Now sounding a bit testy, Tassos said, 'I repeat, how can you say that?'

'Let's begin with where we're standing. If this project goes forward, there's no doubt in my mind that a new airport capable of landing international commercial-size jets will be built somewhere on this island.'

'There's already one on Mykonos, less than an hour from here by boat.'

Jack nodded. 'I get your point, but do you think that's going to satisfy governments who are investing billions, if not trillions, in this project, if – and I emphasize *if* – they view Syros as their front line in a coming digital global war?

'There will be a constant flow of high-level technical, operations, management, and you-name-it personnel flying in and out of Syros. And at some point, critical equipment will fail or require an update in a time frame that can't be met by ships or dare be entrusted to airport transfers.' Jack looked at a dour-faced Tassos. 'I'm sorry if what I said offended you, but you asked for my opinion.'

'I'm not offended. Just crotchety by nature.' Tassos sighed. 'So, what else do you see in your crystal ball?'

'At a bare minimum the project needs warehouse space to secure supplies and spare parts, and offices, housing, and other needed support for all the personnel necessary to supervise, operate, maintain, and secure their systems on a twenty-four-seven basis.'

Tassos shook his head in agreement. 'I heard earlier today from a friend, who attended a meeting on Monday with the Consortium's lawyer at the Municipal Port Fund, that the Consortium proposes rebuilding Lazaretta to serve as the underwater cable connection point for all its off-island privately generated power sources, and to house transformers, computer servers, and related equipment. On top of that, reconstruction is to provide enough onsite space for conducting necessary day-to-day operations, and some sort of dedicated community social hall or performance space. The Fund is expected to vote to approve the Consortium's proposal today.'

'Great,' cursed Andreas. 'But what about housing for all the new workers?'

'The lawyer told the Fund that the Consortium was prepared to build housing and hire locals, but the details of its housing proposal were the subject of an evening meeting on Monday between the lawyer and members of the affected community. It deteriorated into name-calling over whether housing should be built on the site of the ruins of a long-abandoned orphanage. Despite that, I'm told that proposal will likely also be approved. There's simply too much money backing this up to stop it.'

'If all that's true,' said Jack, 'the new Lazaretta space soon will be bursting out of its current footprint.' He looked at Andreas. 'And that doesn't count all the housing.'

'I guess you're not putting much stock in the Consortium's promise to hire locals,' said Andreas.

Jack laughed. 'I've no doubt the technology driving the Consortium is Chinese. Just look at their reputation for what's happened when similar Chinese-backed entities have brought infrastructure development projects to other countries. The record is filled with examples of Chinese workers being brought in to do the serious work, while locals are kept poorly trained or confined to low-level positions. Nor is it in their nature to entrust non-Chinese with access to technology as valuable to China as its greatest state secrets. At best, some Syros locals might obtain junior management positions supervising their Greek support staff. Above that level, management positions will most likely be all Chinese.'

'How do you come up with these opinions on what the Consortium is up to?' grouched Tassos.

Jack replied much like a professor addressing a hectoring student. 'Let's take it as a given that the Consortium intends to make Syros its metaverse base of operations. I say that because it publicly admits to that. Indeed, it's wrapped itself in the cloak of metaverse because it knows that's a buzzword for things few understand but everyone wants to be in on.'

He paused, as if considering what to say next. 'The big question is how do they plan on exploiting their metaverse presence? Considering the predilections of its members, I think political messaging will play an obvious and significant role. But the crucial question to answer is how ominous and powerful a presence do they intend on being? And that's what alarms me.'

Jack pointed at Lazaretta. 'Based upon the assumption that properties the Consortium is acquiring on Evia will be turned into wind farms or the like, and that the new underwater cable it's prepared to pay for will carry all of that power to Lazaretta, we're looking at far more power than a property the size of Lazaretta's footprint would require for what today would be considered a reasonable metaverse presence.'

Jack paused again. 'Put differently, for what it publicly *claims* it has in mind, the amount of power the Consortium is amassing is like using a sledgehammer to drive a thumbtack into a corkboard.'

He looked at each face. 'Analysts at one of the world's largest tech giants believe that global computing infrastructure needs to be *one thousand times* more powerful to comfortably sustain the metaverse. Bottom line, in my judgment there's something very big afoot here.'

Tassos looked at Andreas. 'Well, that sure makes things simple. I guess we can all go off to lunch.'

Jack smiled. 'If you'd like a more complicated analysis, I can give you one, but my bottom line remains the same. What precisely it may be that the Consortium has in mind I can't say as yet.'

'What about other uses?' asked Andreas. 'Do any come to mind that would require power on the scale you see here?'

'Nuclear facilities for one, but I can't imagine Consortium members thinking they could surreptitiously build something as obvious and controversial as that in another country. Then there's the massive power requirements of cryptocurrency mining, but why go through all the expense, red tape, and intrigues Lazaretta presents, when any one of the Consortium members could quickly and easily put up such a facility at home for a fraction of the cost of doing so here?'

Andreas fluttered his lips. 'As I see it, we've got three inciner-ated bodies serving as potential proof of how merciless the project's participants can be in pursuing their project goals, local Syros officials anxious to find a magic bullet for restoring their island to its old glory, and three of the most autocratic, ruthless, and wealthy nations on earth driving it all.'

Tassos sighed. 'Not sure where that leaves us. I was hoping for a definitive answer on how to get us out of this metaverse mess.'

'Such is real life,' said Andreas. 'There's no convenient game reset button. Each of us has to live with the consequences of our reactions to what life throws at us.'

'On that cheery note, at least allow me to give you and Jack a ground-level look at Lazaretta.' Tassos turned toward the terminal.

'I'm parked outside. Jack, I understand this is your first trip to Greece since leaving as a child. Perhaps you'd like a quick tour of parts of our beautiful island, starting with lunch in my native village of Kini? All at no cost to you.'

'That sounds terrific. Thank you.'

Andreas did not react as enthusiastically. 'Did Lila speak to you?'

'Why do you ask?'

'Because it sounds a lot like what she said to me just the other day.'

'Well, I'm sure Jack's happy to hear that at least one of us listens to your wife.' With a twinkle in his eye, Tassos added, 'Or perhaps I should say, his Aunt Lila.'

Jack sat in the front passenger seat and Andreas in the back, as Tassos wound along the one-kilometer, well-paved spur road leading from the airport down to the main road.

Jack pointed to a modern, well-maintained two-story building on the right, displaying a banner above its entrance bearing the English words CHOPPER RIDERS CLUB over a small insignia. 'I guess after this morning's ride, I qualify for membership.'

That brought a deep laugh out of Tassos, followed by his stopping the car and backing up in front of the building. 'Look more closely and you'll see a pair of hitching rails.'

'For horses? Donkeys?'

Tassos laughed harder. 'No, for choppers.'

'I don't understand.'

'Look at the insignia on the banner.'

Jack and Andreas each turned to look at the insignia, and simultaneously burst out laughing.

'Chopper, as in motorcycles,' said a still-laughing Jack. 'Not helicopters.'

'You're not the first one to make that mistake,' said Tassos. 'I take it as a constant reminder that things often aren't what they appear,' he added, starting back down the road.

'Sounds like the sort of mindset we all could use at the moment,' said Andreas.

The road twisted on down the hill, offering broad vistas of property west and south of Ermoupoli.

'How close are we to Lazaretta?' asked Jack.

'Up ahead by two car dealerships this spur road runs into a main road leading into the port. We'll take a right there, and head north for a minute before turning right again just before a petrol station. From there it's about three minutes to Lazaretta.'

'Is that important?' asked Andreas.

'I'm not sure it is,' said Jack, 'but I noticed a lot of undeveloped land west and south of here that might play a part in the Consortium's plans. That is, if I'm correct that it has a much bigger project than Lazaretta in mind for Syros.'

'I know the land you're talking about. A lot of it is farmland or protected,' said Tassos.

'Understood, but I suspect protections can be undone by new laws, and loyalty to one's ancestral farmland can be changed by money.'

'I'd like to disagree,' said Andreas, 'but from experience I can't say that doesn't happen.'

'Nor can I,' said Tassos. 'Even here on Syros where we're outspoken and at times aggressive in our efforts to preserve our island.'

'Aren't most islanders everywhere that way?' said Jack.

'Nope.' Tassos glanced over at Jack. 'Where are your people from?'

'Athens.'

'I mean what islands.'

'No idea.'

'What's your last name?'

'Diamontopoulos.'

A broad smile burst across Tassos's face. 'Welcome home, fellow Syrianos.'

'What are you saying?' asked Andreas.

'The manager of the factories of the Ladopoulos family that perished in the tragic sinking of the *Sperchios* was Periklis *Diamontopoulos.*'

'*Mazel tov,*' said Andreas.

Less than five minutes later, Tassos pulled to a stop and parked in front of Saint Haralambos church.

Jack got out of the car and stared at the crumbling walls next to the church. 'This place really is in ruin.'

'A lot of that's attributable to decades of locals stripping its walls of stones for personal use,' said Tassos.

Jack did a slow 360-degree turn. 'What are those tanks off by the airport?'

'They're used by a bunkering company to store fuel oil and gas oil.'

'What's a bunkering company?'

'It fuels ships. Bunker is the maritime term for fuel.'

'So, it's like a gas station for boats?'

'Big boats,' smiled Tassos, 'and where the fill-ups occur at sea. The company has operations in Syros and Piraeus.'

'And those big metal pipelines I saw running along the shore road leading here and along the shore in front of Lazaretta are part of that operation?'

'That's what I understand,' said Tassos. 'If you think it's important, I can check for you.'

'No need. I'm just musing to myself that if the island saw enough economic development benefit in allowing five huge fossil fuel tanks and attendant piping to be erected in the heart of this beautiful harbor, practically on top of a treasured symbol of the island's glorious past, it's not much of a reach to imagine at least that much official cooperation getting behind a deep-pocketed, one-hundred-per-cent clean-energy business venture promising not only a huge economic boost to the island, but restoration of the treasured Lazaretta to its original state.'

Jack let out a deep breath. 'You asked for my opinion. Well, here it is. I doubt it will come as a surprise to either of you. If you're looking to stop this project, you better do so ASAP, because from what I can see, once the island's political and community leadership gets behind it, and the money starts rolling in, there will be no stopping it.' He shook his head. 'No matter how far the Consortium deviates from its original commitments to play nice on the island, it will expand exponentially as an economic driver of the island, with cultural changes likely to follow.'

'I fear we might already be there,' said Andreas. 'As I see it, unless someone on Team Consortium screws up big time, the party's over.'

Come Monday, it most certainly will be for me, Andreas thought.

THIRTEEN

Andreas, Jack, and Tassos spent an hour together walking about the property, ever alert for snakes and other unwelcome critters. By far the most unwelcome of all were the thoughtless generations of pillagers, vandals, and defacers who came before them.

'Did our little hike give you any more ideas?' asked Andreas as they walked back to the car.

'The place is pretty much as it appeared in photos and videos I'd seen posted to the internet. What would be interesting, though, is the opinion of a geologist or civil engineer on the feasibility of creating a basement and sub-basements within the current footprint. That would add a lot of additional capacity for transformers, servers, and the equipment needed to keep them cool.'

'But it would add a lot to the cost,' said Tassos.

'Hardly a concern if it's truly a cost-is-no-object project.'

Andreas shook his head. 'I keep asking myself why is the Consortium willing to throw so much money into rebuilding what any developer with sense would call a tear-down project in a location without a scintilla of historical or cultural significance for any of the Consortium's partners? The only answer I can come up with is they view Syros as so desperate to reassert itself on the Greek national stage – if not an international one – that by offering to restore one of its most revered buildings in a manner that also promises to fulfill the island's economic and status desires, Syros will allow the Consortium to do as it wishes with its metaverse project.'

'A modern-day deal with the Devil,' said Jack.

'And fits in with your opinion that once this project gets started, there's no stopping it.'

'Hey, guys,' shouted Tassos. 'Don't malign my island.'

'I'm not maligning your island, just trying to figure out "why here,"' said Andreas. 'Yes, it's beautiful, has a proud history, and its people are charming, but Syros is not a tourist hotspot, and Syrianos long ago realized their island can't possibly compete with Piraeus on shipping's world stage.'

'Fine, apology accep—' Tassos stumbled over a loose rock. 'Damn it.'

'Are you OK?' said Andreas.

'Yeah, but let's get out of this rubble and off to Kini for lunch.'

'What and where is Kini?' asked Jack.

'It's an old fishing village due west of here over the mountains. It should take about ten minutes to get there.'

'That's if Tassos is driving,' said Andreas. 'For most sane folk it takes closer to twice that.'

'Just sit back, enjoy the ride, and let me do the driving.'

He also served as tour guide, telling tales linked to many of the places they passed. After Lazaretta, they met up with the main road headed into the port, but turned west at a rotary on to a two-lane road running by Syros General Hospital. From there the road snaked its way up, over, around, and down largely untouched beige-gray to golden hills – some adorned in patches of green and others merely with green dots – all leading on toward a picturesque cove encircled by a classic Cycladic village at the edge of the turquoise sea.

And for each new vista, Tassos had a story.

The road ended at the beach, where Tassos turned right on to a brief stretch of beachfront road before parking beside the last taverna on the road. Not far past the taverna, a jetty for small boats ran west, snuggled up against a cliff face marking the northern edge of the cove.

'Here we are,' announced Tassos. 'Welcome to my favorite beachfront taverna, with not a tourist in sight. This place is utterly mobbed in August. But now, it's heaven.'

'Kini is Tassos's heaven. He's spent his life here.' Andreas waved toward a modest fisherman's house atop the far end of the cliff side boundary. 'That's Tassos's home. It and that large mansion with three massive archways closer to us are the two oldest buildings on that side of the cove.'

'Just to be sure Jack doesn't confuse the mansion with my castle; the mansion's bright white and my house is pale green.'

'Now that you've set the table for us, Mr Local, the pressure's on you to choose the menu for Jack's first meal back in Greece.' Andreas looked at Jack. 'Assuming that's OK with you.'

'Sounds great.'

'Any restrictions on what you eat?' asked Tassos.

'None. Neither medical nor religious.' Jack smiled. 'But thanks for asking.'

'Great,' said Andreas, clapping his hands together. 'Let the welcome-home meal begin.'

'With *tsipouro*,' said Tassos.

Andreas paused. 'Since one of you is a civilian, and the other's back home and clearly off duty, that leaves only me to pass on the booze. But what the hell, I'm the boss. So, I hereby declare myself off-duty.'

Jack smiled. 'I never realized how much fun police work could be.'

'Oh, yes, just one laugh-filled moment after another.'

'Ask him if it's still fun on Monday,' quipped Tassos.

'What's happening on Monday?'

Andreas waved him off. 'Not your problem. Let's just chalk it up to traditional office politics that I'd prefer not to get into now.'

'My feelings too,' said Tassos, waving to a waiter. '*Tsipouro*, Stephanos. The biggest bottle you have. We have a lot of serious business to discuss.'

'And stories to tell,' added Andreas. 'Some of which might even be true.'

Jack smiled. 'I can't wait. Truth is so overrated these days.'

'Not to mention reality,' added Andreas.

'Well, hang on to your appetites, fellas, because what's about to come out of this taverna's kitchen is reality in its truest form.'

'Bring it on,' said Jack. 'I'm starving.'

Tassos smiled as he slapped Jack on the back. 'Challenge accepted.'

True to his word, Tassos ordered a meal grand enough to please a king . . . and large enough to feed his army.

Greek *choriatiki* salad with local cheese and olives; pureed fava beans topped with onions and capers; fresh baked bread; creamy, spicy dips of *tzatziki* (yogurt, cucumber, garlic, and dill), *melitzanosalata* (eggplant), and *skordalia* (garlic); grilled octopus; black-eyed peas with smoked mackerel and fresh tomato; beets and local soft cheese; eggplant baked with fresh tomatoes, cheese, and spices; chickpeas and spices baked in a clay pot; fried calamari; grilled sardines; oven-roasted goat with vegetables and herbs; panna-cotta-style local cheese custard topped with *vyssino* sour cherry preserve; and, of course, melon to finish off the meal.

Lunch lasted long enough for the three of them to finish off an entire liter of *tsipouro*, plus a dozen beers, and yet remain – for the most part – no more than pleasantly buzzed.

They spent the hours talking about whatever subject came to mind, running from their respective childhoods, first loves, favorite football teams, tragedies they'd endured and weathered, up through and including each's yet-to-be-realized life goals. It was the life-goals topic that brought them around to talking about the Consortium.

'Jack,' said Tassos, still nibbling at the watermelon and nursing his beer, 'you're the youngest of us, meaning you've likely got the widest open future ahead of you, so, what do you think the future has in store for you and the world at large?'

Andreas laughed. 'The classic deep and meaningful sort of question you expect to hear after way too much drinking.'

'Hey, some of my finest philosophical discussions have come at moments like this.'

'I bet,' said Andreas. 'Jack, do you care to answer our play-ground Plato's question on where life is headed?'

Jack smiled. 'Sure, but can I order some coffee?'

Tassos waved for the waiter. 'Stephanos. Coffees all round, please. Greek coffees.'

'Actually,' said Jack, 'I have no problem trying to answer that question, because it's one I've pondered practically every day since my mother died.' He looked at Andreas. 'Not to sound hokey, but Anna is the answer to my wildest dreams and aspirations. She's my soulmate and has given direction to my life.'

'There's no reason to get into any of that with me, Jack. I already think you're great for my niece.'

'Thanks, but that's not what I was getting at. Until meeting Anna, I wasn't sure if I should aim for a traditional job in the software industry, one that pays well with good benefits; accept an offer from a leading investment banking firm that holds out the promise of hitting the jackpot if I can pick tech start-up winners; or continue working to establish my own business as the leading go-to independent problem-solver for whatever the digital age might throw at you.'

'Are you saying Anna has you thinking about giving up your business?'

Jack shook his head no. 'Just the opposite. She's wildly alive with ideas and dreams of what she'd like us to accomplish in our lives. She's made me realize we must be willing to take risks and trust our instincts to lead us to wherever we're meant to be.'

The waiter set a coffee down in front of each man.

'And where's that place for you?' asked Tassos.

'I'm not sure yet, but from what I see happening in the digital world, I've little doubt technology has a future in store for us that will change the world as we know it.' Jack took a sip of his coffee. 'And I want to be involved in that as a player, not a fungible chip in the game.'

'Bravo, Jack,' clapped Tassos. 'That's quite a goal you've set for yourself.'

'Thanks, but now I've got to prove to myself that I'm up to playing in that league.'

'How do you propose doing that?' asked Andreas.

Jack took another sip of coffee. 'By doing my best to help you.'

'Preferably by Monday,' said Tassos.

'That's the second time you guys have mentioned Monday. Don't you think it's about time you told me what's going on?'

Tassos looked at Andreas. Andreas shrugged, picked up his coffee, and nodded.

'In order to get more time to pursue his investigation without revealing his suspicions to his superiors, and risk political meddling or worse, Andreas reached an agreement with his boss, the Minister, that if he can't come up with proof supporting his suspicions by Monday, he'll resign from the police.'

'Jeez, no wonder you guys are drinking so much. The pressure's on.'

'Don't worry, it's not your problem,' said Andreas.

'Of course it is. Over the phone I told you what I thought the Consortium might have in mind, but you wanted something stronger than that from me. That's why you flew me over here ASAP. Well, I've done that, and have told you within a reasonable degree of professional certainty that in my opinion the Consortium is preparing to launch a major metaverse operation on Syros.'

'Thank you,' said Andreas. 'That's been a big first step.'

'You're welcome, but we still have to determine the Consortium's agenda once its operation's up and running.'

Andreas nodded. 'Figuring out what the bad guys specifically plan on doing once they're operational is an admirable goal, but

I think it's safe to conclude that whatever it is won't be to encourage democracy and inclusion.'

'Amen to that,' said Jack.

'That brings us to an entirely different can of worms,' said Tassos. 'How can we do anything to stop them?'

Andreas looked at Jack. 'The other day you shocked me when you described the awesome potential power in the hands of whoever controls the metaverse. Today, you've confirmed that the Consortium is aggressively preparing to do just that.' He picked up his coffee. 'Let's assume we confirm our worst suspicions and lay bare the Consortium's wicked intentions before the world. My question then is: how will our succeeding in doing all of that prevent the Consortium from going forward with its plans for Syros?'

Jack looked surprised. 'Do you actually believe Greece would allow a project to go forward within its borders intended to give three of the most autocratic nations on earth potential control of the metaverse?'

'I share your disbelief at the thought, but as you've expressed to me, virtually all the world's biggest players want in on the metaverse game, hoping to control it for their own selfish purposes.'

'But this is an effort to control minds for political purposes, not sell products or services.'

'True, but just imagine how the Consortium will use its unlimited funds, and strongest propaganda operations on earth, to convince the free world that it's doing nothing different from what politicians, governments, businesses, and public service organizations everywhere do every day.'

'And what is that?' asked Tassos.

'Using messaging efforts, ranging from subtle product placement to hard-edged direct pitches, to bombard constituencies that they hope to bring around to their way of thinking.'

'But the Consortium countries don't have free and independent media. They would never permit those who challenge their doctrinaire line reciprocal access rights to their metaverse.'

'You make a good point, Jack, but many in the free world have been led to believe by their own leaders that much of their native press is fake news, not to be believed. That lends considerable credence to the Consortium countries' argument that western media is no different than their own.'

Obviously flustered, Jack asked, 'Are you saying we should just call it a day and let the Consortium have its way with the world?'

Andreas ignored Jack's emotion. 'Not at all. I'm just pointing out how mismatched we are up against this triad of ruthless, savvy, and likeminded adversaries hiding behind the Consortium. We need to find a way to tear it apart from the inside. Or at least make their metaverse plans too politically hot for Greece to host.'

'How do you suggest we do that?' asked Tassos.

'I wish I had an answer. But for now, all I can think of is to keep pulling as hard as we can on whatever loose threads we find dangling from their Consortium cover.'

'Like the three dead arsonists,' said Tassos.

'Yes, and whatever Jack and I pick up at our dinner party tomorrow night.'

'What dinner party?' asked Jack.

'The one where you, your aunt-to-be, and I put on our most sincere, fawning faces and spend the evening subtly fishing for leads that might help to bring down the Consortium.'

'I assume you're going to tell me how I'm supposed to do all that.'

'Absolutely I will,' said Andreas. 'As soon as I figure it out for myself.'

'*Yamas*,' said Tassos, raising his glass.

'*Yamas*,' said Andreas, doing the same.

'*L'chaim!*'

Tassos offered to drive Andreas and Jack back to the airport, but Andreas refused, pointing out how that would require Tassos to undertake a round trip over precarious roads, while in a bit of a precarious condition himself.

To his credit, Tassos didn't play the macho Greek role of insisting booze never affected his driving. Instead, he said he'd give his car to a friend to drive them to the airport. He did insist, though, that they take a different route back, one that completed a circle running south from Kini, east across to the other coast, and north to Ermoupoli and the airport.

When Andreas said he wasn't interested in wasting hours touring around the island, Tassos pointed out that he and Jack needed the additional time to sober up. If not, he faced the risk of the pilot spreading locker-room talk about the Chief Inspector of Special

Crimes stranding him in the middle of a nowhere airport for half a day, while he went off to get shit-faced drunk with his friends while on duty.

Andreas accepted Tassos's suggestion, after grudgingly admitting that claiming he wasn't on duty didn't appear the best strategy for salvaging a career already under fire.

Tassos's friend was an obliging ex-cop who knew not to press for small talk. He'd also been told by Tassos to make a point of noting the villages they passed through and to make strategic detours to beaches or sites he thought might be of interest to Jack.

To accommodate Andreas's desire to sleep rather than tour, Jack sat up front, leaving the back seat to Andreas. Jack stayed awake the whole trip, listening courteously to the driver softly point out the main sites and offer answers to any questions Jack had.

They climbed east out of Kini, turned south off the main road, and headed toward the inland village of Danakos, in the process gaining a final panoramic view down across the mountains to Kini, still snugly tucked up against a blue and white sea.

Danakos sat midway between the beach town of Kini and the self-proclaimed number-one Syros beach resort of Galissas. Danakos's scattered greenhouses, hardworking farmers, and dedicated stock raisers offered a distinctly different vibe from its beach-based cousins, one formed by generations of agrarian lives lived amid the golden-brown rolling hills and cultivated green that covered much of undeveloped Syros.

They passed through the tranquility of Danakos and the theme-park promise of Galissas on to Finikas beach, the second-largest port on Syros. Finikas also served as a popular place for fishing boats and yachts seeking shelter from north winds, as well as for tourists looking for time in the sun.

Upon leaving Finikas they entered the architectural gem of a village known by two names: Della Grazia and Posidonia. Without question this was the place to be during mid-nineteenth-century Syros summers. Here the wealthy of Ermoupoli and elsewhere built magnificent mansions and elaborate gardens, many of which had been restored to their old glory.

Then it was on to Megas Gialos, once among the least developed places on the island and likely its longest beach. With the opening of a new coast road, its desirable location, and sandy beaches,

Megas Gialos became an instant magnet for the sort of development that now lines its beachfront.

On reaching Vari, a farming community on the northern leg back to Ermoupoli, the driver pointed out that close by the bay of Vari stood the sites of the oldest settlements on Syros, dating back to between 4000 to 3000 BCE.

The last seaside village they passed before reaching the airport was Azolimnos, a tiny beachfront village popular with tourists and locals alike less than five kilometers from Ermoupoli.

By the time they arrived at the airport, Andreas had slept off most of his buzz, and Jack had seen more than enough beachfronts to last him for this trip.

Back on the helicopter, Andreas asked Jack what he'd missed while napping.

'Do you want the long version or the short?'

'Let's start with the short and see where we go from there.'

'I saw loads of golden-brown hills, stark gray mountaintops, and more shades of green bursting out of fields and orchards than I could ever have possibly imagined growing up in New York City. And all of that against a bright blue sky and deep blue sea.'

'So, you're saying I didn't miss much.' Andreas chuckled.

'You're clearly from the "if you've seen one beautiful sunset you've seen them all" crowd.'

'Not really.'

'Do you want to hear the rest of my take on what I saw?'

'Ah, the other shoe is about to drop.'

'The beaches are beautiful, and the sea is drop-dead gorgeous, but in my humble opinion, the developed parts of virtually everything I saw on the way back to the airport could use somewhat of a charm makeover. Much of what I saw struck me as derivative of dated beach resort style, or just plain run-down.'

'That's a bit harsh, wouldn't you say?'

'It's just my opinion, based upon where I was taken. I've no idea how representative what I saw is of other places on the island. But there are also New York beaches that deserve the same criticism.'

'A lot of what you're referring to went up in the nineteen-fifties, sixties and seventies across many parts of Greece, during times when building construction more often than not opted for functional mediocrity over charm.'

'I'm sad to hear that.' Jack sighed. 'I wish I'd had the chance to spend time wandering about Ermoupoli and Ano Syros. I'm intrigued by what I've seen of them from a distance, read about them, and heard in Tassos's comparison of them to Venice, less canals and plus steps. All of that suggests a different experience from the one I had, because it makes me think of the outlying locales more as suburbs of Ermoupoli than rival, unrelated villages.'

'That's a perceptive take, Jack. One no doubt shared by many who know Syros well and love it as the Grande Dame of the Cyclades. We'll have to arrange to get you back here soon.'

'Even after my take on the island's most popular beach communities?'

Andreas grinned. 'I like a man who speaks his mind even though it might land him in a Greek prison for slandering our national image.'

'Don't get me started on America's current image. Landing in a New York prison would likely be even worse.'

Andreas grinned again. 'I think you and Lila are going to get along famously.'

'I'm happy to hear that, but why?'

'Because you both know how to make me laugh when the subject is an emotional downer.'

'It's an acquired skill,' smiled Jack. 'But while we're talking about downer subjects, when are you going to tell me more about tomorrow night?'

Andreas brought his finger to his lips and nodded at the pilot.

'I just wanted to know what time the movie starts. I'd hate to miss any of it.'

'Trust me, you won't. And I can assure you, you'll find it a thriller from beginning to end.'

FOURTEEN

'Yianni, building security just dropped off a small package at my desk addressed to you. It's been scanned.'

'Who's it from?'

'No idea. Some local messenger service delivered it,' said Maggie.

'Does the delivery ticket have a sender's name on it?'

'Let me check . . . Bruce Lee.'

Yianni jumped up from his desk chair and raced down the hall to Maggie's desk.

'I assume from how fast you got here that you know what's in the package.'

'If we're lucky, it's about the three who died in the fires.' He shook the package. 'It's light and something's rattling inside.'

'Security said it's a thumb drive.'

'Where's the Chief?'

'He's on his way back from Syros. But I think he's going straight home.'

'Tell him to call me when he checks in. I'll see what's on the drive.'

'Will do.'

Yianni had hoped the inmate would come through, but never expected it to be this quickly. Some revolutionaries are far better organized than he'd imagined.

He carefully opened the package, taking care not to tear the wrapping paper in case something on the other side of the paper might be important. His instinct proved partially correct. On the other side was an image of Bruce Lee kicking out through a wall.

This guy has a sense of humor.

Beneath the wrapping, in a box of the sort that would hold a small bracelet, sat the thumb drive.

Yianni said a quick few words of prayer as he inserted the drive into his desk computer.

The video opened without sound or titles, not that he'd expected any, but it did have a running date and time stamp. What Yianni hadn't expected was the high-definition quality of the images.

The drone soared high above forested ground until it detected human presence. It would then swoop in, hawk-like, for a closer look. If someone were found, the drone operator would mark the coordinates and resume surveillance from on high until a new reason for a closer look presented itself.

The footage supported the inmate's story about drones being used to observe vast areas of forest. Whether the people targeted in the video were later involved in acts of arson was not answered. At least not in the first thirty minutes of video Yianni watched.

He'd been hoping for something helpful, something that might give him an angle on identifying the three dead. So far, he'd seen nothing faintly resembling helpful. It was as if someone had sent him the most boring outtakes from a seriously uninteresting travel documentary.

In a literal flash, all changed. The camera caught a bright light coming at it from below. At first Yianni thought it might be someone laser-targeting the drone for kicks. But the flash was too inconsistent to be a laser. A car windshield?

Yianni was not alone in his curiosity, for the drone immediately homed in on the source of the flash and dived in for a closer look. He was right, it was a car windshield.

On a parked silver Porsche.

He leaned forward in such a hurry to get a closer look that he almost fell out of his chair. The drone circled the car, marked coordinates, paused for an unobstructed view of its license plate, and hovered long enough to see no one in the car. This time, though, the drone didn't abandon the scene and fly off as it had in other instances of likely human presence. Instead, it rose higher in the sky, hovered, and switched to another type of recording. Yianni himself had used such thermal imaging in his Navy SEAL days. Its purpose was to detect hidden human presence, using body heat.

'This is one sophisticated operation,' Yianni said aloud.

As the drone hovered, Yianni counted. He'd reached five when Maggie stuck her head in the doorway.

'Any luck so far?'

'It's just starting to roll in. We might have hit the jackpot.'

Maggie stepped inside and looked at the screen. 'What's that?'

'Infrared. Here, it's picked up on five probable human images.'

'Dead or alive?'

'All alive. So far.'

They stared at the screen in silence.

The images stood bunched together under what the other camera had shown to be tree cover. They could be seeking shade to hide from the sun or cover to hide from eyes in the sky. Two minutes passed and no one moved. The drone retreated to a higher position in the sky, as if leaving the scene, but kept its camera riveted on the five. A minute later, two of the figures split off from the other three and headed in the direction of the Porsche. The drone switched back to traditional video and zoomed in on the Porsche. Two men, one dressed in a suit and tie, and the other in jeans and a work shirt, walked out from the tree cover, got into the car, and drove off, the suit behind the wheel. The drone did not follow the car but dropped down to hover where it had been parked.

'Damn fool didn't follow the car,' muttered Yianni.

The video zoomed in on the three people still under the trees. All men, dressed in plain cotton drawstring trousers and tops. They didn't seem to notice the drone or perhaps didn't realize what it was, for they paid no attention to it. Rather, they busied themselves filling three knapsacks with what Yianni took to be identical, wildfire-starting paraphernalia. Once packed up, they hurried off in three separate directions, two by bikes, one on foot. The drone followed the one on foot. He stopped walking about a kilometer from where he'd left the others.

Coordinates appeared on the video, but this time with a legend: THEY DIED BY FIRE, BUT NOT BY ANY THEY STARTED.

The screen went blank.

'I hereby apologize to the drone operator for criticizing his or her decision to ignore the Porsche.'

'I take that to mean you're pleased,' said Maggie.

Yianni kept fidgeting with his computer to capture, enlarge, and print several images from the video. 'Yes, I am. I wish I had more answers, rather than so many more questions, but on balance, a definite yes.'

He pointed at the screen. 'We now have the Consortium's lawyer off in the middle of a soon-to-be-burned forest, meeting with three men likely to later die in forest fires, and an unidentified fourth man chummy enough with the lawyer to be with him at the meeting and riding around in his Porsche.'

'Any idea who he might be?'

'From the photo,' Yianni pointed at the close-up he'd created of the fourth man, 'it's grainy, but clear he's a big guy. And from the images caught by the drone of the three presumed victims, they look to be Chinese.'

'Some coincidence.'

'Only if you're into fairy tales. My money's on the fourth man linking a lot of bad stuff back to the Consortium.'

'Including the three Chinese deaths?'

'I think we'll soon be calling them murders.'

'When will that be?'

'As soon as I can confirm with my friends in the Fire Service what the three were stuffing into their backpacks.'

'How do you plan on proving that?'

'Me? I'm a simple detective. I'll leave that to the Chief.'

'That reminds me. I spoke to him while you were watching the video. He's on his way home and will call you from there.'

'How did Syros go?'

'Let's just say about the same as your past hour.'

'Meaning?'

'Nothing is like it seems, and all hell's about to break loose to prove it.'

Jack stood in awe at his introduction to Andreas and Lila's home. The rare old residential apartment building on historic Irodou Attikou in downtown Athens stood across the street from the National Garden, next door to the Presidential Palace, and just up the road from Panathenaic Stadium – the site of the first modern Olympic Games.

That in and of itself was impressive, but their elegantly decorated, full-floor penthouse apartment and its breathtaking views utterly blew Jack away. He'd heard of palatial homes tucked away in parts of New York City, but he'd never been in one. Up until now, the thought of a three-bedroom apartment on a high floor in Manhattan had been his idea of living the high life.

'Welcome to our home, Jack,' said Lila, smiling broadly from the doorway to the apartment as Jack and Andreas stepped off the elevator.

'Thank you, Mrs Kaldis.'

'Please, it's Lila.'

'Yes, ma'am.'

'Don't mind him,' said Andreas. 'He's hung up on being polite to older folk no matter how many times I tell him there's no need to be so formal.'

'Well, this old folk thinks it's charming.'

'I didn't mean you're old,' grinned Andreas.

'Too late, you've already dug yourself into that hole, so drop the shovel.' Lila hooked her arm in Jack's. 'Come, let me show you to your room. Your bags are there. I didn't bother to have the maid unpack them because we didn't have your permission to do so.'

'That's very kind of you Mrs . . . Lila.'

'Now you've got it,' smiled Lila, dropping her arm from his. 'I hope you don't mind that we've put you in a bedroom on the children's side of the apartment. It has a great view of Lycabettus Hill.'

'I'm sure it will be fine. Thank you.' He paused. 'Would it be OK if I took a shower now? I feel like I've been in transit forever.'

'I know the feeling well. There's a full bath in your room. Take all the time you need, and whenever you feel up to resuming the march, you'll find us on the other side of the apartment.'

'Thank you.'

'No need to thank us, but you're welcome. Consider our home your own.'

Don't I wish.

When Jack joined up with Lila and Andreas, they were hanging up on a telephone call with their children.

'Tassaki and Sofia are off with my parents on a long-planned trip to their flat in London. They'll be back on Monday and are excited to meet their new cousin Jack.'

'As am I them.'

'They told me to say hi,' said Andreas, putting down the phone.

'I hope you didn't cut the call short because of me.'

'Not at all,' said Andreas. 'Frankly, I was surprised at how long they endured our asking them to tell us what they did today, and everything they plan on doing next.'

'Every child everywhere gets those questions from their parents in one form or another,' said Lila. 'It's a natural instinct.'

Jack nodded. 'Even if they don't appreciate it now, someday they'll realize how nice it was to have had someone in their life care enough to ask those questions.'

Lila froze for an instant. 'I'm sorry, that was insensitive of me. I—'

Jack held up his hand. 'Please, you said nothing wrong. I'm long past the point of feeling uncomfortable when people talk about their parents. In fact, listening to those sorts of conversations is how I've gained perspective on what it's like to grow up with parents.'

'Whoops, I forgot to call Yianni back,' said Andreas.

'Shall we leave you alone?' said Lila.

'No, please stay. What he has to say might influence how we approach tomorrow night's soirée at the Cirillo home.'

'Oh, heart be still, I can hardly wait.'

Andreas put the phone on speaker and dialed.

Yianni answered on the first ring. 'Chief, I was wondering when I'd hear from you.'

'Blame Lila and Jack for distracting me.'

'I assume they're on with us now.'

'Yes.'

'Good. They need to hear this if they'll be interacting with Cirillo.'

'That sounds ominous.'

'Because it is.' Yianni launched into a brief description of how he'd come to receive the drone video, and what the relevant segment contained.

'You're certain it was the lawyer?'

'It was his car for sure, and from the angle of the drone footage it certainly looked like him.'

'Any word yet from the Fire Service on what the three likely victims were putting into their backpacks?'

'Yes, the sort of stuff amateur arsonists would use, like gasoline.'

'Why's that amateur?' asked Jack.

'Because it vaporizes when you pour it out of its container, and when you add the flame it can explode all around you.'

'Ouch,' said Lila.

'But they also had matchbooks and cigarettes, which are used by arsonists to create a crude form of delay device. You tuck a lighted cigarette between the book's rows of match heads, and when it burns down to the heads, the book bursts into flame, and everything goes wild from there.'

'Sure sounds like amateur hour to me,' said Jack.

'Which may be precisely what whoever's behind the fires wanted it to look like,' said Andreas. 'But the fires that later killed the three were anything but amateurish.'

'Then how can you prove they were murdered?' asked Jack.

'Unless we have another lucky drone revelation or can squeeze a confession out of someone like Cirillo, I doubt that we ever will. The fires set by the three were purposely intended to look amateurish, and their later elimination was staged by professionals who knew how to avoid raising suspicions or leaving unwanted clues of it being anything other than accidents by amateurs who got what they deserved.'

'You're saying Cirillo and his people will get away with murder,' said Lila.

'That they might get away with one of their crimes – likely the most heinous – doesn't mean they'll get away with all their crimes. Sometimes you've got to settle for less justice in order to get some justice.'

'I can't stand the thought of that,' said Lila.

'I know,' said Andreas. 'But it's how the real world works in a democracy.'

'And the Consortium wants to eliminate even that imperfect system of justice,' added Jack.

'Excuse me, folks,' said Yianni, 'but since the only one on this phone call not comfortably ensconced at home is me, unless someone objects, may I ask what more you want me to do today, Chief?'

'If you'd like to join us in person while we discuss how to approach tomorrow night, you're more than welcome to come over.'

'Only if you want me there.'

'Why the sudden lack of enthusiasm?' asked Andreas.

'Because Toni's planning to spend the weekend with me in Athens.'

'And you need to clean your apartment,' chuckled Lila.

'How did you know?'

Lila smiled at Andreas. 'From experience.'

Andreas jumped in. 'Request granted. See you tomorrow.'

'Bye,' said Yianni.

'So, what's your take on how we handle tomorrow night?' asked Lila.

'It's simple. We do whatever it takes to get Cirillo bragging about his relationship with the Consortium, including running interference for any of us who gets him talking.'

'That's *all* we have to do?' said Lila.

'Any suggestions on how we get him talking?' said Jack.

'Just be your normal charming selves, but focus your attention on what he has to say, and flatter him constantly, without being too obvious.'

'As I said before, *that's all we have to do?*'

'If you have a better plan, I'm all ears.'

'Absolutely not, darling, you are the man, and your ideas are brilliant. I can't wait to hear more.'

Andreas turned to Jack. 'See what I have to put up with?'

Lila feigned a pout. 'I'm just rehearsing my best sycophantic moves for tomorrow evening.'

Jack smiled. 'This is going to be fun.'

Lila looked at Andreas and nodded toward Jack. 'I really like this guy.'

Andreas stared at her and smiled. 'At least we agree on something.'

Anna's generally easy-going good nature had run up against the inevitable angst of a daughter about to seek parental approval for her choice of spouse.

She wasn't close enough to anyone in her dorm to have that conversation, and her friends back in Greece didn't know Jack, so they couldn't offer her anything more than a pep talk.

Tomorrow afternoon she would fly to Greece. The last thing she wanted to do was spend the ten-hour flight biting her nails over what awaited her back home. She needed to talk to someone who could help her get her head straight.

That's how she ended up first thing Wednesday morning in Solona's garden, tearful and running on about the fears she held over what Jack and she were about to confront with her family.

Solona waited patiently for Anna to finish. 'Does Jack feel the same way?'

'Jack,' Anna sniffled, 'is a rock. He's enchanted by my uncle and aunt.'

'That's good. But how does he feel about your mother and father?'

'He hasn't met them yet. He's been busy with my uncle since the moment he landed.'

Solona nodded. 'The police uncle?'

'Yes. Today he dragged Jack practically all over the island of Syros, and tomorrow he and his wife are taking Jack with them to some big party in a chic Athens neighborhood.'

'Sounds like he's having fun.'

'That's what I thought, but he said it's work.'

'Work?'

'The person throwing the party is someone the police are investigating, and they want Jack's opinion on what the host might be up to.'

'Well. He must be excited to be asked to help the police solve a big mystery.'

'Yes, he is.'

Solona shrugged. 'Then what are you worried about?'

'I don't understand.'

'Jack's obviously made a good impression on your uncle, and your uncle sounds like the sort of man who'll tell that to your mother. Perhaps you should consider what Jack's now doing as auditioning to play a lifetime role as your husband.'

Anna blinked.

'From what you've told me, I'd say Jack's got the part, now it's just up to your uncle – the director – to sell it to your producer parents. I'd say he's in line to become a big hit.'

'Are you sure?'

'Are you looking for a pep talk or the truth? The truth is relationships can end for many reasons, but having known Jack for years before you met, having been there at the moment you two first set eyes on one another, and having listened to each of you separately go on about your feelings for the other, I'd say you've got a better chance than most at making it all work.'

'How good a chance?'

'I'm not an oddsmaker. But I'm profoundly impressed at how you each carry a deep concern for the wellbeing of the other. Let's just say I've already started saving for your golden wedding anniversary gift.'

Anna laughed. 'You're such an upbeat soul.'

'Let's make a pact. Call me as soon as you land in Athens to tell me whether you were able to resist dark thoughts while crossing the Atlantic, and I promise that each day you're in Greece I'll light a special candle to assure your happy and smiling return.'

'But that will be around three in the morning New York time.'

'Don't worry, I'm used to those hours.'

Anna leaned over and kissed Solona on the forehead. 'Deal.'

FIFTEEN

Despite the cavalier attitude Andreas had displayed the night before over how to handle tonight's party, he'd spent much of the morning at home with Jack and Lila preparing for every contingency he could think of. Plus a few possibilities suggested by them.

As Andreas saw it, success depended upon getting Jack into a conversation with Cirillo about the metaverse. Making that happen might depend more on luck than planning, but Andreas felt it bettered their odds to spend the morning play-acting potential scenarios, if only to learn what plainly wouldn't work.

Two and a half hours into the routine, with Lila cast as wife Jill, Andreas playing Panos, and Jack acting as himself, Jack said, 'Why don't I just ask him straight out whether he believes that, in a quest to dominate human kind through the metaverse, a foreign nation is justified in torching thousands of acres of Greek forest-land, bribing countless Greek officials for permission to change the face of Greece's second-largest island, and murdering three of its own one-and-a-half billion citizens.'

'That does have a certain dramatic flair,' said Lila.

'Yes,' said Andreas. 'Just enough to get him killed.'

Jack blanched. 'Killed?'

'We're just playacting here, but tonight it's real, and I've no doubt that if Cirillo thinks for a second you could potentially threaten his and his Consortium clients' plans, he'll have you murdered.'

Lila's jaw dropped. 'How can you ask Jack to take such a risk?'

'Ask him. I'm not forcing him to do a thing. I'll run the risk myself, if necessary, because that's my job.'

'This evening is getting worse the more you talk about it,' said Lila, biting her lip.

'That's why it's important we all do just as we rehearsed and avoid last-minute inspirations we haven't played out.'

Lila turned to Jack. 'Why are you doing this?'

'I must say that hearing a single misstep could cost me my life did take me by surprise, but on reflection, I've subconsciously accepted that risk all along.' He smiled. 'After all, we're talking about changing the world here.' He swallowed. 'But seriously, this is about the destruction of democracy. If that happens, we'll *all* die a slow death, even if we get to live out our natural lives.' Jack shook his head. 'That's not for me.'

'Good man,' said Andreas, clapping him on the arm. 'I suggest we call it a day on the prep. It will either work or not based upon what we've done so far. So, rest up, and let's plan on getting there around ten. That will give Cirillo enough time to play super host, have a few drinks, and hopefully drop his guard.'

'Works for me,' said Jack.

'Me too,' said Lila, 'with one minor addendum.'

'Being?' said Andreas.

'A trip to church to offer a major prayer.'

'Amen.'

The northern Athens suburb of Old Psychiko stood as a refuge of peace, greenery, and high walls for foreign embassies, exclusive private schools, and the upper echelon of Athenian society. A few nearby neighborhoods and one or two to the south might claim to be equally desirable, but none could argue to be more exclusive.

Psychiko's confusing array of one-way streets, winding every which way about its tree-lined slopes and hills, was designed that way for a reason: to keep out casual passersby. But it hadn't worked as well on the new-money crowd. They flocked to the neighborhood, favorite GPS app in hand, sending prices through the roof for houses they often tore down to build grander homes than their neighbors'.

Although Andreas was familiar with the neighborhood, and Lila had grown up playing here, they still used Google maps to find their way to the Cirillo house. The street was packed with cars, and not a parking valet in sight. Andreas squeezed up on to the sidewalk to park and stuck his official police business placard on the dash.

Lila pointed at it. 'Refreshing to see you use it when you actually are on police business.'

'I assume you'll cease with the sarcasm once we're inside.'

The Cirillo home stood across the street from two high-walled Eastern European embassies and up the road from the compound of one of Greece's most highly regarded families. Compared to its immediate neighbors, the three-story white stucco house seemed modest. But it was encircled by a three-meter-high black wrought-iron fence nestled up against lemon trees, bougainvillea, and oleander strategically planted between the fence and five meters of manicured grass, effectively curtaining the house from the curious.

They made their way through an ornate leaf-and-tendril iron gate on to a flagstone walkway leading to a pair of rose-and-gold marble pillars framing a massive front door. Lining each side of the path stood two, true-to-size replicas of the seventh-century BCE marble Lions of Delos.

Andreas didn't have to look at his wife to know what she was thinking. He held the front door open for Lila and Jack. As they stepped into an entry foyer made entirely of white Dionysus marble trimmed in gold inlays, and packed with more replicas of classic Greek sculptures, he heard Lila mumble, 'I don't believe what I'm seeing.'

'You did say she's from Texas, didn't you?' joked Jack.

'Let's be nice, folks, and keep our eyes on the ball,' said Andreas. 'Remember, tonight it's all flattery and no snide commentary.'

'So, you're asking me to ignore my years of work at the Museum of Hellenic Art, and praise this . . . this . . .'

'Yes,' whispered Andreas.

Lila sighed. 'Do you mind if I quietly scream to myself for a moment, just to rid my conscience of any need to speak the truth?'

'Lila, darling!' came a voice bellowing across the large room at the end of the foyer.

Lila forced a smile. 'Jill, darling, how wonderful to see you again, and I can't believe what you've done with this place.'

'Easy there, my love,' whispered Andreas.

Lila forced a broader smile. 'I just love what I've seen of it.'

Jill McLaughlin Cirillo ignored the man she'd been talking to and raced over to greet Lila just as she, Jack, and Andreas stepped out of the foyer into what many would call a giant living room. From its grand marble appointments, slew of gaudy decorative objects, and gilded furniture, a better moniker might have been 'nouveau riche playpen.'

'Lila, my dear,' said Jill, kissing her on both cheeks while expertly balancing a three-quarters-full glass in one hand. 'I was so worried that something might have happened to you when you weren't here on time.'

'I'm so sorry. You know how much I detest being late, but my husband and his nephew were delayed by last-minute business matters. I'm sure you know how that is.'

'I certainly do.' She turned to face Andreas and Jack. 'And who are these two extraordinarily handsome men?'

'Shh, or you'll give them such swelled heads it will make them impossible to live with.'

'Hi, I'm Lila's husband, Andreas, and this is my nephew, Jack.'

Jill put out her free hand. 'A pleasure to meet you.'

Jack and Andreas shook her hand. 'Likewise.'

'Now, gentlemen, if you'll excuse us, I'm going to borrow your lovely lady for a short time. I want to show her the rest of my home and introduce her to some wonderful people.'

'That's fine with us,' said Andreas.

'But don't worry, I won't leave the two of you standing around alone and unmanned. Come, let me introduce you to my husband.'

Jill whisked Lila across the room, her glass held straight out in front of her like the bow of an icebreaker, and pressed her way through a mass of men standing around her husband holding court by the bar.

'Darling, sorry to interrupt, but I want you to meet my dearest friend, Lila Vardi.'

Lila stuck out her hand to shake his, but instead Panos took her hand, bent over, and kissed it, all the while fixing his eyes on hers.

Lila seemed to shudder for an instant, but then exploded in a broad smile. 'My, how continental you are.'

Panos nodded. 'Great beauty brings that out in me.'

'A real charmer, isn't he?' said Jill. 'This gentleman is her husband, Alex and—'

'Andreas,' corrected Andreas.

'And their nephew, John.'

'Jack,' he corrected again.

'Whatever,' said Jill, swishing her highball glass in the air. 'Be a darling, won't you, Panos, and include these two handsome fellows in whatever sort of conversations you men have on occasions like this.'

And with that she turned, took Lila by the arm, and led her away.

After an awkward second or two, Andreas extended his hand toward Panos. 'A pleasure to meet you. You have a beautiful home.'

'And you have a beautiful wife.'

This is not going well. The guy's an asshole. 'Thank you.'

Ignoring Andreas, Panos went back to telling some story about how he got laid in college by the wife of one of his professors so often that when the professor found out, he offered to give him an A in the course if he promised to stop. 'I guess you could say I got an A in intercourse.'

Everyone laughed, though it took a stiff but discreet prod from Jack for Andreas to join in.

Men soon drifted away from the scrum at the bar, leaving Jack, Andreas, and a couple of clearly inebriated hangers-on as Panos's only audience. He stared at Andreas through glassy eyes. 'So, lovely lady's husband, what do you do for a living?'

Andreas smiled. 'I work in a government office.'

'Oh, you're one of those sorts.'

Andreas had to force his next smile. 'Yes, sir, that's me.'

Switching his gaze to Jack, he said, 'And you, young man, what do you do?'

'I teach.'

'Oh, another silver-spoon winner of the birth lottery who gets to do whatever he likes without worrying about having to make a living off of it.'

'Me? Silver spoon?' Jack laughed. 'I was orphaned by age eight with not a penny to my name. Whatever I have these days I owe to myself and no one else.'

Panos looked surprised. 'I assumed you were like your aunt. Born rich. That sort doesn't know what it feels like to bust your ass, hoping to beat the odds.' He took a swig of his drink. 'So, what do you teach?'

'Nothing that would be of interest to you. It'll sound like technical gibberish.'

'Humor me.'

Jack shrugged. 'I specialize in solving digital problems.'

Panos blinked twice. 'What sort of problems?'

'All kinds.'

'Can you be more specific?'

Jack reached into his jacket pocket and pulled out his business card. 'My work concentrates on the metaverse.'

Panos hesitated for a second. 'What's the metaverse?'

Jack smiled. 'I told you that what I do is too technical for party talk. I lead a very boring life.'

'Just tell me, what is the metaverse?'

Jack sighed. 'Think back to the darkest days of our shared pandemic times, when so much of the world felt isolated and afraid of what would happen next. Now imagine if, in the midst of all that, you're able to live a full, rich, and unimpeded life. One where you're free to share and satisfy your deepest desires, hopes, and dreams with as many or few like-minded souls as you choose.' Jack paused. 'Could I trouble you for a glass of water?'

'Of course.' Panos snapped his fingers to get a barman's attention, pointed to Jack, and said, 'Water.'

He looked back at Jack. 'Continue.'

'Where was I?'

'You were telling me where our world is headed.'

'Oh, yes, inescapably into the metaverse. Look at all the people who cannot stand their day-to-day lives. They long for an alternative to the real world. Until now their only choices were alcohol or drugs. Now they have a third alternative. A simple, non-invasive escape from reality via the metaverse.'

The barman handed Jack a glass of water.

'Thank you, sir.' He took a sip. 'And if you doubt where our world is headed, just look where all the big tech players are placing their bets. I've no doubt the metaverse is the future for our world, and I plan on being in on the ground floor.'

Panos smirked. 'And how do you plan on doing that.'

'By teaming up with those currently incapable of competing head-to-head with Big Tech.'

Panos looked puzzled.

'There are deep-pocketed players anxious to get in on the metaverse gold rush . . . both private and government actors. Every one of them properly worries about investing in technology that won't be supported by the uber powers who ultimately will dominate a vast and rapidly expanding metaverse, thereby condemning their investment billions to shrivel up and die a lonely death on a soon-to-be-forgotten island of deserted technologies. That could have been avoided had they not allowed their own hype to cloud their early decision-making, as so many learned in the FTX cryptocurrency exchange disaster.'

'That's quite a pitch you have there. But what makes you think you can help change the result? Investments in new technology are always a crapshoot.'

'It's all a matter of perspective and experience. For example, think of yourself as the captain of your own ship sailing in uncharted waters. You're confronted by bad weather and looking for a safe port in which to ride out the storm. You decide the best thing to do is follow the other ships who seem to know the seas, and bet on taking your lead from the big, modern ones, because they have the most to lose.'

Jack paused to take another sip of water. 'But that analysis fails to take into account that the big ones are likely better equipped than most to ride out the storm head on, and more likely have the financial wherewithal that affords them to lose the most.'

'What are you saying?'

'Were it my ship, I'd look to see where the local fishermen sought shelter. Their livelihoods – indeed, very lives – depend on making the right decision. They may not make as much as their bigger-boat brethren, but employing a fleet of maneuverable smaller vessels has a better chance of keeping you in the game should you bet wrong . . . which we all do at times.'

Panos smiled. 'I put my faith and money on the big boys.'

'Like the *Titanic*?'

A flash of anger reached across Panos's face, but it mellowed into a smile. 'I have a friend who I believe would enjoy talking with you. He's also into this metaverse stuff but comes at it from a different perspective – the perspective of those "uber powers."'

'So, you do know about the metaverse?'

'Only in passing, but I found your take very interesting. Are you doing any work here in Greece?'

'Not yet, though I'm certainly open to it, and would appreciate any introductions you could make for me.'

'Then why are you in Athens?'

'I'm here to meet my fiancée's family.'

Panos looked around the room. 'Is she here?'

'No, she arrives tomorrow morning from New York.' Jack looked at his watch. 'She should be about to board her plane at JFK soon.'

'Come, let me introduce you to my friend. He's over there talking to my wife and your aunt. That should serve as credentials enough for him to talk to you.'

'Credentials?'

'He works for the Chinese government on matters similar to

your interests. He's just reluctant to talk shop with strangers. But I think he'll enjoy talking with you.'

'I'm sure that I will. What's his name?'

'He likes to be called Victor. Something about him once being told he looked like an American movie star named Victor who used to run around in movies in nothing but a loincloth.'

'Victor Mature?'

'I don't know, but if that's what he wants to be called, I suggest you go with it. He can be a bit dismissive, especially of Americans, and certainly when he's attempting to impress women – which he always is – so don't take it personally. Put all that aside; he really knows his stuff.'

When Panos led Jack away, Andreas stayed put. He'd stayed as silent as one of the Cirillo entryway statues during Jack's back and forth. There was no way of telling where things were headed with this Victor character added into the mix, but one thing was certain: for now, there was nothing Andreas could do to help move things along except fade off into the background.

It's up to Jack now.

Panos correctly predicted Victor's icy reaction to what he perceived as a new man crowding in on his efforts to wow the two ladies he'd been monopolizing for nearly a quarter of an hour. He warmed up a bit when Lila referred to him as her nephew, but once identified as an American, paid him little mind and intensified his efforts at focusing his practiced smile on Lila. Efforts that Jack sensed had already worked their magic on Jill.

Jack waited patiently for an opening, but none came until a server offered him a pork roll that Jack courteously refused.

'Are you an American vegan?' asked Victor, dismissively.

'No,' smiled Jack. 'A Greek-American Jew who doesn't eat pork.'

Victor's eyes widened. 'A Jew? You're a Jew?'

'I assume you're not going to ask me to prove it in front of these ladies.'

Victor missed the circumcision joke but pressed ahead. 'I've never met a Greek Jew before.'

'There are fewer of us than there once were, but we're still here.'

'We share much in terms of reverence for our ancestors, a long and distinguished culture, highly valuing education, a penchant for business, a love of the arts, and of course, being persecuted for being different.'

'Shall I call you cousin?' Jack smiled.

Victor paused, then smiled back and extended his hand. 'Absolutely, Cousin Jack.'

From that point on the two men never stopped talking to each other. The ladies faded away, but neither man noticed. They talked for what seemed hours about cultural and socio-economic similarities and differences, plus their respective views on the metaverse, its history, and where it was headed.

When Jack finally insisted he had to leave, Victor extracted a promise from him that they'd get together again before Jack left Athens, and bring his bride-to-be with him.

Jack promised.

Victor bowed and Jack reciprocated.

'A pleasure and honor to meet you, cousin,' said Jack.

Victor smiled. 'The pleasure is mine, cousin,' he said, and gave Jack a surprise hug.

Jack met up with Andreas and Lila saying their goodbyes to Panos and Jill at the front door.

Panos pulled Jack to one side. 'I knew you and Victor would hit it off.'

'You were right, thank you.'

'I can tell he has wonderful things in store for you. Just don't forget who's responsible for all that's about to happen.'

'Don't worry, I won't.' Jack paused. 'And I don't think Victor will either.

'Well, Mr Diamontopoulos, I'd say you were the star of the evening.'

'I second that,' said Andreas. 'I didn't dare say a word once you got cooking with Panos. And when he took you over to meet that guy Victor, all I could think of doing to help was cross myself three times and say a prayer.'

Jack laughed. 'That earned you a welcome assist, sayeth the Jewish kid.'

'I couldn't believe how his entire demeanor changed the moment you said you were Jewish,' said Lila.

'I have to admit that was a calculated risk. I had no idea how it would play with him, but from the way he was treating me up until then, I figured what did I have to lose?'

'But what made you think he'd treat you differently once you said you were Jewish?'

'It's a long story, but a college friend of mine who went to work for an American Fortune 100 company doing business in China once told me a story about an experience he'd had in China at the launch of a ship the Chinese had built for his company. Though the Chinese treated him with the full respect due him as the representative of their client, everything got kicked into an entirely different gear when he happened to mention at a dinner that he didn't eat shrimp for religious reasons. When someone asked if he was Jewish, he said yes, and the reaction of his hosts was much like Victor's to my turning down the pork roll.'

Jack paused to laugh.

'What's so funny?' said Andreas.

'I love pork rolls.'

'You little hustler,' said Lila.

'Speaking of hustlers,' said Jack, 'I think Victor and Panos share a competitive passion for the ladies.'

'You think so, huh?' Lila giggled. 'If you ask me, especially for one lady in particular.'

'You?'

'But of course.' She rolled her shoulders. 'But I'm talking about reciprocated passion.'

'The wife?'

'Yes, you should have heard her going on and on about how handsome and charming Victor is. Plus a few winks between drinks about how *fit* he was that suggested a lot more.'

'Funny, he never talked about any of that with me. He was all business, and deeply into what I considered an honest dialog on every subject – except politics. He never admitted to what his dealings were with Panos, but he openly agreed that whoever controls the metaverse – or even a large percentage of it – will have oversized influence on the direction of our world. By the way, aside from his native languages, he admits to being fluent in Greek, English, French, and Spanish.'

'Why do you say, *admits to*?'

'Because I think he also speaks Russian.'

'You seem in awe,' said Andreas.

'I am. And anyone who cares about where our world is headed best be too. From my conversation with Victor, it's clear the

Consortium is involved in cutting-edge artificial intelligence research, and he's the sort of adversary we'll be up against in competing for the hearts and minds of generations to come.'

'That's a thought-provoking observation if ever I heard one,' said Lila.

Jack's voice took on a serious tone. 'Everything we know about utilizing the internet is about to change due to the rapid development and influence of chatbot technology. And before you ask, think of a chatbot as a *chatty robot* computer program capable of communicating with human users through speech and text in a manner indistinguishable from human-to-human conversation. We're all somewhat familiar with rudimentary chatbots from when we ask questions of our smart phones and immediately receive answers. Chatbots employ artificial intelligence neural networks modeled on the neural network of the human brain and draw upon the vast amount of data out there on the internet as their knowledge base.'

'Uh, could you put that in more understandable terms . . . at least for me?' said Andreas.

'Bottom line, to meet a human user's written or spoken request, computer algorithms analyze what's available on the internet and instantaneously produce the sought-after blog, academic paper, sonnet in the style of Shakespeare, simulated work of Picasso, lines of computer code, product design, made-up images in the form of photographs, and so much more. In the gaming world, human-sounding chatbots bond with human players in situations where only the latter risks reprogramming.'

'It sounds ominous on so many levels,' said Lila. 'I can't help but wonder what will happen to artists, musicians, and writers if a few words spoken by anyone with access to that kind of program instantaneously results in a bestseller-level book, hit album, or masterpiece painting.'

'Not to mention how forged photographs, videos, and documents could be misused, or how many white-collar jobs will become obsolete,' added Andreas.

Jack shrugged his shoulders. 'And there's a darker side yet to be addressed. With internet data serving as the basis for generating a chatbot's reaction, the amount of internet attention a particular point of view receives could influence the response. Radical groups can automate their hate speech in such a manner as to make it appear as if millions of humans share their positions, thereby leading the program to provide well-presented but fake information to its users. I've no doubt the Consortium's metaverse project is prepared to use chatbots as an integral and substantial part of its plans. That also explains its hunger for additional energy. Chatbots require a lot of it. Once again, though, all the big international tech entities jockeying for commercial dominance in that arena, aided by politicians hosting their own agendas, will be cited by the Consortium in defending against any challenge to its use of widespread chatbot technology as part of its metaverse project.'

'What do you suggest we do about all this?' asked Lila.

Jack sighed. 'I'm off duty, folks. I plan on getting as good a night's sleep as I can with what's left of it, and making it to the airport in time to meet Anna's plane at ten in the morning.'

'I like that plan,' said Andreas. 'And yes, you've earned the morning off.'

'Plus, a bit of the afternoon,' added Lila.

'The early afternoon,' Andreas countered. 'Monday's fast approaching.'

'A lot can happen between now and then.' Jack yawned. 'But I'm sure we'll figure out a way to handle it. After all, so far so good.'

'Puh, puh, puh.'

It was after one in the morning when Panos's cell phone rang. He looked at the number and cursed as he answered. 'Only you would have the balls to call me this late, after missing our party.'

'I'm sorry, but I'm still in the office. There's nothing in the world I was looking forward to more than attending your party, Panos, but something came up today regarding a major event on Monday that could change the direction of my career.'

'Most would say your being a deputy minister in the Ministry of Citizen Protection at your age has you on the right course.'

'Thank you, but this is a very big deal. Please do give your wife my apologies.'

'I will when I see her. She's still up having a nightcap with our house guest.'

'Any exciting news or gossip come out tonight?'

'None that I know of. Jill probably picked some up from her new best friend.'

'Who's that.'

'Some socialite named Lila Vardi.'

Pause. 'How did she come to be there?'

'I don't know, the two of them met recently and hit it off. She showed up with her civil servant husband and nephew in tow.'

'Did you get her husband's name?'

'Alex, or something like that.'

Dittos swallowed deeply. 'Andreas, as in Andreas Kaldis, Chief Inspector of GADA's Special Crimes Unit. The same husband of Lila Vardi who's promised my Minister that by Monday he'll be in the position to confirm his suspicions that there's a major international threat posed by yet-unnamed persons. Kaldis claims those persons possess substantial power, influence, and wealth, and are somehow tied into the wildfires that decimated much of Greece's forests. Kaldis told the Minister he had an expert flying in from America whom he promised could confirm Kaldis's suspicions by this coming Monday. They were all over Syros today. That's what's kept me at the office. Trying to find out what they found out.'

'Son of a bitch. *Jack.*'

'Huh?'

'Oh, nothing. I just remembered a guest's name that I'd forgotten earlier. Well, thank you for calling. I wish you the best of luck on Monday, and I'll pass along your regrets and apology to Jill. Bye.'

Panos hung up before giving Dittos a chance to sign off.

'I'm as good as dead,' mumbled Panos to himself. 'The moment Victor learns what Jack's doing, I'm dead. Period. End of story.'

He needed a plan to keep Victor from ever learning about his major screwup and security breach. He'd saved himself once before, when the three barely clothed Chinese illegals introduced by Victor, and used by Panos to set fires made to appear amateurish, thought themselves smarter than he. They'd insisted on getting a share of any profits made off those fires. Panos had ended those negotiation efforts through a combination of poisoned beverages, a thorough dousing of three bodies with accelerants, and placement of each body in a separate location guaranteed to sustain long, slow burns.

I'd better see if the guy who ended it for the three Chinese is available for another job.

But that wouldn't work this time.

Or would it?

SIXTEEN

Delta Flight 202 out of New York's John F. Kennedy airport listed 10:05 a.m. as its arrival time in Athens, but few believed it. There always seemed to be a delay on one end or the other that made tight connections through Athens a risky bet. But none of that bothered Anna, for she had no connecting flight. Her text to Jack on departing JFK read: *Will meet you outside baggage around 11. Can't wait. Xox Your future bride. :)*

By ten thirty, Anna's anxious bridegroom was standing right where she'd told him to be, courtesy of a ride from Andreas, who said that with all he'd put Jack through, he felt obliged to give him a ride to the airport and be there with him to welcome his niece back home.

Jack stood glued behind the railing separating arriving passengers from the hordes waiting to meet them outside baggage and customs. He scanned every face passing through that restricted area's automatic exit doors, hoping the next one would be Anna's.

Andreas bought two coffees at a nearby *kafenio*, and gave one to Jack, who nodded a quick thank-you, never taking his eyes off the exiting passengers.

Andreas smiled at his memories of waiting for Lila in this very spot. It was clear how much Jack loved his niece. Andreas couldn't wait to see Anna's face light up on first seeing Jack waiting for her.

By eleven Jack was wired for her to show up.

By eleven fifteen he was biting his lip.

By eleven thirty, Andreas had left Jack to speak to the customs and immigration sergeant on duty just inside the exit doors.

The repeated shuffling of the doors between open and closed added a dramatic staccato rhythm to the images Jack watched of Andreas in animated conversation with the sergeant.

Then a grim-faced Andreas waved for Jack to join them.

Something had gone wrong.

*   *   *

When Andreas first spoke to the sergeant, he told Andreas that Anna's flight had arrived on time, all passengers had been processed through immigration, and all baggage delivered to the appropriate carousel.

Andreas then asked the sergeant to please have someone check on whether any bags off Anna's flight remained unclaimed, but he refused, saying that wasn't his job. Andreas showed him his credentials, but the sergeant still balked. That led to a hard-edged warning from Andreas that if he wanted to play tough guy, he soon may not have a job, or at the very least, find himself transferred to Greece's wild northern border where he'd get to spend his time chasing down human traffickers and drug smugglers rather than looking for lost luggage in Athens.

The officer cursed Andreas but made the call.

Andreas waved for Jack when the sergeant told him two bags had not been picked up. Both Anna's.

'Jack, this kind gentleman is now going to escort us to his commander's office.'

'Why? What's wrong?'

'Nothing we know of yet, which is why I want to speak to the officer in charge.'

The sergeant waved for someone to take over his position at the door, then walked them back through baggage claim and along the corridor behind passport control to a group of offices.

'He's in there. Can I get back to work now?'

'Yes, and thank you. Sorry about before, but my niece seems to be missing.'

'No hard feelings. We tough guys have to learn to take as good as we give.'

Andreas smiled. '*Touché.*'

'What was that all about?' asked Jack.

'Not making unnecessary enemies. He was just being grumpy, and so I had to be grumpier.'

'I meant about Anna missing.'

'That's why we're going in here. I know you're anxious but let me do the talking. If they think you're a civilian, they might not be as open as I want them to be.'

'What's that mean?'

'Just don't say anything unless I tell you to.'

Two men in uniform crowded around a third sitting at a desk.

The two stood up straight as Andreas and Jack walked into the office.

'May I help you?' said the sitting man.

'Are you in charge?'

'Yes.'

Andreas showed him his ID. 'I'm Chief Inspector Andreas Kaldis, head of GADA Special Crimes. I'm here to inquire about my niece who was onboard Delta Flight 202 out of New York but has not cleared immigration or picked up her luggage.'

The man behind the desk looked at the two others, then at Andreas.

'Did you say Andreas Kaldis?'

'Yes, why?'

'What's your niece's name?'

Andreas told them.

'Because we just escorted your niece to the private vehicle you'd arranged to meet her in order for her to avoid the hassle of going through long immigration lines and baggage claim.'

A distinct chill darted up Andreas's spine. 'Gentlemen, let's take this from the beginning, because I never made any such request.'

The taller of the two standing men walked over to another desk, picked up a paper, and handed it to Andreas.

'What's this?'

'A directive we received by email from your Ministry that we were to assist your niece through immigration and escort her directly to a vehicle waiting for her in our parking area. Her bags were to remain in baggage claim to be picked up later by . . .' He struggled to find a name. 'Jack Diamantopoulos.'

Jack's eyebrows raised but he said nothing.

'Didn't that strike you as suspicious?'

'It's not common, but I wouldn't call it suspicious. It happens regularly enough with VIPs that we have a procedure. The subject must clear immigration, and any bags remain subject to customs inspection until claimed and released.'

Andreas shut his eyes, then drew in and let out a deep breath. 'I want to see all CCTV video of my niece from the moment she got off the plane. I also want every bit of tape you have on the vehicle, the driver, and anyone else involved in picking her up.'

'What's this all about?'

Andreas swallowed, as he edged closer to Jack. 'There's been a kidnapping.'

Jack's knees seemed close to buckling, but he kept his balance and braced himself with a hand on Andreas's shoulder.

'Let's start with me talking to anyone who had any contact with my niece, the vehicle, the driver, etcetera. As of now this is a full-blown kidnapping investigation, meaning everything else is on hold.'

He thought to add how the survival rates of kidnap victims are often calculated in terms of hours but decided against alarming Jack any more than he already was.

Or I am.

Andreas had Maggie running down the source of the email from the Ministry, and Yianni rushing out to the airport to help chase down and interview potential witnesses.

He'd ignored a message from Lila wanting to know where they were, and two from his sister asking the same question. All hell had broken loose, and he simply couldn't spare the time those calls would require. All he could think to do was ask Maggie to make those phone calls as soon as she had an answer for him on the email. Hopefully his family would understand.

Jack hadn't moved from the immigration office. He sat in a chair staring off in a daze at nothing in particular. His mobile rang and he ignored it. It rang again. He looked at the number. It was Solona. He answered but didn't speak.

'Jack? Are you there?'

'Yes.'

'What's wrong? I was supposed to hear from Anna the moment her plane landed, but that was hours ago, and I still haven't heard from her. I've called her a dozen times but there's no answer.'

'She's been taken.'

'Taken? What do you mean taken?'

'Kidnapped.'

'What?! How do you know?'

'I know.'

'Have you heard from the kidnappers?'

'Not yet. But we will.'

'But why Anna?'

'Because of me. Because of the threat I pose to the plans of some very powerful people. They want me to disappear.'

'This sounds crazy.'

'But it's very real.' He seemed about to cry. 'I never thought for a moment that what I do for a living might jeopardize Anna's life.'

'Well, now is not the time for self-recriminations. This is when you must be strong. If not for yourself, for those who are as worried to death as you are.'

'You mean her parents?'

'Among others.'

'They don't know yet.'

'*What?* So why don't you tell them? This is not a time to hide the truth from them.'

'But I've never met her parents.'

'That makes this the perfect time to change all that. This is when all who care for Anna should come together, share their hopes, and gain strength from each other to maintain themselves through this ordeal.'

Jack said nothing.

'I repeat, this is not a time to hide. Hiding is too much like mourning. God willing, that time will never come.'

Jack brought his hand up to his forehead and shed a tear. The shorter officer handed him a tissue. Jack nodded thanks.

'I love you, Jack. Keep in touch. Call me any time, day or night.'

Jack cut the call, drew in and let out a deep breath, and made a phone call. To Lila.

Jack delivered the news to Lila as if Andreas had asked him to make the call. She was as stunned and alarmed as Jack had expected but did not lose her composure. When he asked for Anna's parents' phone number, Lila offered to make the call for him. Jack thanked her, but said he felt it his responsibility to do so.

Only Anna's mother, Gavi, was home when Jack called. At first he thought to make unrelated small talk, and call back when her father would be home. That way they'd have each other to comfort themselves at the bad news. But as he introduced himself to Anna's mother, he realized that was the cowardly route, bringing no good to anyone. So, he told her the truth.

The long, dead silence on the other end of the phone had Jack thinking she'd fainted. But then he heard a distant, weak voice asking whether her brother was searching for Anna. Jack told her that he was and had every available cop in Athens doing the same. She asked if Andreas had any idea who might have taken her daughter, and Jack said he'd not yet spoken to Andreas about that but would let her know as soon as he had any news.

She thanked him and hung up.

Jack then called Lila to tell her he'd spoken with Gavi, and that her reaction worried him. She seemed in shock or close to it. Lila said she'd leave at once for her sister-in-law's home.

He'd just hung up with Lila when Andreas walked into the office, followed by Yianni.

'We have a plate number on the limo that picked her up,' said Yianni. 'It's registered to a limo service based in Piraeus. A unit's on its way there now. We also have CCTV photos of the driver. Maggie has the office running the images through facial-recognition software as we speak.'

'If that doesn't yield a match, try EUROPOL's database,' said Andreas. 'The CIA's too. If this involves who I think it does, any bad-guy driver won't be local.'

'Who do you think's behind this?' asked Jack.

'Likely the same as you think.'

Jack nodded. 'The Consortium.'

'But how would they know about Anna and her flight information?' asked Yianni.

'I was introduced many times as the fiancé of Andreas's niece, and in my conversation with Panos, and possibly Victor, I mentioned she was arriving from New York this morning on a direct flight. That's all they would need to find her flight.'

Andreas clenched his fists, then took a deep breath. 'OK. This is not a time for anger. I'd better call my sister and tell her what happened.'

'I already spoke with her. Lila too.'

Andreas studied him. 'What did you tell them?'

'That Anna appears to have been kidnapped from the airport by someone claiming to have been sent by the Ministry to pick her up, and that you're doing everything possible and then some to find her.'

'What were their reactions?'

'Lila went to be with your sister at her home, and your sister wanted to know who you thought did this. I told her you hadn't said, but I would let her know when you did.'

Andreas exhaled. 'Good work. Thanks.'

Andreas's cellphone rang. 'Maggie, what do you have for me?'

'The email was legit. It was sent from the deputy minister's office.'

'I'm going to kill the son-of-a-bitch.'

'Uh, before you do that, listen to me. The email was sent by Dittos's secretary. She composed it and typed it up.'

'But why the hell would she do that?'

'She received a phone call very early this morning from a woman who said she was the assistant to a close personal friend of Dittos, and that he had a small favor to ask. He wanted to impress some important people with his ability to get their daughter VIP treatment in Greece, and would greatly appreciate it if he could arrange for her to be whisked through immigration and into a limo he'd hired for her.'

'This sounds crazy,' said Yianni.

'It gets crazier. The secretary called Dittos at home, and he told her not to bother him with the details. She should just get the name and information from his friend's assistant, type up a directive to Customs and Immigration, sign his name to it, and send it off ASAP.'

'Who was the friend asking Dittos for the favor?'

'The friend's assistant said she was calling on behalf of Panos Cirillo, but no one bothered to verify whether he knew anything about this.'

'How neat for everyone,' Andreas growled through clenched teeth. 'Panos gets to claim he knows nothing about this, and we have no way of proving otherwise. I'm willing to bet Panos will claim he has no such assistant to make a call to Dittos's secretary. Would we by chance be lucky enough to have a recording of any of those calls involving his alleged assistant?'

'I asked,' said Maggie. 'No.'

'That leaves us to locate the limo driver. If he's not involved, he's going to need a far more creative story than he dropped her off somewhere and has no idea what happened to her after that. Anna's far too streetwise to be let off in a strange place with people she did not know. She'd raise holy hell, and never go willingly.'

'But she did get into the limo,' said Yianni.

'That's different. Government officials led her to it straight from immigration.'

'We even showed her a copy of the email from the Ministry naming you two,' interjected the short officer, nodding at Andreas and Jack. 'She said she couldn't wait to thank you for making her feel so important.'

The blood drained from Jack's face. 'Oh please, God, let me be wrong.' Jack yanked his cellphone out of his pocket. 'I was so exhausted last night that as a matter of habit I turned off message notification. And in my excitement this morning at getting to the airport, I forgot to turn it back on.' He looked at his phone. 'A dozen unread messages from Anna.' He scrolled through them. 'Nine about how excited she was.' He read the last three to himself, shut his eyes and shook his head. Then read them aloud.

Can't believe Uncle A's big surprise. I feel like a movie star skipping the line and led to my own limo! With champagne! THANK YOU both.

The driver is very nice. He said I should open the champagne and toast our life together. I said I don't drink this early in the morning, he laughed handed me a bottle of water to use instead. And so, TO US!!

I'm sleepy. It was a long flight. Driver says we'll be there soon. I can't wait to see you. But maybe I'll take a little nap. Xx A.

Jack's voice quivered. 'How could I not have checked for Anna's messages? If I had, none of this would have happened.'

'Or it could have turned out a lot worse. We don't know what her abductors were prepared to do,' said Andreas.

'What we do know,' said Yianni, 'is that they likely drugged her, which means they plan on keeping her hostage.'

'What kind of drug?' asked Jack.

'Most likely liquid ecstasy injected into a sealed water bottle. It's a favorite of kidnappers and date rapists. Puts you out and you don't remember a thing when you wake up.'

'You don't think they—'

Andreas interrupted Jack before he could finish his sentence.

'No, I don't. This is all about business, not sex. The deal they want to make requires the return of Anna unharmed, in exchange for our agreeing to walk away from exposing the Consortium for what it is.'

'When do you think we'll hear from them?' asked Jack.

'As soon as they reach a place where they think they're safe.'

'Where would that be?' said Yianni.

Andreas glared at both of them. 'Nowhere.'

Anna didn't know where she was but felt extraordinarily sleepy and wanted to be with Jack. She was supposed to be with him by now. That's what the driver had told her when she lay down on the back seat to rest.

The thick, humming noise of the motor must have stirred her awake. It was a much louder and different sound from what she'd heard before falling asleep. Now she felt her entire body shake, and no longer was she lying down, but sitting up strapped into a seat. She tried to open her eyes but her muscles wouldn't respond. That's when she gave up the struggle, and let the looping whirl of the motor drift her back to sleep as she kept repeating to herself:

I'll be with Jack when I wake up . . .

Andreas, Yianni, and Jack made it back to GADA from the airport in near record time. The building was abuzz with the story of bad guys kidnapping Andreas's niece to obstruct an investigation. It struck at the heart of every cop in the place with *there but for the grace of God go I* thoughts. Even off-duty cops were out scouring the city for the limo and kidnapper.

It still came as a surprise to Andreas that when he walked into his office, Maggie told him the limo had been found. It was abandoned five kilometers from the airport, in a field local police described as an unofficial helipad used by private helicopter services.

Andreas passed on asking why such an unofficial location – one undoubtedly illegal and used at times for patently unlawful activities – was allowed to continue serving as such. He already knew the answer.

'What do we have on the driver of the limo?'

'According to the dispatcher, the limos are privately owned and operated. She said her company serves as a clearing house for calls for service. I sent her a photo of the driver who picked Anna up at the airport and she said that's not her owner-operator.'

'How can she be so sure?'

'Because the driver in our photo is white, and the owner-operator of the limo is black.'

'Find an address for the owner and get someone over there, stat, asking why he wasn't driving his limo this morning and who was.' Andreas bit at his lip. 'And when you're done with that, find out the name of the helicopter company that met the limo, details on the customer who leased it, where the copter went, who was in it, and what happened to whoever was driving the limo.'

'Will do, Chief. The two cops who discovered the limo said the driver was nowhere to be found, and no one saw the chopper land or take off. *But*, over the past several months, they'd received a rash of complaints from neighbors about helicopters landing in that field at all hours. Though local police never caught anyone in the act, virtually all of the complaints mentioned helicopters emblazoned with the name of a helicopter taxi service operating between Athens and Mykonos and its logo "Rapid and Discreet."'

Yianni called the owner of the company and described GADA's urgent need for his help in saving the life of a kidnap victim. Yianni's plea was met with, 'Sorry, but we never discuss our private clients, even with the police.'

Yianni responded calmly. 'I see. Well, allow me to put it to you this way, sir. Unless you provide the information I'm requesting within the next three minutes, police will be knocking on your door in ten to seize all your personal and business records and impound all of your company's aircraft, based upon your decision to impede a kidnap investigation, and our having reasonable cause to believe you're an accessory not just to kidnapping, but to drug- and human-trafficking activities. Plus, of course, there will be significant fines and penalties for illegal air operations.'

'Go to hell. I'm not afraid of you. I've friends to take care of assholes like you.'

'I look forward to receiving their names. I'm certain they'll thank you appropriately for dragging them into a drug-dealing, human-trafficking, tax-fraud mess of your own making at the potential cost of a young woman's life.' Yianni paused. 'Two minutes fifteen seconds left and counting.'

Ultimately, Yianni gave him an additional minute to gather and deliver the information he wanted.

The owner said arrangements had been made today around dawn from an ID-blocked phone by a woman whose voice sounded a bit scrambled. She told him there would be two passengers, a man and a woman, and the man would pay the pilot in cash in advance. The owner had never done business with the caller or passengers before, and when Yianni asked for their names, the owner gave them to him.

Yianni asked if the passengers had shown ID to the pilot. The owner laughed. 'As if cash customers would give us real ones if we'd asked.'

He said that according to his pilot, the man and woman were the only passengers. The pilot described the woman as around twenty and 'out of it,' a not uncommon condition on flights involving party island passengers. The man he described as 'a tough looking guy in his mid-thirties.'

Yianni asked for and obtained the pilot's telephone number and told the owner to keep the helicopter out of service and not to clean it until his forensic people examined it later that day. He also instructed him not to delete his call records on the phone used to speak with the woman who booked the flight.

As soon as he hung up with the owner, Yianni called the pilot and arranged to speak with him on a WhatsApp video chat. The pilot confirmed that his passengers were the man and woman in the photographs Yianni showed him. He also said the man did not engage in any conversation the entire time but kept checking on the woman he'd carried from the limo and strapped into the seat behind the pilot.

The man had given him a piece of paper bearing the coordinates to an empty field on Mykonos in a sparsely populated, heavily boulder covered, rural area of Ano Mera. It was a delicate landing, and when they finally touched down no one was there to meet his passengers. Still, the man hurried to remove the woman from her seat. As he was about to lift her out of the helicopter, the pilot asked him whether he should call them a taxi. The man loudly barked three words: 'No, do not.'

'So, you did speak with him?' asked Yianni.

'I'm sorry, but I never thought of that as a conversation.' He paused. 'But come to think of it there was something weird about that moment.'

'What was it?'

'I could tell he understood my Greek, and when he barked those three words it was as if he were giving me a military command, but only his last two words were in Greek. His first word – a most emphatic "No" – was not Greek.'

'What was it?'

'*Nyet.*'

SEVENTEEN

'So, now we likely have a Russian involved,' said Andreas after Yianni finished reporting on his conversations with the helicopter folk.

Yianni held up his smartphone. 'It ties in with the text message I just received from the uniforms who went looking for the limo owner-operator. They found him tied and gagged inside his house. He claimed a big Russian guy showed up at dawn this morning and told him either to give up his limo keys or his life. The driver took the keys option, and the Russian tied him up. He'd never seen the Russian before, nor does he ever want to again. He's really scared.'

Maggie shook her head. 'Just imagine how scared poor Anna must be.'

'I'd rather not,' said Andreas. 'Maggie, see what you can find out from the limo dispatcher about past clients of their driver, especially any who might have known his home address.'

'We're sounding a bit desperate,' said Yianni.

'Only because we are. There are thousands of homes and rooms where they could hide her on Mykonos. But if they get her off the island, they could take her anywhere.'

'We're searching for the proverbial needle in a haystack,' said Yianni.

'No,' Jack spoke suddenly. 'We're searching for an eighteen-year-old girl who, when under pressure, thinks and acts like her uncle.'

All eyes shifted to Andreas.

'Then let's start looking for breadcrumbs. If Anna can figure out how to avoid being drugged twenty-four-seven, she'll try to find a way to call our attention to where she might be. Let's keep our eyes, ears, and noses open to anything out of the ordinary. I want every available cop, fireman, port worker, you name it, out searching every potential hiding place on Mykonos for any sign of Anna or the Russian, including every private plane, every ferry, and every vehicle boarding a ferry. I'm talking stem-to-stern searches.'

'And what will you be doing?' asked Maggie.

Andreas clenched a fist. 'Jack and I will be paying visits on some folks who may not have liked me before, but most definitely won't like me after.'

To describe Andreas as storming into Dittos's office would be akin to describing running with the bulls in Pamplona as a stroll in the park.

Closely trailed by Jack, Andreas rushed past the secretary's desk, yanked open the closed heavy wooden door, pointed at Dittos, and shouted, 'I've come for you.'

Eyes wide open and mouth agape, Dittos's voice abruptly cracked in the middle of whatever he was saying to the two young men sitting across from his desk.

'Kaldis, have you gone mad?'

Andreas pointed at the two men. 'Out. *Now.*'

Dittos cried out to his secretary, 'Call security!'

The two men paused.

'I said *OUT.*'

The men tripped over each other while getting out of the office.

Andreas nodded Jack toward the door. 'Close it and lock it.'

'I'll have you arrested,' said Dittos, struggling to regain control of his voice. 'You're finished, Kaldis.'

Andreas pointed to the array of photographs adorning the walls showing Dittos posing with persons he regarded as important. 'I suggest you start calling your friends, because you're about to need them all.'

'Is that supposed to be some kind of threat?'

'No, just a precursor to me about to warn you of your rights before I arrest you as an accessory to the kidnapping of an eighteen-year-old woman.'

Hearing the charge seemed to give Dittos a rush of confidence. 'You *are* insane. I have no idea what you're talking about.'

A knock on the door was followed by a shout. 'Open up, it's the police.'

'Hurry up, there's a mad man in here!' yelled Dittos.

Andreas pointed for Jack to sit down on a sofa by the door, as he walked toward Dittos, reaching into his pocket and pulling out a single-page document that he dropped on to the desk.

'You're right: there is a mad man in here. A *very* mad man.

Because the girl whose kidnapping you engineered with your official directive happens to be my niece.'

Dittos looked down at the copy of his morning email to Customs and Immigration.

At the sound of the door lock click, the door swung open and three men in body armor, with guns drawn and aimed at Andreas and Jack, told them to put their hands above their heads.

'I'm Chief Inspector Andreas Kaldis of Special Crimes and I'm here to arrest this man on charges of kidnapping.'

'Let me see some ID,' said one of the police.

'Gentlemen,' said Dittos, clearing his throat. 'That won't be necessary. You've shown exemplary skill and courage in responding to this surprise security readiness test. I shall personally put a commendation in each of your files. Chief Inspector Kaldis and I are proud to serve as part of this ministry with you.'

The three lowered and holstered their weapons and glanced at each other as if everyone in the room were mad. One thought to thank Dittos, followed by the two others, and all hurried out of the office, closing the door behind them.

Dittos was breathing so quickly that Andreas thought he might hyperventilate, but he did not tell him to relax. Rather, Andreas kept staring down at him, waiting for him to speak as he read and reread the document on his desk.

'I had absolutely no idea this was your niece, or that the request was part of a kidnapping plan.'

'But I'm mentioned by name.'

'I never knew that anyone's name other than the girl's would be in the email. You can ask my secretary.'

'We already did. But that's a rather convenient way of making you seem an innocent favor-giver taken advantage of by a scheming friend.'

'But I was.'

'So, who's the friend?'

'I think I need to speak to a lawyer.'

'Ah, yes, continue being loyal to your scheming friend rather than help us save the young woman's life.' Andreas shook his head and sat down across from Dittos. 'You do realize that if you don't fully cooperate, I'm leading you out of here in handcuffs, with a full-scale perp walk and media feeding frenzy to follow.'

Dittos shut his eyes. 'Panos Cirillo.'

'Who else?'

'I don't know who else was involved. He made the request.'

'Personally?'

'No, through his assistant to my secretary.'

'Do you know his assistant?'

'No.'

'Do you know if he has an assistant?'

'No, but I assume he does.'

'Could his wife have made the phone call?'

'Jill?'

Andreas nodded.

'I guess so. She is rather aggressive when it comes to promoting herself in the VIP community.'

'But this wasn't a true VIP favor. It was a set-up for a kidnapping.'

'But maybe she didn't know it. After all, I didn't.'

'When's the last time you spoke with Panos?'

Dittos hesitated.

'You're starting to piss me off . . .'

'I'm just trying to remember our conversation. It was today after one in the morning. I called to apologize for missing his party, and he mentioned your wife's name as an important guest, which led me to mention who you were.'

'What sort of mention?'

Dittos dropped his head to his chest and seemed on the edge of sobbing. 'I told him who you were, that you were investigating a major international threat posed by persons of substantial power, influence, and wealth somehow tied in to our recent wildfires, and had an expert flying in from America who you'd promised our Minister could confirm your suspicions by this coming Monday.'

'What else?' said Andreas, visibly struggling to restrain himself.

'That if your expert couldn't confirm your suspicions to the Minister by Monday, you'd resign.'

'And everything would go away?'

'No, I never said that.'

Andreas now felt himself verging on hyperventilation. 'And what did he say in response?'

'Nothing that made any sense to me.'

'Just tell me.'

'He cursed, "Son of a bitch. *Jack.*"'

Andreas exhaled. 'I'm not done with you yet. But if you're holding anything back that might help us rescue my niece, I can assure you . . .' He let his voice trail off.

Dittos nodded. 'I understand. I'm so sorry, I had no idea.'

Andreas ignored his comment. 'Where is Cirillo now?'

'I have no idea.'

'Can you think of anyone who might know.'

'His wife, Jill, or perhaps his Chinese friend, Victor.'

'Don't talk to anyone about our conversation, and if Panos Cirillo, or anyone tied into him, tries to reach you, let me know immediately.

'Do you think the girl is in real danger?'

'Let me put it to you this way. Start praying and don't stop until she's back safe and sound in her fiancé's arms.'

Andreas stood and headed for the door.

Jack let him pass before rising from the sofa. He stood in place, staring directly into Dittos's eyes. 'Pray as if your life depends upon it . . . because it does.'

Andreas decided to arrive unannounced at the Cirillo home. The day was edging toward sunset, and once night fell, the advantage would shift to the kidnappers.

He called Yianni for an update and to brief him on where things stood with Dittos. Yianni asked why no one had yet made a ransom demand.

'Because the kidnappers don't feel safe yet. They're still trying to find a place to hide. My guess is this was a last-minute operation. That's not to say it's not dangerous, but it seems more improvised than thought through.'

'Why do you say that?' asked Jack.

'Unless the Russian knew Mykonos well – but no one there has recognized his photo, so I doubt that's the case – someone met him at the copter's landing field. He also must have realized the police soon would have that exact location. That means whoever met him knows the island and had a place ready for them to hide.'

'They must be in hiding by now,' said Jack.

'Yes, but not in the safe place they ultimately have in mind.'

'Why do you say that?'

'There are thousands of places to hide on Mykonos, but with the all-hands-on-deck mobilization we've put into effect, we just might find them. After all, escape by plane or ferry is a non-starter, plus photos of Anna and the Russian now plaster the island.'

'Are you saying the kidnappers will try to get off the island as quickly as possible?' asked Yianni.

'Yes, but not during daylight hours. Too many people tend to turn up in the most unexpected of places on Mykonos, any one of whom might recognize them and alert the police. Even the most deserted of beaches presents a risk of discovery, because virtually every home with a long-range angle on a beach, likely has bored owners glued to powerful binoculars hoping to catch intimate moments among unwary participants.'

'So, they move Anna tonight . . .' said Jack.

'Which is why we're headed to the Cirillo house. I want to speak to the wife.'

'Why not the husband?' asked Yianni.

'Because I doubt he'll be there.'

This time the front gate to the Cirillo home was locked, and no one responded to Andreas's efforts on the intercom buzzer, or Jack pressing on it for a solid minute.

'I know someone's in there,' said Jack.

'How do you know?'

'Instinct.'

'I'll try the number Lila gave me for the wife's mobile.'

No one picked up, and the phone clicked off without giving Andreas the opportunity to leave a message.

'I'd say she's not in the mood to talk.'

'What do we do now?'

'Not much we can do.'

'I have an idea.' Jack searched along the foot of the fence until he found a rock the size of a baseball.

'What do you plan on doing with that?'

Jack walked back to the front gate and waved the rock at the security camera. He held his other hand up, showing all five fingers, and slowly closed them, one finger at a time. When he'd closed all the fingers into a fist he leaned back and, with his other hand, whipped the rock over the gate and through a second-story window, instantly setting off a burglar alarm.

'What the hell are you doing?' yelled Andreas.

'Getting the attention of the lady of the house.'

'And a whole lot of other folks.'

'I know.' Jack walked away from the gate and returned with another rock. This time he held up two fingers. Then went through his five-finger countdown, followed by lofting the rock though a downstairs window.

'I really should stop you,' said Andreas.

'Yes, you should,' said Jack, picking up a third rock.

As he started his countdown for the third rock, the front door to the house swung open, followed by a string of Billingsgate curses spewed with the wild-eyed energy of a woman in exercise clothes holding a drink in her hand.

'Good evening, Mrs Cirillo,' said Andreas.

The curses continued unabated.

'We've been trying to reach you on a life-or-death matter.'

More curses.

'Mrs Cirillo, please open this gate or I'm afraid the young man with me will drive my police car right through it and into your house.'

The cursing continued as Jill stumbled more than stomped from her front door to the gate, waving her glass about as if preparing to throw it.

'Are you assholes crazy? I'm upstairs exercising, and you start throwing rocks through my windows. I'm going to sue you both.'

From her whiskey breath, glazed bloodshot eyes, and utter lack of make-up, Andreas guessed that her form of exercise involved a lot of booze and very little sleep.

As she fiddled with the gate, she struggled to focus her eyes on Andreas. 'I don't have my glasses with me, but aren't you Lila Vardi's husband?'

'Yes.'

'Then what the hell are you doing here with that rock thrower?'

'Let's go inside and talk.'

Andreas led her back into the house and on to one of her sofas. 'Where's your husband?'

'Why don't you tell me? You're the big detective.'

'Where's your husband?'

'No idea. He was gone when I got up this morning.'

'What time was that?'

'I was up by ten.'

'Not earlier? Like dawn perhaps?'

'No, I never get up at dawn. Not since I was a schoolgirl. I hate dawn. It reminds me of my chores on the farm where I grew up.'

'You're happy to be off the farm?'

'Couldn't be happier.'

'I guess you'd do just about anything to stay happy.'

She offered a coquettish attempt at a smile. 'Wouldn't anyone?'

'What time this morning did you call the secretary of your husband's buddy, my deputy minister, to request a favor for a VIP friend of your husband?'

'What makes you think I did anything like that?'

'That, plus arrange for a helicopter service for two to Mykonos.'

'How do you know that?'

'Did you also arrange for the limo driver?'

'What limo driver?'

'The one who kidnapped my niece and this man's fiancée.'

The glass she'd been clutching fell from her hand on to the marble floor, shattering in every direction.

'Kidnapping? You can't be serious.'

'I'm very serious. So serious that unless you can convince me otherwise, I'm about to arrest you as an accessory to kidnapping.'

'That miserable lying bastard. He told me he'd planned all of this as a surprise for your niece, to impress you and your wife with our generosity. He said he learned last night that your niece was arriving this morning on a flight from New York, then connecting through Rafina on a ferry to Mykonos to stay at Lila's parents' home. The plan was for her fiancé to show up with her bags at the helipad and fly off to Mykonos together.'

'Is that why you booked the helicopter for two?'

'Of course, why else would I?'

'To include the limo driver.'

'I know nothing about any limo driver. My husband told me he'd taken care of all ground transportation arrangements. I was only to help with the immigration people thingy and booking the helicopter.'

'If everything was so innocent, why the voice scrambler?'

'I thought it was silly too, but whenever Panos asks me to make calls posing as his assistant he has me use it. He fears people might recognize my voice and think less of him for using his wife as a secretary.'

'How often do you act as his assistant?'

'Not often. Only when he has a problem.'

'Interesting.'

'Why?'

'Because now you both have a problem, and if I don't find my niece safe and sound, you'll have a *much* bigger problem.'

'Is that a threat?'

Andreas turned to Jack. 'You've been quietly taking all this in; what would you say to the lady's question?'

Jack smiled. 'Sounds more to me like a personal guarantee.'

'Well, now that your question's been answered, do you care to tell me who might know where we can find your husband?'

'The only person I can think of who might know is Victor.'

'Do you have an address or phone number for him?'

'Only a phone number,' which she recited from memory.

'One last thing. I'm sending a team to monitor all your incoming calls in case your husband tries reaching you. I expect you'll cooperate.'

'Do I have a choice?'

'There's always a choice, if you can handle the consequences.'

'I'm used to consequences.' She shook her head and sighed at the broken glass. 'But I'm tired of that life.' She jerked her head back against the sofa and shut her eyes. 'Yes, I'll cooperate.'

'A wise choice.'

Jill's face dropped into a pout. 'One of the few I seem to have made.'

Jack spoke up again. 'It's a good time for you to start down that road. After all, wise choices save lives.' He leaned in toward her. 'And who doesn't want to live?'

Jill blinked. 'Are *you* now threatening me?'

Jack smiled, but before he could respond Andreas jumped in, 'Thank you, Mrs Cirillo, for your cooperation. We'll leave your home as soon as the phone-monitoring technicians get here.'

She pushed herself up from the sofa. 'Stay as long as you like. I'm going to make myself a drink.' She walked out of the room.

Jack turned to Andreas as if to say something, but Andreas put his index finger in front of his closed lips and mouthed, 'Later.'

*   *   *

Once in the car, Andreas turned to face Jack before starting the engine. 'What did you want to say to me back in the house?'

'That she's not as dumb as she acts. My guess is she knows her husband uses her when there's nasty business involved that he won't trust to just anyone. But I also don't think she had any idea this episode involved a kidnapping.'

'Anything else?'

'That's not to say she wouldn't willingly participate in kidnapping if she thought it necessary to maintain her lifestyle, such as it is.'

'That sounds about right,' nodded Andreas, turning on the ignition. 'Though I have an additional observation.'

'What's that?' asked Jack, facing the side of Andreas's face.

'I admire the way you kept quiet during my questioning, despite what I'm certain were nearly irresistible urges to jump in.' Andreas turned to catch Jack's eyes. 'But don't think for a minute that I missed the – shall we say – *signals* you directed at Dittos and Mrs Cirillo. I hope you aren't serious.'

Jack tightened his jaw. 'With all my heart and soul, I hope I never have to find out.'

EIGHTEEN

Andreas tried several times to call the number Jill had given him for Victor, but there was no answer. After leaving a second message for him, Andreas called Yianni, told him to find the address connected to that phone number, and check if anyone there could help them locate Victor.

His next call was to Tassos.

'You've been a busy boy,' said Tassos, answering on the first ring.

'Once again your sources are impeccable.'

'Maggie says the same about you.'

'Jack's here with me. We've been chasing down potential leads on Anna's whereabouts without much success.'

'Maggie told me Anna's likely stashed away for now on Mykonos, but soon will be transferred to some sort of boat.'

'Why a boat?' asked Jack.

'Because if it's a big enough boat,' said Tassos, 'you can hide practically anything on it, and make it virtually disappear in any number of ways.'

'Any ideas spring to mind on where to find the bad guys before they disappear?' said Andreas.

'I'll ask around about any strange goings-on, or sightings of Panos. My guess is he's staying near to wherever Anna is. Though I can't imagine anywhere close enough to risk her later being able to identify him as her kidnapper. After all, she's the prize he must protect if he wants to pull off whatever he has in mind.'

'Thanks for the pep talk,' said Jack, 'but I'm well aware of the likely consequences if Anna can identify him. More importantly, I'm sure she does too.'

'That's why we've asked the Coast Guard to keep a close eye on after-dark water departures from Mykonos,' said Andreas.

'How effective will that be?' asked Jack.

'We'll know the answer to that come morning.'

'Don't worry, kid,' said Tassos. 'We're tougher and smarter than they are. We'll find her. And that's not a pep talk. It's a commitment.'

Andreas's mobile signaled another call coming through. 'It's Yianni. I've got to take his call. Bye.'

Tassos clicked off.

'Yianni, give me the good news first.'

'The government has shut down all helicopter traffic in or out of Mykonos until sunrise tomorrow, and the Coast Guard has added patrols to randomly check boats seeking to leave Mykonos waters, effective immediately.'

'Good work. Any bad news?'

'No new bad news, except we still haven't found that guy Victor. But I have a question, Chief. What can Panos possibly hope to achieve by kidnapping your niece?'

'I've wondered that too. My best guess is that he thinks we've tied him to the murder of the three arsonists, and he's panicked at the thought that what we know might be enough to crater Greece's support for the Consortium's plans. Panos is understandable considering who's behind the Consortium, because if the project dies because of him, he's likely the one who'll face the consequences.'

'So, he comes up with the idea of kidnapping your niece as a way of getting her uncle to walk away from the investigation?'

'Thereby allowing all of the Consortium's plans and hopes to continue rolling merrily along for the greater glory of all mankind.'

'Plus, of course,' added Yianni, 'dropping all kidnapping and other charges lurking out there upon the safe return of your beloved niece.'

'That's what I'm thinking. Panos must really feel his ass in a vise to come up with this craziness. It simply can't end well for him.'

'With all due respect, I hope his planning isn't as haphazard as you suggest,' said Jack.

'If it helps rescue Anna, I'm all up for another opinion. Let's hear it.'

'Based on Dittos's description of his late-night, post-party conversation with Panos, I'd say that phone call is what set Panos off into panic mode.'

'Agreed,' nodded Andreas.

'Panos also knows from that conversation that if you don't come up with the proof you promised your Minister by Monday, you're off the force. If that happens, the person most likely to take charge of your investigations will be his buddy, Dittos. Panos could see that to mean all he has to do to make his problems go away is make sure the proof you promised to give the Minister never gets to him in time. And what is that proof? *Me*.'

'You?' said Yianni.

'Yes, I'm the big expert from America come to debunk the Consortium's plans on Monday. What better way to discourage me from showing up than to kidnap my fiancée? Monday comes, I don't show, Andreas is out, and Anna walks free on Tuesday. All without a single ransom demand or call being made or hair on her head being harmed. Just a girl who took off to party over the weekend on Mykonos, thanks to the kind logistical arrangements of a family friend. No harm, no foul, no kidnapping. Any different story from her is attributed to her heavy drug use over the weekend.'

Andreas stared at Jack in silence. 'That's an ingenious and persuasive theory, but it only works if Panos's mind is as sharp as yours, and his self-confidence level high enough to pull it off. Otherwise, what we're seeing is panicked felons looking for a way to save their skins. With that type, everything can turn to shit in the blink of an eye. At best, we're dealing with killers willing to incinerate their victims, who are desperately afraid of their own people. Should they for any reason, rational or not, suddenly see Anna's continued existence as a liability . . .' Andreas did not finish his sentence.

'Jack's theory does offer another explanation for why we haven't yet heard from the kidnappers. They don't want to be seen as kidnappers,' offered Yianni.

'OK, folks, I'm as much into hope and prayer as any of us, but this isn't a time to be feeling rosy about the future. It's the time for hard-ass police work, and plenty of it.' Andreas drew in and let out a giant breath. 'Bottom line, our marching order until Anna is safely back in Jack's arms is as follows: *Hope for the best and prepare like hell for the worst*. Period, end of story.'

Anna struggled to stay awake. She knew she was being drugged. It had to be something in the water because she couldn't recall when she last ate. The limo driver kept bringing her bottled water, but never food. She had no idea why she'd been taken. At first, she thought she might have been raped, but no one had touched her other than to carry her from one place to another.

She tried convincing herself it all must be a case of mistaken identity. Someone else must be the intended target. But then she remembered the paper the immigration people showed her when they led her to the limo. The paper with her uncle's and Jack's names.

I am the target.

Her heart raced wildly as her mind ran through images of her life ending at any moment. She sensed panic had set in and had to regain control. There was no one to rely upon but herself. Anna struggled to take charge of her breathing, to calm her heart rate.

She thought of her uncle, and how he must be turning the world upside down to find her. She thought of Jack and how worried he must be. She must let them know where she was. But how, when she didn't know herself? She needed a plan. But whatever her plan, its first step must be to stay awake.

Anna looked at the half-liter bottle of water lying next to her. If she didn't drink all of it before the driver checked on her, he'd likely force her to drink it, or drug her in some other way.

She twisted her body to move her legs, but they wouldn't move. That's when she realized her ankles were handcuffed to the foot of a bed, and that she lay upon a soft mattress. She struggled up to a seated position as best she could, opened the water bottle, and carefully emptied it on to the part of the mattress recently covered by her torso. She then lay back to cover the newly created wet spot with her body.

That's when she heard footsteps outside the door to her cell or whatever sort of room she was in. Panic returned, but she shut her eyes, feigned being asleep, and prayed whoever was coming wouldn't notice the wet spot on the bed.

Someone picked up the empty bottle and replaced it with a full one.

'How is she?' said a male voice from outside the room.

'Sleeping,' said the voice Anna recognized as the driver's.

'Good. Keep her that way. I don't want her conscious when we leave for the boat.'

'Don't worry. I put enough in the new bottle to keep her out cold for six hours at least.'

'That should work. We'll make a break for it as soon as the Coast Guard backs off on its search for her. I doubt they'd search our boat anyway, but no reason to take a chance.'

'Why's that?'

'Because it's a local fisherman's caïque. A wave by the captain to the Coast Guard is likely all it will take to get him past a checkpoint.'

'Then what?'

'We head west for about an hour to hook up before sunrise with the ship that can get us far away from Greece, if necessary.'

'What about her?'

'Either we get what we want, or we'll be dumping our incriminating evidence into a very deep sea. And without a body, let them try and prove we did anything more than give the poor girl a lift to Mykonos.'

'By "we" you mean me,' said the driver.

'Correct. But you Wagner Group mercenary-types are used to that sort of risk. Besides, you'll be out of Greece and on your way home a hell of a lot richer the moment we know whether she lives or dies.'

'It can't come soon enough.'

The door closed.

Anna could hardly breathe. She had to get her mind out of panic mode and focus on planning. She needed a place to start. They'd mentioned Mykonos, and that soon they'd be heading one hour west. What lay one hour west of Mykonos?

She focused as hard as she could on her memories of sunsets with her uncle and his family on Mykonos. She struggled against the prodigious efforts of her subconscious to distract her from the crisis of the moment with memories of happy times. She needed to recall what lay one hour west of Mykonos . . .

Her eyes opened wide. *Syros.*

Though the plans called for Jack to move into Anna's parents' home the day her plane arrived in Athens, Andreas changed all that in light of what had happened. He saw no need to pile additional pressures on to Jack and Gavi. But he did stop by his sister's home with Jack for them to meet and console one another as best they could.

Gavi's first words sought hopeful news on Anna. When neither could offer anything new, she asked for Jack and her brother to pray with her. The three sat in a circle, each holding hands with the others in whispered prayer.

When Andreas's phone rang, and he excused himself to take the call from Tassos, Gavi reached for Jack's free hand, and the two of them sat side by side immersed in prayer.

Andreas stepped outside. 'What's up?'

'A couple of things. But first, I hope you and Jack are doing OK. I didn't mean to be so direct in my earlier conversation with you.'

'Frankly, you weren't direct enough. And I think Jack understands the score.'

'My greatest fear is the kidnappers will panic and do away with Anna in a way that leaves no evidence that she's dead, or was even kidnapped, as opposed to simply disappearing on her own accord . . . perhaps to escape a fiancé she couldn't stand.'

'Yeah, there are all sorts of scenarios a sharp lawyer could come up with to get a client off.'

'On the news front, Mykonos is a madhouse with boats, and there's any number of strange goings-on involving women, boats, and shipboard surreal experiences.'

'In other words, business as usual.'

'All of which brings me to one interesting bit of news.'

'You are such a drama freak,' quipped Andreas. 'Get on with it, please.'

'I'm not sure you know this, but the island of Gyaros, which lies sort of equidistant from the northern tip of Syros and the spot where Tinos and Andros nearly touch, is off limits to the general public, and getting close to it for any reason, including fishing, is forbidden by the Coast Guard.'

'In the hope of concluding the history lesson aspect of this conversation,' said Andreas, 'as I recall, it's also arid, uninhabited, unpopulated, and since the days of the early Roman empire primarily served as a place of exile for the politically undesirable. Why anyone would want to go there, other than of course to pay tribute to it as the place where you got your start in police work as a prison guard, is a mystery to me.'

'You forgot that it's also been used for target practice by the Greek navy and hosts the largest population of monk seals in the Mediterranean.'

'So, what's your point?'

'I'd asked a buddy who captains a ferry running between Rafina and Mykonos to let me know if he noticed anything suspicious. His sea route runs past Gyaros's eastern shore, and over the past two days he's noticed the same mega-yacht anchored off the old Gyaros harbor.'

'Why would a mega-yacht be there?'

'That's what had my buddy wondering.'

'Can we get the Coast Guard to search it?'

'I doubt that. It's not blocking any sea lanes, and not close enough to shore to warrant a Coast Guard warning to move off, plus it's owned by a very rich and connected Middle Eastern gentleman who claims that his diplomatic status gives his yacht diplomatic immunity from seizure or delay.'

'You don't say.'

'I thought that might interest you.'

'What can the Coast Guard do for us?'

'One thing they won't do is board it and risk setting off an international incident, at least not without more than wild-ass conjecture to go on. Besides, with all the units they've sent to Mykonos to join in the search for Anna, they're strapped for people.'

'How about dropping a couple of their port police off close by the Gyaros harbor to keep an eye on the yacht until midday? By then we should know if a boat joins up with the yacht.'

'Or a helicopter lands on the yacht's helipad,' added Tassos. 'I'll see what I can do.'

'I know you'll try your best.'

'I'll get back to you as soon as I have any news.'

'Thanks.'

Andreas shut his eyes as he ended the call and steeled himself for stepping back inside his sister's home bearing a positive outlook and attitude.

Despite how he felt at that moment.

As Andreas stepped back inside his sister's home, Jack walked out to take a call from a number he did not recognize.'

'Hi, Jack, it's Solona.'

'Oh, hey. I didn't recognize your number.'

'That's because I'm using the phone on a chartered plane.'

'A plane? What are you doing on a plane?'

'I'm headed to Athens.'

'You're heading *where*?'

'The Grande Bretagne, across from Parliament.'

'But why?'

'Once you told me what had happened to Anna, I knew I couldn't stay in New York. After all, I introduced the two of you, and feel as if we're family. I also counseled each of you to go to Greece, which makes me feel somewhat to blame.'

'You don't deserve *any* blame.'

'Thank you, but I feel I do. Any word yet on where she is?'

'No. The best guess is Mykonos. But she'll likely be moved by the kidnappers tonight to somewhere else.'

'And what is the name of the likely kidnapper-in-chief? I know you told me, but I forgot.'

'Panos Cirillo. He and his wife Jill McLaughlin are quite a pair.'

'Tell me all about them.'

As succinctly as possible, Jack told her all he knew about the Cirillos, what they'd done, and where things stood now.

'Who are the other potential players?'

'The only potential one I know of is a man named Victor. Though he's Chinese, he likes to be called Victor.' Jack told her what little he knew about the man.

'Darling Jack, I know how adrift you must feel, but all of us working together will find a way to rescue Anna. I should be landing shortly. You can call me on my mobile then. Just let me know if you learn anything more about the potential kidnappers or their plans. As I shall alert you should I discover anything that might be helpful. And if for any reason you need to speak to me sooner, call me back on this number.'

'Thank you, Solona,'

They hung up. Jack paused for a moment before going back inside. Why would Solona think she could help?

Well, at this stage, all thoughts and prayers were welcome.

On the ride back to Andreas's place, Jack told Andreas of his call from Solona, and how they'd met.

'Sounds strange,' said Andreas, 'that she would come over here thinking she could help with a police investigation in a foreign country she doesn't know. If you'll excuse me for saying this, she sounds like a bit of a wacko. '

'But she's not. She's a seriously genuine person, with different views on life than most. She's also tied into the world of the uber-rich, where everyone at the top seems to know everyone else.'

'Do you trust her with Anna's life?'

'Why do you ask?'

'Because if what I'm about to tell you gets back to the kidnappers, they might just kill Anna and bury her at sea in darkness.'

Jack shut his eyes. 'Yes, I trust her.' He opened them again.

'Fine, I'll take your judgment on that. So, here's what I just heard from Tassos.' He told Jack about Tassos's mysterious yacht, including its name, and why it might be connected to Anna's kidnapping. 'Do you think any of that might be useful for your friend?'

'I don't know, let's ask her.' Jack called Solona and passed along Tassos's information on the yacht.

The instant Jack said the name of the yacht, Solona shouted, 'I know that boat! I've been on it several times with my friend. The owner is a powerful, close friend of his country's ruler, but I can't imagine him involved in a kidnapping.'

'Why not?' said Jack.

'If you'd told me he'd used his yacht for organizing a wild, over-the-top weekend orgy for major international business and government leaders, I'd agree. He's known for that. Even tried a couple of times to get me to participate.'

Andreas's eyes popped open.

'Which, of course, I declined. But something as heavy-handed as participating in a kidnapping that involved his yacht. Uh-uh. No way.'

'Do me a favor,' said Andreas in English. 'Please don't say a word of this to anyone or try to contact the yacht owner. If the kidnappers plan to rendezvous with his yacht, it could be our best chance to save her. And based on what we've been able to gather so far, if by some stroke of luck Cirillo happens to be with her, it's our best shot at tying him to the kidnapping.'

'Understood, but how does the wife fit into all of this? She must know something.'

'She's playing the innocent, unknowing spouse,' said Andreas, 'despite her role in setting Anna up and arranging the escape by helicopter.'

'Oh well, some women just are that way. Please don't hesitate to ask me for any help you might need. I might just surprise you.'

'We won't,' said Jack.

'And you already have,' added Andreas.

'Thanks. Bye.'

Jack looked at Andreas after Solona hung up. 'I told you she's a unique soul.'

'I can't wait to meet her.'

Jack chuckled. 'I can't wait to see Lila's expression when you do.'

It was after midnight when the buzzer sounded from the front gate at the Cirillo home. Jill had dozed off on a downstairs sofa and at the buzzer began yelling for someone to answer the door. But the only other people in the house were the police technicians, and they were under orders to stay with their equipment in the basement.

The buzzer rang again. Jill pushed herself to her feet and staggered toward the front door and outside to the gate. An attractive blonde woman dressed in Dior couture and literally bedazzled in diamonds stood on the other side of the gate smiling, a black Maybach limo behind her.

Jill's first reaction was that she'd finally overdone the drinking, and this was her first alcoholic hallucination. But then her hallucination spoke to her.

'Jill, Jill McLaughlin, is that you?'

Caught off guard, she answered, 'Yes, but who are you?'

'Think of me as a dear old Texas girl trying to help out a sister who's got big trouble brewing back home.'

'Why are you here?'

The woman looked back toward the chauffeur before leaning in and saying, 'I know it's late, but I think it's best we talk in private. For your sake.'

'My sake?'

'Yes. It has to do with your previous husband.'

'Which one?'

'The one before your current one.'

'Is he all right?'

'We really should talk inside.'

Jill hesitated, but ultimately opened the gate. The woman walked right past her and into the house, waving. 'Come on, dearie, I'm not going to bite you.'

Jill trailed her inside, slamming the front door behind her. 'OK, you're inside. So, tell me what's so important that you're knocking on my door at,' Jill looked at her watch, 'close to one in the morning.'

'It has to do with money. The money you get from your husband, and properties you received in your divorce settlement.'

Jill looked at the partially full glass of whiskey on the nearby coffee table but didn't reach for it. Instead, she sat down on the sofa. 'Tell me more.'

'If your divorce settlement was like that of most who marry powerful rich men, there's a provision in the agreement that, should you bring disrepute to the husband's family name, there will be serious financial penalties, up to and including the total elimination of alimony and reversion of transferred properties.'

'So what?'

'I understand you continue to use the McLaughlin name as opposed to your new husband's name.'

'Again, so what?'

'You're on the cusp of irreversibly tarring the long-respected McLaughlin name, not just in the state of Texas, but internationally.'

'What are you talking about? Is this some sort of extortion hustle? You should know that my husband is a lawyer. He won't stand for this. He'll draw and quarter you.'

'Now, now, don't get yourself in a tizzy until I've told you what your problem is. I'm not talking about you being exposed for shagging the occasional pool boy or business associate of your husband. I'm talking about your being tried and convicted for kidnapping and murder.'

'What?' said Jill, leaping to her feet. 'You're insane. Get out of here.'

The woman shook her head, reached into her clutch, pulled out a card and held it out for Jill to take. 'I was given this card and told that the person whose name appears on it is digging into your and your husband's involvement in serious criminal activity. I don't know the woman, but I've been told she's the most prominent gossip columnist in Greece.'

Jill stared at the card.

'So, if you won't at least listen to what I have to say, you'll be blind-sided big time by the Greek media.'

Jill took the card and sat down. 'So, what do you have to say?'

The woman sat down next to her on the sofa. 'It's simple. Being accused of kidnapping the niece of a Chief Inspector and of the scion of one of Greece's most prominent families is big news, even bigger should she not be returned alive and well. But add to that the cold-blooded murder by fire of three immigrants as part of a land grab and arson scheme orchestrated by your husband, and you'll be catapulted to the tippy top of the world's most disliked list. It might be different were you the innocent unaware spouse of a Doctor Jekyll and Mister Hyde husband, but that's not the way this is shaping up.'

'What do you mean? That's what I am . . . if what you say is true.'

'Dearie, don't you see that you're the one being played in this domestic scenario? Every contact tied into the kidnapping is through you. The email from the Minister's office, the helicopter arrangements, all went through you. There's nothing linking your husband to any of it.'

Jill began nervously biting at her lower lip.

'But wait, there's more: I'd bet that all documented contacts with anyone tied into the three murdered immigrants ran through you alone. Did hubby make you call them with instructions on where to be and when? And did fires just seem to coincidentally start where you directed them?'

Jill sat frozen in place for nearly a minute.

Solona shook her head at Jill. 'Girl, you've got some deep problems. Your whole life's about to explode and your scheming lawyer husband's going to walk away, leaving what remains of your good looks to rot away in prison. And when you get out – if you get out – you'll be penniless.'

'I want to talk.'

'To whom?'

'The uncle.'

Andreas's mobile kept ringing. He let it go into messages, but after the fourth round of buzzes, Lila yelled, 'If you don't answer it, I'm going to flush it down the toilet.'

'It won't fit.' He picked up the mobile and said, 'Kaldis.'

'Hi Chief Inspector, it's Solona.'

'Solona?'

'Yes, Jack's friend.' He looked at the clock: it was one thirty in the morning. 'Is everything OK?'

'Actually great. Sorry to call so late but I had a bit of trouble getting your mobile number. I think we should meet.'

Andreas stared at the phone. 'Um . . . I'm home in bed with my wife.'

At that remark Lila turned on the light and sat up in bed.

Solona laughed. 'And I'm sitting on a sofa across from Jill McLaughlin Cirillo in the living room of her lovely home. She's anxious to talk to you immediately and in person. I strongly suggest you take her up on the offer.'

'I'll be right over. Bye.' He put down the phone.

'You'll be right over where?' asked Lila, with a slightly suspicious tone.

Andreas hurriedly began pulling on his clothes. 'To meet your girlfriend Jill McLaughlin, who's with Anna and Jack's friend Solona. But don't worry, I'm taking Jack along as a chaperone.' Andreas stepped into his shoes, grabbed his jacket, and headed out of the bedroom in the direction of Jack's room.

'Darling,' he heard from behind, 'take care.'

NINETEEN

Andreas had set a likely land-speed record for getting from his home to the Cirillos'. His red-lights-be-damned approach to driving had Jack gripping the door handle as Andreas ran on about how in the world Solona could have convinced Panos's wife to turn on him.

'I told you she's a special person,' said Jack. 'She has a natural instinct for finding whatever it takes to get a person to open up. It's a gift.'

'Let's hope it helps Anna.'

'And pray.'

The gate and front door to the house were unlocked, so Andreas did not bother to buzz or knock. As he and Jack walked through the front doorway, Solona rose from the sofa and turned to face them.

Casting a broad smile, she said, 'Hi, Jack, and hello to you too. Uncle Andreas, I presume?'

It is said there are some people in this world so beautiful that a mere glimpse of them can make your heart stop. Andreas felt his miss a few beats.

Jack looked stupefied. 'I've never seen you look so beautiful.' All her piercings were gone, her hair honey-blonde and coiffed.

'I'll take that as a compliment.' Solona smiled at Andreas. 'Thank you for coming on such short notice. Mrs Cirillo is anxious to help your investigation in any way that she can. She believes she's been as much a victim of her husband as our dear Anna.'

She looked at Jill. 'Don't you, my love?'

Jill nodded, biting at her lip.

'Come sit beside Jill as you ask your questions.' Solona sat on a sofa across from where Jill sat and patted the space next to her for Jack to join her.

Andreas sat where he'd been told, trying to gather his thoughts as he did. He looked at Solona, smiled, and put his smartphone on the coffee table separating the two sofas.

'Perhaps you could tell us what transpired before we arrived.'

'Certainly.' In less than ten minutes, Solona precisely described all she and Jill had talked about, stopping after each point to obtain Jill's verbal agreement with her description. 'That's when Jill asked to speak with you.'

'Thank you,' said Andreas, nodding at Solona. 'So, Mrs Cirillo, how may I help you?'

In a more frightened than threatening snarl, Jill said, 'Help *me*? I'm here to help you.'

'Even better yet.'

She paused. 'My husband is trying to destroy me.'

Andreas said nothing.

'I had no idea whatsoever that he was involving me in a kidnapping.'

'Well, now that you know he has, what are you offering to help us save my niece's life and you to avoid an accessory-to-murder charge?'

Jill's hand began to shake. 'I think I know who the limo driver is.'

'Who is he?'

'He's a Russian that Panos met on one of his first trips to Moscow. A former mercenary who spoke Greek and acted as his bodyguard there. Panos liked him so much he arranged for him to work for him here in Greece.'

'Do you have a name and address for him?'

'He lives somewhere off Omonoia Square, and Panos always called him Ivan. I don't know if that's his real name.'

'What makes you think he's involved?'

'Because he does all of my husband's dirty work.'

'What kind of dirty work?'

Jill shut her eyes. 'Perhaps I should get a lawyer.'

'You're entitled to one,' said Andreas flatly.

Solona spoke softly, 'But knowing what you know about your husband's mercenary friend Ivan, do you think going the lawyer route will help save that poor girl's life?'

Jill looked down at her hands. 'I never wanted to be a part of any of this. I just wanted a better life. To be a respected member of the community.'

'As I see it, my love,' said Solona, shaking her head, 'there's only one door remaining in that direction. All others open to a dead end or worse.'

Andreas watched Solona's eyes catch Jill's attention and hold it until Jill spoke again.

'The Russian managed the men who set the fires.'

Andreas sat up straighter on the sofa. 'How do you know that?'

'Because sometimes the two of them would watch television coverage of the fires and talk to each other as if I weren't around to overhear. My husband would say things to him like "Great job you did;" "Now we'll get that property;" and "How did you ever pull that off?"'

'Anything more specific than that?'

'Once I heard him say, "Too bad about the Chinese, they did good work."'

'Which Chinese?'

'I don't know.'

'You're not being very helpful here.'

'I assume they were talking about the Chinese my husband had me texting specific coordinates to for locations in Greece, with a copy sent to Ivan.' She dropped her head. 'And a mutual friend once told me how valuable my husband and Ivan were to his project.'

'Valuable in what way?'

'They did whatever it took to make things happen.'

Andreas did not hide his frustration. 'It's way after two in the morning. I need better answers.'

'*Fine!*' she barked. 'He said Panos picked the places to burn and Ivan arranged to set the fires.'

'Did Ivan actually set the fires?'

'Not that I know of. But I wouldn't be surprised if he did. My friend said he'd provided my husband and Ivan with a crew of Chinese.'

Andreas shook his head. 'This all seems a bit far-fetched without your naming names. Like, who's this mysterious friend who confides in you? How does he know your husband's business? And why would he tell you what you claim he did?'

'Simple,' said Jill, looking to Solona as if for reassurance. 'I was fucking my husband's business partner, and sheets yield secrets.'

Andreas simply nodded. 'I assume you're referring to Victor.'

Jill assented.

'Did Victor happen to tell you what happened to your husband's Chinese crew?'

'Just that one day they up and disappeared without a trace. But by then they had nothing more to do. All the necessary fires had already been set.'

'Did Victor have anything more to say about your husband?'

'Only that he had a bright future.'

'Doing what?'

'Working for the Consortium that Victor represents in Greece.'

'Where do you think your husband is now?'

'I've no idea. But I truly wish I did, so that I could tell you where to catch the bastard.'

'What about Victor?'

'What about him?'

'Do you think he's involved in the kidnapping?'

'I doubt it. He has no stake in Panos beyond using him as his lawyer.'

'And you, of course.'

Jill snickered. 'I'm just one of many to Victor. It's nothing more than that. In fact, this weekend he's away at some wild stag party on a private yacht.'

Andreas glanced at Jack, then back at Jill. 'Do you know the name of the boat?'

'No.'

'Could your husband be headed there?'

'I have absolutely no idea. But why would he want to take a kidnap victim to a party?'

'Why indeed?' asked Andreas. 'But, at this hour, nothing would surprise me.

'Isn't that the truth,' said Solona.

Andreas stood up and nodded to Solona and Jill. 'Thank you, both. And if anything more comes to mind, Mrs Cirillo, please let me know at once.' Andreas handed a card to Jill.

'Uh, do you happen to have an extra card for me?' Solona asked. 'Just in case something comes to mind?'

Andreas handed her a card. He hoped he wasn't blushing.

After saying goodnight to the ladies, Andreas drove home at a far more relaxed pace.

'I think it's fair to say that your friend Solona is a force of nature.'

'I told you you'd be impressed. She's hard not to like. And I don't mean just because she's pretty.'

'I must say she makes quite a first impression.'

'You'd be amazed how differently she dresses back in New York. I've never seen her look like this before.'

'I'd say she knows how to dress for her audience. She had the perfect high-end look for gaining Jill McLaughlin Cirillo's respect.'

'Not to mention getting our attention.'

'Yes,' laughed Andreas. 'She does know how to flirt.'

'Don't take that seriously; she was just playing with us.'

'Don't wreck my delicate male ego with the truth,' Andreas told him.

'Fine, I'll change the subject. Do you or do you not believe Jill?'

'As I hope was picked up on my recording, she's practically admitted to involvement in setting the fires, or at least in having knowledge of who set them. But arguably only in hindsight, not knowingly beforehand. Still, she's hanging out there as a potential accessory to arson, if not murder.'

'Then why in the world did she decide to turn on her husband in a way that sticks her own neck out as far as she has?'

'From what I gathered through Solona's description of their conversation before we arrived, Jill thinks she's been set up by her husband to take the fall for all of his crimes, and she's looking for a way out.'

'What about her involvement in Anna's kidnapping?'

'Tougher question. The facts support both her involvement and her claim she had no idea that what she did was part of a kidnapping plot. Her innocence claim gains considerable support from the fact her primary contribution to the scheme did nothing more than request that our deputy minister authorize the central element of the kidnap.'

'Do you think Dittos is involved?'

'If I did . . .' Andreas smacked the steering wheel. 'No, I don't. He's just a butt-kissing, highly manipulable bureaucrat doing whatever he can to ingratiate himself to anyone he thinks important or powerful.'

'And still no ransom demand.'

'Nope. My guess is they likely don't feel safe yet, possibly combined with some sense that we must already know what they want. That sort of thinking doesn't make a ransom demand as urgent as it is to those who kidnap for money.'

'Then again, there's my theory,' said Jack.

'Yes, there is, and for the record, I'm rooting for that one. Not the part about me losing my job, but Anna showing up unharmed on Tuesday.'

'So, what do we do now?'

'My hope of catching a couple of hours' sleep were blown out of the water by your friend's call. Not that I'm complaining. But I'm headed back home to take a shower and check in with Tassos on how surveillance is going on the mega-yacht.'

'Can you imagine if that's the same boat Jill said Victor boarded, and that's where the kidnappers are headed?'

'I already have. If Victor and others onboard are involved in the kidnapping, when we show up with the cavalry, a lot of folk are going to be desperately trying to eliminate any evidence linking them to Anna on that boat.'

'Do you think they'd . . .' Jack didn't finish his thought.

'Don't lose hope. Just prepare yourself for the possibility of being called upon to do some rather unorthodox things to make this end well.'

Jack crossed his arms and nodded. 'Unorthodox works for me.'

Anna's ploy to avoid drinking water had helped her clear some of the cobwebs from her thinking and allowed her to focus on potential escape scenarios. But every brilliant thought ended with the same incontrovertible conclusion: Being handcuffed by her ankles to a bed in a locked room, with no windows or vents, and at least two men outside the only door, offered her no chance of escape. At least none from here.

The small, battered knapsack that she carried everywhere was gone, and along with it her iPhone, iPad, and ID. All she had with her now was her Apple watch, strapped to her left wrist under the sweatshirt she'd worn on the flight. The driver must have missed it. Jack had given it to her as an engagement gift, and the thought of that moment made her tear up.

Having discovered a possible link to the outside world, Anna obsessed over finding some way of using her watch to reach out for help. But there was no connection to be made, and she feared draining the battery and ending her fragile connection to hope. So, she switched the watch to low-power mode, then turned it off at 2:15 in the morning.

Not long after, she heard the door open, and two men walked into the room.

'Are you sure she's asleep?' asked a male voice.

'Take a look for yourself,' said the driver, in a Russian accent.

The beam of a powerful flashlight hit Anna squarely in the face and fixed on her closed eyes. She did not budge. Next, she felt a hand running along her body, squeezing and pinching her most sensitive parts.

'I told you she was out cold.'

'Jeez, her bed is soaked.'

'What do you expect? I've been pumping her full of water since I picked her up. And she's had no bathroom privileges for over sixteen hours. You'd piss your pants too.'

'Fine, then you carry her to the car. Do you think we should drug her some more?'

'The last dose I gave her was pretty heavy. It should last for six more hours at least. Do you want to risk killing her?'

'No. Dead she's no good to us. Just get her out of here.'

Anna kept her eyes tightly shut, let her body go limp enough to be manipulated in any manner the men chose, and fixed her mind on ignoring how they touched her. The driver uncuffed her ankles and swept her up and over his shoulder as if she were a pillow.

Twenty seconds later she heard a car door open and a front seat slide forward. She felt herself being dropped on to the back seat of a small vehicle. The driver turned her on her side facing forward, bent her at the knees to fit her legs inside, and slid the seat back snug against her legs. Someone sat in that seat and slammed the door shut.

She heard another door open and close. Then someone tossed a bag on top of her, heavy enough to almost make her cry out. But she didn't, and then realized it was her knapsack.

'Where are we headed?' asked the driver.

'Up north, by the old mines. There's a beach we can reach with this Jimny. The boat will meet us. The Coast Guard never patrols there.'

'What do we do with the car?'

'Just leave it. I borrowed it from an American colleague who only drives it when he's here, and he lets me use it from time to time. I'll just tell him someone stole it and let him call it into the police. By then we'll be long gone.'

Anna had hoped once outside the room there'd be some way
to scream or signal for help, but she'd not seen a single headlight
in front or behind them since she'd been put on the back seat. And
now they were on a bumpy road that had her rolling partly off the
seat on to the floor. Neither of the two in front seemed to care.
She just lay there, as limp as a sack of potatoes.

Perhaps the captain of the boat would help rescue her. At least
being at sea would give her more escape options. Or so she prayed.

When they finally stopped and the headlights turned off, all was
black.

'We're lucky there's no moon,' said the driver.

'There's the boat,' said the other man.

'Does your fisherman captain know about our third passenger?'
asked the driver.

'Of course he does. I told him. Besides, he's not stupid. Her
picture and yours are all over the place, so the moment he saw
you he'd know who you are. But don't worry, I'm paying him for
his silence, as he is for mine.'

'I don't follow.'

'I saved his son from a murder-rape conviction involving a
fourteen-year-old girl.'

'What makes you think that will keep him from gossiping with
his buddies about you, a big-time lawyer, caught up in a
kidnapping?'

'Because I know who did what his son was accused of and,
more importantly, I can prove it.'

'Why should he care?'

'Because he's the one who did it,' chuckled the lawyer.

The driver laughed.

Anna shivered. She would find no escape here.

The classic Aegean caïque is a small fishing boat made of pine,
primed in orange, painted white, and trimmed in bright colors. It's
rigged for sail, with a sharp prow and broad rear beam hosting a
dominating tiller at its stern. It's built to survive rough seas and
remains a living historic symbol of the traditional Mediterranean
boatbuilding craft, despite the ever-broadening influence of plastic
and fiberglass.

None of that mattered to Anna. All she wanted was an opportunity to escape, but in the middle of the night, in the middle of

the sea, she saw little chance. Her last glimmer of hope faded
when the driver handcuffed her ankles together, pressed her far
up into the bow, and covered her with fishing nets.

'If the Coast Guard stops us, you'd better get in there with her.
I'll cover you with the nets.'

'How nice and cozy that will be,' said the driver.

'Don't get any ideas, Ivan. We need her unharmed.'

'What I have in mind won't harm her.'

'Whatever you have in mind will harm her. So don't even think
about it. If we succeed, we'll both be set for life.'

'Don't worry about any of that,' said the fisherman. 'The Coast
Guard already stopped me on my way over here. They searched
the ship and aren't going to do it again, especially not in the middle
of the rough seas we'll be hitting crossing between here and Tinos.'

'Terrific,' said the driver. 'But I have a question.'

'What is it?' said the man.

'What makes you think that in the middle of the night you, me,
and the girl can board a mega-yacht owned by one of the most
influential men in the Middle East?'

'Good question.'

'So, what's the answer?'

'We've been invited to a party.'

'Huh?'

'Well, at least I've been invited. But it's the kind of party that
showing up with a drugged out, pretty young woman and a strapping guy is welcomed.'

'Panos, I think you're out of your mind. She's been kidnapped.
What makes you think they won't just call the Coast Guard?'

'Kidnapping is just another means to an end for some folk, and
I suspect our host falls into that category. Besides, it's an important
step toward implementing a plan that will make his patron among
the most powerful rulers on earth. There's no way he'll risk
obstructing that effort in any way.'

'If you're wrong?'

'I'm not, so stop worrying. Once we're on the yacht I'll make
the call that will get this all straightened out.'

'And if not?'

'Our host also happens to be adept at doing away with incriminating remains. Something you didn't quite do with the Chinese.'

'We didn't have to,' said Ivan. 'They were illegals with no IDs or ties to Greece, and their burned-to-a-crisp remains meant no photos to show around for someone to possibly recognize. They were quickly written off as illegals hiding out in places caught up in the wildfires, who likely started the fires and earned a fate they deserved.'

'This one's not nameless or unidentifiable,' said Panos, 'which is why if her uncle doesn't do what I tell him, she disappears. Completely.'

Anna heard every word. She was no longer panicked or afraid but determined to survive.

At any cost.

'Any news?' asked Andreas, holding the phone against his shoulder as he worked at his kitchen stove, scrambling eggs for Jack and himself.

'Not yet,' said Tassos. 'The two men the Coast Guard dropped off on Gyaros said they weren't spotted by the yacht, even though the yacht's sidelights and mast lights lit up the sea all around them. But nor have they seen any sea or air activity around the yacht. It's been calm as far as they can tell, and—'

Tassos abruptly stopped. 'Hold on a minute. I've got to take this call.'

Andreas kept scrambling the eggs with one hand, but now held the phone in his other.

'That was one of the guys on Gyaros,' said Tassos, back on the line. 'They've picked up faint lights headed their way from the general direction of Mykonos.'

'What kind of boat is it?'

'No way to tell for sure, but from how slowly the lights are moving, and how few and close together they are, their best guess is a fishing boat.'

'I thought fishing is prohibited off Gyaros.'

'It is.'

Andreas stopped stirring the eggs. 'We've got to get the Coast Guard to intercept that fishing boat before it reaches the yacht.'

'That won't happen. The fishing boat is maybe ten or fifteen minutes away from the yacht, and there's no Coast Guard vessel in the area. Not even the two guys on the island have a boat.'

'If that's the case, once they hook up, we can't let either boat go anywhere until we've had the chance to board and search them.'

'You're about to create an international incident. Many of the people on the yacht likely have diplomatic immunity.'

'Screw them and their immunity! If my niece is held hostage on that boat, you damn well better believe I'll be making an international incident.' Andreas paused to calm his voice. 'I'm leaving for Gyaros as soon as I can get to a helicopter. What are the chances of your Coast Guard buddy getting an armed offshore patrol vessel and other support there ASAP? If Anna's on that yacht, and it makes it to international waters . . .'

'Pretty good. I'll ask him to get the Coast Guard underway as soon as we get off the phone. Just let me know when you're in the air.'

'What makes you think he can do it?'

'He's a Coast Guard Vice-Admiral.'

A bit of tension faded from Andreas's voice. 'You never fail to amaze me. Thanks.' He hung up and looked at Jack. 'Ready for another helicopter ride?'

Jack nodded. 'I can't believe all this is happening just to get you to drop your investigation into the Consortium's metaverse plans.'

Andreas abandoned the eggs, headed for the door, and waved for Jack to follow. 'Since the dawn of time, world domination has been a powerful motivator for taking outrageous risks.' He hit speed dial on his phone. 'I'm calling Yianni to meet us at the heliport.'

'What's the plan?'

'To surprise them before they surprise us.'

The helicopter pilot promised Andreas they'd make it to Gyaros in thirty minutes. Andreas passed that on to Tassos, who said an armed Coast Guard patrol vessel had already engaged the fishing vessel and was about to board it and search it.

'What about the yacht?' asked Andreas.

'It hasn't moved.'

'Good. Tell them not to let it budge a centimeter.'

'They're prepared to keep it from moving until you get there. Their pretext is, that by having spent so much time anchored in a forbidden area, authorities are on their way from Athens to address the situation personally.'

'Anything that keeps that yacht from leaving Greek waters works for me,' said Andreas, excitement tightening his voice. 'And do let me know if they find anything on the fishing boat.'

'Of course, but I wouldn't hold out much hope on that score. It had already met up with the yacht and was headed back to Mykonos when the Coast Guard stopped it.'

'Just let me know if they find anything.'

'Will do.'

Andreas looked over at Jack and Yianni, and held up crossed fingers.

Two sets of crossed fingers flashed back at him.

As Panos saw it, he'd come up with the perfect plan. He'd been invited by the owner of a mega-yacht to join a wild, week-long party onboard, where rendezvousing in darkness off a small inconspicuous boat, in an utterly deserted area, was standard operating procedure for many invited to these sorts of clandestine affairs. The remaining partiers likely came onboard by helicopter, but no matter: whether arriving by boat or copter, all shared the same desire to avoid prying eyes and paparazzi.

Panos's decision to arrive with an attractive, disoriented young woman and a tall strapping man to share his quarters, rather than confining himself to those companions provided by the host, also was not out of the ordinary for the host's free-wheeling guests.

This was where the cruder of the world's movers and shakers came to play in secret, their confidentiality guaranteed by their host, no matter their choice of vices. Never had any authority dared challenge the inviolate sanctity promised by the owner to all who attended.

As Panos saw it, the party gave him a week tucked away from any risk of discovery. More than enough time to exchange the girl in return for no further interference with his clients' project. Or, if necessary, to dispose of her body without a trace.

TWENTY

Flying over a populated Greek island in a helicopter during the darkest part of a moonless night might lead some to feel trapped in a tunnel of stars: the true ones glittering above, the man-made shimmering below. But for Jack, the points of light arrayed across the heavens lighted a path across the wine-dark Aegean to a barren, lightless place known as Devil's Island – and Anna.

He said a silent prayer, repeating over and over the five-word mantra he used whenever passing over water – *I am not on a boat* – knowing all the while that soon would change.

'Gentlemen,' said the police pilot, 'off to port are the lights of the Coast Guard patrol vessel, on course toward our target. The yacht's still anchored in the same location.'

'If Anna's onboard, you'd think they'd have left by now,' said Yianni.

'I'm going with my gut on this one. She's on that boat,' said Andreas.

'Where do you want me to land, Chief?' asked the pilot.

'I don't see us as having much choice. If you put us down on the island, we'll have no way of getting on to the yacht until the Coast Guard arrives. And once you do, the yacht will know we're here and, if Anna's onboard, will take off immediately.' Andreas paused. 'Or get rid of her before we can board.'

'What are you saying?'

'I want you to put us down on the yacht's helipad.'

'*What?* Without permission from the boat or help from its crew? It's pitch-black down there.'

Andreas leaned over and patted the pilot's shoulder. 'That's why the good Lord created landing lights.'

He gave Andreas a quick glance. 'And prayer.'

Andreas smiled. 'Thanks, I know you can do it.'

'Need I point out,' said Yianni, 'that once we get on the yacht, and the chopper takes off, the boat could leave with us on board?'

'Nope, no need to mention that.'

'OK, then what's the plan once we get on the yacht?' asked Yianni.

'It depends. Just follow my lead.'

'In other words, improvise.'

'You got it.'

Jack said a second silent prayer, praying that the shaking fear he felt deep into his bones would not overwhelm him. His thoughts ran back to something Andreas had said to him before his first helicopter flight. *There's no rule requiring you to be sad or blame yourself when your thoughts drift to loved ones who've passed on.*

Jack could have done nothing to save his mother, and he could not now allow his panic-laden memories of those horrible moments to jeopardize Anna's rescue. He must concentrate on finding a way to channel his anxieties into saving the love of his life.

Or die trying.

The sea was relatively calm, and first light had not yet broken when the helicopter's landing lights blazed above the bow of the yacht. They literally lit up the ship, and two crew members dressed all in white, one a young attractive man and the other a young attractive woman, came racing to the helipad. Touchdown went smoothly, disembarkation by the passengers was a non-event, and takeoff took place without incident.

Andreas, Yianni, and Jack were now on their own.

'Are you guests?' the woman asked loudly, over the chopper's engine noise.

'No,' shouted Andreas, pointing up at the helicopter still hovering above the yacht. 'We're from the organization whose name is emblazoned across the side of that flying machine.'

The woman appeared flustered and started talking into her headset.

Andreas couldn't hear what she was saying but didn't have to. He knew she was calling for instructions on how to handle unexpected police visitors.

'Sir,' said the woman. 'Please follow me. The captain would like you to join him on the bridge.'

She led them from the bow to a staircase, and up two levels to the bridge. According to a layout of the yacht Andreas had found on the internet, the owner's quarters were directly above the bridge level, giving him a front-row seat to their arrival.

A starboard door aft of the bridge marked CAPTAIN'S QUARTERS slid open and a tall, fit-looking man dressed in white, with jet black hair and a bushy, Tom Selleck-style mustache strode though the doorway. He looked to be in his early forties and flashed a brilliant smile.

'Gentlemen, welcome aboard. I'm afraid you've caught me at an inopportune moment. We're preparing to sail at first light. I understand your helicopter has departed . . . If you can't make other arrangements, I'd be more than happy to lend you one of our Zodiacs.'

'That is so very kind of you to offer, Captain. Especially since you don't even know why we're here.'

The captain flashed that smile again. 'Your reason doesn't matter to me. You have no right to be here under any circumstances. Indeed, your landing on my ship without permission constitutes a breach of my country's sovereign immunity. An act which I can assure you will not go unreported through appropriate diplomatic channels.'

Andreas looked around the room, and then back at the captain. 'Funny, I didn't know you had a law degree.'

The captain held on to the smile and shrugged. 'If that's the way you want to play it, we'll treat you as pirates.'

'Well, I have a few ideas on how to treat you, Captain. But I suggest you put your pride and bravado back in your pants and check with your radar guy on what's headed your way.'

Anger flashed across the captain's face. 'Bosun, send an armed detail to the bridge immediately.'

'Tsk-tsk,' said Andreas, taking out his mobile and calling Tassos.

'What's up?'

'The three of us are onboard the suspect boat but the captain has opted not to cooperate. Instead, he's chosen to call us pirates and sail off to who knows where with us as prisoners under armed guard. Could you possibly arrange for our colleagues to let him know it would be better to play nice?'

'Done.'

Andreas put his phone back in his pocket as four men armed with AK-47s marched toward them.

'Lock these three pirates below,' barked the captain.

Andreas laughed. 'You're serious, huh? Well, all I can say is your owner and his very important guests are going to be deeply pissed off at you for the media shitstorm you're about to bring down on this floating whorehouse.'

'Get them out of here *now*!' yelled the captain.

'Uh, Captain,' said a mate manning the radar. 'You ought to take a look at this.'

His smile long gone, the captain whirled on his mate, but Andreas spoke first.

'I agree with him. You should look.'

The captain pushed past Andreas to the mate's station. 'What is it?'

'A ship's headed straight for us,' said the mate.

'To be more precise,' said Andreas, 'it's a Hellenic Coast Guard offshore patrol vessel fitted with heavy machine guns and other nasty surprises for use against discourteous sea captains attempting to kidnap a Hellenic Police Chief Inspector, a detective, and two civilians. With *kidnap* being the operative word.'

The captain's anger had him spitting out his words. 'You wouldn't dare board or seize this boat.'

'Well, you've already been boarded, and as for what I might dare do . . .' Andreas pinned him with a glare. 'You've *no* idea what I'm capable of. I suggest you tell your boys with the toys to back off before I decide to arrest all of them for armed assault on police officers acting in the line of duty.'

'You're bluffing.'

Andreas pointed toward the bow. 'Take a look.'

As first light and distant clouds off to the east had turned the Aegean sky to fire, across the dawn-painted sea steamed a battle-ship-gray patrol boat, straight at them.

'Are you people mad?' cried the captain.

'Yep. Just let me know when I can speak to your boss in an effort to resolve this matter quietly.'

'I will never allow you to speak to my owner. I'm hired to protect him.'

'Well, you're not doing a very good job of it, Captain, and any minute now he's going to hear it for himself.'

As if on cue, a bullhorn roared across the sea from the Coast Guard vessel. 'This is the Hellenic Coast Guard. You're ordered to immediately stand down your armed men and make ready to be boarded.'

The captain looked desperately from the vessel to his armed men.

Andreas shrugged. 'I warned you.'

A short, pudgy, silver-haired man in a purple velvet bathrobe trimmed in gold braid, bearing the name of the boat embroidered in gold over the left breast, stormed up behind the guards. 'What the hell is going on here, Captain?'

The captain started to speak, but Andreas cut him off. 'I'm Chief Inspector Andreas Kaldis, head of Greece's Special Crimes Unit, and I came onboard in connection with a matter of grave concern to my government, but your captain has refused to listen to what I have to say.'

The man spoke calmly. 'This ship is a sovereign entity. You have no right to be here.'

'Am I correct, sir, that you are the owner of this magnificent yacht?'

The owner stood up a bit straighter. 'Yes, I am.'

'Well, then you should know that this vessel has no right to claim sovereign immunity. Only vessels *owned* by a sovereign nation can make that claim, no matter whether its owner has diplomatic immunity.'

The owner stared at Andreas, then turned to the captain. 'Send your armed men away. And confirm to the Coast Guard that you have done so. I will be with this gentleman in my apartment.'

The captain started to object, but the owner raised his hand and he fell silent.

Andreas looked at Yianni. 'Keep an eye on the captain. Make sure he doesn't do anything suicidal.'

'I resent that,' blurted out the captain. 'I've only done what I saw as necessary to protect my ship. Nothing more, nothing less.'

'For your sake I hope your claim of innocence holds up, but frankly, Captain, up until now everything you've said and done has you looking more and more like an accessory to kidnapping.'

'What are you talking about?' The captain looked pleadingly at the owner. 'He must be crazy.'

'Then explain this to me, Captain,' said Andreas. 'Three of us boarded your ship, but when I accused you of kidnapping two cops and two civilians, you didn't even correct my math. Either you knew there was another kidnapped civilian onboard or you can't count.'

The captain blinked twice. 'I wasn't paying attention to what you were saying. I just wanted you off my ship.'

'I want the same . . . and we'll all be gone the moment you deliver to me the kidnapped young woman *and* her two abductors.'

'I know nothing about that.'

'You should. They're on this boat.' Andreas reached into his pocket and pulled out three photos. 'Here's the girl and her kidnappers. Recognize any of them?'

Before the captain could answer, the owner spoke up. 'Chief Inspector, I think it will be more productive for all concerned if you and I continue this conversation in private.'

'That's fine with me, so long as your Captain doesn't attempt communicating with anyone but the Coast Guard while we're away.'

'He won't,' said the owner, turning his head to stare the captain dead in the eye. 'Will you?'

'No, sir.'

'Make sure that he doesn't, Yianni.'

'Come, Chief Inspector, it is time for us to talk frankly.'

'And truthfully.'

For most of Andreas's non-married life, the closest he'd ever been to a super yacht – let alone the much larger mega-yachts – was strolling past one in a Greek island harbor. Each time that he did, it amazed him how much money some people had. Once married to Lila, they often spent time as guests on such floating palaces, and now what amazed him was how much money *so many* people had.

The owner's apartment occupied the two highest-level living quarters on the ship and, from its sheer size, over-the-top appointments, and priceless fine art adorning the walls, was undoubtedly meant to overwhelm visitors.

The owner pointed out the upper-level bedroom suite area as they passed through an elegant salon on the way to the deck lounge area, where he motioned Andreas toward a pair of matching gold-embroidered canvas deck chairs. 'Pick whichever one you'd like.'

As they sat, a steward asked Andreas, 'Would you like coffee, sir?'

'That would be very nice, thank you,' nodded Andreas.

Once the steward left, the owner crossed his legs and studied Andreas in silence.

Andreas said nothing, waiting for him to speak.

'My normal reaction to such an outrageous breach of international courtesy, if not law, as you and your colleagues practiced in boarding my vessel without permission, would be to assume this was just another form of sanctioned piracy engaged in by officials in some parts of our world looking for a pay-off to go away.'

'I've heard of such practices.'

'But what intrigues me about you is I don't sense that's what you're after.'

'Your instinct is correct.'

'Then what is it that you really want?'

'It's just as I said to your captain. The immediate return of a kidnapped Greek girl and surrender of her two captors.'

'Yes, I heard all that. But you can't be serious.'

'I couldn't be more serious.'

'Please show me what you offered to my captain.'

Andreas handed the three photos over as the steward returned with a silver tray containing a coffee service and pastries for two.

The owner held the photos face down until the steward had placed the tray on a table between the two men and left them alone. He turned the photos over and studied them.

'Rather than engaging in a frivolous back and forth over who is or is not on my ship, I can tell you that if you're only interested in these three, I can't help you, because I know all of my guests, and to the best of my knowledge none of these three is onboard.'

'Let's start with a simpler answer to a simple question. Do you know any of the three in those photos?'

'Why would I?'

'Only you know the answer to that question, but if I don't get an answer, the Hellenic Coast Guard and my Hellenic Police colleagues and I will require a list of everyone on this boat, guests and crew, and search every millimeter of your ship.'

'And if I refuse?'

'We can arrange to have your ship impounded or towed to Syros where no one will leave your ship until properly identified and interviewed.'

'That's outrageous.'

'So is kidnapping and human trafficking.'

The owner raised his voice now. 'How *dare* you accuse me of such behavior?'

Andreas reached for a coffee. 'I accused you of none of that, but shouting your denial adds nothing to the truth of what you have to say. So, allow me to repeat my simple question: do you know any of these three?'

The owner glared at Andreas.

Andreas took a sip and smiled. 'Very good coffee.'

'I do not appreciate your veiled threats or feeble attempts at repartee.'

Andreas feigned shock. 'Veiled? I'd hardly call it veiled. Or for that matter a threat.' He put down the coffee, leaned in across the table, and spoke softly and deliberately.

'It's obvious to me that when a person of your eminent status, who proudly represents his country on the international stage, is found concealing a kidnapped young Greek woman and her captors on his half-billion-euro yacht, amid a guest list of the world's movers and shakers, an insatiable international media feeding frenzy will follow on an order not seen since the 2018 assassination of journalist Jamal Khashoggi in the Saudi consulate in Turkey.'

'What makes you think I know anyone in those photos?'

'You cut off the captain before he had a chance to look at them, and just now you hid the photos from your steward.'

'One can't be too careful about what you allow your staff to see. Gossip runs rampant on a boat filled with guests such as mine.'

'I'm certain that's true. Which is why I'm talking with you in private. Neither of us wants gossip turning into front-page news. All I want is the girl and her captors. Then you can go about your business.'

The owner returned to the photos. 'Yes, I do recognize one of the men. But not because he's on my ship. He is a lawyer with whom I've worked in the past. He's also been on my boat before, so some of my people might recognize him. He may have been invited to join us, but he wasn't onboard when I went to bed.'

'When was that?'

'After three in the morning.'

'We believe he came on board within the past hour or so, along with his accomplice and the girl.'

'What do you base that on?'

'We have reason to believe they left Mykonos aboard a caïque since impounded by the Coast Guard after rendezvousing with your ship.'

'Reason to believe is not proof.'

'But it is probable cause for a search.'

The owner picked up a walkie-talkie from the table and pressed a button. 'Did anyone come onboard last night after three, other than the three in the police helicopter?'

He paused.

'Send whoever met them up to me on the bridge at once.'

He put down the walkie-talkie and stood up. 'I may owe you an apology, Chief Inspector. Three persons did arrive around the time you said. The two crew who helped them board are on their way up to the bridge. They'll know where they put them. Hopefully, they're your three persons of interest.'

Andreas jumped up. 'Let's go.'

By the time Andreas and his host reached the bridge, the space was crowded by the captain and his bridge detail, a fully armed four-member Coast Guard boarding unit, Yianni and Jack, and the two crew members summoned by the owner, all waiting for orders on what to do next.

Andreas showed the two crew members the photos and they immediately identified them as the three who'd come onboard. They'd put them in guest quarters closest to the prayer room in a lower level of the ship.

Three minutes later, the boarding unit, Andreas, and Yianni were outside the door to those quarters. Andreas quietly slid the pass key into the lock and nodded to the lieutenant in charge of the boarding unit before twisting the key and slamming the door open for the Coast Guard to storm into the room.

It was empty, with not a sign of anyone having been there.

An enraged Andreas stormed back ahead of the rest to the bridge where the owner, the captain, and Jack waited.

'Nothing, no one, not a sign of life in that room. I don't know what sort of game you folks are playing, but time is up. I want a list of every passenger and every room they're in.'

The owner smiled. 'You're right. Time is up. I've endured enough of your insults and boorish behavior.' He handed Andreas a phone. 'It's your boss.'

'Minister?' said Andreas into the phone.

'Not yet,' said Dittos into his ear. 'I don't know what madness is possessing you to cause such an egregious breach of international law, but as your superior I order you to cease and desist immediately and *get off that boat now.*'

'Sorry, we have a bad connection . . .' Andreas whipped the phone out through an open porthole and into the sea.

'Thank you for that,' Andreas said to the owner. He turned to the Coast Guard. 'We've just been ordered to conduct a thorough search of every centimeter of this vessel for the three people in the photos. Lieutenant, your unit will take the lead in that, and there are to be no exceptions from the search. If anyone refuses to cooperate fully, my detective or I will arrest them. Hop to it. A young Greek girl's life depends on us.'

'I'll have you destroyed,' shouted the owner.

'Lieutenant, start upstairs in this guy's apartment,' Andreas said, pointing at the apoplectic owner. 'Pay particular attention to his upstairs bedroom suite. No telling what you'll find in there.'

'I'll have you shot!'

'Sorry, wrong country. But one more outburst from you, and you'll spend the rest of this search gagged and in handcuffs. By the way, close up your bathrobe. You're minimizing your image.'

'May I add something?' said Jack, drawing in and letting out a deep breath.

'Feel free.'

Turning to face the owner, Jack shook his head, and in a flat calm tone said, 'Sir, I don't understand why you're going to such lengths to protect people who are destroying your nation's metaverse dreams.'

'Who are you?'

'I'm the man charged with evaluating your country's Syros-based metaverse project with China and Russia.'

'I don't know what you're talking about.'

'Well, let's just say that your conduct is making it appear that your country is complicit in the murders committed by the men you're so strenuously protecting.'

'Murders?'

'Yes, three, at least. And from the clumsy way you're trying to protect these non-countrymen of yours in their kidnapping efforts, I seriously doubt that you're endearing yourself to the powers-that-be back home, who care far more about how they're regarded in the world at large than about your party guests.'

'You don't know what you're talking about.'

'Why don't you ask your guest Victor whether or not I do?'

The owner blanched. 'Victor? I don't know any Victor.'

'Of course you do,' smiled Jack, still calm. 'You likely even know him by his true name, not just his nickname. He's often your guest on this boat. You know him well. He's who represents China in the metaverse Consortium you claim to know nothing about. Trust me on this. Speak to him before you do something to make yourself your country's national scapegoat for losing out on the irreplaceable opportunity of becoming a twenty-first-century true world power.'

The owner began chewing at his lower lip. 'How do you know Victor?'

'Call him and find out. You'll also likely learn that, if you don't return the girl safe, sound, and unharmed, I will spend the rest of my life working to destroy you.' Jack paused. 'And your family.'

Andreas leaned in so that only the owner could hear him. 'Me too, and yes, that's a promise, not a threat.'

Ivan had carried the seemingly insensate Anna aboard the yacht while Panos joked with the two crew members who'd greeted them about her unconscious state.

'Don't worry, we have spares onboard if you need them,' laughed one crew member.

Panos tipped them lavishly, as well as the steward who was waiting for them in their room to greet Panos as an often-returning guest.

Anna shuddered. These strangers were not people she could trust to help her. She prayed she wouldn't be drugged again – and that she'd find better souls to help her. But she had no idea who to trust. Nor could she think of a way to alert any who might be out there that she'd been kidnapped.

Between the residual effects of the drugs and recurrent anxiety over her predicament, Anna had a tough time thinking at all. She tried keeping up her spirits with thoughts of Jack and Andreas working to find her. But she also knew time was running out, and she'd have to take a risk soon. Delay was no longer in her favor.

She heard one of the two crew members who'd shown them to

their room mention that it was next to the prayer room. She took that as an encouraging sign, because if she somehow attracted the attention of a prayerful person to her predicament, that might lead to her rescue.

Her hopes were buoyed when she heard a helicopter landing above their room. But they soon sank when it quickly departed. Then came a rapid knock on the door and a quick muffled conversation between the steward and Panos.

Panos closed the door. 'Cops are on board. They're looking for us. We've got to get out of this room to a place where we can hide until they're gone.'

'How did they find us?'

'There's no time to worry about that now. We need to hide.'

'But where?'

'The steward will be back in a couple of minutes to show us.'

'Letting her live is getting more dangerous by the minute,' said Ivan.

'Actually, the opposite will be true if he doesn't hide us well enough . . . But let's see where he takes us. Some yachts have ingenious hiding places.'

'For what?'

'Jewels, cash, arms, drugs, people. You name it. Mega-yacht owners and those who charter their ships generally have something they want to hide from pirates, customs officials, or spouses, and so ship designers come up with all sorts of ingenious hideaways. If worse comes to worst, we can do away with her wherever we end up hiding. Doing it that way will give us time to get away – before anyone notices the smell.'

Two quick knocks on the door.

'There he is,' said Panos.

Ivan swept Anna up off the bed and over his shoulder. 'Let's get out of here.'

Anna had the same thought.

TWENTY-ONE

Victor and the owner entered the bridge in lock step, Victor impeccably dressed in yachting white slacks and a blue and white striped tee-shirt, the owner still in his robe.

'Jack,' said Victor, his voice ringing with concern. 'What is all this craziness I'm hearing about a kidnapping and murder involving Panos?'

'It's not craziness. It's fact. Panos and his Russian colleague kidnapped Anna and brought her on to this ship. They're trying to end a police investigation tying them to the murder of three Chinese workers you arranged to work for them.'

Victor pointed at Andreas. 'I see your uncle from last night is also in on this.'

'I will be his uncle once we safely get my niece off this boat, but for now you can call me Chief Inspector.'

'Chief Inspector, I had absolutely nothing to do with the men Jack says were murdered, other than supplying them as workmen to Panos. Nor did I have anything to do with any kidnapping or have any idea that Panos and the two others would be on this boat. I packed up and left Panos's home around two this morning and arrived here by helicopter an hour or so later. I went straight to bed and wasn't awake until twenty minutes or so before my friend here,' nodding toward the owner, 'came pounding on my door wanting to know all about Jack.'

'What did you tell him?' asked Andreas.

'That I'd met him last night at a party at Panos's home, that he is a very impressive, respectful young man who I took a liking to immediately. He has a vast knowledge of many things, particularly the metaverse, and I was considering offering him a job.'

'Now that's a twist I never expected,' said Jack. 'But let's talk about how to find Anna.'

'Certainly,' said Victor.

Looking at the owner, Andreas said, 'So, sir, how do you suggest we go about finding my niece on your boat?'

'No idea. You're the experts.'

Andreas turned away from the owner and looked directly at
Victor. 'I'm beginning to get the impression that you and your
buddy in the bathrobe are trying to run a good-cop, bad-cop routine
on me to justify neither of you doing anything to help us find my
niece.' He paused to catch Victor's eyes. 'Which means she will
likely die.' Andreas's eyes turned to ice. 'If that happens, I can
assure each of you that your metaverse and yachting days in Greece
will be just as dead, and that I'll be doing everything in my power
to make whatever remaining days you spend on earth a living hell.'

The owner started to reply, but Victor silenced him with a few
words in a Middle Eastern language Andreas did not recognize.
Victor softly but firmly continued speaking to him in that same
language. The owner replied, and they spoke briefly.

Victor turned back to Andreas. 'My friend meant no offense.
He misunderstood the assistance you were seeking from him. He
has no way of knowing or learning whether some of his crew
could be complicit with Panos in this horror. Panos is a well-known
tipper who has made friends over previous stays among the notoriously underpaid crew, some of whom would probably protect him
from discovery in ways and places my friend doesn't know. The
crew members know the ship far better than he.'

'That doesn't help us,' Andreas said flatly.

'I realize that. All he can think of that might help to rescue
your niece is the use of the ship's emergency loudspeaker system.
It's capable of broadcasting messages throughout the ship.'

Andreas wrote off most of what Victor had to say as pure BS.
But realistically, there was little hope of getting the owner to do
more than remain neutral in this confrontation. And Victor seemed
to have done that.

'Yes, that will help. Thank you, both.'

Now, what to broadcast?

*Ladies and gentlemen, this is Chief Inspector Andreas Kaldis of
the Hellenic Police. There is no reason to be alarmed as we are
not onboard to interfere with your festivities. We are here to rescue
a young woman named Anna, who was brought onboard against
her will. Once we find Anna safe and sound, you may all resume
your activities. Until then, please stay in your assigned state rooms
or workstations while the Hellenic Coast Guard continues its
search for Anna. Anna, if you can hear this message, Jack and I*

are watching for a sign that you are safe. If you can safely send one, do it now.

The words sent chills running throughout Anna's body. She'd been crammed for what seemed an eternity into a closet-like space, pinned between Ivan behind her, and Panos in front. At first, she thought she might suffocate. Then, as the minutes ran on and breathing regulated, she felt hands groping about her body. Hands were now inside her leggings and under her sports bra. Her captors no longer seemed to care if they caused her harm. Perhaps because they no longer expected her to survive.

She wanted to scream but knew that would only hasten her demise.

The message played again. '*Jack and I are watching for a sign.*'

But what sign could she give them? All her electronics were in her missing knapsack . . .

That's when she thought of her new watch.

She had to turn it on without the men noticing. The man behind her was now aroused and groping at her more aggressively. Perhaps he'd become distracted enough with her body not to notice the slight movement her hands required to turn on her watch and remotely ping her missing phone. She didn't know how pinging her phone might help, but at that moment – on the verge of her seemingly inevitable death – that was all she could think to do.

Andreas asked the lieutenant to station his Coast Guard detail at locations most likely to reveal sounds triggered from well-hidden positions. He prayed it would work far more than he believed it would.

Jack and Yianni remained on the bridge with Andreas, listening for any sounds the ship's two-way broadcasting system might pick up. Andreas's message to Anna had played three times, without the slightest sign of a response.

'She must be gagged and tied up,' said Andreas.

Jack stood nearby, chewing nervously at his lip.

Ping.

Jack swung around, looking for the source of the sound. 'Did you hear that?'

'What?' said Andreas.

'A very soft ping.'

'No, where'd it come from?' asked Andreas, looking around them.

'It must be from over there,' said Yianni, 'where the Coast Guard piled up their gear bags while you were off meeting with the owner.'

Andreas hurried over to the bags and began rooting through them. 'What the hell's this?' He was holding up a well-worn knapsack.

'That's Anna's!' Jack rushed over to take it from Andreas.

'How did it get here?' asked Andreas.

'The Coast Guard must have brought it on board from the fishing boat,' said Yianni, 'but in the ensuing craziness, shouting, and phone tossing, neglected to mention it to us.'

Jack pulled an iPhone out of the bag and hit a few keys. 'She pinged this phone from her watch.'

'Are you sure?'

'I'm positive someone did. We should ping her back.'

'That risks alerting her kidnappers,' said Andreas.

'But we've got to do something to let her know we heard her signal.'

'The best way to do that will be by finding her. Can you think of a way to use her phone to do that?'

'As a matter of fact, I can . . . assuming that function is turned on for her watch.'

Jack fiddled with her phone for a moment, then smiled. 'Found it. Now, the phone will lead us to wherever Anna is, or rather to her watch.'

'We'd better update the Coast Guard.' Andreas texted a message telling the lieutenant to assemble his unit on the bridge ASAP.

'I'll need some help from someone familiar with the boat's layout to know precisely where she is,' said Jack.

'Bosun,' said Andreas to a crew member standing nearby. 'Would you please take a look at the phone my friend is holding and tell him where on this boat is the place shown on the screen.'

The bosun glanced at the screen and pointed toward the bow and down. 'It's in the prayer room, on the lower two decks, next to the anchor room.'

For the first time in a very long time, Andreas felt a sense of hope. Trouble was, he knew this was perhaps the worst time to feel that way. Too much could go wrong, too quickly.

The prayer room drew Muslim worshippers to perform *salat* five times a day: at dawn, midday, afternoon, sunset, and evening.

Anna's phone had led them there, but when Andreas and the others arrived, the room was empty, and virtually bare except for prayer rugs lined along the floor, facing a wood-paneled wall spanning the entire bow end of the two-story room.

'She's got to be in here,' shouted Jack. 'Look at the screen.' With a shaking hand, he thrust the phone in Andreas's face.

Andreas lightly pushed Jack's hand away. 'I know, but there's no use yelling. It'll let the bad guys know we found them, and they could still do her great harm.'

A near-hysterical Jack swung around to face the paneled wall. 'Did you hear that? I swear it's Anna trying to speak. She must be in there, *behind that wall.*' He shouted louder: '*If you can hear me, Anna, make a sound.*'

Yianni stepped up to the wall and began tapping along it, from port to starboard.

'It's likely all going to sound hollow, what with the anchor room behind it,' said the lieutenant. 'And noises carry through hollow spaces in strange ways around ships.' He pointed to his sergeant. 'But if you're interested, she has something that might be of assistance.'

The sergeant held up a fire axe.

'Thanks, but we're not quite yet at the point of demolishing the wall of a prayer room on this particular yacht,' said Andreas.

A piercing siren flooded the room, sending the Coast Guard and cops into instinctive defensive positions.

'Well, we are now,' said Jack, taking the axe from the sergeant, stepping up to the wall, and swinging with all his might.

Yianni raced up next to Jack and shouted over the siren. 'Be careful. If she's in there you don't want to take her out with the axe.'

Yianni grabbed hold of a bit of fractured paneling, and started yanking at it with his bare hands, soon joined by his Coast Guard brethren, all peeling away at the wall in the direction of the siren.

Seconds later they saw a man's arm, grabbed it, and yanked Panos out on to the floor. That's when they saw Anna struggling to breathe as another man's hand gripped her mouth and nose tightly shut.

'Let her go!' yelled Andreas. 'She can't breathe!'

Ivan didn't.

Jack stepped up and, with a hard swing of the axe, severed Ivan's free arm at the elbow.

Yianni and the Coast Guard sergeant pulled Anna away from Ivan, now screaming more loudly than the siren.

The Coast Guard medic took hold of Anna and yelled for a colleague to bring oxygen. 'And once you've done that, put a tourniquet on him.' He motioned toward Ivan.

No one offered to do it sooner.

'Can someone please turn off that siren?' pleaded the medic as he started oxygen flowing to Anna.

Jack knelt and pressed a button on Anna's watch screen and the siren stopped. 'When I bought the watch, I thought the siren was just another sales gimmick. Who would have guessed it would save her life?'

'No, Jack,' said Andreas. 'The watch only gets an assist. You're who saved Anna's life.'

With that, both men embraced.

And cried.

In the hour following Anna's rescue, the medic and the yacht's onboard sick-bay staff performed a thorough medical examination and declared her in good physical condition.

They did not conduct tests or offer opinions on the state of Anna's psychological wellbeing.

During that same hour, the yacht's onboard surgeon worked to stabilize Ivan while the Coast Guard arranged for a medevac helicopter to transfer him to Syros General Hospital under armed guard. Tassos would meet the helicopter at the hospital to ensure Ivan was kept under close police surveillance in strict isolation from all but designated medical staff.

The owner and captain were nowhere to be found, but the entire crew treated Anna, the police, the Coast Guard, and Jack as if they were visiting royalty, telling them to use the owner's salon as if it were their own.

Andreas took that generous offer to mean the place must be crawling with listening devices that their host hoped would pick up some hint of Andreas's next move.

Andreas only wished he had one to share.

All he could think of was getting Anna safely back home to

her mother and father. He wondered how Gavi would take to Jack now that her little girl – who grew up believing one day that Prince Charming would come to her rescue – had just experienced her dream come true.

Andreas smiled at the two of them cuddling on the sofa, hugging, crying, laughing, kissing. He looked over at Yianni, who watched the same scene, biting at his lip as he did.

'Well, folks, are we ready to shove off?' said the lieutenant, walking into the salon. 'The prisoner and two of my sailors are on the medevac, waiting for orders to take off, and we're all packed up and ready to sail you on to Syros.'

Andreas shot a nervous glance at Jack. 'Are you all right with that, Jack?'

'After what I've just been through – make that what Anna's been through – my childhood fear of boats is a thing of the past.'

'Happy to have been of help, my love,' said Anna, with a wink to her uncle as she rose from the sofa.

'Ah, my favorite niece's sense of humor is back,' said Andreas, jumping up to hug her, and dragging Jack into a big family hug.

The others waited patiently for the hug to finish, then followed the lieutenant out on to the deck from where they'd board the Coast Guard vessel.

Victor was waiting for them on that deck.

'Jack, I don't know what to say. An apology is not only meaningless under such circumstances, but would suggest I had something to do with what happened to your dear Anna. The owner and his captain are too embarrassed to say anything, but they don't know you as I think I do.' Victor cleared his throat. 'I want you to know that from the bottom of my heart I am sorry for what happened, and that I will do whatever I can to see that those responsible are held fully accountable. Perhaps not under Greek law, for that is not my place. But I vow that they shall be held responsible for their actions wherever I do have influence. This offense to you and your family shall not go unpunished.'

Victor bowed his head. 'I don't expect you to respond, but I did want you to know my honest feelings.'

Jack said nothing but looked to Anna, who nodded. Jack continued toward the Coast Guard boat, passing silently by Victor, but softly touching him on the shoulder as he did. As Anna passed by Victor, she did the same.

Neither likely saw Victor's tears, but they might have heard his softly spoken three words, 'Thank you, Cousin.'

Though dead tired from catching only snatches of sleep on the boat ride to Syros and a late-afternoon helicopter flight back to Athens, Andreas stayed with Lila at his sister's home until the very end of what turned out to be a celebration of life unlike any he'd ever witnessed before.

Upon Anna and Jack walking into her home, Gavi invited the entire neighborhood to welcome not just her daughter back home, but her 'wonderful husband-to-be.'

Among a seemingly endless parade of well-wishers bringing food and drink, Gavi hardly let go of Jack's hand the entire time, kissing him so often on the cheek that you'd have thought he was her son and Anna the new member of the family.

Andreas had never been prouder of his sister than he was tonight. Especially as he watched her confide a secret in Jack and Anna she'd never before told her children.

'I was named after my great grandmother on my mother's side. She was slaughtered by the Nazis in Thessaloniki during World War Two.' She leaned in, took the two by their hands in hers, and squeezed them. 'Because she was Jewish!' She kissed them both.

Jack burst into a broad smile.

'Mazel tov,' said Andreas. 'And on that joyous wish of good luck, Lila and I must say goodnight. It's already Sunday, and I've a lot of sleep to catch up on before a big meeting on Monday morning.'

'Oh, wow . . . I lost track of time,' said Jack, his smile fading.

'Don't worry,' said Andreas. 'After what we've been through, the meeting will be a piece of cake.'

'No . . . that's not what I meant. Yesterday was the anniversary of my parents' deaths.'

Anna hugged him. 'The Fates protected you from thinking about any of that so you could concentrate on rescuing me.'

Jack smiled. 'And in the process gave me a joyful memory to replace the sad ones I've carried for far too long.'

'Never underestimate our Greek gods, dear Jack,' said Lila.

Jack squeezed Anna's hand. 'Never.'

TWENTY-TWO

I t was mid-morning when Andreas showed up unannounced at
Dittos's office.

'Hi,' Andreas smiled. 'I'm here to see the Deputy Minister.
I'd like to speak with him before I meet with our Minister.'

The secretary cautiously rose from her chair and edged toward
her boss's office door, as if unsure whether the Rottweiler she'd
seen in action before now planned to lick her hand or go for her
throat.

She opened the door just wide enough to slip inside and closed
it behind her.

Three minutes later she emerged. 'The Deputy Minister will
see you now.' She skirted out of Andreas's path, and back to behind
her desk.

'Thank you,' said Andreas, strolling up to the door, knocking
twice, and waiting for Dittos to call for him to enter.

'Good morning, Kaldis. I must admit I'm surprised to see you
so early in the morning on your final day on the job.'

Andreas closed the door and stood there. 'I see you're as up
on developments as you've ever been.'

'What's that supposed to mean?'

'Do you remember that episode on Friday in which your office
played a key role in the kidnapping of my niece?'

'As I told you back then, I had nothing to do with any kidnapping, and never knew she was your niece. I was only helping a
friend obtain VIP treatment for an arriving international air
passenger.'

Andreas nodded. 'And on Saturday, do you remember ordering
me off the boat of a man whom I gather is another friend of
yours?'

'Of course I do. You created an international incident aboard
the private property of one of the most influential people on earth.
In fact, it's a subject I intend to raise with the Minister when we
meet later today to discuss your replacement. My recommendation
will be to dismiss your entire unit.'

Andreas could see Dittos rising to what he truly thought would be a career-making moment in his upcoming meeting.

'Well, I don't know how to break the news to you, but after admittedly disobeying your instructions, my band of pirates and I discovered the kidnap victim and her two kidnappers hidden in a compartment in the yacht's prayer room.'

Dittos practically leaped out of his chair. 'What? I knew nothing about any of that!'

'That seems to be a standard line of yours. I suspect that you'll also claim it's sheer coincidence that the two kidnappers now under arrest happen to be your buddy Panos – for whom you made your airport arrangements – and his Russian pal who snatched my niece at the airport.'

'This is all an outrageous subterfuge, intended to distract attention from your utter incompetence in conducting the wildfire investigations.'

'As a matter of fact, I have some news for you on that score, too. Your buddy Panos was behind a number of those fires. He told the Russian where to set them, who to use, and ultimately who to murder to cover their tracks.'

Nervously sitting again, Dittos repeated, 'I know nothing about any of that.'

Andreas smiled. 'I wouldn't have expected you to say anything different. The trouble is, the facts are mounting against you, and if pushed, who knows what Panos Cirillo might say about your involvement in his affairs. So far, he's played the prudent client, and refused to say even a word without his own lawyer present, but my sense is that's all going to change once it sinks in that everything he's worked for his entire life is gone – vanished – in a flash. That's when rage will take charge and compel him to take down whoever he can with him.'

'How could you possibly take his word over mine?'

'That's sort of where I'm heading with this. The best thing you have going for you is that I'm currently the cop charged with making recommendations to the prosecutor on what happens to you next.' Andreas smiled. 'That being the case, I think the wisest course of action would be for you to resign immediately and recalibrate your career goals.'

'What?' Dittos barked indignantly. 'Why would I do that?'

'I know you fervently dislike me, but not every cop subscribes to

my philosophy when looking at a string of events linking someone such as yourself so convincingly to arson, murder, and kidnapping.'
With his eyes blinking wildly, Dittos nearly screeched, 'What philosophy is that?'
'Never attribute to malice that which can be explained by sheer stupidity.' Andreas opened the door and paused. 'Before deciding on what to do next, I suggest you think long and hard about how hubris brought down Panos.' He turned and, with a nod to the secretary, left Dittos alone to contemplate his future.

Andreas debated whether to call the Minister to set up an appointment or wait to hear from him. He chose the latter.
It was late afternoon when the call came through from the Minister's office asking that Chief Inspector Andreas Kaldis report to the Minister's office ASAP.
When Andreas arrived, he was immediately shown into the Minister's office. It was just the two of them.
'You've had a busy weekend, I hear,' said the Minister.
'I'd say that sums things up in a rather understated but tidy sort of way.'
'Thank God your niece is safe and sound.' The Minister gestured for Andreas to sit in a chair across from him.
'With a very big thank-you to the Hellenic Coast Guard.'
'Yes, they do great work. So, why don't you tell me, in your own words, everything that's happened since you promised to resign by today if you didn't come up with satisfactory results in your top-secret investigation.'
'Everything?'
'Yes, everything.'
Over the ensuing forty-five minutes, the Minister did not speak, but stayed keenly focused on every word Andreas said.
When Andreas finished, the Minister leaned back in his chair. 'Frankly, I'm surprised you didn't strangle my deputy.'
'The thought did cross my mind, but I figured I'd leave him to do that for himself.'
'Well, it worked. He was in here about an hour after you paid him a visit, concocting some story about how he could no longer work in a ministry where his professionalism wasn't respected, and thus he had no choice but to resign, effective immediately. Leaving you to retain your current position, I should add.'

Andreas exhaled. 'Thank you. I think it best, though, that under the circumstances someone outside of my unit decides if any recommendations should be made to a prosecutor concerning Dittos's possible involvement in crimes connected to my unit's wildfire investigations or my niece's kidnapping.'

'I agree.'

Andreas paused. 'I have one question. Perhaps I shouldn't ask it, but curiosity will kill me if I don't.'

'You've earned the right to ask any question.'

'Why did it take so long after Dittos resigned his position this morning for you to meet with me?'

The Minister leaned across his desk. 'What you and your crew have unearthed has the potential to cripple what many in our government see as the means for launching our economy to levels once thought inconceivable. It's not for me to take it upon myself alone to make such a consequential decision.'

'I assume you're talking about the Consortium's metaverse project.'

The Minister nodded. 'It's a project that everyone I've spoken to desperately wants to go forward. Landowners who sold or leased their burned-out land want it to go forward, contractors set to erect the wind turbines and lay the cables all want it to go forward, communities clamoring for economic development in their regions all want it to go forward, not to mention the banking and investment communities smelling the scent of money flowing in from all around the world.'

'In other words, the only ones likely not on board are those who don't take kindly to arson, murder, and kidnapping as acceptable practices in the pursuit of commercial goals. Not to mention those who'd prefer hitching their futures to economic saviors favoring democracies over autocracies.'

'Come on, Andreas, you know that's over the top. You nailed the guys responsible for arson, murder, and kidnapping. Take the accolades and move on.'

'Why? How do we know this Consortium crew hasn't committed *more* crimes in the name of achieving world domination?'

The Minister shook his head. 'Businessmen do the same sort of things every day to achieve their goals. They might call it public relations, political contributions, or advertising, but let's be real. Virtually everything happening on our far-from-perfect planet has to do with one tribe trying to convince the members of another tribe that their tribe's way is better.'

'But my tribe expects your tribe to play by the same rules, and the Consortium guys don't believe in playing by anything other than their own rules.'

The Minister sighed. 'So, how do you suggest we change these differing tribal attitudes?'

'I'm not suggesting you or I can. Though I think you'd probably agree that the sort of business-as-usual attitude you're espousing explains why so much of the world is confused between what's truth and what's not.'

The Minister shrugged.

'But what I can say with relative confidence, Minister, is that unless the Consortium gets its act under control, Greece will find itself as a ground-zero target for the world's grievances over where this brave new metaverse takes us. And that isn't going to be pretty. For anyone.'

'I guess that leaves you and me to respectfully disagree over the future direction of our world.'

'While sharing hope that somehow, somewhere, someone finds a way to make it work out for all of us.'

The two men shook hands.

'Amen.'

A week had passed since Jack arrived in Athens. Shortly after lunchtime, he showed up at Andreas's office.

'Hi, Jack,' said Maggie. 'Welcome back to the trenches. I thought by now you'd have had your fill of police work.'

He smiled. 'This is purely a social call. I've had more than enough police adventure to last me a lifetime. I was wondering if Uncle Andreas is around.'

'I see you've picked up on a new label for the Chief.'

'It's hard not to, what with Anna always saying, "Uncle Andreas this, Uncle Andreas that."'

'Who's calling me by my favorite moniker?' said Andreas, coming down the hall toward his office. 'Jack! What a surprise. If I'd known you were coming, I'd have waited before going to lunch.'

'That's OK. I already ate.'

'Were you off with Lila and Anna? I heard they went shopping together.'

'No, I had another appointment. They went with Solona.'

'Aha,' said Andreas. 'The three of them have become fast friends.'

'Yes, Solona adores Lila. She said they're exchanging fashion tips.'

Andreas stood in the doorway to his office. 'That should be interesting.' He waved for Jack to join him inside.

Jack started to close the door.

'No need to do that. Maggie will pester me to death to repeat whatever you tell me.'

'But I've come to ask you for advice.'

'More reason for her to pester me. But, OK, close it.'

Andreas sat behind his desk, and Jack took a chair across from him.

'So, what's on your mind?'

'We're leaving for New York on Saturday.'

'We'll miss you.'

'Well, that's the point. You might not be missing us for long.'

'I don't follow.'

Jack exhaled. 'I've been talking with Victor over the past couple of days, and we just had lunch together. He's offered me a very interesting proposition.'

'I assume we're talking about the same Victor who's been humping his close friend's wife and is the likely brains – if not brawn – behind supplying now-murdered Chinese workers to Panos and Ivan.'

'Yep, the very same.'

Andreas nodded. 'I just wanted to make sure we know who we're talking about. I assume you've heard the adage to be aware of Greeks bearing gifts. These days I think it's more applicable to Chinese.'

Jack smiled. 'For all of those reasons, plus a few more, that's why I'm here for your advice.'

Andreas leaned back. 'OK, tell me what sort of deal this devil has offered you.'

'Just a few preliminary questions. Do you believe Victor played any knowing part in Anna's kidnapping?'

Andreas exhaled. 'No, I do not.'

'What about in the deaths of the three Chinese workers?'

Andreas exhaled again. 'According to Cirillo's wife, Victor knew what they were doing, but nothing she said directly implicates him in their murders. Though I wouldn't put that sort of thing past him. Certainly not past his Russian and Middle East partners.'

'What about in the burning of the forests?'

'Not as a participant in the actual burning, but as far as going along with using fire as a means for gaining control of properties the Consortium desired, a definite yes.' Andreas sighed. 'But to be perfectly fair to a foreign criminal, Greeks have been doing the same thing for generations to get around development laws.'

'All of that agrees with my take on him.'

'So, what has he offered you?'

'A proposition that's too good to be true.'

'Ah, the very worst kind.'

'In a nutshell, he wants me to assume operational supervision responsibility for the entire Syros metaverse project.'

Andreas stared at Jack. 'And did he happen to tell you why he wanted you, a non-Chinese, to assume such a role in a project shared with Russians and Middle Easterners?'

'Not just non-Chinese but a Greek-American Jew.'

'I was going to get to that part next. Aren't you the one who told me how only Chinese have a realistic shot at progressing in a Chinese company?'

Jack nodded. 'That's what I've heard and read. It's also a point I raised with him directly.'

'And his response was?'

'He could only guarantee that I'll keep my position for as long as he holds his own in the Consortium. But so far, his guidance has been followed by the Consortium partners. The Russians no longer have an operational role in the Consortium, following their blunder in choosing Ivan as their undercover watchdog meant to keep an eye on Panos – who turned out to be a lapdog.'

'Ivan's now claiming diplomatic immunity and demanding to be turned over to the Russian Embassy.'

'From what Victor told me, Ivan will wish he'd opted to stay in a Greek prison. He's the Kremlin's scapegoat for its loss of status in the project.'

'What about Victor's friend, the yacht owner?'

'He's to continue throwing his parties and gathering vital intel and other opportunities for his country.'

'I can only imagine.'

'But he's only to serve in a reporting capacity and cannot participate in any operational activity except on the express instructions of his benefactor.'

'Do you believe that BS?'

'Honestly, even if it's all flat-out lies, it's not the sort of thing that would affect the role Victor has in mind for me.'

'And how do you evaluate that proffered role in the context of your own life goals?'

'It's the chance I'd always hoped for – getting in on the ground floor of my area of expertise, in a way that allows me to play with the big boys on a level field. It's that life-changing opportunity worth taking a risk for I'd spoken about when we got drunk together on Syros.'

'But what about the subliminal messaging part that's so important to the bad-guy governments who want to use the metaverse to change the world order?'

Jack shrugged. 'After all I've seen of the players involved, and their reach into governments, I've concluded the project's going forward in Greece whether I'm involved or not. The simple truth is our democratic governments regularly play footsie with autocrats at the same time as they criticize them for all sorts of human-rights abuses.'

'I sadly must agree with you on that.'

'This opportunity at least gives me a shot at influencing the messaging. Otherwise, it's likely the most rabid who'll get to run the show. This is my chance to start things off on a more moderate footing, hoping any success we have following that path influences those who later lead.'

'If anyone but you had told me what you just said, I'd say it's all pie-in-the-sky talk by someone whose ego has him believing he alone can change the world, or, more likely, just a bunch of self-serving rationalizations put forth by someone anxious to justify his morally questionable work.' Andreas spread his arms open wide. '*But*, I have too much respect for your judgment and know for a fact that no one can say you're not going into this with your eyes wide open. You know better than almost anyone precisely what your prospective employers are capable of. So, all I have to say to you is, good luck.'

'Thanks, Uncle.'

'Do you mind if I ask what they're offering you?'

'A lot of money.'

'That's a good start.'

'But with the job based in Syros, we'll have to move to Greece.'

'What about Anna's studies?'

'They'll arrange for her to transfer to the college of her choice in Athens or anywhere in Greece and will pay her tuition.'

'Sounds good to me, if it's good for her.'

Jack nodded. 'Plus, they'll provide a place for us in Syros, while allowing me to commute from Athens by helicopter if I choose.'

'I see you've become used to helicopters.'

'Thanks to you.' Jack laughed.

'Your future mother-in-law must be pleased.'

'Anna describes her as over the moon. She's already making plans to redo Anna's old bedroom for us to stay in when we're not in Syros.'

'Let the good times roll,' laughed Andreas. 'But on a more serious note, how does Anna feel about giving up her lifetime dream of living in New York City?'

'She's not giving it up. I won't let her. In fact, Anna's been pressing me to take the job. We both see this as a once-in-a-lifetime opportunity for us to contribute something meaningful to the world, while likely setting us up for life in the process. There will be other chances for us to live in New York. Another chance like this won't likely come again.'

'Is she just saying that not to make you feel guilty?'

'She's convinced me that's not her motivation.'

'How did she do that?'

'By giving me an ultimatum. If I don't take the job, she won't marry me.'

Andreas shook his head and smiled. 'Sounds like my Anna.'

Jack paused. 'She has only one caveat.'

'What's that?'

'No surprise limo rides. *Ever.*'

That evening, after Andreas had returned home, and the kids were in bed, he asked Lila to come sit with him as he looked out upon the Acropolis.

'Something on your mind?' Lila asked, dropping down next to him on the sofa.

'Yes.'

'Are you still bothered by that Cirillo case?'

'Not directly. Cases don't get to me once I've sent them off to a prosecutor. I've done my job, now it's up to others to do theirs. It's no longer my worry, especially with Anna safe and sound.'

'OK, then, what has you so pensive?'

'It's a conversation I had this afternoon with Jack about a job he's been offered.' He paused. 'By the Consortium. Specifically, Victor.'

'What kind of job?'

'Does that really matter if the point of the exercise is to assist in undermining democracy?'

'Wow, that must have been one heavy conversation.'

'That's what's troubling me. It wasn't.' He reached for Lila's hand. 'He came to me for advice and, rather than discouraging him, I acted more like a cheerleader rooting him on to greater glory.'

'What's wrong with that? Do you think he's going to put himself in legal or physical jeopardy?'

'I hope not, though considering the players, there's always that possibility. But he already knows that.'

'So, what's bothering you?'

'No matter how I cut it, the bottom line is he's going to work for the bad guys.'

'Doing bad things?'

'Not directly. But if he's successful at his job, the Consortium will succeed at its purpose.'

'And that will be Jack's fault?'

'Some might say that, yes.'

'As I recall, you warned your Minister of the risk posed by the Consortium, and he told you to back off, because it's considered by our government as too valuable to the Greek economy.'

'Essentially, yes.'

'So, why should Jack be denied the opportunity offered by an entity protected by our government?'

'Because it's the right thing to do.'

'We're living in a world today that's moving so quickly, in so many directions, all at the same time, that it's hard to tell what's right and what's wrong. For good or for bad, our government is backing the Consortium's project. If you have confidence in Jack's moral compass, why discourage him from pursuing his big opportunity?'

Andreas sighed. 'Perhaps you're right, and this is a providence-driven opportunity for Jack to use his past as inspiration for a better future. Maybe for us all.'

'And in the process, making your niece very happy.'

'Not to mention her mother.'

Lila smiled. 'Yes, we must never forget the importance of making mothers happy.'

Andreas leaned over and kissed his wife on the cheek.

'Never.'